Double Crossed

Vengeance

A Novel By

Tony Gray

SINCERITY

Published in the United States by Sincerity Press, an imprint of Sincerity Publishing, a division of Sincerity Media Group, LLC. - Nashville, Tennessee

ISBN: 978-1-7352720-3-0 (Hardcover)
ISBN: 978-1-7352720-4-7 (Paperback)
ISBN: 978-1-7352720-5-4 (eBook)

First Edition

Design by GL2

"Sooner or later, everyone sits down to a banquet full of consequences."

-Robert Louis Stevenson

Prologue
New Orleans, Louisiana

Stenson Beckett found himself trapped inside the darkest corner of a broken heart. At 28 years old, his life should have never turned out like this. He had endured enough trauma for many terrible lives. Yet this devastation tempted him to doubt everything good he believed. What was the point of being a kind person when all it brought was suffering to himself and those he loved?

Locked inside his bedroom, lit only by a pale moonlight, wicked slats of blue violation cast over him like a phantom voyeur begging to see him to cry. The room appeared as if a prison might when the criminals were asleep. Quiet. Scary. Lonely. Cold.

Dust particles floated through the air more freely than his mind; frozen between two frames of a horror movie filmed in a living hell. Somehow, he had found the light before in the darkest moments of his troubled life. But this was different. Hopeless. Hurtful. Helpless. Sad.

This done could not be undone. There would be no going back or rewinding tape. No amount of prayer would change this deadly deed. Like a tattoo artist's needle, it was an exclamation point leaving an indelible mark to join the countless other scars that defined his life. Marks he would never remove or forget, if only...

Stenson questioned if he could take anymore;

not one more loss or stab to his heart. Friends could not pierce the veil concealing his pain; the overwhelming sadness like a widow watching love pass through life's eternal final door.

It terrified those who cared because this was not the man they knew and loved; the warm-hearted human being who gave so unselfishly to the world. The harm befallen him was undeserved. Now he stood on a precipice; a high cliff from which they were afraid he may jump. They felt as helpless, with nothing to do but pray for Stenson Beckett and his broken heart.

[Knock]

"Go away," Stenson mumbled.

[Knock] [Knock]

"Go away, I said."

[Click]

The latch slowly turned.

"I swear to God, go away!" Stenson roared.

Undeterred, the door inched open. Stenson raised his head with an angry glare. The silhouette of a slightly hunched figure stood in the doorway. The shape seemed familiar yet unfamiliar, as if déjà vu. Without invitation, the shadowed intruder stepped inside.

In a warm baritone voice from the past, the violator asked, "Stenson?"

The slanted blue rays met a cragged face outlined by an orange halo backlighting the figure from the hallway light. It revealed an old man with a long gray beard.

It couldn't be.

"Haggerty?" Stenson quivered in disbelief.

"Yes," the figure calmly replied.

"But I thought you were..." his voice trailed off.

"Dead?" the violator suggested.

Stenson gulped. "Yes."

"I was dead long before I met you, boy. You gave me life and a reason to live," the sage informed.

"But your will? Your estate? You left everything to me."

"I gave you the chance you deserved, boy," the wise old man explained.

Stenson bowed his head. With a trembling voice of defeat, he quietly admitted, "I have failed you and myself."

"You have not failed, boy. You have given up," the wizard-like character replied. "Your work has only begun if you find the courage to face the challenges before you now and throughout your long life, until you are a much older man than me."

"I am afraid I will fail again, Haggerty," Stenson confessed.

"My boy, you have a heart that cannot be defeated. There is goodness in you. But it is you who must believe."

Two Years Earlier...

Chapter 1

Monroe County, Alabama

Standing inside the church vestry, Robert "Brick" Brickhouse adjusted the long black tie of the groom's tuxedo. He noticed an uneasy expression on his best friend's face.

"You look like a Secret Service Agent in this outfit," Brick suggested. "All you are missing is a pair of dark sunglasses."

"And a gun and a badge," Stenson replied, "Besides, I would have looked like I was going to prom if I wore a bow tie," the groom explained, justifying his choice of neckwear.

"I don't remember much about my prom," Robert admitted.

"Is that the one you took the twins and spiked the punch bowl that got you kicked out?" Stenson recalled the humorous story.

"Yeah, that was the one. Those girls got the better of me that night," the big marine confessed.

Close as brothers and thicker than thieves, Stenson Beckett and Robert Brickhouse served together in the United States military. Stenson had been a communications specialist in the Army, while Robert served as an old-fashioned grunt in the Marine Corps.

They became inseparable and the closest of friends after Stenson risked his life to save that of his best man. He rescued the big marine from a burning Humvee after an improvised explosive device tried to erase Robert from existence. In a spontaneous act of bravery and blind courage, Stenson pulled the burning soldier from the inferno and dove on top of him to extinguish the flames. In an ironic twist of fate, Stenson was shot in the buttocks. It earned him the Purple Heart, which became a running joke among those who knew the hilarious details. Whenever anyone asked Stenson how he got the award, he would simply say he was shot rescuing a dumb marine. He would never reveal the location of his injury or which dumb marine.

"Nervous?" the burly survivor asked with the sly smile of some all-knowing Cheshire cat.

"I am terrified," Stenson admitted, understanding the finality of the commitment he was about to make.

"Luna deserves someone better than me," he chagrined, as if he was the most unworthy peasant in the village who was about to marry a princess.

"Are you kidding?" Robert shot back with rhetorical disbelief. "You are perfect for Luna LeRoux. Only magic or fate could put you two together. You're like peanut butter and jelly. You were meant for each other," Brick reassured with a playful punch to the nervous groom's chest.

Built in 1810, the original First Baptist Church of Colored People served the slaves of Monroe County, Alabama. It was part of a dark past in Southern American history nobody wanted to acknowledge and everyone wanted to forget. Many slaves wore the scars of their attempts to escape the chains that bound them. Stenson Beckett wore them too.

As an 8-year-old boy, Stenson witnessed his racist, viciously violent, alcoholic father kill his mother when he ripped a knife through her throat. With his brave heart, Stenson tried to fight his dad to save his mother from the brutal attack. But the hateful man was too big and strong, and the little boy almost lost his life that terrifying night.

The horrifying experience of witnessing hate-filled rage take the life of the person who truly loved him, who cared for him and showed him goodness in the world, was both a lesson and a curse. The scars of lost innocence ran deeply within Stenson, and the boy, now a man, vowed to live his life on the side of righteousness rather than sin.

Rather than face his father in court as the key witness at his criminal trial, Stenson ran away. It was too terrifying for the youngster to be in the presence of the evil man. As a result, the charges were reduced from a lifetime in prison to 15 years for manslaughter.

That was when he met a hermit-like old-man, Lucious T. Haggerty, who found the boy trespassing on his land by a stream reading a Cub Scout manual trying to teach himself how to fish. After the recluse learned of the trauma the child had endured, he befriended the youngster and allowed him to stay there camping by the stream. Other violators would have been shot on sight. But Haggerty sensed something special in the determined kid.

Haggerty was more of a father to Stenson than his biological father ever was. The old man also knew the trauma of losing people you love with the loss of his wife and son many years ago. Those losses turned a once proud man into a recluse and caused him to shut out the world. Like Stenson, Haggarty wore painful scars, too.

Over the years, Haggerty and the boy fished together and shared stories. The old man would reminisce about better times decades ago when he was a happier man. They had a special bond, like a grandfather and a grandson. One day Haggerty discovered two hunters ready to abuse the little boy by the stream and he murdered them with his double-barrel shotgun without question or remorse. That was the last day Stenson saw Lucious T. Haggerty when the old man insisted he must run away again. The old man nobody understood loved Stenson Beckett, and he loved the old man too.

Fifteen years later, a lawyer found Stenson working at O'Malley's pub in the French Quarter of New Orleans after he was honorably discharged from the Army. To Stenson's astonishment, the attorney informed him he was the sole beneficiary of Lucious T. Haggerty's estate.

The church they stood in today bearing the same name as the original was built with proceeds from Stenson's inheritance. The church, a new cemetery, and Haggerty's home were gifts from Stenson to serve those less fortunate. The rest of the land was dedicated as a preserve for boys and girls to camp on and enjoy the same fishing streams that saved his life.

Robert Brickhouse and the bride, Luna LeRoux, knew Stenson's dark past and the kindness he held in his heart. It was one of many reasons they loved him and the reason she was destined to marry the wonderful man. Despite the pain Stenson had endured, he held virtues that seemed lost in a harsh, often cold and uncaring world.

Stenson met Luna in kindergarten when they were both five years old. As children, they walked to school together and talked about things as children do. They played in a treehouse they built and were proud to be a Cub Scout and Brownie. When tragedy struck young Stenson's life, they lost touch after he ran away.

They reconnected years later when Stenson was in the Army stationed overseas. Stenson had spoken of Luna so often to Robert Brickhouse that one day the big marine persuaded him look her up. She was beyond surprised and overjoyed to hear Stenson's voice when he called. Luna had thought of him fondly over the years and wondered how he was doing and if he was safe. From that moment on, their friendship rekindled as if they had never been apart.

Brick recalled the day when Luna walked through the door and Stenson laid eyes on his childhood friend after so many years. She was stunning at 24 years old. With a petite 5' 4" frame and strawberry blonde hair, she had an athletic body like a soccer or volleyball player, only to later learn she played Lacrosse in college. Robert would have called her hot if not for upsetting Stenson by noticing how beautiful his childhood friend had become.

Luna was equally memorized seeing Stenson in person again. He was much taller, buff, and handsome than the little boy she remembered. But there was something unmistakable; he still had a charming smile with a twinkle of kindness that sparkled in his eyes. Her heart melted that day and continues even now.

It amused Robert to see how shy Stenson was around her and how he felt unworthy of her love. Brick and Luna knew Stenson was the only man for her. This peanut butter and jelly sandwich was perfectly made.

Justin "JC" Carter sauntered into the church vestry, accompanied by his best friend, Anthony "Big Tony" Gallo. Robert took one look at Justin and shook his head in disgust. Since JC and his band of misfits double-crossed Brick and Stenson two years ago, Robert wanted to kill Justin Carter. However, Stenson would not allow him to do it since they had called a truce and become friends after the war was over; a war in which Stenson and Brick had won.

However, Robert had not forgotten or forgiven what JC did that set off a chaotic tit-for-tat of paybacks that almost got everybody killed. It seemed the big marine did not possess the same level of compassion or forgiveness as Stenson Beckett.

"What are you wearing?" Brick bewilderingly questioned the mocha-colored man.

"A fly blue suit," JC replied as if Brick was color blind.

"You know we are dressed in black tuxedos, right?" Robert reminded Justin as if it was Talk to an Idiot Day.

"You guys look like you are going to a funeral, but I'm gonna look sharp up in this joint," JC crowed.

"The only funeral is going to be yours if you don't go home and change clothes!" Brick growled.

Stenson and Big Tony chuckled at the silly disagreement over apparel. Stenson did not care if people showed up naked to this affair. His only concern was how he would get through the wedding.

Justin Carter's life began as difficult as Stenson's. His 16-year-old mother abandoned him at the hospital shortly after he was born and diagnosed with HIV, the human immunodeficiency virus. JC spent his first eight years of his life in a hellish orphanage with buildings resembling a civil war prison. Children bullied him constantly for being the only black kid, and it frustrated Justin to see every other child adopted except him. He concluded at that tender young age nobody wanted a black boy, especially a sick one like him. He felt like the puppy at the shelter who watched all the others find a home while he asked why not him? JC resented the color of his skin, hated his disease, and wondered why God hated him for simply being born?

Like a broken toy, a fact he still hides today, JC ran away from the orphanage of unwanted souls to live on the streets of Devereaux Parish, Louisiana at eight years old. Anthony Gallo met JC when he discovered a group of white school children bigger and older than JC taunting the scared little boy as he sought shelter in a box behind a school. The boys were ready to beat JC up for fun that day. But Anthony Gallo would have none of it, and used his intimidating size to scare them away. He warned the boys if they ever bothered JC again, they would have to deal with him and there would be hell to pay.

It is how Anthony Gallo earned the nickname, "Big Tony". Since then, JC and the gentle giant with a teddy bear heart have been best friends, and as inseparable as Stenson and Brick.

JC huffed from the vestry to change clothes, throwing up a middle finger at Brick on his way out.

Robert comically asked Stenson, "Has he lost his mind?"

Stenson shrugged with a hearty laugh and said, "Maybe?"

JC passed Zabrina in the hallway. "What's up hooker?"

The Asian lady shot her hand in the air in a slapping gesture, causing JC to flinch. "Boy, don't make me hurt you!"

Zabrina Chao and Justin often teased each other this way. They were business partners, the unlikeliest of friends, and enjoyed playing rough. She grew up in North Korea as Pok Kyung-Wook. Her parents spent everything they saved, sold everything they owned, and borrowed even more to pay Chinese traffickers to smuggle their only child to a better life in the United States with the hope of joining her some day.

During the perilous month-long journey crammed inside a shipping container, many people died. After Zabrina arrived at the Port of New

Orleans, the smugglers demanded more money from her. In a strange land with a language she did not understand, her innocence was ripped away when they forced the 16-year-old virgin into prostitution.

The night Justin Carter met Zabrina, he found her crying in a dimly lit alley. With a brotherly instinct, JC sat down next to her against a damp brick wall and asked why she was sad? Through pouring tears, Zabrina revealed the last money she owed the smugglers was stolen by a customer after he savagely beat her and left her for dead. She told JC she no longer had the will to live this shameful life forced upon her. At that moment, all she wanted to do was curl into a ball and die.

Her confession shredded JC's heart with a pain he knew too well. He convinced her to stay with him and Big Tony in a hotel room that dank night in New Orleans. For some unknown reason, Zabrina, a woman who trusted no one, especially men, trusted Justin Carter. Later, JC and Big Tony pooled their money and paid off the smugglers to free Zabrina from the chains that bound her once and for all.

It is how the friendship between these broken toys began. Over the next two years, they built an amazing nightclub named Club Empire in New Orleans. However, their success was short-lived after they made the almost fatal miscalculation of stealing from another group of misfits: Stenson Beckett and Robert Brickhouse. In a back-and-forth game of cat-and-mouse, JC, Big Tony, and Zabrina lost everything after Stenson & Co. destroyed them in a publicly humiliating stink-filled way.

After the chaos ended and the war was won, Stenson felt sorry for JC and his friends. He returned the money they had drained from their bank accounts to help them rebuild. As far as Stenson was concerned, they had learned their lesson. He understood Justin Carter's heart and knew the pain of defeat. They were kindred spirits, and Stenson did not want to be Justin's enemy or destroy his dreams. It is the reason Stenson would never let Robert Brickhouse kill JC.

Robert actually liked the guy in his twisted biker-marine kind of way. But he would never let Justin know he cared. Something like that might ruin his bad boy reputation. Yet there was no denying such a bizarre twist of fate that brought this band of crazies together and how they became friends. Without question, they would do anything for each other, any time or place no matter the cost or consequences.

Deep reflections of troubled pasts were interrupted when Pastor Jackson entered the room. The minister noticed the angst on Stenson's nervous face and offered a wide, gap-toothed grin. He had seen that deer-in-the-headlights look before on many grooms.

Stenson introduced his best man to the minister. "Pastor Jackson, this is Brick... I mean Robert Brickhouse."

The men shook hands. Robert could not resist asking the pastor about his name. "Stenson told me your name is Samuel L. Jackson?"

The pastor laughed the enquiry. "It is. But not the same as the actor. He is Samuel Leroy Jackson, the rich one who curses a lot. I am Samuel Lamont Jackson, the poor one who prays for people who curse a lot."

The funny explanation broke the tension filling the room. Pastor Jackson gave Stenson a reassuring pat on his shoulder as he excused himself to take his position at the pulpit.

"Hi darlings," came a deep, sexy voice from the hallway. The guys smiled knowing it belonged to Soni James, a transgender woman who always cracked them up with her introductions. Standing seven feet tall in high heel shoes, Soni entered the room wearing a soft pink bridesmaid gown, florescent fuchsia wig, matching fingernails and lipstick so illuminated the guys wondered if it included batteries.

Soni asked Stenson, "Are you ready, baby?"

He smiled with less confidence than a condemned man heading toward the gallows. "As ready as I ever will be, I guess," the groom anxiously replied.

Soni turned her attention to Robert Brickhouse. "Oh, Brick, you look hot! Give me a kiss."

She enjoyed teasing the big marine who always seemed hilariously uncomfortable whenever Soni was around. He put on his macho act to ensure she knew which team he played for.

"No, thank you. I haven't brushed my teeth," Robert told the gigantic black woman.

Everyone loved Soni, who was Zabrina's best friend and hair stylist. She and the guys were playful with each other and nobody cared, or even noticed, she was transgender. To them, she was simply one of the girls; albeit a very tall, muscular, funny girl.

"Alright babies, I need to adjust my panties before the ceremony starts," Soni told them before patting Robert's backside as she left the room.

Brick looked at Stenson in shocked disbelief, not believing Soni had touched his butt. The groom roared with laughter at the funny expression on his best man's face. Now he was ready to marry Luna LeRoux if Robert Brickhouse did not require therapy first.

The big marine gathered his composure and wrapped his muscular arm around Stenson's shoulders. He said, "Let's go, boy. We are about to celebrate the happiest day of your life!"

The men strolled out of the vestry and down a long corridor past children's artwork hung upon the walls. They reached a wide gathering area facing two wooden doors that had been transplanted from the original house of worship built in 1810.

Beyond this threshold, there would be no turning back. They paused momentarily while Robert adjusted the groom's tie. Stenson stood up straight and looked Robert in the eyes. With a joyous boyhood smile, he said confidently, "Let's do this."

The doors swung open as if to announce the king had arrived. The only things missing for a coronation were trumpets, a court jester, throne, and a shiny crown. But as Robert thought about it, he knew Justin Carter was there. So scratch the need for a court jester. JC could play two.

Brick escorted the shaking groom down the aisle whose knees wobbled like a scarecrow from the land of Oz. Robert noticed JC had returned wearing the appropriately colored suit. Justin stood alongside Big Anthony Gallo on stage. Across from them were Zabrina, Soni James, and Luna's former college roommate who was a fashion model with a Bachelor of Science degree. Brick made a note to knock the drool off JC's face with his fist when he arrived at the stage. But then he reconsidered it since it was a wedding and checked his pocket for a handkerchief.

Stenson and Brick arrived at the stage to assume their positions. Robert stood alongside Stenson to his right, followed by JC and Big Tony. A few moments later, the rear doors opened to announce the bride had arrived.

The audience stood, craning to get a glimpse of the beauty tightly clutching her father's arm. Luna's tummy filled with butterflies as she caught the first glimpse of her future husband awaiting her arrival at the end of a walk she had dreamed of all her life.

When the wedding march began, Luna looked at her father with a childish smile that said, "Daddy, I love him."

With her heart fluttering, almost beating out of her chest, Luna LeRoux took those first sacred steps toward forever. Stenson felt unsteady on his feet, praying he would not faint. She was the most beautiful woman he had ever seen.

Robert Brickhouse steadied the groom and whispered, "You are a lucky man."

When Luna and her father reached the foot of the stairs, Stenson took three solemn steps down. Luna's dad, with an abundance of pride, released his only child to the man he knew would love and protect her for the rest of their lives.

Stenson stared at Luna's beautiful eyes through the thin, white veil covering her face. How could it be that such an amazing person would love such an imperfect soul as him?

With an illuminated smile that glowed more brightly than the most beautiful star Stenson had ever seen, Luna squeezed his hand. Together, they climbed the steps and turned to face each other. Every heartbeat pulsed through bodies in perfect sync.

Pastor Jackson approached and stood between the couple. He opened a well-worn bible to a marked page and removed a folded piece of paper. He cleared his throat.

In a booming voice, the pastor announced, "Dearly beloved we are gathered here today to get to this thing called love. Electric word love and this love between Stenson Beckett and Luna LeRoux will be forever and that's a mighty long time. They will be filled with never-ending happiness and will always see the sun, day or night."

JC seemed confused and whispered to Brick,

"Did the pastor change some words to a Prince song?"

The interruption annoyed Robert who was caught up in the moment. The big marine whispered, "Shut up, JC. What prince? Do you see any royalty here?"

The vows reached the high-point of the service where the couple exchanged rings. Robert removed a velvet box from his coat pocket and opened it, presenting it to his friend.

Stenson removed the simple Platinum band and placed the symbol of his love into the palm of his hand.

Pastor Jackson asked the groom in a commanding voice, "Stenson Beckett, do you take this amazing woman to be your wife through sickness and health? To have hot, passionate love with her day and night and make lots of good looking babies?"

The audience looked at each other with an expression of, "What did he just say?"

Stenson gazed into Luna's crystal blue eyes, not even realizing what the pastor just asked him, and placed the ring upon her delicate finger.

Proudly he said, "I do."

Pastor Jackson winked at Stenson while JC nudged Brick and whispered, "I like this pastor. I am going to attend his church."

Brick punched JC in the crotch. "This church would burn to the ground if you attended JC!"

The pastor turned his attention to the bride and asked, "Luna LeRoux, do you take this amazing man with a heart of gold who built this church and has a manhood the size of a prize-winning bull worthy of making your smoking hot body scream in delight to be your beloved husband?"

JC nudged Brick again and said, "These vows aren't like any I've ever heard."

Robert Brickhouse sharply turned to JC and

grumbled in a low voice. "Boy, if you don't shut up, I vow to beat you all over this stage before this ceremony is over!"

Luna giggled at the vow and placed the ring on Stenson's finger. With a radiant smile and a twinkle in her eyes, she said, "I do."

The attendees waited in anticipation for the final decree. Pastor Jackson looked at the happy couple and boomed so loud God could hear, "I pronounce you as stone-cold-pimp and holy-hottie-ho... I mean husband and wife!"

The couple laughed out loud. They knew Pastor Jackson planned these funny vows especially for them and they loved it. The pastor said with his toothy grin, "Stenson, rip that veil off that fine lady and lay some love down!"

The church erupted in cheers and applause when the couple kissed. Brick was so delighted he almost kissed Big Tony after witnessing the amazing scene.

JC told Robert, "Bro, I think that was the actor playing the part of a pastor. Give him an Academy Award for his performance. Best wedding vows I have ever heard. But he didn't curse. Must be a PG wedding."

Brick shook his head and laughed. He wrapped his burly arm around JC's neck and said, "Come on idiot, we've got a party to attend."

The celebration was raucous. Attendees danced the night away to a DJ playing classic hits. It was fun to see since Robert Brickhouse and Big Tony danced so badly they appeared to be having medical emergencies. Nobody noticed or cared. They were overjoyed celebrating a peanut butter and jelly sandwich this good.

When the bride and groom cut the cake, they playfully put more on each other's face than into their mouths. Later, Luna sat in a chair while everyone gathered around. Whistles and catcalls erupted when Stenson kneeled down and lifted Luna's dress to expose her garter. Paster Jackson, who had a few drinks, yelled from across the room, "She's hot Stenson. I'd hit that if you weren't married!"

The single ladies gathered into a group behind the bride. Luna turned her back and tossed the garter over her shoulder. Soni, at seven feet tall, easily caught the prize without even jumping.

Brick, who'd also had a few cocktails, yelled from the crowd, "Come on, Soni. That's not fair! You should be at basketball game. A men's basketball game!"

Soni laughed at Robert's remark and stepped aside. She returned the garter to the bride for a second attempt. Luna threw it again and this time it landed in the hands of her former enemy, Zabrina Chao. Big Tony yelled from across the room, "Yo, JC your girlfriend caught it! When are you two getting married?"

JC ignored Big Tony's remark. He hated Zabrina, and she hated him. They were simply business partners who argued about anything and everything. Besides, JC told himself Zabrina Chao wasn't attractive enough for a handsome guy like him and Zabrina knew JC was too dumb for her.

Tipsy from the drinks he'd consumed, JC approached Pastor Jackson. He asked, "Dude, you sure you aren't the actor? You look and sound like him."

Pastor Jackson looked at JC with contempt.

"Do you see me wearing pastor clothes?" the pastor replied. "Am I standing in a church? And did you see me pull up in one of my ten Rolls Royce cars?"

Justin thought about it for a moment after a sip

of his drink and concluded, "Yeah, I guess you are a pastor. Because the actor has to be better looking than you and richer if you don't have ten Rolls Royce cars and he does. He probably has a big house, too."

"What's your name, boy?" Pastor Jackson demanded.

The pastor was wound up. Instead of waiting for JC to reply, he answered his own question.

"I heard those boys call you JC? What's that stand for, Just Crazy?" the pastor asked.

Pastor Jackson took a long swig of his drink and pointed at JC, looking more like a killer than a saint.

He said "Let me tell you something, Just Crazy. That actor has 10 mansions and more money than you will ever see in your simpleton life and he has way more women and a much bigger bible than you! Now get out of my face before you need some prayers!"

JC mumbled as he stumbled away. "No way he's the actor. That guy didn't say one curse word. He is lame compared to how cool the actor is."

"I heard that, Motherf…" The pastor screamed from across the room, catching himself before completing the sentence.

Paster Jackson took another swig of his drink to calm his nerves before glaring at JC and exclaiming, "You are pressing your luck, Just Crazy!"

After the party was over, the newlyweds thanked their guests as they prepared to leave. Everyone gathered outside to throw popcorn instead of rice, since someone suggested it was better for the birds.

Brick noticed JC eating the popcorn.

"What are you doing?" Robert asked JC.

"I am hungry. They've got more inside. Get you some," Justin replied.

Robert knocked the cup of popcorn out of JC's hand and pushed him into the bushes.

"Your popcorn is over there. And wear the right color tie next time!"

Chapter 2

Wedding guests waved goodbye as the limousine pulled away, headed towards a small bed-and-breakfast on the outskirts of town. With the buzz behind them, Stenson and Luna finally had time to relax. Stenson leaned over and kissed his wife.

"I love you, Mrs. Beckett," he sweetly confessed.

Butterflies tickled her toes hearing her husband say her new last name. Secretly, she had practiced signing, "Mrs. Luna Beckett," long before Stenson proposed. From a tender young age, when little girls dream of marrying a handsome prince, Luna LeRoux had always known Stenson Beckett was the only Prince Charming for her.

Now here she sat with her husband and forever best friend. This knight in shining armor and the most handsome guy in the world, proved to her fairytales of childhood dreams really can come true. She wanted to pinch herself.

Luna wrapped her arms around her Stenson's neck and whispered, "I love you too, Mr. Beckett. You've made me the happiest girl in the world." She kissed him so deeply that electricity coursed through their bodies. She offered him a playful wink with mischief in her eyes that teased there would be more of that soon.

Like most modern couples, they had been intimate before their marriage. In fact, Stenson lost his virginity to Luna when he was 22 years old. They began dating soon after they laid eyes on each other again when Luna came home from college to see her old friend who had recently been discharged from his military service.

She was amused the first time she saw her husband naked and saw the war injury on his backside. She teased Stenson saying she was a lucky girl because other women didn't have a guy with two butt holes. She told him it was especially sexy because he earned it being a hero.

From the time they were children, Luna and Stenson had always been open and honest with each other. She felt guilty knowing she was the only girl Stenson had ever been with romantically. She even suggested Stenson could be with another woman before they married, and he was stuck with her for the rest of his life. He appreciated the offer but politely declined, telling her she was the only girl for him. Quietly, she was relieved that was his answer, because she would not have been happy if some hoochie stole her man because she was better in bed.

By bachelor party standards, Stenson's was quite tame. All he wanted to do was to go out with the guys to O'Malley's pub for games of pool, listen to some old-fashioned country music, and throw back a few beers. But no matter what they did, trouble seemed to find these double-crossing friends. Why not add a bar fight to Stenson's bachelor party to liven things up?

It all began when Robert Brickhouse overheard a drunk biker tell six equally drunk bikers at a nearby table, they would be better in a fight than the U.S. Marines. It seems Brick took exception to the remark when the loudmouth guy compared the marines to the lower part of a woman's anatomy using a term not found in medical school.

Without saying a word, Robert arose from his seat and moseyed over to the bikers' table. He tapped Mr. Motor Mouth on the shoulder and told him he was a biker, too. Then he offered to buy the guy a beer.

Brick said, "I agree, bikers can fight."

The man smiled at the acknowledgement but changed his tune when Brickhouse continued, "But I am prouder to be United States Marine. Here's your beer!"

Brick grabbed the bottle and smashed it over the biker's head so hard it shattered, knocking the bloodied man unconscious before his chair fell backwards onto the floor. The other bikers around the table were stunned at the unexpected turn of events.

Brick roared, "Semper Fi!"

With that, the fight was on. Stenson, Big Tony, and JC jumped from their seats and into the fray. Tables smashed. Glasses, chairs, and anything not nailed down became a weapon, including the dart board. The biker who was hit with it was in more pain when Brick removed a dart and stabbed him in the shoulder. With a sinister grin, Robert announced the score. "Bullseye!"

Stenson leaped from atop the bar into a pile-driving move like a professional wrestler in a championship match. He landed with his elbow squarely to the center of a biker's sternum, which made an eerie crack. Meanwhile, Brick had another biker's body wrapped in a submission hold. When the man tried to tap out, Robert reminded him this wasn't Mixed Martial Arts. Brick snapped his arm like a toothpick, which caused the biker to yell in a high-pitched squeal like a little girl watching a horror film. His eyes rolled back into his head before he passed out at the sight of the bone protruding out of his skin.

JC and Big Tony showed a couple of bikers how well they played pool when sticks broke over their backs, noses, and heads. JC winced when he saw how hard Big Tony jammed a pool cue into a biker's crotch. He was certain that guy wouldn't be making any little biker babies with those scrambled eggs.

In less than two minutes, the battle was over. One biker remained conscious attempting to point his nose forward from the left side of his face where it currently resided.

Robert leaned down and said to the man, "It looks like you didn't appreciate JC's pool game and nose job service. He always messes things up. Here, let me fix that for you."

Robert yanked the man's nose in the opposite direction, where it now pointed to the right. When the biker screamed in excruciating pain, Brick taunted him. "I thought you bikers were tougher than marines? I was on fire in combat and you are crying over a broken nose? You are such a baby."

He pointed at Stenson and asked the funny breathing biker with the crushed sternum, "You see that guy? He served in the United States Army and saved my life. You let an Army radio operator beat you up? Be thankful he didn't put more moves on you. He loves watching professional wrestling, and you boys ruined his bachelor party."

The bar was a total wreck, but not nearly as messed up as the loudmouths scattered on the floor. It wasn't long before police arrived and informed the guys there's a law against smashing a bottle over a man's head for running his mouth. After Brick explained they disrespected the United States military, an officer who had served in the Marine Corps told Brick he would have loaned him his nightstick and taser.

But since the law is the law, Robert, Stenson, JC, and Big Tony were cited for disturbing the peace. The officers did not see any reason to take two veterans and their friends at a bachelor party to jail for getting a little rowdy and taking out the trash. Besides, it would be too much paperwork. They told the guys to go home before the ambulances arrived and they would take it from there.

Luna's bachelorette party was more fun and less destructive than Stenson's chaotic event. However, when she told him she and the girls went to a strip show, Stenson began to pout. She was tickled at his response, then revealed it was a drag show where Soni James was performing in a Vegas-style cabaret act.

The revelation made Stenson chuckle. He said, "We should have sent Brick to that party. You know how much Soni likes him. Although Brick might have started a fight with her if she grabbed his junk. And considering how big Soni is, Robert would have a hard time explaining how he got beat up by a girl."

It was late when they arrived at the bed-and-breakfast. Stenson picked up his petite wedding-dress-wearing wife and carried her across the threshold. He accidentally stepped on the hem of her dress and stumbled, crashing them both onto the floor.

The older couple who owned the bed-and-breakfast were fast asleep. But the crash caused such a stir, lights turned on and a man's voice called from a bedroom at the end of the hall.

"Everything, alright out there?"

Stenson and Luna, a little tipsy from the champaign, giggled.

Stenson replied, "We are good, Mr. Johnson. Go back to sleep. We'll see you in the morning."

They quickly rushed up the creaky stairs into

the bedroom. Stenson and Luna could not wait to get this wedding party started, but there was a delay when Stenson struggled to remove Luna's dress with all its straps, hooks, buttons, and lace. He was a man on a mission and determined to chew it off, cut it off, burn it off, or whatever it took to get this woman out of that garment as quickly as possible. Amused, Luna helped him because she intended to keep the dress and not have to explain her husband's anxious wedding-night destruction to her children when she passed it down.

The evening was filled with passion and a lot of love. After Stenson and Luna had exhausted each other, they sat back on their pillows with sweaty expressions of "Wow, that was great!".

Luna said, "Too bad neither of us smoke."

Stenson replied, "I am so relaxed, I could smoke Bob Marley."

'Our wedding vows were funny," Luna mused. "Pastor Jackson must have done that especially for you, since you built the church."

"Or he did it for you because he knew you are a fan of Prince music," he said.

"He was talking crazy at our wedding, I thought the actor had kidnapped our pastor," Luna remarked.

"Did you hear him call JC, Just Crazy?" Stenson asked.

"That was hilarious," Luna replied. "Better than when you used to call him Jesus Christ."

"That's before I knew him very well," Stenson joked. "Just Crazy is a way more fitting nickname for JC. Did you notice he wore the wrong color tie?"

"At least it wasn't one of his shiny track suits and gold chain outfits he normally wears. He dresses like an outcast from a rap video sometimes," Luna remarked.

The next morning, Stenson and Luna joined the

Johnsons downstairs for breakfast.

"Have a nice rest?" Mr. Johnson asked the couple with an all-knowing smile.

"Yes, Mr. Johnson. It was delightful," Stenson coyly replied.

"That's good," Mr. Johnson said. "I thought those enormous rats I heard upstairs last night might have awakened you and your lovely bride from such a blissful sleep. Mrs. Johnson and I thought the ceiling was going to cave in."

Mr. Johnson winked at Stenson while Mrs. Johnson offered a congratulatory smile to Luna's blushing face.

Chapter 3

New Orleans, Lousiana

Stenson was convinced his wife had lost her mind when she suggested Peru for their honeymoon. Before Stenson, Luna, and Brick were friends with JC, Zabrina, and Big Tony, they were mortal enemies. In an escalating attempt to outwit the other, Zabrina arranged for a charter flight that left Luna stranded in the Amazon rainforest. If not for a little jaguar cub Luna named Mi Amiga, she would be dead right now. The feline guided her to the village of the Matsés tribe, also known as the Jaguar people, who, until 1969, nobody knew existed.

While Luna may not be clinically crazy, Stenson wondered if he was for agreeing to go on this trip. He vividly recalled how terrified Luna was for 10 days lost in the sweltering heat with bugs big enough to ride on and snakes that could swallow you whole. Despite his concerns, Stenson would do anything for his wife. And if that is where Mrs. Wild Kingdom wanted to go, then he would take her as long he remembered to pick up the largest can of bug spray he could find and research how to mud wrestle anaconda.

They landed on the same grassy airstrip in the jungle where Luna's ordeal began two years ago. After four treacherous bouncy hours rumbling through the Amazon rainforest in an SUV equipped to deal with the nausea-inducing conditions, they reached their destination.

University professor Dr. Aaron Fletcher and members of the Matsés tribe met the group with great fanfare when they arrived. The village elder greeted Luna where they exchanged welcoming bows of respect. Matsés women surrounded her and exclaimed, "Luna!" to their long lost friend. The chief placed two warrior hands upon Stenson's shoulders. With a wide toothless grin in a language he did not understand, Stenson knew it meant, "Welcome to my home".

Suddenly, Stenson became alarmed when he saw a large animal rush toward Luna from the corner of his eye. Instinctively, he jumped between the predator and his wife, only to realize now he was the prey. The large spotted feline halted one pounce from Stenson's head and let out a ferocious growl that warned him to get out of her way.

Luna turned to see what the commotion was about and immediately recognized the creature. She exclaimed, "Mi Amiga!"

The beast ran past Stenson, who stood so frozen that only his eyeballs moved. The cat jumped up and placed her paws on Luna's shoulders, almost knocking her down. She licked her face with the same rough tongue Luna remembered when she first met the wonderful creature. Mi Amiga was not a kitten anymore. She was a full-grown Jaguar now.

Realizing he would not be this evening's Jag food, Stenson walked over to Luna and reached out to pet the cat. Mi Amiga growled another warning at him that said she did not give him permission to come any closer or touch her. Stenson retracted his hand quickly since he was fond of having two hands and noticed the size of the animal's teeth.

Luna said sweetly to the feline, "It's okay, Mi Amiga. This is my husband. He is nice."

Somehow, the animal understood Luna, while

Stenson wondered if he married Dr. Doolittle. Mi Amiga licked Stenson's hand in a conciliatory gesture as if to say, "She likes you, so I won't kill you right now, but I will have my eyes on you, buster."

The tribe held a grand celebration that evening. Women braided Luna's hair in their traditional way and sang traditional songs; the men painted Stenson's face as that of a warrior. They ate a feast of wild boar, piranha, and exotic fruits gathered from the forest.

Stenson became tipsy drinking a jungle brew. He sat by the fire and listened to the tribesmen tell animated tales of wars and great hunts. He did not have a clue what they said. He simply laughed when they laughed and raised his cup, exclaiming, "That was a great story. I am drunk!"

Stenson admired how content Luna was talking with the Matsés women by firelight through Dr. Fletcher's translations. The jaguar, Mi Amiga, laid at Luna's feet like a large house cat. Occasionally, women would look over at Stenson and giggle at his painted, drunk face. Luna probably told them the story of him being shot in the butt or some other wild tale. He did not mind because he was as content as her and had to admit Luna was right. This truly was a magical honeymoon.

They returned to New Orleans and resumed their normal lives. Stenson managed O'Malley's pub in the French Quarter with Robert Brickhouse while Luna got back to her job as an I.T. Security Analyst at a large technology firm.

A few months later, Stenson found Luna on the sofa when he arrived home from work. She was usually in bed by then since he worked late and she so early. He sensed something was wrong.

"You are up late. You okay, babe?" he asked.

"I am fine, just a little sick to my stomach," was

her icky reply.

Stenson sat on the sofa next to her.

"Can I get you something?" he asked.

"No, just hold me," Luna said with a green-around-the-gills smile.

She snuggled up to her husband and laid her head on his chest. Stenson stroked her hair They were quiet for a few minutes before Luna looked up and asked, "Do you love me, Stenson?"

Not knowing if he should laugh or wonder where this was going, he replied, "Of course I do! What kind of silly question is that?"

Luna enjoyed seeing the look of bewilderment on her husband's face. She knew he loved her. She gazed into his worried eyes and said after a long pause, "I'm glad you love me because I am pregnant."

Stenson leaped off the sofa as if he had been shocked with a cattle prod, tossing Luna onto the floor like a sack of potatoes. She burst out laughing.

"You are what?!?" Stenson yelled, making sure he heard her correctly.

"I am pregnant!" she joyously repeated as she rose to her feet.

Stenson raised Luna into the air and planted the biggest kiss on her lips that he had ever given her.

"I love you, Mrs. Beckett!" Stenson proudly proclaimed.

"Are you happy?" she asked.

"Are you kidding?" he replied. "Words cannot explain how happy I am... for both of us!"

A few weeks later, Stenson accompanied Luna to a medical appointment with her obstetrician. He watched with bewildering curiosity as the physician moved a white wand-like device across Luna's stomach. Everyone stared at a monitor which showed the inside of Luna's body lit up in florescent colors.

Stenson did not know what he was seeing. It looked like a blob from a 1960s acid trip until he leaned closer to make out a tiny head and tiny little fingers and tiny little feet. The physician looked up and said, "It appears you are having a son."

Stenson wasn't sure how the doctor made out that portion of the anatomy, but he almost melted upon hearing the news. Once he regained his composure, the father-to-be leaned over and kissed his wife's lips and then her tummy, getting some of the jelly on his lips. He even hugged the doctor like she had something to do with it. It was a precious moment. Stenson and Luna were soon to be parents.

* * *

If there was a word for unbearable scents, "funky" was it and that word perfectly described how nasty Club Empire smelled after Stenson and his crew destroyed the place when they set off several wretched stink bombs during their most publicized black-tie event. JC did not blame them. He had to admit, Stenson & Co. put the final nail in their coffin after months of deadly tricks. It was Zabrina's terrible idea to scam Stenson and Brick, which set off the cat-and-mouse game. They started the fight and Stenson finished it. It was that unpleasantly and smellfully simple.

It was water under the bridge, so JC thought. After he and Stenson buried the hatchet, Stenson proved there were no hard feelings when he returned $800,000 of the money his hacker girlfriend, now his wife, siphoned out of their bank accounts to help them rebuild.

JC regretted scamming Stenson. They had come from similar backgrounds as runaways; Stenson, after witnessing the murder of his mother, and JC fleeing an evil orphanage of unwanted kids. As JC considered it, that had to be one ingredient that made Stenson such a good person. He used his injustice to do better things in the world. Stenson never asked for as much as a thank you when he did saintly deeds. JC admired him for that.

He often wished he was more like Stenson. He admitted to himself that he was a work in progress. Things were improving after he reconnected with his mother during one of his darkest days of his life.

After they lost Club Empire and became the laughingstock in town, JC realized there was more to life than his flashiness and fakery. He understood, in part by watching how Stenson did things, that friendship and love were more cherished than any of the falsehoods he had previously lived.

His friends did not care what clothes he wore, except for Robert Brickhouse. Nor did they give a thought to what car he drove or how much money he had. Big Tony Gallo had been with him from the beginning and never asked for anything in return but his friendship. And Zabrina, while they would often go after each other like cats and dogs, JC loved her toughness and resolve. Zabrina was like a sister or that girl you pick on because you like her but do not have the courage to admit.

His Hispanic friend, Jesús Alvarez, and transgender friend, Soni James, taught JC that he was not the only person in the world to be picked on or discriminated against. Many people were maligned for different reasons. Who was he to judge or feel sorry for himself? In some ways, they had it tougher than him.

Another thing he admired about Stenson; He didn't care what color people were, or their nationality or orientation. Stenson liked people for being themselves and having good hearts. He saw past their human flaws. Stenson was truly a friend; that one-in-a-million kind anyone would be lucky to have in a lifetime.

Now it was time to pick up the pieces. Past was the past and a bright future lay ahead. It started with cleaning up this wreck of a place. JC grabbed a mop and pushed it across the sticky floor of his once beautiful nightclub. Lost in his thoughts, he did not notice Big Tony walk in.

"JC, what are you doing? I've never seen you pick up a mop in your life," the lumbering teddy bear of a guy said with an approving cherub grin.

"Time to turn a new leaf. I have been full of myself for way too long," JC told the big man.

Tony Gallo grabbed another mop. "Any thoughts about what we should do now?"

"I have a few," JC said. "Let's get together with Zabrina after we clean up this mess and see what that crazy woman has in her thick head."

* * *

Back at O'Malley's, Stenson was on cloud nine. He had a beautiful wife, a child on the way, amazing friends, good health and a bit of money. Life could not be better.

It was mid-afternoon on a sweltering summer day, and the French Quarter was quiet. Only locals stayed around this time of year because nobody cared for the heat of a Louisiana summer that stuck to you like dirty napkin pulled from a sewer.

Robert was behind the bar talking with Stenson when Fallon O'Malley, the pub's owner and former member of the British Special Air Service (SAS), walked in. Fallon pulled up a seat next to Stenson and ordered a pint of Guinness. The men traded small talk before Fallon asked Stenson if he could speak with him in the office.

Fallon sat behind the desk and asked, "So how does it feel to be an expectant father, my boy?"

"I was less nervous when I was in combat," Stenson joked.

"You'll be alright, mate. I remember when the missus gave birth to our first child. I was terrified. How's Luna?"

"She is great. Glowing and preparing the nest," he said.

"Ah, nesting. I remember it well," Fallon reminisced.

"The reason I wanted to talk to you, Stenson, is I am thinking of retiring and need to do something with the bar. I have grandkids now and my wife and I would like to travel a bit and spend more time with them."

Stenson worried Fallon was about to tell him he'd lost his job. It wasn't the news he wanted to hear with a kid on the way.

"I wondered if you would be interested in taking the place off my hands?" Fallon proposed.

Stenson was relieved and stunned at the suggestion.

"I would love to, Fallon, but I don't have that kind of money."

"It wouldn't cost you a thing, Stenson. I want to give it to you. Brick and you have done a remarkable job running the place, and your sales are better than mine ever were when I was in charge."

Stenson laughed. "Well, Brick's biker friends drink a lot of beer."

"What about your kids?" Stenson asked.

"They have fancy careers and families," Fallon opined. "They have no interest in owning a pub."

He continued, "I know you don't make a lot of money here since I am the one who pays your salary," Fallon said in an honest jest.

"And with a child on the way, I thought it would be an opportunity for you to have a little more stability. I've got a military pension and if you sent me a little money each month, that would go toward my rainy-day fund. What do you think? You can even change the name of the place if you like?" Fallon suggested.

"I don't know what to say, Fallon. Are you sure about this?" Stenson asked.

"Absolutely, Stenson," Fallon reaffirmed.

"I would say yes in a heartbeat, Fallon. But I need to talk to Luna if that's okay? We make every decision together. I hope you understand."

"Of course, Stenson. That is something I admire about you. You always consider other's feelings before your own," he replied. "Take your time and let me know what you decide."

Fallon stood up and shook Stenson's hand as he left. Stenson looked around the room and thought about the future. Could his life get any better than this?

* * *

The guys tossed ruined furniture and wasted equipment into a giant pile in the parking lot. Predicably unpredictable, JC felt compelled to pour gasoline onto the heap and set it ablaze, despite Big Tony saying it was not a good idea. The unbelievable stench emanating from the garbage did not improve the funky odor. It was so bad that even the flies stayed away. The guys covered their noses as they watched their dreams burn away.

They returned to the club and found Zabrina in the office upstairs. She looked at them and said, "I hope none of you expect to get a date. You smell like a dumpster fire."

JC quipped, "You don't smell too good yourself,

and you are wearing perfume."

The malodorous misfits joined Zabrina around the table. JC wanted to share his ideas of what they could do with the place should they choose to rebuild. She rolled her eyes knowing this would be crazy to hear the outrageous malfunctions zooming around JCs silly head. Every idea JC came up with was terrible. What would it be now; a petting zoo for sharks or alligator mud wrestling?

"What have you got, moron?" Zabrina hesitantly asked.

"Why don't we do something that combines everything we like?" the out-of-the-box thinker suggested.

"None of us like the same thing," Zabrina reminded. "For example, you like sports and I hate sports."

"Exactly!" JC exclaimed.

Zabrina did not know where this was going, but let his randomness continue.

"You love fashion and know sex appeal, considering your previous occupation," he poorly explained.

Zabrina was ready to knock JC across the room to bring that up. Strike one, she thought.

"Big Tony loves food." JC continued.

Anthony Gallo rubbed his stomach and smiled with a hungry grin.

"Let's create a bar concept with a sexy twist." JC suggested.

"They've got that already. It's called Hooters, and I am not walking around here wearing a halter top and shorts." Zabrina warned.

"Why not? You do it anyway," JC observed.

Big Tony laughed. "Touché. He got you on that one, Zabrina."

Zabrina ignored their fashion commentary about

her clothes and asked, "What makes us different?"

"Well, for one, we will have the prettiest servers in all of New Orleans, but not dressed in tacky outfits; something more upscale. Second, we will have better food. It might not actually be better, but we will charge more for it. And because it costs more, people will perceive it is better. Maybe a cigar bar, music venue, sports bar kind of thing. It could be three venues in one."

"What, no bowling alley or ice-skating rink?" she sarcastically whipped.

"Nah, too hot for ice skating in New Orleans. Miniature golf might be fun, but it will take up a lot of room. We may need to rent the warehouse next door," JC rationalized.

Now Zabrina did not know if JC was messing with her or if he really considered those other ideas. It was hard to tell with him. But his idea wasn't terrible, outside of the bowling alley, ice skating rink, and miniature golf.

"What do you propose we call this place, genius?" Zabrina asked.

"Why don't we call it JCs?" he replied.

Zabrina and Tony laughed out loud.

JC felt embarrassed. "Well, it's better than a black guy, an ex-hooker, and their fat friend."

"Hey now, watch it, JC," Big Tony warned. "This fat friend can toss your skinny butt over that balcony if you mention my weight one more time."

Zabrina chuckled. Then she suggested, "What about Fats—New Orleans, if Big Tony doesn't mind? It plays on the city's nickname, the Big Easy, and music roots."

"I don't mind that kind of fat," Tony Gallo said. "I like it."

"What about you, moron?" Zabrina asked JC.

"Why do I get tossed over a balcony if I joke

about Tony's weight, but you can name our place Fats, and he likes it?" JC wondered.

"Because she's prettier and smarter than you, JC," Big Tony explained.

"Well, let's sleep on it," Zabrina suggested.

"Can we still have a shark tank?" JC teased as they walked out the door.

Zabrina laughed at JC again. "Tony, feel free to toss him over the balcony. Maybe falling on his head will make it clear I said no."

Chapter 4

Luna noticed Stenson sitting on the sofa watching TV when she arrived home from work.

"You're home early," she said as she laid her keys on the console table in the hallway and walked into the living room.

"Is everything okay?" Luna asked.

"It's great when I see the most beautiful girl in the world walk through the door," he cheekily complimented.

"Oh, you like fat women who waddle now?" Luna suggested with a pregnant "What are you up to?" grin.

"I took off early. There is something I want to talk to you about," he told her. "Come sit down."

Luna kicked off her shoes and plopped onto Stenson's lap. She wrapped her arms around him and leaned over to peck his lips with a playful kiss.

"What does the future father of the year want to tell the most beautiful fat girl in the world?" Luna asked Mr. Charisma.

"Can I call you Big Mama now?" her husband jokingly replied.

She slapped his arm. "You better not!"

"Just kidding. Actually, Fallon stopped by today. He is thinking of retiring and wants to get rid of the bar."

A concerned look overcame Luna's face. "Does that mean you will be out of a job?"

"Quite the contrary, if you agree?" Stenson suggested.

"Agree with what?" she curiously asked.

Stenson deadpanned, "He offered to give me the bar."

"Wait. What? Give you the bar?" she repeated.

"Yeah, give it to me. Fallon asked if I would send him a stipend each month to supplement his retirement. He didn't even name an amount. He also said I can change the name of the bar if I want. But of course, I told him I would have to talk to you first. What do you think?"

"I think it is great! Of course it will be a lot of work. But it is not like you haven't been running the place for a couple of years, so it wouldn't be much different. Will you change the name?"

"No, I don't think so. I like the name O'Malley's even if I'm not Irish. Besides, Fallon put a lot of heart into making it what it is today. I will keep it like it is. Are you sure you are okay with it?"

"Stenson, you are successful in everything you do, and I support you. You have my blessing if you want to do it. And thank you for thinking of me before you agreed."

"Always, Luna," he replied. "What do you say we go out for a nice dinner to celebrate?"

"Sounds good to me. I am starving! Remember, I am eating for two," she reminded him. "And if I hear one more fat joke, you are sleeping on the sofa in your new bar!"

The next day, Stenson asked Brick to join him in the office. He shared the news of Fallon's offer to take over the the bar. Robert was surprised by the generous offer. Then Stenson asked if he would like to become the new manager. Stenson suggested it would come with a raise.

"A raise?" Brick said. "I would dance on the bar

wearing a hula skirt for a raise."

"That is why I am giving you a raise so you won't do that," Stenson joked. "Besides, you are my best friend and I couldn't think of anyone I would trust more than you to run the place, even though I will have nightmares thinking of you in a hula skirt with coconuts over your breasts."

"I would rock that outfit!" Brick proudly proclaimed.

Later that day, Stenson met Fallon O'Malley at his attorney's office to complete the transfer of the pub. Stenson called Brick after they were done to invite the big marine to join them for a late lunch in the Quarter. The three former soldiers reminisced over beers with tall tales of wine, women, and county jails. It was a pleasant afternoon celebrating among friends.

Fallon was in unusually good spirits after he left the restaurant. He was delighted Stenson would take over the bar and, knowing Robert would help him run it. Now he looked forward to spending more time with his wife and family to make up for all the time he missed.

* * *

It was agreed the new venue would be named "Fats—New Orleans". Zabrina wasn't keen on the idea at first, but after considering it further, she realized the concept had possibilities. They would divide the former Club Empire space into three separate venues: a high-end sports bar, cigar bar, and a live music venue. It allowed them to cater to a wider clientele and offered more revenue streams than they had before.

Z was an expert marketer, and the team liked the preliminary plan she designed. While she often chastised JC over his intelligence, she knew he was actually a smart guy. Even though he was naïve, Justin had natural instincts. However, it did not excuse some of the silly things he did with his money, like buying a shrimp boat or outrageous cars and expensive clothes.

Zabrina understood JCs flamboyance hid the hurt boy inside a man's body. She often felt sorry for him and how his life began. While she would not admit it, she secretly admired how he had grown in the last few years. It began when he gained confidence after they built Empire. Together, she, Big Tony, and JC had created something special. No single one of them could have done it. It took all three. And where she saw the biggest turning point in his life, where JC truly grew, was when he met his mother after 25 years.

He reconnected with her in his darkest hour after they lost the club. So much of his heart was restored. His mother explained she made the heart-wrenching, terrifying decision to abandon him at the hospital when he was born out of love. She believed someone would adopt her son and provide him with a better life than she could as a sixteen-year-old unwed mother. When she explained the disease he carried was caused after she was raped by a heroin addict hiding in a train car when she ran away from home to prevent her mother from forcing her son into an unborn grave. He felt ashamed for blaming his mom for so many years.

In many ways, those heroic ways, JC was like his mother; a wonderful person who was hurt as a child and despite the pain tried to do what was right even though to others it may seem wrong. And when JC's mom explained to him about the vivid dream she had before he was born, that told her that the little boy she carried would one day grow up to be a great man, she knew it was true. Though it hurt her to sacrifice like she did to bring JC into this world, she did it with unconditional love and would do it all over again. Zabrina knew his mother was right. One day, that funny guy will be a great man.

The thought of parents made Zabrina miss her own. It had been eight years since she left North Korea and four since she had spoken to them on an illegal Chinese phone. In her last conversation with her father, she detected tension in his voice. When she asked if everything was okay, he reassured her that all was fine. Her mother was a little more forthcoming and revealed authorities had interrogated them about their daughter's whereabouts. Rumors had circulated that she had escaped the country with the help of a Chinese gang.

While North Korea could not adequately feed their own people, they did not like when anyone escaped. Better to suffer together than let one of their citizens find out the world was better than the daily hardships they faced. The last thing the regime wanted were former North Koreans returning home to expose their lies. Maybe it was jealousy or self-preservation, but it is very hard to keep a secret in North Korea. Eyes and ears were everywhere, and you did not know who to trust. If a person believed it would benefit them to provide information that may help themselves, they will do it in a heartbeat. And that concerned Zabrina the most. She spent many sleepless nights worrying about her family.

She pushed those dark thoughts aside. There were more pressing things to do, like getting their business up and running again. She asked JC to join her in the office to review their plans. He was wearing a white tank top and red jogging pants when he walked in. She noticed how much more muscular he was from the stick figure she met a few years ago. He was gawky then, but after spending time in the gym he was built more like a professional athlete.

JC noticed her stare. "Like what you see?"

Zabrina quickly looked away, embarrassed JC noticed her admiring his frame. "Shut up and get over here, moron. And for your information, I have seen better bodies on pencils."

JC ignored her remark. "What ya got?"

She rolled out architectural plans across the table.

"These are design ideas for Fats the architect dropped off," she said.

"When did we hire an architect? I drew some stuff on a napkin," JC bragged.

"He is a friend and former customer of Club Empire. He felt sorry for our loss and liked the idea of us rebuilding rather than putting our tail between our legs and running away," she explained.

"He offered his services as a way of donating to the cause. And before you say a word, no, I didn't sleep with him."

JC grinned. "I didn't say a word. But if he is giving us free architectural services, I bet he wants to sleep with you, but I wonder why? He must be a cheap architect."

Zabrina slapped JC on his arm.

"Boy, a monkey wouldn't sleep with you," she jabbed.

"Our architect is a monkey?" JC joked.

They were both tickled at the idea their architect was a monkey that won't sleep with JC, but would sleep with Zabrina.

Big Tony walked into the room. "What are you two laughing at?"

"The wicked witch is being funny," JC replied. "Look at this," he said, motioning him over.

Tony looked at the plans. He said, "I am glad to see you two are on speaking terms again while secretly plotting ways to kill each other."

They all chuckled. The truce between Zabrina and JC never lasted very long. Big Tony had watched JC and Zabrina tease each other from the first day they met. He was convinced there was more to their relationship than either pretended or understood.

Zabrina pointed to an overlay and explained, "We can divide the building into three venues, an upscale sports bar, cigar and wine bar here, and a music venue on the far end."

She continued. "These won't be large spaces, but I like the idea they are intimate. We can cater to different crowds and rent the entire place for VIP events like we did it before."

"Great idea, but how much will it cost?" JC asked.

"Believe it or not, I ran some numbers and we can squeeze it in for under $800,000, the money Stenson returned. We salvaged the kitchen equipment, which can serve all venues. The lighting and sound system from Empire can go into the music space. The rest we build ourselves or buy used."

She said, "We may not make a salary for a while, but we can reopen. We should make money soon enough if all goes well. And many of our servers and bartenders want to come back and agreed to work for tips until we get on our feet."

JC and Tony were impressed.

"What do you want us to do?" JC asked.

"I want you two sweaty bozos to go home and take a shower. You stink!"

Chapter 5

Luna was in a nesting phase late into her pregnancy with motherly instincts signaling her to prepare for birth. Stenson also found himself in a doting stage too with cues beckoning him to nurture the mother of his child.

Stenson wanted to spend more time with Luna during her last term and asked Robert Brickhouse if he would assume his management responsibilities at O'Malley's Pub for a few months. Brick did not mind. He was overjoyed for the couple as if he had something to do with the pregnancy—which in some ways he did since it was he who encouraged his best friend to call the girl after so many years that got this love story started. The big marine would do anything for Stenson and Luna. Besides, evenings were when his biker buddies stopped by the bar and they were a rowdy crowd. No sense in exposing an expectant father to the chaos that might break out among those wild friends.

Despite Stenson's pleas for his wife to stop working weeks before she was due, she insisted on continuing to work until she gave birth. She planned to take several months of paternity leave after their child arrived, and she still had things to do.

Stenson did not dare argue with her. After all, a person must be crazy to argue with a pregnant woman. She might get that crazed look in her eyes like parrots do when they are about to explode and rip a piece off you when their pupils flare wide. "I said no!" she might say. Luna's hormones were flaring, and Stenson was bright enough not to ask again. He would keep this parrot happy if it was the last thing on earth he could do.

Most nights, Stenson would have dinner prepared when his pregnant wife and mother-to-be arrived home. While he never claimed to be an expert in the kitchen, he enjoyed cooking for her. Luna often teased him that they could never divorce. She said she would starve to death because the only thing she could cook was burned toast.

Luna loved the attention from her husband. She felt blessed to have a guy like him. Pregnant or not, Stenson Beckett would always be the same loving man. Despite everything he had endured in his life, he remained the most gentle, caring, thoughtful, and funny person she had ever known. She knew more than anyone the details of her husband's dark past and understood the pain he hid deep inside.

She remembered vividly when they were kids the abuse he received from his violent, racist, alcoholic father. Stenson would often show up for school with bruises or a black eye. She would ask him what happened and he would shrug it off like it was nothing. To have witnessed such a violent end to his mother's life at that tender age would have scarred anyone. And to make matters worse, police had circumstantial evidence never proven in court that his father was behind the explosion at his grandparents' home that killed his mother's parents. In one fateful, deadly evening, Tug Beckett destroyed everything Stenson loved in the world.

The goodness in Stenson came from his mother's DNA. Luna was convinced it was one of the ingredients that made him the man he is today; courageous, tender, and strong. He strove to be a better man; the kind of man his dad never was to him.

His father was released from prison after serving 12.5 years of a 15-year sentence for "good behavior" which incensed Stenson. He believed the man should have received the death penalty or at least spent a miserable lifetime behind bars.

He blamed himself for the early release of his father after running away at eight years old rather than testify in court for fear of seeing the evil man again. It would have been difficult enough for an adult to face a murderer in court and much more for a child. While nobody blamed Stenson, he blamed himself. Maybe that was why Stenson was so brave today. He sought redemption for his dark past. Wherever he saw injustice, he would fight for what is right, no matter the consequence or price he must pay.

Nobody knew if Tug Beckett was alive or dead to this day after he vanished upon his release from prison, nor did anyone care. As far as the people who knew Tug Beckett, it was one less scum-of-the-earth to torture the world. But women have intuition and Luna believed Tug's existence on this earth, or lack-thereof, may have been perpetrated by her husband. She believed when Stenson learned the man had sired another boy after reading a newspaper article about Tug Beckett's arrest for domestic violence against the mother, something inside of him may have snapped. Luna knew Stenson's moral compass pointed true. It would not have been revenge for his mother's death. For that, he would let God decide. But if he had erased the evil man, it would have been because Stenson would never let what happened to him happen to another child. Period.

It was another reason she admired Stenson. Anybody who had experienced the same trauma as him would have changed. But somehow, it made Stenson stronger and more convicted to be a better person, husband, father, and friend. She often wished his mother were alive so she could thank her for raising such a wonderful son and instilling in him goodness the world desperately needed today.

Luna's son moved inside her belly. It was the weirdest sensation and felt like the child was having a wrestling match, or rearranging her intestines to find a comfortable spot to lay his head on her bladder and prop his feet up on her rib cage like she was a human lounge chair. She laughed to herself and wondered if she had gobbled a Smurf at lunch.

She was due any day, and her stomach had grown as large as a beach ball or a small weather balloon. The thought of having a baby stretch her lady parts sent a shudder running up her spine. As if having eight pounds of bouncing baby boy playing with her guts was not enough; oh wait, there is an encore!

Everything about her body had changed. She was tired of waddling whenever she walked and eating for two. The fat she gained, stretch marks, and gigantic rear end had to go. Even though Stenson reminded her every day how beautiful she was, in her mind she was ugly and obese. She did hope, however, to keep her breasts, which had grown quite impressive from the B-sized she wore before. "Lose the fat, keep the boobs," Luna told herself. She must admit, life could be funny sometimes.

She logged off her computer and grabbed her purse and keys then toddled out of the building toward her car, feeling like a walrus looking for a new place on the beach to sun. When she reached her SUV, she discovered a flat tire.

"Oh, great!" she said out loud.

She phoned Stenson to ask for help. Fifteen minutes later he showed up with Robert Brickhouse,

Justin Carter, and Big Tony Gallo. All she needed was a tire change, and her husband brought a calvary of mechanics. Did these tough guys plan on lifting her vehicle manually instead of using a jack? She chuckled watching the boys go to work like a NASCAR pit crew repairing a wheel in record time. Robert became irritated with JC fumbling to remove the lug nuts.

Brick said, "Give me that before I bash you over the head with a tire iron," he told JC.

Besides her husband, the rest of the guys treated Luna like their little sister. It was comforting to know so many amiable, albeit crazy men looked after her. AAA could never provide this kind of service.

After they finished, Stenson invited the pit crew to their home for dinner. Luna enjoyed having a house full of hungry people to feed, especially this motley crew. She noticed one person missing from the crowd. Zabrina Chao was not there. She and Luna had never formerly made up like Stenson and JC did. They weren't unkind to each other, just never spoke about what happened before. Luna asked JC why Z had not come over?

"Zabrina thinks you hate her," Justin replied.

"Nonsense, invite her over," Luna insisted.

JC phoned Zabrina, and soon she arrived. Luna answered the door and greeted her with a big, pregnant hug. They shared a few private words together, and that was all it took for Zabrina to know there were no hard feelings and she was always welcome in their home.

The pair rejoined the rest at the group at the table. Luna surveyed the room. She smiled thinking this was how it should be sharing a meal together as friends.

After the guests left, Luna told Stenson, "That was nice. I will do the dishes."

He looked at her like she was crazy and emphatically stated, "No, you won't, young lady. You are going to sit your gigantic butt on that sofa and watch one of your chick flicks while I clean up this mess."

"I know you did not call my butt gigantic," Luna jokingly said.

"I was thinking Titanic, but that boat sank," Stenson quipped back at her with a teasing wink.

Luna knew there would be no point in arguing with a proud father-to-be. She walked into the living room and found a cozy spot on the couch, and flicked on the TV. Half an hour later she said, "Uh oh."

From the kitchen, Stenson called out, "Uh oh, what?"

"I believe your son is ready to meet you. Either that or I have just become the new Niagara Falls.

Luna stood up to reveal her water broke through her soaking wet spandex pants. Stenson looked over and dropped the pan he'd been washing and immediately transcended into full freak out mode. He ran to their bedroom and retrieved a suitcase they had prepared for this moment. Then he grabbed his coat and keys and rushed out the door. A few moments later, he returned and asked Luna, "Aren't you coming?"

She laughed and said, "I guess so, unless you plan on birthing this child yourself?"

Speeding like a madman with his emergency flashers on, no red lights, stop signs, or werewolves would prevent Stenson Beckett from getting this laborious woman to the hospital in record time.

He screeched to a stop in front of the emergency room door and rushed inside. Moments later, he returned with a nurse and a wheelchair. He helped his wife out of the car and into the rolling chair.

Luna did not know what all the fuss was about. She wasn't the first woman to have a child. Try explaining that to a first time, father. Stenson acted as if this was the immaculate conception. All they were missing were three wise men, a manger, and a donkey. And if Stenson did not calm down, Luna was convinced he would find a mule.

"Honey, relax," she suggested. "It will be hours before the baby arrives and I don't need my husband going into cardiac arrest and laying on a table next to me. Breathe Stenson.Breathe."

"I thought I was supposed to say that to you," he replied, so unfocused that he completely missed Luna's little joke.

She was tickled seeing her husband like panicking this. He was normally such a calm guy even in the wildest situations, But right now, Stenson was on a different planet and he wondered how his wife could be so calm when he was on DEFCON 3?

A nurse shooed Stenson out of the delivery room while they prepared Luna. She ensured him they would take good care of his wife and would call him when the baby was ready to arrive.

Stenson made her promise. "Don't forget, okay?"

The nurse smiled and reassured him she would not forget; she had done this before. After Stenson left the room, the nurse told Luna she never tired of seeing first time fathers lose their minds.

Stenson phoned Brick from the hospital lobby to inform him the baby was on the way. Soon after, the waiting room filled with all their crazy friends. Stenson paced like a person with a mental disorder. Robert considered punching him in the forehead to knock him out so the boy could relax. But punching his best friend was probably not the best idea. Since he didn't have a tranquilizer gun or the will to steal some hospital pharmaceuticals, Stenson would have to walk this anxiety off. As Brick watched his best friend pace, he was convinced the hospital would need to replace some floor tiles because Stenson was wearing them out so badly it looked like the runway of an aircraft carrier deck. If that baby did not arrive soon, it would be Stenson Beckett needing an arresting cable to keep him from flying over the edge.

Stenson complained, "I wish Luna would hurry!"

Soni James, their trans friend tried to explain it was not up to Luna, it was up to the baby when he was ready to enter the world. Stenson told Soni he would have a conversation with the child about why it took him so long to arrive.

After a few torturous hours of Stenson saying the clock must be broken because every minute felt like an eternity, a medical assistant entered area to summon the impatient dad. He leaped from the chair and almost knocked her over as he rushed by. She grabbed him by the shirt tail and said, "Hold your horses. You don't know what room she is in."

He released her grip and shouted, "I will find her!"

The nurse looked at Stenson's friends and asked, "Is he always like this?"

Robert shrugged. "Not always."

She caught up to Stenson after he ran into the wrong delivery room.

"You're not my wife!" he exclaimed.

The lady with expanded legs yelled at Stenson, "You're not my husband!"

The nurse grabbed him by his earlobe since grabbing his shirt tail did not work. She led him to another room where she instructed Stenson to don a pale blue cap, gown, and a mask. He scrubbed his hands, then washed his face. The nurse told him he didn't have to wash his face since he would wear a mask. But it was okay unless he planned on washing his hair. She explained that is what the cap was for. Then Stenson asked what about his shoes? The nurse told him this was not NASA and he could put his shoes back on.

Stenson slid his hands into pair of latex gloves and entered the delivery room. Suddenly, a strange thought came over him when he noticed he was dressed like the doctors and nurses. He surely hoped they weren't expecting him to deliver this baby. If so, it was way out of his league!

A lump as large as a golf ball formed inside his throat when he laid eyes on Luna lying on her back with legs spread wide open in stirrups on the delivery table. Luna saw him enter and offered a strained, loving smile. Her breathing had become, "Woosh, whoosh, whoosh" which told everyone it would not be long.

Stenson joined her beside and took his wife's hand. She squeezed him tightly and looked deeply into his eyes.

She whispered, "I love you."

Stenson felt as if he would melt on the floor after hearing those three lovely words. He fought back tears to be the stronger one in this room. It was for naught, because the true hero clutched his hand. Stenson returned her gentle smile with one of his own and whispered, "I love you more."

It was such a cherished moment between these two friends, lovers, and soon-to-be parents.

Their obstetrician informed the couple Luna was moments away. The doctor asked Stenson if he wanted to see the miracle of birth to stand behind her. Stenson leaned down and kissed Luna's cheek. Then he reluctantly released her hand. From that moment on, time went into slow motion.

His mind flashed to when he and Luna were kids.

He thought of their laughter and the fun they had; of the heartfelt secrets they shared; of the first time he saw her again after so many years. He fondly remembered their funny wedding and precious moments that made their lives so rich. A warm smile filled his face as he watched the movie play inside his head.

A voice broke through his beautiful memories, saying, "Mr. Beckett? You may lean a little closer to have a better look," a medical assistant encouraged the melting man.

Stenson craned closer to see his son's head beginning to crest. Luna's doctor coached Luna to pace herself as she took faster puffing breaths. Through a strained cry, she pushed hard to free the child's head. Stenson felt faint and could not help but cry at the sight of his son's tiny face for the first time. Luna continued to breathe deeply, then she pushed again. The baby's shoulders emerged with a painful relief. A few more minutes of deep breathing, then Luna took a final breath. She gave one more agonizing push and screamed like an opera singer, hitting the highest notes as she freed her son from his protective cocoon. Stenson was awestruck with emotions of love and minuteness like he had never felt. Stenson Beckett, Jr. was finally here!

He could hide it no longer and burst into tears. Stenson did not care who saw him cry. It was the most beautiful thing he had ever witnessed in his life. The doctor cut the umbilical cord to release the child from the last physical bond he shared with his mother. Now the little boy was on his own. A nurse took the baby to clean while another attended to Luna. Stenson returned to his her side. She shared her husband's tears of joy. They were parents now. What a beautiful day!

The nurse returned their son to Luna and gently

laid the child wrapped in a pale blue blanket into her arms. Luna gave her son a kiss on his tiny forehead and said, "Hello, Stenson Beckett, Jr."

Hearing those words, "Stenson Beckett, Jr." made Stenson feel proud and terrified at the same time. He promised himself, his wife, and God Almighty his son would never endure the childhood he had.

"He's so tiny," Stenson admired.

"He's not that tiny! Trust me," Luna replied with a smile like she had just won a battle. "You didn't have to push him out of your butt!"

Even in this moment, Luna still had her fun a sense of humor. Stenson was asked to leave the delivery room so medical staff could attend to his wife. He kissed Luna's lips and his son then returned to the waiting room and triumphantly announced, "I have a son!"

Cheers erupted. Hugs, handshakes and high fives were shared around the room with the new father who beamed with a smile so wide you would think it might break.

"How is Luna?" Zabrina was the first to ask.

"She is great!" Stenson replied. "She came through it with barely a whimper. I cried more than she did," he admitted.

"She is a tough girl," Zabrina said. "I should know, since my hair still hasn't grown back completely after the prank she pulled on me."

Everyone laughed, recalling the time when Luna placed hair remover in Zabrina's shampoo as an act of revenge before they were friends.

"What's his name?" JC asked.

Stenson looked down at the floor sheepishly.

"Stenson Beckett, Jr. It was Luna's idea."

"That's great!" Brick exclaimed, "Couldn't have named him after a better man!"

The comment made Stenson feel even more

awkward and overwhelmed. Like a ton of bricks, he realized more than ever how important his responsibility was now. The friends chatted around the waiting room until a nurse told Stenson his son had been moved to the nursery.

"You want to meet my kid?" Stenson asked proudly.

Of course they did!

The gang of misfits walked down the cheerfully colored hallway of the maternity ward. They arrived at three large windows peering into the nursery. The room was lined with three rows of cribs, three rows deep, with incubators on each side. Two nurses flitted around the room attending to newborns. Stenson scanned looking for his son. While babies look similar when they are born, Stenson spotted his in the second row, third from the right.

A nurse noticed Stenson pointing excitedly and knew this was a first-time father. She removed the baby from the crib and walked over to the window, holding him for everyone to see.

"Aww, what a beautiful child," Zabrina gushed.

"Good thing he didn't get your looks, Stenson," Brickhouse teased.

"He's definitely got his mother's good looks," Stenson proudly agreed.

After a few moments of admiration, Stenson suggested everyone should go home. He told them he planned to spend the night with Luna while she recovered.

"We will leave after we smoke one of these." Brick said as he removed a fistful of cigars he had brought for the special occasion.

The gang walked outside into the parking lot where Robert handed out stogies. They passed around a lighter, igniting their salute.

Robert said, "Here is to my best friend, his lovely

wife and handsome son!"

"Here! Here!" they exclaimed. Everyone took a long drag on the cigars causing Zabrina and Big Tony to choke and gasp for air. After more hugs and congratulations, everyone left except for Robert who stayed behind with Stenson. He placed his burly tattooed arm around his best friend's shoulder and said, "I am proud of you and Luna, buddy. This will be a day we all remember."

While Robert was a bear of a man who could be gruff with people sometimes, underneath that tough exterior was a genuinely nice guy who Stenson was proud to call his best friend.

"Can I get you anything before I go?" Robert asked.

"Maybe a toothbrush. In the rush, I forgot mine. Luna might throw me out when I kiss her in the morning and my breath smells like a wolf."

"Good thing I don't have to kiss you," Brick joked. "I will bring you a toothbrush so you don't end up sleeping on my couch."

Robert hugged the new father and told him to give Luna his regards. Stenson took another long drag on his cigar as Brick walked away and savored the moment. Today, he knew he was a very blessed man.

The next morning a nurse stopped by Luna's room to offer the parents instructions about caring for a newborn. Stenson studied the pamphlets as if there would be a test afterward. He could not resist asking the nurse about the instructions regarding breastfeeding.

"You have a pamphlet on nursing a baby? Doesn't that kind of come naturally to a mother and child?"

The nurse replied, "You'd be surprised. We just make sure we cover all the bases, especially for new mothers and curious dads like you."

Stenson left the room at the conclusion their newborn class to allow Luna time with their son while she fed him. As he walked to the administration desk, he was simply amazed how miraculous women are to give birth to a child and feed them with their own bodies. He had never really thought about that before and suddenly felt inadequate compared to her.

When he returned to the room, Stenson watched Luna nurturing their child with a memorized gaze. After the baby was finished feeding, Luna asked her husband, "Do you want to change his diaper?"

It did not occur to Stenson he would be on diaper duty this soon. He had never changed a baby's diaper before and now he felt like he needed to review the pamphlet again.

Luna handed him the tiny child who felt so delicate in his arms. As he stared into his son's face, Luna encouraged Stenson with a playful tease, "Come on dad, you've got this."

He carefully laid his son inside the bassinet while Luna gingerly climbed out of bed to watch. When Stenson noticed her getting up, he suggested she lay back down.

She replied, "Nonsense, I am sore, but I am not dead. I want to see you do this, tough guy."

He smiled with fake sense of confidence hiding his terror and reassured his curious wife, "I've got this."

He unwrapped the pale blue blanket from around his tiny son and removed the tape of a disposable diaper. The smell and unusually colored runniness made Stenson dry heave like he was going to vomit. Luna laughed out loud.

"What's the matter, honey? Haven't you seen a newborn's poo-poo before?"

Trying to play it cool, Stenson said, "I am fine.

It's just the smell and the color. What did you feed this child?"

Luna placed her hands on her hips and said, "What do you think I fed him?"

Stenson chuckled, then disposed of the soiled diaper and wiped his son's bottom with a moist towelette. When Stenson leaned down close to see how to attach the diaper, his son peed in his face like a little water fountain.

Luna roared. "I guess he wasn't done."

"Very funny, Junior," Stenson told his son. "You haven't been here 24 hours and already you are giving your dad a hard time."

Luna told Stenson the nurse informed her he had washed his face before entering the delivery room.

"You should have waited," she joked as she handed him another toilette.

Stenson managed the diaper without too much difficulty. He told Luna when he was a baby, his family was so poor they could not afford disposable diapers. He wore cloth diapers with safety pins. He is surprised he doesn't have more holes in his backside other than a gunshot wound.

"Oh, how times have changed," Luna remarked.

After they arrived home from the hospital, they noticed a bottle of Champaign wrapped with a baby blue bow and two glasses. Alongside it sat a gift with a card on the coffee table. The couple wondered how it got there.

Stenson opened the card and read it aloud. "To a wonderful family and your new edition. Cheers! -MM"

Stenson and Luna looked at each other. They immediately knew how special this gift was when Stenson showed her the card.

"Is that who I think it is from?" Luna asked.

"There is only one ghost we know who can sneak in and out of somebody's home without being noticed and has those initials," Stenson replied.

The gifts were from the Mystery Man, the hooded character who helped them get their revenge on JC and his crew for various tricks they pulled over the years. To this day, nobody knew who the person was or how they did such mysterious things. But it was no surprise and a little exciting to know the Mystery Man knew about the birth of their child and snuck into their locked home to leave gifts. If Santa Claus had a spooky brother who dressed in a black hoodie, it would be the Mystery Man.

The gift would have to wait. They had a baby to attend to now. Stenson and Luna spent months preparing the baby's room. It wasn't until Stenson watched Luna gently lay Stenson Jr. into his crib that the room felt complete. Their tiny son looked up at them with bright blue eyes and wonderment on his tiny face. Luna and Stenson stared at the amazing miracle with an overwhelming sense of pride. They stared at the little boy until he drifted to sleep.

Stenson wrapped his arms around his wife and gave her a tender kiss. He said, "You made a beautiful baby, Mrs. Beckett."

With a gentle reminder and a soft kiss, Luna replied, "We made a beautiful baby."

They returned to the living room and sat on the sofa. Stenson handed Luna the gift from the Mystery Man.

"Would you care for a glass of champaign, my dear?" he asked in the voice of a British butler.

"I would love one, kind sir." she replied as she unwrapped the present.

"Aww," Luna said as she held up a pale blue jumper.

"The Mystery Man has nice taste," she admired.

"But how did he know we had a boy?"

"Some things remain a mystery. He has great taste in wine, too. This stuff isn't the cheap stuff."

Luna made a toast. "To my wonderful husband and his beautiful son. You have filled my life with more joy than a girl deserves."

They tinkled glasses and took a sip. It had been an exhausting 30 hours. The couple went upstairs to their bedroom where Stenson tucked in his wife in and rolled the baby's bassinet by her side. He climbed into bed next to her and held Luna close, never wanting to let her go. As he laid there, he was filled with pride and felt complete. They were really a family now.

* * *

Early the next morning, Stenson's phone buzzed on the bedside table. He saw it was the big marine calling. He climbed out of bed so as not to disturb Luna who had awakened several times during the night to attend to their son.

He went downstairs to answer the phone. He whispered, "Do you know what time it is?"

"Well, good morning to you, too!" Brick cheerfully roared, ignoring Stenson's question.

"Mind if I come over?" Brick asked.

"Sure. I will put some coffee on," Stenson replied, wondering if Brick needed more coffee, as cheerful as this bulldog was.

"Make sure you put on pajamas," the marine instructed.

"I should come to the door naked, so you will let me go back to sleep," Stenson joked before he hung up the phone.

A short time later, there was a quiet knock. Stenson opened the front door to see the grinning Marine with arms filled with presents.

Stenson whispered, "What is all this?"

Robert entered the foyer and said, "Don't get excited. None of it is for you. It is for my nephew."

"Oh, you are an uncle now?" Stenson teased, since Robert isn't biologically related.

"What is he going to call you, Uncle Brick?" Stenson inquired.

"Nah, Uncle Robert would be okay," Brickhouse said, since it seemed he had already decided what he wanted Stenson's son to call him. Stenson skipped reminding Brick the child was born yesterday and it would be awhile before he could talk.

"Can I see him?" Brick asked anxiously.

"He's in our room. I don't want to wake Luna. But it's probably time to change his diaper, so I will bring him into the baby's room." Stenson said as they tiptoed upstairs.

Stenson returned with his son in his arms and laid him into the crib. Robert gazed at the sleeping child and whispered. "He seems so happy."

"Yeah, he probably knows his crazy uncle is here, and he's putting on a show for you," Stenson suggested.

After Stenson changed the baby's diaper, they returned downstairs to the kitchen where he poured two cups of coffee.

"Sorry, but you weren't the first one to bring a gift," Stenson told Robert as he walked to the living room and returned with a card and handed it to Brick.

"No way!" Robert exclaimed after reading the note. "How did he... never mind. We both know how he operates. That was nice of him, though. But if he ever breaks into my place, he is likely to get shot."

Stenson laughed. "It would be more like, 'Where did Robert go? He simply vanished one day.'"

They both knew it was true because with the

Mystery Man, anything was possible.

Chapter 6

Construction progressed steadily, transforming the former Club Empire into three new entertainment venues, collectively named Fats — New Orleans. JC, Zabrina, and Big Tony of JZBT Enterprises toiled like a family of beavers building a dam they hoped would not leak like the last one.

Zabrina juggled the money, project management, human resources, and marketing while JC took on the role of general contractor. He wasn't qualified to do the job, but after Zabrina became exhausted watching him skulk around moaning about not having a fancy title, she conceded. His primary role was to stay out of people's way and ensure their construction schedules remained on track.

Big Tony did whatever was asked without complaint. He would assist moving heavy items or run errands to pick up food or supplies. Anything Tony did was accomplished with a cheerful attitude, unlike JC who complained about everything.

"Hey, you over there," JC would yell. "You sure you are using the correct screws?"

One day Zabrina overheard him barking orders and said, "Leave those people alone, JC. The only screws you know about are loose in your head!"

Jesús Alvarez, their previous cook from Club Empire, rejoined the team to assist setting up the kitchen. He would often try out new menu items on the construction crew, which was Big Tony's favorite part of the day.

Even though the grand opening remained a few months away, Zabrina wasted no time promoting the new venture. After the colossal disaster that took Club Empire down and ruined their reputations, Zabrina was eager to get ahead of this resurrection with a narrative of her own.

A television crew planned to visit the construction site the following day. Zabrina was prepared for the inevitable questions about their spectacular demise by diverting the conversation toward their bright future. She was an expert at turning negatives into positives; so good, in fact, that she should have been a politician.

"Yes, the unfortunate fumigant disbursement at our previous establishment occurred after a malfunction of an organic environmental control system using clean, renewable energy. It was a demonstration of how businesses and the community can work together to solve important social issues without adding additional burden or expense to our government, which lowers taxes for the average citizen and improves their quality of life. I am proud of the work our team has done and look forward to making New Orleans great again when we open our exciting new entertainment venue, Fats—New Orleans!"

What she really said was, "Stenson and his friends set off the funkiest stink bombs in our club during the most import and highly publicized black-tie event we ever hosted. Patrons running out of Club Empire vomiting all over their pretty clothes, with burning eyes, and screaming obscenities was caught on live television and spread across social media like wildfire, making us the laughingstock of New Orleans and around the world. We hope you have forgotten the embarrassing incident because we are building a new place and hope you will visit because we are broke and don't know what else to do."

Zabrina always seemed to be in damage control mode, especially when JC was around. He begged her to allow him to appear on camera during the interview. Since she never knew what nonsensical things he might say, she instructed JC to look busy and, by all means, keep his mouth shut.

The next morning JC arrived wearing a shiny red track suit with white unlaced sneakers, a gold construction hat tilted like a fedora, gold chains hung around his neck, and an imitation Rolex watch to polish off his look.

Zabrina was flabbergasted. "Who dresses like that at a construction site?" she asked the shiny track suit man.

"I do!" JC proudly crowed.

He said, "You told me to look busy. You didn't say how I should dress," he emphasized.

She shook her head. "You should be in a rap video on an oil rig as a member of DJ Dummy and the Funky Freaks."

"You are the freak," JC taunted.

She shot back, "And you are the dummy!"

Zabrina could not be mad at him. JC was kind of cute, in a have-you-lost-your-mind kind of way. And it was his idea for their new concept. Besides, she was happy to see him acting like his old crazy self again rather than the sullen guy he was a few months ago.

When the news crew arrived, the reporter suggested interviewing Zabrina with construction activity in the background. JC huffed when he was asked to get out of the shot because he kept smiling at the camera while hammering a board without a nail. Not to hurt his feelings, the cameraman said the hammering was too loud. JC offered to "air" hammer or use an unplugged circular saw instead. Zabrina sharply told JC he should stick his tongue in an electrical panel, since he knew as much about electricity as any other construction job.

After Zabrina's interview was finished, the crew filmed B-roll footage and conducted additional interviews with Anthony Gallo and Justin. Big Tony's interview went much like his normal persona; it was shy and reserved. However, JC was a much different story when the reporter asked him to describe their new venture.

JC said, "Man, this is going to be dope like skippity doo on a rope! You know what I mean?"

The reporter appeared confused. She did not understand a word he said. "Skippity do what?" she wondered before asking him again.

JC looked at Zabrina whose eyes were burning a hole through his shiny red track suit like a magnifying glass under the bright New Orleans sun.

This time JC said, "This place will be the balls! I mean gigantic balls! The biggest balls New Orleans has ever seen, I am telling you! Have you ever seen balls this big?" he asked the young female reporter who was clearly in shock.

"Cut!" the reporter instructed the cameraman.

"Was that good?" JC asked.

Zabrina grabbed JC by the arm and pulled him aside. She warned him if he said one more dumb thing, she would bash his nonsensical head with a construction shovel. Zabrina walked back and asked the reporter to give him one more chance.

For the third time, the reporter repeated the question. JC gave a wide smile and calmly replied, "How would I describe it? Simply amazing!"

Finally, Zabrina and the reporter were satisfied; maybe not satisfied, but at least relieved. As the crew packed equipment, Zabrina apologized for her partner's erratic behavior. She explained JC had not taken his medication that morning. The reporter asked if his medication affected the way he dressed? Zabrina said no and told the journalist even an elephant tranquilizer could not fix that.

Everyone gathered in the office later that evening to watch the interview on the 10 o'clock news. To Zabrina's relief, it came off well, especially since they did not use JCs first two takes.

"Man, I look pretty on camera," JC bragged. "I should have been a male model."

"Yeah, a male model on planet Lost Your Mind," Zabrina quipped.

"I looked fat," Big Tony critiqued.

"Television always makes people look 10 pounds heavier, Tony. You looked great," Zabrina complimented Big T.

"Yeah, now you are 380 pounds of greatness," JC crowed.

"Watch it!" Big Tony warned. "I will crush you like a shiny track suit wearing bug with this 380 pounds of greatness if you mention my weight again, JC!"

Silkroad International Shipping
New Orleans, Louisiana

"Check this out," Kenny Wu told David Pham as he motioned him over to see the news program playing on the TV in his office.

"Isn't that the girl we smuggled here?" the Chinese-American businessman asked his lieutenant as they watched the interview together.

"It looks like her," Pham agreed. "If I recall, her name is Pok Kyung-Wook. She goes by Zabrina Chao now. She's the woman we brought from North Korea years ago who those guys paid off the rest of her debt, remember?"

"Yeah, the fat dude and the black guy. I remember," Kenny recalled.

"Looks like she is rolling in dough now. I don't believe she's paid us enough to bring her to America with all the opportunity this country provides," Kenny realized.

"Well, she paid us what we asked for. Her parents gave up everything to get her here. Then we hit her up for more after she arrived and forced her into prostitution. I believe she's paid enough," Pham justified.

"Be that as it may," Kenny argued. "But I believe she owes more. Success like that does not come cheap."

Kenny Wu was born Su Dingxiang in the United States to a Chinese mother who was the mistress to his father, a powerful Chinese businessman named Wu Kong. Until the mid-1980s, Kong led one of China's largest and most ruthless crime syndicates in Hong Kong with connections to the mainland.

Wu Kong banished Kenny's mother to the United States after he discovered she was pregnant. Sending her to the U.S. served two purposes; to keep her out of his way and provide him with a naturalized son he might later use to expand his dirty deeds of human trafficking, drug smuggling and other acts of ill repute.

Growing up, kids constantly teased Su Dingxiang about his name, calling him "So Ding-Dong". He legally changed his name to Kenny Wu after he turned 18. "Kenny" because it was western sounding, and "Wu" because his biological father was a powerful man. It also hid the fact that Kenny had little confidence in himself and hated being teased.

David Pham, his chief operations officer and number two in the organization, was born in South Korea and immigrated to the United States with his parents when he was 4 years old. The pair met when they attended university together.

Kenny held a burning desire to reconnect with his father from a young age. His mother never spoke of the man and if Kenny asked she would turn away with some impolite Chinese phrase he did not understand. He knew nothing of Wu Kong except what he read in glowing business stories he found online. But one thing was clear; He and his mom were destitute as he grew up and his father was a wealthy and influential man.

Wu Kong was also known by another name from his gangster days: Sun Fang or "Rising Tiger". He was the shrewd CEO of Sun Fang International, a global conglomerate of corporations operating companies throughout the world in a broad range of industries, from technology to finance and everything in between. If it emanated from Asia, Sun Fang had his sticky fingers in all of it.

Kenny would learn that was not where the Rising Tiger's career began. In Kong's early days, he was involved in every illegal activity known to man. After making such considerable money that was harder to hide, Kong went public with his wealth. He was smart enough to start business as a front company to keep law enforcement and authorities away. It was a convenient way to launder his illicit proceeds and keep politicians, police, judges, and other influential people at bay.

Over time, Wu Kong used his street smarts to climb bamboo ladders that led him to the pinnacle of success he sat upon today. He owned everyone of any importance and killed those who got in his way. If he could not buy their loyalty, Sun Fang had them dismissed. He was intelligent and so well insulated, like the American mob that nobody dared move on Kong because they all knew beneath his success was a stone-cold killer.

Maybe the apple did not fall far from the tree. In some demented father-missing way, Kenny wanted to be like his infamous dad.

Arranging a meeting with Sun Fang proved to be no simple task. Wu Kong's first reaction upon hearing the news of his bastard American son, Dingxiang's request to meet him in person was to get rid of him. He was simply another in a long list of illegitimate kids; one more who showed up expecting a handout, a piece of his empire, or Buddha forbid, daddy's love. Yet, the longer Kong thought about it, this son may be more useful alive than dead.

Hong Kong

Kenny arrived in Hong Kong a few days before the Chinese New Year in 1998. It was the year of the Tiger, which Kenny found ironic considering his father's nom de guerre. He had never visited Hong Kong or mainland China before and barely spoke the language. He was a watered down western version of Chinese. So bad, in fact, that the Chinese people he encountered looked upon him with disgust.

Hong Kong was filled with energy and more modern than he expected. The airport and subways were high tech, more so than his home in New Orleans, which had no subways because if you built one it would float up like the above ground graves.

He admired the brightly lit skyscrapers across Victoria Harbour from his vantage point on Kowloon Peninsula. After a young Chinese businessman pulled up in front of a convenience store in a brand-new Lamborghini, there was no mistaking the amount of money that flowed through this town. Hong Kong was the financial capital of Asia, and Kenny was certain his father had his hands in much of it.

A black Mercedes SUV arrived at his hotel at precisely 9:00 AM. An attractive Chinese lady wearing dark sunglasses dressed in a black blazer, white blouse, and a tight-fitting skirt with matching high heel shoes approached Kenny in the lobby. With a stern, unsmiling glare she confirmed, "Su Dingxiang?"

"Yes?" he sheepishly replied even though he hadn't heard his birth name in years.

"Come with me," she instructed.

Kenny followed the fierce woman outside the hotel where a Chinese man dressed like a secret service agent stood by the vehicle. He patted Kenny down, then nodded for him to enter the SUV.

"Get in," the icy woman commanded.

She climbed inside next to Kenny and looked straight ahead. It was apparent the woman was not much for small talk, so Kenny did not even try. Minutes later, they were coursing through zig-zag streets of the financial district up a mountain to a place named The Peak. Kenny had researched the place and knew it to be some of the most expensive real estate in Hong Kong.

Finally, the curt woman spoke. "When you meet Sun Fang, you are not to speak to him unless spoken to. You are not to make eye contact with him. You are to look down at all times. Do you understand?"

"Yes," Kenny nervously affirmed.

The SUV drove through double black iron gates with golden tiger emblems posted on each side, past a security checkpoint with more intimidating men and up a long winding driveway until the car stopped front of the massive estate. Two guards opened the rear doors of the vehicle, where the woman stepped outside along with Kenny Wu who was frisked again.

"Follow me," the woman instructed.

She briskly led Kenny up a flight of steps flanked
by two other men in black and marched through the
open doors, past a marble fountain between a double
curved staircase and down a long hallway filled with
priceless art. They entered another room through a
set of French doors leading to a patio overlooking
an elaborate garden with a pink flamingo-filled lake.

"Sit here," she directed, pointing to a specific
chair around a circular marble-top table.

"May I get you something to drink? Tea or
coffee?" she asked out of obligated protocol.

"Actually, I would like a Coke if you have one,"
Kenny replied.

The Chinese woman stormed away mumbling,
"Stupid Americans."

She returned with a silver platter holding a
porcelain pot with matching cups and saucers. She
placed it in the center of the table. She removed
a single can of Coca-Cola and unceremoniously
slammed it down in front of Kenny with such
disdain for either his choice of beverage or simply
because she did not like the guy. Probably both.

Kenny said, "That pot looks antique."

"It is from the Ming Dynasty. Don't touch it!" the
woman warned him before she whisked away.

It felt so surreal as Kenny admired the gardens.
He noticed men strolling the estate with automatic
weapons slung over their shoulders. He could not
hide the tremble in his hand as he picked up the
soda can and spilled some of the brown liquid on
his crisp white shirt. He used his tie to wipe the stain
away, hoping his father would not notice and think
he was a slob.

As he waited, Kenny wondered what drove him
to be in Hong Kong, sitting at his billionaire father's
home? Did he have a death wish? If so, he didn't
have to go far with as many gunmen as this place

had roaming around.

To his left a pair of doors opened with a sudden purpose.Kenny startled to attention in his chair, bumping the table with a noticeable sound of alarm. He looked over his shoulder to see a well-dressed man stroll in, followed by two stern-looking men who remained on either side of each door as if to prevent escape.

Dressed in a crème-colored suit and crisp white open-collared shirt, the man approached the table. Kenny rose to his feet and bowed his head to avert his eye contact, remembering the warning from the unfriendly woman.

Wu Kong returned the gesture with a slight nod of his own and sat in a chair pulled out for him across from Kenny. He gestured for him to sit while an attendant poured two cups of tea from the priceless porcelain pot. Kong acknowledged his approval and signaled the servant to leave. Nothing was said for several moments while the elder Wu gazed toward the gardens.

"How do you like Hong Kong?" Wu Kong finally asked.

"I... uh... it is not what I expected," Kenny sputtered. "It is very nice."

"What did you expect, a dirty place with poor people?" Wu Kong inquired with a tone of wicked sarcasm in his voice.

He turned his gaze toward Kenny with the steely eyes of a tiger summing up its prey. "There is a certain element of that within our belly, but China is on the rise and will soon be the most powerful nation in the world."

Kong took a sip of his tea. "What brings you here?"

It was less of a question, rather more of an inquisition to the condemned. Kenny hoped his father did not notice the shaking ancient teacup he held in his hand.

"I don't know, really. I guess I have always wanted to know who my father is," Kenny replied.

Studying the boy like a serpent, Kong took another slow sip of his tea.

"Is that all?" he hissed.

"Yes, that is all," Kenny desperately tried to assure.

Kong returned his gaze to the flamingos.

"Your mother is well, I assume?" Kong said.

"Yes, she is well. She works..."

Kong cut him off.

"I know where she works, and I know everything about you," he revealed.

"I know you were terrible in school. Your grades were unremarkable. You have never held a job. And you have very few friends," Kong emphatically summarized.

"I have friends," Kenny said in a hopeless self-defense.

"You have one, David Pham, the South Korean you met at university," Wu Kong stated.

It was apparent he had done his homework. Kenny worried if he knew all this, what else did he know?

"Did you come here to ask me for money?" Kong tempted while staring at the gardens.

"No!" Kenny insisted. "I just wanted to meet you."

Kong returned his steely gaze toward Kenny who was visibly shaken.

"I am sorry. This was a mistake. I will leave," Kenny said, rising from his chair. A man in black stepped forward in case Kenny made another sudden move.

"Sit!" Wu Kong demanded as he waved the guard away.

"I will tell you when you may leave."

Kenny returned to his seat.

"What do you want to do with your life? Work some meaningless job and always be disrespected while barely getting by?" Kong asked.

"No," Kenny sheepishly replied.

"Do you think all you see around you was easy for me to achieve?" Kong questioned.

Without waiting for an answer, the elder Wu continued.

"I was born to a poor farming family in mainland China. My parents toiled in the fields to barely make ends meet. We lived in poverty. I wanted more for myself, and I worked hard to get it. No matter what I had to do or who got in my way, I built the success you see. Do you have that kind of tenacity? Would you do anything to succeed?"

"I would," Kenny assured.

Kong returned his gaze to the gardens and pondered the situation. This boy, this bastard son of his, was not like his other children. He was less ambitious, and moldable, the Rising Tiger thought to himself.

Taking another sip, Kong asked without looking at Kenny, "How would you like to work for me?"

"Father, I don't believe I am qualified. You have seen my grades," Kenny truthfully replied.

"Maybe so, but I recognize something in you that schools cannot teach. You have fire in your eyes. The same fire I had all those years ago."

Kong continued. "I have many sons, by many women; Some no longer exist in this earthly place. But none of them had the same burning desire I recognize in you," Kong acknowledged.

"What would you like me to do, father?" Kenny asked.

"Anything I say," the Rising Tiger replied. "It will begin with several tests to see if you are up to the task. Go home and wait for my people to contact you."

Wu Kong rose from his chair. With an icy glare, he warned, "But never mistake my generosity for weakness. If you ever cross me, your time on this earth will be short."

He left the patio followed by his guards. The Chinese woman in the tight-fitting skirt returned.

She told Kenny, "Let's go."

The car was silent as they drove down the mountain peak. When they arrived at Kenny's hotel, a man in black opened the door, motioning Kenny to get out. Before he exited, the Chinese woman handed Kenny a business card.

"We will be in touch," she said, then the darkened window rolled up.

Kenny watched the SUV drive away, then looked at the card, which read, "Sun Fang International, Ming Bou–Special Assistant."

The card contained a phone number, but no postal or email address. Kenny tucked it inside his jacket pocket knowing this card is not one to lose. He returned to his hotel room and collapsed upon the bed. This had been the most terrifying experience in his life. Never had he been in the presence of power such as this. Kenny knew from this moment onward his life would forever change. Staring at the ceiling, Kenny realized he had made a deal with the devil, a deal he could not refuse as the illegitimate son of Wu.

Chapter 7
New Orleans, Lousiana

"You sure about this, Kenny?" David Pham asked his boss after Kenny shared his intentions for Zabrina Chao.

David reminded him, "Remember when your father warned you to remain low key? Once they have paid their debts, walk away. That is how your father has always done things and why he is so rich. People who are on the hook to him always pay. He knows how to crank the screws and has a ton of tools at his disposal. But once they've settled their debts, he lets them live to see another day."

"Times have changed, David. We've been working for my father for 15 years, and what do we have to show for it?" Kenny asked. "Sure, we have nice houses, cars and a little money, but nothing like the old man."

"He's been at this game a lot longer than you, Kenny, and he earned his money the hard way. Now his businesses are legit. We are low on his radar, and I prefer to keep it that way. Do I need to remind you that your father is a very dangerous man?"

"His 'Honor among thieves' is non-sense. This is a new generation and I am the new way of doing things. My father is a dinosaur," Kenny rationalized.

"You should watch what you say, Kenny. Your father seems to see and hear everything," David reminded.

Kenny never understood how his father knew so

much, not only about his business activities, but also his personal life. Once when Kenny was accused by a woman of drugging and raping her, he got out of it with the help of his father's high-powered attorneys and paying the lady a large sum of money to keep her mouth shut. As much as he tried to keep the incident hidden from his father, somehow Kong found out and came at him with a fury worthy of his Rising Tiger nickname. Wu Kong warned Kenny if his family name or reputation were ever tarnished, that would be that last of him, no questions asked. So, David was right. He better watch what he said. Sun Fang's network of spies seemed infinitely more intelligent than the CIA.

"Don't worry it, David. He is simply using us to get a spiff from our income. Father doesn't know the inner workings of what we do."

"That may be true, Kenny, but your father expects something from every deal we do, regardless," David reasoned.

"If he catches wind of something like this, there may be hell to pay. He set us up in this business and he can easily take it away, especially if we get his name caught up in one of your schemes. His success is due to how low-key he remains and how well he is insulated he is, so you better watch out."

Kenny replied, "Trust me, he will never find out."

"I hope so, for your sake he doesn't," David flatly replied.

* * *

A month had passed since Luna gave birth and the couple were feeling a bit stir crazy at home. Stenson suggested they have a date night and go out for a nice dinner. Her parents were several hundred miles away, so Luna wondered who would watch their son.

"Who can we get to babysit?" Luna asked her husband.

"Robert?" Stenson suggested.

"That big lug? Do you think he knows anything about caring for a one-month-old?

"He'd love it, Luna. Robert calls me multiple times a day, asking how his nephew is. He never asks how I am, but occasionally he asks about you."

Luna chuckled. "Why do I have a feeling when we return there will be rock music blaring and our son will have his first tattoo?"

Stenson laughed at the thought. It was possible.

"Robert is a teddy bear," Stenson defended his rough-around-the-edges best friend. "But I hope he doesn't bring anymore gifts. We are running out of places to store them like that miniature motorcycle he brought last time."

Robert Brickhouse loved their son. He didn't have any children of his own and in some ways Stenson felt this would be good training for the day he did. It would be nice for them to get away as a couple for a few hours and let Brick spend some quality time with his nephew. They certainly did not have to worry about their son's safety with that big marine around. However, the refrigerator was another story. Robert liked to snack almost as much as Big Tony Gallo, so they better stock up.

"I'll stop by the bar and ask Robert if he wants to babysit after I pick up groceries," Stenson told his wife.

"The groceries can wait," she said. "You've been stuck with me for a month. Go visit your buddies and have a beer or two. You have my permission. But grab some groceries later if Robert agrees to babysit. That marine can put away some food."

"Thank you, boss!" Stenson enthusiastically said like a kid whose mom gave him permission to go out and play.

After her husband left, Luna knew Stenson was right. Just because they were married parents now didn't mean they didn't deserve some quality time together once in a while. And who knows? Maybe they would make another baby later. Then Luna thought about it and told herself, "Well, maybe not this soon."

Stenson was greeted with catcalls and cheers from the regular patrons when he walked into O'Malley's pub. Based on their reaction seeing him for the first time in a few months, they treated him as if he was a prison escapee joining the other convicts for his first beer since going on the run.

Robert yelled from behind the bar, "Look who it is. Stenson Beckett, father of the year!"

He slid a cold draft down the polished bar to his best friend and walked over with a beer of his own.

Stenson said, "I see you didn't burn the place down while I was away."

Robert clinked his beer to Stenson's and took a sip.

"I couldn't do that. Then where would I get free beer?" Robert asked, "What brings you to this shady side of town?"

"I missed your ugly face," Stenson told him with a grin.

Robert brushed the foam from his nose. "You saw me yesterday and the day before."

"And your looks have not improved. I was hoping today would be better," Stenson joked.

"Actually, I came by to ask you a favor. Luna and I wondered if you would like to babysit your nephew Saturday night while we go out for a little one-on-one time?"

"Me, alone with your child? What do I know about babies? I can barely handle these out-of-control bikers, and they are adults," Brick admitted.

"There is nothing to it. You already know how to hold him after the first few times we thought you were going to crush the kid with your enormous biceps. We just need to show you how to change his diaper. Luna's got breast milk in the fridge so you can feed him."

"Oh, no! That's where I draw the line. I puke at the sight of doo-doo," Robert stated emphatically.

Stenson replied, "You have seen blood and guts on the battlefield, and seeing a little baby's number two makes you queasy?"

"It's different on the battlefield. Most of those people I didn't like, and I was responsible for a few of their blood and guts being exposed to the fresh air. But seeing the bowel movement of someone I like is a different story. I like you, but I don't want to see yours either," he clarified.

Robert took another sip of his beer and thought about it. "But for you and Luna, I will be happy to babysit. Just don't be surprised if I show up wearing a hazmat suit. And I hope I don't accidentally put Luna's breast milk in my coffee."

Stenson laughed at the thought. "You should try it in your cereal."

"Uh, no thank you," Robert replied. "I like my cereal just the way it is."

"Your nephew will enjoy spending time with his favorite uncle. But please don't bring him any more toys. You have spoiled the child enough. And Luna said no loud rock music or tattoos."

Brick chuckled. "She is such a party-pooper. Luna will probably have the boy listening to Mozart if we leave it to her. Warn me when you are on the way home, so I will have classical music playing and don my angel wings."

"You an angel? Now, that's funny!" Stenson said

as he toasted the big marine.

* * *

Fats buzzed with activity. People scurried full tilt in different directions trying to finish the remaining tasks before their soft opening in two weeks. It was late afternoon when Zabrina found JC and Big Tony looking over the plans for the sports bar area.

"Hey guys," she said. "I need to pick up some things for the office. You bozos want something to eat?"

"I am always hungry," Big Tony said.

"What about you, Twiggy?" Zabrina asked JC.

"I'm on a diet. Gotta keep up my loving weight for all the hotties." JC teased his nemesis.

"You hear that, Tony? He called you a hottie, because I know he wasn't talking about me. I am way too hot for that pencil stick." She egged JC.

"Whatever, evil woman. Get me the regular," JC instructed, ignoring her twiggy remark.

"I will spit in yours, JC," Zabrina told him as she winked at Big Tony to signal she would not spit in his.

Zabrina left the guys to their work and made several stops before arriving at JC and Tony's favorite sandwich shop in a sketchy part of town. She never felt comfortable in this neighborhood, but the guys swore they made the best sandwiches in New Orleans.

It was 8:00 P.M. and dark. She never understood why the owners did not light the parking lot except that they were cheap. Given her previous occupation, she found herself in many dark places in sketchy neighborhoods, but none gave her the creeps like this. Even though she knew how to take care of herself, something about this night made her feel uneasy. She could not pinpoint the source of her anxiety, but shrugged it off as exhaustion or lack of sleep.

She killed the engine and went inside. After she left, her spider senses tingled. She picked up the pace as she walked more briskly toward her car. From the corner of her eye, she noticed a black sedan following her down the aisle with its headlights off. She clicked the button to unlock her vehicle. Before she reached the handle, an arm wrapped around her neck from behind and placed a cloth over her nose and mouth, preventing her scream. In a panic, she dropped the bags of food, her cellphone and keys as she struggled to get free before she fell unconscious.

* * *

"It was nice of Robert to babysit for us tonight," Luna said, gazing into her husband's candle-lit eyes.

"I didn't have to twist him arm," Stenson said, clinking a glass of wine to Luna's.

"I miss times like this with you," the loving husband said.

"Do you regret we had a baby, Stenson?" she asked sincerely.

"No way! That was the best decision we have ever made. I am the luckiest man in the world. Of course, I knew things would change when we had a baby. But I never want us to forget our romantic side."

"We never will," Luna ensured with a twinkle in her eyes.

* * *

"Where is Zabrina?" JC asked Big Tony.

"I don't know. She's been gone for hours," Gallo replied. "My stomach is growling like I swallowed a motorcycle."

JC's phone rang, and he saw it was Zabrina's number.

"Where are you?" he asked.

A male voice replied, "She is with me."

"Who is this?" JC demanded, completely surprised.

"Don't worry about who I am. If you care to see your friend again, you will do exactly as I say," the voice warned.

JC was silent. He placed the phone on speaker so Big Tony could hear the ominous conversation.

"You will bring a bag containing $500,000.00 to the St. Claude Avenue Bridge at 2:00 AM," the mystery voice instructed. "If we even sense the police or anybody else is involved, we will kill her. It's that simple. Understand?"

JC tried to process what he just heard.

The mysterious voice repeated, "Understand?"

"I understand," JC said. "2:00 AM. St. Claude Avenue Bridge. 500k."

The phone went dead. He looked at Big Tony with an ashen face that had more questions than answers.

"Who was that?" Tony asked, as confused as JC.

"It has to be those Chinese smugglers we paid off. They kidnapped her wanting more money. Who else could it be?"

"Nobody that I can think of," Tony agreed.

"How much do we have in the safe?" JC asked.

"I don't know. Zabrina handles the books," Gallo replied.

They went upstairs to the office. JC opened the safe and counted out $450,761.39 of their remaining cash from the money Stenson had returned. JC stared at the pile on the table and said, "We are $50k short."

"Where are we going to get that kind of money at this time of night?" Tony asked.

The men looked at each other.

"Stenson," JC said. "He's the only person we know who may have the funds to cover this."

JC dreaded asking Stenson Beckett for something like this after all he had done for them, but he had no other choice. He picked up his phone and called Stenson while Big Tony stuffed the money into JCs gym bag.

A cheerful voice answered. "JC, my man, how are you? Say hello to Luna. We are having dinner."

In a polar opposite voice, JC replied in a more serious tone, "I am sorry to bother you at dinner, Stenson. Is there some place where I can speak to you privately, like now?"

"Yeah, sure JC," Stenson looked at Luna with concern.

"What's going on?" he asked.

"I can't say over the phone. Can you meet me in a few minutes at the diner near your home? You know the place."

"Sure, JC. I will meet you there in a few minutes."

Stenson hung up and told Luna something was going on with JC and it sounded serious. He wasn't sure what, but it must be important enough for him to call him like this. He told her JC asked to meet now and he needed to leave. Stenson apologized to Luna and promised to make it up to her.

"It was good while it lasted," she said with a disappointed look and understanding smile.

"Go. I will grab the check and get a ride home," she told him.

"I am sorry, babe," Stenson said, giving her a kiss. "I will be home as soon as I can."

Stenson left the restaurant and drove to meet JC, who was standing by his car in the diner parking lot.

"What's up, JC?" Stenson asked while shaking his hand.

JC cut to the chase. "Listen, I hate to ask you this,

Stenson, but can I borrow $50k? It is an emergency."

"Whoa, fifty grand?" Stenson confirmed.

"When do you need it?" he asked.

"Now. And please don't ask why," JC replied humbly. "I don't want you any more involved in this than loaning me the money, and I promise to pay you back."

Stenson knew this was serious because JC would never reach out to him like this. He had too much pride.

"Of course, JC," Stenson said. "Meet me at the bar in forty-five minutes. Come to the back door."

"Thanks, Stenson," JC said. "You don't know how much I appreciate this."

Stenson watched JC drive away. He was scared and Stenson knew it. He saw it in his eyes.

Stenson drove to the bar and called Luna on the way. "Babe, there is something serious going on and JC doesn't want me to know or be involved in it but he needs cash immediately. I am headed to the bar."

JC phoned Stenson when he arrived at O'Malley's. "I'm out back."

A moment later, Stenson opened the rear door and let JC inside. They headed to Stenson's office where he pushed a bag across the desk.

JC didn't have to open the bag or count it. He knew what he asked for was there. He hesitated before he picked it up and said, fighting back tears in his eyes, "Thank you Stenson, for not asking questions."

"Be careful, JC. And whatever this is, if it's too hot for you to handle, know Brick and I have your back," Stenson reassured.

JC knew Stenson and Brick had his back, and that was why he didn't want them involved. He and Big Tony would handle this insanity themselves.

Chapter 8

Crunching gravel beneath Anthony Gallo's tires echoed the unpleasant thoughts grinding through JC's mind. The 4x4 truck rutted down a pothole-filled service road beneath the east side of the St. Claude Avenue Bridge. The clock on the dash read 1:52 AM.

The weather fit their mood like a custom suit made by the devil; it was dark, foul and eternally angry. Fog rolled in from the river like a soggy blanket covering the Lower Ninth Ward. Big Tony parked the truck leaving the headlights on to search the distance for trouble ahead. Words were unspoken among these telepathizing friends. They checked their weapons. Tony gripped his trusty black Smith & Wesson .45, while JC polished a chrome Tanfoglio 9mm with 17 rounds of hollow point love.

Six hours ago was a normal day and now here they sat under a bridge on a nasty night ready to give a half million dollars to kidnappers to get their business partner back. It crossed JC's mind that this could be a setup by Zabrina. But why? She could have taken the money and run away a long time ago. She was as invested as anyone and sought redemption like the rest. That idea made no sense.

Nobody had more motivation to kidnap Zabrina than the smugglers they paid off two years ago. As much as JC and Tony wanted to kill these hostage-taking, ransom-loving gangsters, they would prefer to get Zabrina back without murder charges or more danger than required. Money, they could replace; or even figure out a tricky way to get it back. But tonight, all they wanted was for this to go down smooth and easy. "Here is your money. Give us the girl."

Simple? Yeah, right. When had anything been simple for them? The pits of their stomachs knotted like twisted wash rags warning them to be prepared for anything. They checked their weapons again. It was 1:58 AM.

"Let's do this," JC said as he reached into the backseat and grabbed the duffle bag. Tony chambered a round into the S&W and tucked it into his waistband behind his back. JC walked in front of the vehicle and set the bag down. Big Tony joined him to his left and folded his arms across his barrel-sized chest. Backlit by the headlights, they stood silently waiting.

Moments later a black sedan pulled onto western end of the service road, followed by a white, windowless cargo-style van. The vehicles stopped when they were 50 yards away. Three doors opened and three darkened silhouettes stepped out. JC and Big Tony kept a running tally of the bad guy count.

A shadowy figure stepped in front of the car. He turned to have words with the men who stood behind him JC and Tony could not hear. Then he started walking toward Justin and Big Tony with a slow, yet determined pace. JC picked up the bag and stepped forward with an equal gate. The men stopped when they were 10 yards apart and stared at each other like two cowboys in a Western movie waiting for the draw.

"Where is she?" JC barked.

"You have the money?" the man questioned with the hint of an Asian accent in his voice.

JC held up the bag.

"Now, let me see the girl," Justin demanded.

The shadowy figure raised his arm and gave a slight wave to the van. The side door slid open and a muffled commotion ensued. Two shapes emerged; one struggling and raising hell that was unmistakably an angry Zabrina Chao. The other was a male holding a pistol to her head.

"Bring me the money," the man instructed.

"Give me the girl first," Justin countered.

"No," he calmly said.

"What do you mean, no? I've got the money. Now let her go," JC insisted.

"I said, bring me five-hundred grand and you will see the girl alive. You have seen her alive. Now give me the money," he instructed JC, as if he had missed an important detail of their agreement.

JC was unprepared for this twist of fate. The non-negotiable terms were reinforced when the man stepped inches from JC's face, exposing his cold dark betraying eyes and wicked thin smile. It was checkmate.

Big Tony reached behind his back for his weapon. Before he could remove his gun, he heard a click of a firearm behind his left ear. JC looked over his shoulder to see another shadowy figure standing behind his big friend holding a pistol an inch from Big Tony's skull. Panic set in.

"What's going on? You've got your money. Let her go and we walk away like this never happened," JC nervously proposed.

"Ah, my friend, we have more plans for her. It was a pleasure doing business with you," the betrayer said as he reached down and picked up the bag.

Sensing his only opportunity, Big Tony spun around and grabbed the gunman's arm and pulled the weapon down. Then a shot rang out. As if time stood still, everybody froze until JC watched Big Tony crumple to the ground. Before he could react, JC felt a bashing thud crash into his head, causing him to drop to his knees in blinding pain while another blow from a steel-toe boot crushed into his face. He fell backwards onto the rocky road and through his blood-blurred vision watched the shadowed figure walk away with the bag in his hand. Another silhouette shoved Zabrina back into a van. JC watched the red taillights fade away.

He screamed, "No!!!" before he passed out.

JC regained consciousness while he was being loaded into an ambulance. He vaguely remembered a homeless man said, "I saw everything and flagged the cops down for you. Hang in there, buddy. You'll be ok."

As the doors closed and the sirens blared, JC garbled from his smashed mouth, "Where is my friend? Where is Big Tony?"

The paramedic noticed his blood pressure rising and said, "Your friend is in route to University Medical Center. Please take deep breaths and try to remain calm."

JC hyperventilated unable to speak. He thought as they drove away, "My best friend has been shot! You take a deep breath and don't tell me to calm down!"

Paramedics rushed Anthony Gallo into the emergency room. He had lost a considerable amount of blood and the deep purple color and dropping pressure were dangerous signs. Time was not on their side. They rushed Anthony Gallo into surgery in an effort to save his life.

JC's ambulance arrived 15 minutes later. His evaluation revealed a severe a concussion and lacerations to his face. His left eye was purple and swollen shut. After he was patched up, a doctor suggested Justin stay overnight for observation. JC flatly refused. As long as Zabrina was missing and Gallo was fighting for his life, he had no intention of lying on his back complaining of a headache or a black eye.

Stenson's phone rang. The caller ID read Justin Carter. He answered with a joke, "Yo, JC! What's up? I hope you don't need more money. I am tapped out now."

A long pause followed.

"JC, are you there?" Stenson asked.

"They shot Big Tony," a sad, quivering voice replied.

Stenson's humor disappeared in an instant.

"What? Who shot Tony?" Stenson asked.

Stenson covered the mouthpiece and looked in shock at Luna who overheard his words.

"No time to explain, Stenson. I didn't know who else to call and I am sorry it had to be you. Can you come to University Medical Center?"

"Of course, JC. I will be right there," Stenson said as he hung up the phone.

He looked at Luna with genuine concern. "Tony Gallo has been shot. JC couldn't tell me more. I am heading to University Medical Center."

"I will go with you," Luna suggested.

"Stay here with the baby. I will call Robert," Stenson told her. "I will call you when I know more."

Stenson grabbed his keys and rushed out the door. He called Brick on the way and picked him up at O'Malley's. They found JC sitting in the emergency lobby, looking like a beat-up mummy with his head wrapped in bandages. They sat down next to him. There was a long pause before JC explained Zabrina was kidnapped and the money he borrowed was for a ransom payment. They were attacked, and that's when...

JC looked at the floor, then quietly said, "And that's when they shot Big Tony. They stole the money and kept Zabrina. It was a setup."

Stenson glanced at Robert.

"Who did it?" Stenson asked.

"I don't know, Stenson. But I suspect it was the same gang who smuggled Zabrina from North Korea."

"I thought you and Tony paid them off?" Stenson recalled.

"We did and thought that would be the last we heard from them. But apparently, they've come back for a second helping."

"Where is Tony?" Brickhouse asked.

"He is still in surgery," JC sadly stated.

There was no hiding the worry on JC's battered face. Robert and Stenson were worried, too. This was not some, "Oh we lost the money gambling" or whatever you needed $500k for. This was "Somebody kidnapped Zabrina, stole the money, beat up JC and left Tony Gallo for dead."

This was an entirely more deadly situation and at this moment, neither Stenson nor Brick knew what to do except be there for JC and pray for Big Tony.

Stenson put his arm around Justin and said, "We are here for you, buddy. Whatever you need."

A surgeon wearing green scrubs entered the waiting room.

"Justin Carter?" the doctor asked.

"Yes, I am Justin Carter." JC said as he rose from his seat.

The surgeon told him, "Your friend is out of surgery. He has suffered traumatic internal injuries and lost a considerable amount of blood. He is in stable but critical condition right now."

"May I see him?" JC asked.

"It will be several hours before he's in any shape

to speak with anyone. Police want to talk to him first," the doctor informed Justin Carter.

After the doctor left, two men approached JC and introduced themselves as detectives with the New Orleans Police Department. Stenson and Robert excused themselves after detectives asked to speak to JC alone. They walked outside to the parking lot. Brick lit a cigar and took a long drag.

"How do you want to handle this?" the big marine asked Stenson.

"I guess we let the cops do their job and see where that goes," Stenson replied.

"You know what they say about the first 72 hours of a missing person case," Robert reminded him. "Finding who shot Tony can take forever and trying to prove it even longer. Zabrina doesn't have that much time. Do you think they will prioritize solving the kidnapping of an illegal Asian immigrant who was a former prostitute?"

They both knew the answer to that rhetorical question.

"No," Stenson said. "As much as I don't us to get involved, this is way over JCs head. And you are right about the cops. They will not make Zabrina's abduction a priority. Kiss the money goodbye. Kiss Zabrina goodbye."

"Ain't gonna happen," Brick dismissed as he stomped his cigar on the pavement.

"As much as I don't like JC, I hate kidnapping thieves even more," Robert said. "And you're right, this is way over Justin's head. He and Gallo need our help."

"Let's hope Gallo survives," Stenson replied with concern.

While Robert headed back to the E.R., Stenson phoned Luna. She was shocked when she found out what happened. She offered to see what she could find about the kidnappers, but warned it would be like looking for a needle in a haystack; especially when you don't know which needle or which stack.

Robert and Stenson stayed with JC at the hospital until 4:00 P.M. when a member of the medical staff informed them, "You may visit your friend now, but only for a few minutes."

JC knocked quietly on the door of the intensive care room and let himself in followed by Stenson and Brick. The big guy was groggy but alive and awake. He was attached tubes, drips, and leads to machines that chirped and beeped.

"Nice pajamas," Robert said. "Looks like I am not the only one who has seen you naked."

The joke was a reference to the time Robert and Stenson kidnapped Big Tony and left him tied nude to a tree as revenge for a stunt Tony and JC pulled on them before they were friends.

Big Tony laughed at the remark remembering that night. After he escaped, the only clothes he could find was a big woman's dress he stole from a clothes line. The laughter caused the big man to wince in pain.

He said, "Don't make me laugh, Robert. In case you haven't heard, I've been shot."

Stenson replied, "They tell us you have an extra belly button now, but you will survive."

"Yeah, thank God I am fat, or I would be dead," Big Tony deadpanned.

While they were cracking jokes, JC remained quiet. He felt responsible for what happened to his best friend.

"I am sorry, Tony," JC said in a humble voice.

"From the look of your face, JC, it appears you got it worse than me," Gallo replied.

"What did the detectives say?" Robert asked the guys.

"They want me to look at some mugshots to see if I recognize the man who stole the money," JC told him.

"All I know is he was an Asian guy. He had these evil eyes and a wicked thin smile. If I saw him again now, I would recognize him. But I cannot remember if he was one of the guys we paid off two years ago."

"I was no help when I spoke to the cops. I never got a good look at the guy who shot me. It happened so fast," Big Tony explained.

"As far as Zabrina? They said they will see what leads they can find, but it did not sound promising they would find her in time," JC added.

Stenson assured them, "Luna is digging around to see what she can find. In the meantime, you two heal up. Robert and I will help you find Zabrina."

Brickhouse nodded in agreement. On the drive back to Stenson's house, Stenson asked Brick, "Why kidnap Zabrina? And what would they want with her now? There are other ways they could have extorted them if it was only money they were after."

"I don't know, but whoever is behind this must be a psychopath," Robert replied. "Not only is it kidnapping and robbery, but they've added attempted murder to the list of charges. And don't they know Club Empire is bankrupt? Why would they even think JC and Zabrina had that kind of money?"

"Zabrina is such a great marketer and recently promoted their new place. Maybe the kidnappers think they are worth more than they really are?" Stenson guessed.

"Well, they certainly came up with half a million dollars in a few hours. There aren't many people I know who have that kind of money lying around. By the way, $50k of it was yours."

"Don't remind me," Stenson said.

"Why does it seem like every time I try to help someone, I get dragged into something as off the wall as this?" Stenson wondered.

"I don't know. You are the best dude I know. If I need half a million dollars, I know who to call." Robert kidded.

Stenson laughed. "After this, I couldn't give you fifty cents."

Luna was pecking away on her laptop when the guys walked in. They joined her in the living room feeling exhausted and emotionally drained. A brief story about a shooting under the St. Claude Avenue Bridge made the local news. The story said police had no suspects and asked anyone with information to call a tip line. A lot of good that would do, Stenson thought. The two guys who witnessed it and almost killed didn't know who the attackers were, so who would have more information than them? Stenson turned off the TV.

"JC said the man was Asian?" Luna confirmed.

"That's what he said. He seemed pretty sure of that part, but not much more," Stenson replied.

"He said the guy was well-dressed. Wore a suit. Confident and cocky," Brick told her. "He said he got a good look at him, but wasn't able to identify the guy from hundreds of mugshots he looked at through his one good eye."

"His one good eye?" Luna asked.

"Yeah, the other one is swollen shut," Brick said. "They whipped him good before they stole half a million dollars."

"I wonder why they didn't kill JC after they shot Big Tony?" Luna wondered aloud.

"Good question," Brick agreed. "Would have saved me the trouble of killing him."

"You don't mean that," Luna scolded the big marine.

"I am kidding," Brick clarified. "Just trying to make light of a bad situation. But you are right. Why didn't they kill JC?"

Stenson wondered that too. "There is a lot about this I don't understand. Why did they keep Zabrina? None of this makes any sense."

Luna looked up from her laptop.

"I may have found something," she said. "It's a long shot. But I ran across this flashy Asian guy who owns a shipping company in town. A few years ago, members of a Chinese gang were busted on a human smuggling rap that ran through his company."

"Interesting," Stenson said.

"It seems the gang were bringing illegal immigrants into New Orleans from Asia aboard cargo ships. The CEO, a guy named Kenny Wu, denied any knowledge of their activities and nothing connected him to it other than it was one of his ships. The gang members did a few years in federal prison on immigration charges and were deported to China after their sentence," Luna explained.

"We know that's how Zabrina was brought to the U.S. so it's probably not too farfetched to believe this gang had something to do with her kidnapping," Stenson believed.

"Who is the CEO you mentioned?" he asked.

"Kenny Wu," Luna repeated.

"From the way JC described the guy who set him up, he wore fancy clothes and rode in an expensive sedan. He didn't sound like your average gang banger to me," Stenson remarked.

"Wu is a flashy guy and known well in social circles. He is not afraid of the spotlight. So I would be surprised if it's him," Luna said.

She brought up a photo of Kenny Wu on her laptop. "Here is a photo of him."

"He looks like a prick," Brickhouse quipped.

"It's a longshot," Stenson admitted. "Let's send the photo to JC and see if he recognizes him."

Chapter 9

"That's him!!!"

JC texted the confirmation within moments after receiving the photo of Kenny Wu.

"No way!" Stenson exclaimed after reading the message not believing this could actually be the guy they were looking for. Some well-dressed Asian-American businessman ripped off JC and almost killed Big Tony? It made even less sense than before. But if JC was convinced this is the guy, the question now was why?

"I bet those cops are still under that bridge looking for bullet casings and interviewing fish," Robert guessed. "And your wife found our suspect before the blood stains dried."

Stenson asked, "Why would this high-profile guy have anything to do with Zabrina's kidnapping? Unless that bash on JC's head scrambled his brain."

"JC's brain was already scrambled. It couldn't be worse," Robert remarked.

"We need to deep-dive this Kenny Wu character and find out everything we can because something is off about this," Stenson suggested.

"I'm ahead of you," Luna informed the guys.

"When I discovered him, I also felt there was something that did not add up. Sure, he's a wealthy guy and owns an international shipping company and went to excellent schools. But you had to be born with a silver spoon to achieve the success he's achieved at such a young age. I wanted to know where his money came from."

"What did you find?" Stenson asked.

"His company, Silkroad International Shipping, was founded in 1999 by Sun Fang International, a global conglomerate based in Hong Kong," she explained.

"So, what? Kenny went to business school, rose through the ranks and became CEO and bought the company?" Stenson suggested.

"In a fairytale, maybe. It was set up by Sun Fang International and transferred to Kenny Wu a few years later," Luna shared. "Guess who is the CEO of Sun Fang International?"

"Dracula? He has fangs," Brick jokingly guessed.

"Funny, Robert. But Dracula is afraid of the sunlight and this guy isn't, so you don't get the prize," she informed the burly marine.

"You are partially correct, though," Luna said. "Sun Fang is a real person whose nickname is based on a mythical Asian character, the Rising Tiger. And he also happens to be Kenny's Wu's father."

Stenson and Brick looked at each other as the tale unfolded.

Luna continued. "Wu Kong, also known as Sun Fang, is one of the richest men in Asia. Actually, he's one of the wealthiest people in the world."

"Wait a minute. This Sun Fang or Wu Kong guy is Kenny's father?" Stenson clarified.

"Appears so. But that is where it gets murky. First, Kenny Wu is not his birth name. He was born in the U.S. as Su Dingxiang to a single mother of Chinese descent who immigrated to the U.S. when she was pregnant with him. He later changed his name to Kenny Wu."

"Wanted to be like his daddy, I suppose," Robert

suggested.

"Maybe. But Wu is a pretty common surname in Asia, so that doesn't mean they are related. I could change my name to Brickhouse. That doesn't mean we are related."

"You'd probably have to check with Stenson on that. The way he is looking at us right now tells me he's about to shoot me if you change your name to Brickhouse," Robert joked.

Luna laughed while Stenson wondered where he put his pistol.

"I haven't confirmed Kenny is actually related to Sun Fang or Wu Kong or whatever his name is. But why would he change his name to the guy who gave him a business?"

Stenson was puzzled. "So you are telling me this Wu Kong guy gave him the company?"

"Technically no. It was sold to him. But let's just say the transaction is obfuscated, moving through multiple shell companies until ultimately Kenny Wu owns it now. I'll dig around to see what else I can find." Luna offered.

"Now I am even more confused," Stenson said. "If Kenny Wu is wealthy, what is he doing with Zabrina, and why did he steal half a million dollars from JC?"

"I would offer my thoughts, but I am still trying to figure out what obfuscated means," Brick said, as he looked up the word on his phone.

"Unclear and harder to understand," Stenson explained.

"There is more blurriness because after the company was sold to Kenny Wu, all ties to Sun Fang were severed," Luna informed.

"Did his dad disown him?" Stenson wondered.

"Unlikely," she said. "Sun Fang International is a tangled web. There are so many off-shore entities and foreign holdings around the world that make it difficult, if not nearly impossible to trace anything. It is well insulated, like nothing I've ever seen. But I bet Sun Fang still has a stake in this shipping company, just not publicly."

"Keep the kid on the payroll and use him to gain access to U.S. markets and whatever else he is up to and nobody knows, or can prove Sun Fang is behind it," Robert assumed.

"That is what I thought," Luna agreed. "Or we are barking up the wrong tree?"

"Your hunches are usually correct, Luna. But Sun Fang is not our problem. Kenny Wu is the problem," Stenson pointed out.

"I believe it's time for Mr. Brickhouse and me to take a brief reconnaissance trip over to Silkroad and see what Mr. Wu is up to," Stenson suggested.

"I will text you the address," Luna told her husband.

The guys left Stenson's place and drove over to an industrial area near the Port of New Orleans. They parked in a darkened alley across the street from Silkroad International Shipping, a run-down looking building near the harbor.

"This doesn't look like a place a flashy guy with as much money as Kenny Wu supposedly has would put a business," Stenson observed. "I was expecting something more corporate. Not a dump like this."

"Who knows? Maybe the kidnapping business is in decline," Robert mused.

As they watched the building, Brick asked. "What's the plan?"

"How about we knock on the door and tell Kenny Wu he owes us money and a girl?" Stenson suggested.

"If only it was that easy," Brick replied.

It was a dumb idea, but it wouldn't be the first time one of their stupid ideas worked out. Sometimes they worked because it was the last thing people expected. Stenson and Brick shrugged, then got out of the car and walked across the street. An Asian woman stepped outside to smoke a cigarette.

"Hi, we are looking for Kenny Wu," Brick said to the lady.

She took one look at Robert's tattoos and overall charming persona and threw her cigarette butt to his feet. Robert had a problem with impolite people and since his politeness did not work, he snatched her by her hair and covered her mouth to prevent her scream. It was another bad idea neither Stenson nor the lady expected.

Robert said, "Listen, I don't speak Chinese, so I hope you understand English. First, you should not litter. You are disrespecting my fine city. Second, I asked you where is Kenny Wu?"

He removed his hand long enough for the woman to yell, "I don't know who you are talking about and get your hands off me!"

"Wrong answer," Robert said as he pulled her hair tighter and gave her a lovely tattooed hug.

He growled at the woman, "Listen, if you don't tell me exactly what I want to know, you see that river over there? You will be in it feeding the catfish and that would not be good for your health."

She looked at the river and knew Robert Brickhouse could toss her 90 pound frame into the water with one hand from where they stood.

She blurted, "He's upstairs. Now let me go you animal!"

Brick released the woman who took off running down the street. When she was far enough away, she turned back and yelled at Robert, "You are bad for my health!"

Brickhouse laughed. "Wiser words were never said."

The men stared at the door. "Do you think

they will be polite if we knock?" Brick asked with a mischievous grin.

"Probably as nice as your new girlfriend was," Stenson said.

They looked at the door like a scene from the story of the Three Little Pigs who huffed and puffed. But unlike that story, these pigs used their feet to kick in the door. The splintered surprise caught a gangster by the door off guard. Before he could reach for his weapon, Robert grabbed the gun, like he had done many times in combat, and told the startled man, "Bad idea, my friend." Robert planted a left hook to his jaw which caused him to go down for the ten count... or more because Brick didn't plan to count.

Out of nowhere, more guys with guns appeared. Robert and Stenson dashed outside. They didn't have enough weapons to fight them all. But Stenson remembered he had a tear gas canister in the trunk of his car left over from the days they were fighting JC and Big Tony.

"Cover me!" Stenson told Robert as he dashed for the car. Stenson found the canister through a hail of bullets, which riddled holes into his classic ride. He ran back and pulled the pin, then tossed it through the front door, yelling, "You owe me a new car!"

Pandemonium broke out when the canister erupted. The guys inside coughed and blindly ran for the doors. One jumped out a window. It was quite a comedy how easily Stenson and Robert grabbed their guns when they ran away. Proof that another of their bad ideas actually worked.

Men running around the parking lot with tears streaming from their burning eyes caused Stenson and Robert to laugh out loud at the crazy scene. When the men finally got their vision back, they stared at Stenson and Brick standing there holding a stack of their guns and smartly decided this was not a fight they could win. They took off running down the road, probably catching up with the Chinese smoker lady.

"That was the funniest way we've cleared a room. Glad you had that tear gas canister, Stenson. Could have been a messier situation," Brick told Stenson, clearly amused.

After the smoke cleared, Robert and Stenson returned to the building and walked inside.

Brick hollered, "Kenny Wu, where are you?"

Stenson said, "That sounds like lyrics from a Who song. Wu are you... who, who, woo, woo..."

They noticed a poker table filled with fresh hands and unspent money. Robert flipped the cards over and said, "I win." Then scooped up the money and stuck it in his pocket. The way he figured, Kenny Wu stole their money, and he was here to collect even if it was only a few dollars at a time.

They searched room by room until they discovered an open window in the rear. Looking out, they observed a man shoving a hooded girl into the back seat of a black sedan and quickly speeding away. There was no point in trying to chase the vehicle. By the time they got back to Stenson's shot up car, even if it ran, they would never catch them. But that would not stop Robert Brickhouse from ensuring they never returned to Silkroad International Shipping. He spotted a drum of diesel fuel near a boat dock and rolled it over.

Stenson watched as Brick push the container into the building and unscrewed the cap. Fuel flooded the floors as Robert calmly walked out. He stood in front of the building next to Stenson and lit a cigar.

"Well, this was a bust," Stenson admitted, since they didn't catch Wu or rescue Zabrina.

"All is not lost," Brick said.

After taking a long drag from his stogie, he thumped it into the front door of the building, which burst into flames.

"I think we should go," Stenson advised his crazy friend.

"Sounds like a good idea," Brick agreed.

Since Stenson's decimated car would not start considering how many bullet holes were in it, he said. "I guess we are walking."

"Looks that way," Brick said.

As they sauntered away, Robert told Stenson, "I bet Kenny Wu got the message he should never play poker with us."

Chapter 10

Stenson and Robert "The Arsonist" Brickhouse reached the Beckett home on foot two hours later. Luna was puzzled when they walked through the door eating ice cream cones.

"Hi, Honey, I didn't hear you pull up," Luna said to her husband.

"We walked," Stenson told her as he licked a trickle of vanilla ice cream from his hand.

"I thought you took your car?" she recalled.

"We did," Stenson said, taking another lick of the icy treat.

"Where is your car?" she asked him.

"We left it there. It had some mechanical issues. But I picked you up an ice cream cone on the way home."

Stenson handed her the dessert melting down his hand.

"What kind of mechanical trouble?" Luna wondered.

She was confused because Stenson had recently spent a small fortune having his classic car restored and only got it back from the shop a week ago.

"Busted radiator," Stenson explained.

Brick chuckled. He filled in the other broken pieces of Stenson's car story. "And busted headlights, busted tires, busted windshield," Robert told her. "But his fuzzy dice are okay. I think he can glue the rearview mirror back on."

"Wait. What?" Luna asked, now completely confused.

Stenson explained Kenny's friends were fond of guns and wanted to show Brick and him how they worked with a demonstration on his car.

"Let me get this straight. You were supposed to go there to surveil the place. How did this turn into them shooting your car?" Luna wondered while licking her ice cream cone.

"All we did was knock on the door," Stenson innocently replied.

Robert laughed. "Yeah, with our feet."

"You kicked down the door?" Luna exclaimed.

"Come on. Do you think they would have let us in if we knocked politely?" Stenson rationalized.

Luna was afraid to ask, but dared to say, "Then what?"

"Well, it seems we interrupted their poker game, which apparently upset them. So, they started shooting at us," Robert told her.

"What happened next?" Luna prodded while licking ice cream from her sticky hand.

Robert said, "Remember when we used tear gas on JC and his crew?"

"Yes?" she recalled.

"Well, your husband had a left over cannister in the trunk of his car so we tossed it inside Kenny's place to get the bad guys to come outside and play," Robert elaborated.

"And did they?" Luna knew the silly answer, but felt compelled to ask the guys, anyway.

"Of course they did, Luna," Brick explained. "You know how much your husband and I like to play with bad guys."

"Oh, I know well how you two like to play. That is why I chaperone whenever we go out," Luna told him.

"Tell me you didn't kill anybody?" she implored.

"Heck no, Luna. What kind of guys do you think we are?" Brick replied, clearly tickled by the question because he would have killed them if they hadn't come up with a funnier way to dispatch those goons.

"You two are crazy," she hilariously remarked.

"Then what?" Luna asked, because she knew this story wasn't over.

"After that, they ran away, including Kenny Wu with Zabrina. And since we experienced a vehicle malfunction, we weree could not pursue," Brick stated their minor misstep.

"You mean since Stenson's car was shot to pieces, that kind of malfunction?" Luna clarified.

"Details, details, Luna." Brick admitted, "Yes, your husband's beautiful car that he loves almost as much as you was slightly impaired, and Stenson and I could not chase down a car on foot."

The shock and amusement on Luna's face was priceless.

"So you walked home like this was a normal day?" She summarized in case Robert and Stenson's adventure involved stealing a bus or trolley car and stopping by to pick up ice cream and bought some for all the passengers to apologize for "borrowing" a city vehicle.

They didn't do that, but there was more to the story, as Stenson explained.

"We walked home after the accident at Silkroad."

"Accident?" she verified. "I thought the accident was what happened to your car?"

"Well, that was an accident because I don't think the bad guys meant to shoot my car. They were trying to shoot me and Robert," he clarified.

Luna stared at the men dumbfounded. "You think?" ran through her mind before her husband finished the outrageous tale.

Stenson continued. "Remember how Robert got his nickname, Brick? People think it's because his last name is Brickhouse. But really, he got it when he was a little boy and other kids made him angry. He would drive by their house on his bicycle and throw bricks through their window."

She laughed. "Yes, I remember. Your best friend has been a lunatic since he was a child," she teased.

Brick found the lunatic remark amusing. He liked the title.

"What has that got to do with the accident at Silkroad?" she asked.

"Well, Robert's new nickname is Pyro," Stenson revealed.

"Pyro?" she repeated.

"Yeah. It seems Robert doesn't like impolite people shooting at him or his friend's car, so he burned the place down."

"He what?" Luna asked in disbelief.

Robert defended himself. "Calm down, Luna. It was a small gas leak,"

"Yeah, it was a small gas leak from the barrel of diesel fuel Robert rolled inside the front door of Silkroad and set on fire with a cigar," Stenson enlightened.

"You should have heard Brick singing 'Burn Baby Burn' and 'The Roof is on Fire' all the way home," Stenson joked.

"Oh lord," Luna said, rolling her eyes.

"Hey, those are good songs, Luna. You should add them to your playlist," Brick suggested.

"What am I going to do with you two?" she wondered.

"I don't know. But we need to find Kenny Wu again," Stenson said.

"Really?" she asked with an exasperated look on

her face.

"I found that needle in a haystack the first time and now he is hiding from you and I have to find him again?" she exasperated.

"You guys are not making this easy for me," Luna said.

"That's why you love us," Robert Brickhouse joked.

"Leave it to me to love two of the most dangerous guys on the planet," Luna replied with a silly grin.

* * *

"Can somebody tell me who those guys were that stormed my business and burned it to the ground?" Kenny Wu asked the only person in the room as if he were addressing a crowd.

David Pham replied, "I don't know who they were. I wasn't there. But I have a feeling they are friends of the black guy and the fat one you shot."

"I didn't shoot the fat guy!" Kenny clarified.

It was a matter of semantics that David Pham did not want to argue with Kenny over. Granted, he did not physically shoot the big guy. But one of his men did, and that was all that mattered and beside the point.

"Did anyone get a look at them?" Kenny asked.

"No. Our guys said it happened too fast." David replied, "We had them on surveillance. But I stress the word had because our cameras and the recording equipment were lost in the fire."

"Where is the black guy and fat one? Is he alive?" Kenny questioned.

"I don't know, Kenny," David said.

"You are so impulsive and didn't say anything about shooting anyone when you came up with the hair brain idea to kidnap the girl and hold her for ransom. I told you it was a bad idea, and you did it, anyway. Now I'm supposed to know where those two are? Do I have a crystal ball?"

"You better get a crystal ball and figure out who was stupid enough to pick a fight with me," Kenny fumed.

"Do I need to remind you that you picked the fight with them?" David asked.

"Shut up, David!" Kenny scolded his number two. "I don't care if I picked the fight. All I want to know is who those two were that burned my business to the ground!"

"I will try," David told him.

"No, you will not try. You will find out who they are!" Kenny demanded. "Kidnap the black guy and torture him until you get the information we need. I don't care how you do it. Just do it!"

David walked out of the room thinking to himself he did not sign up for this craziness. One of these days, Kenny would get what was coming to him and sleep in the bed he made.

* * *

There was a knock at the door. When Stenson answered it, a creole-looking man wearing a dark brown off-the-rack suit asked him, "Stenson Beckett?"

"Yes. I am Stenson Beckett," he replied.

The man flashed a badge and told him, "I am Detective Thibodeaux with the New Orleans Police Department. May I come in?"

"Sure," Stenson replied, somewhat surprised.

"What's this about?" he asked the officer.

The detective noticed Luna and Robert in the living room and asked to speak to Stenson privately. They went to the dining room out of ear-shot and sat at the table. The detective began by inquiring about Stenson's car. He told him it should be in the driveway. The policeman informed him that his car was discovered at the scene of a suspected arson. When he asked if Stenson knew anything about it, he feigned ignorance and told him he had nothing to share.

The detective asked about his whereabouts between six and ten? Stenson said he ran an errand with a friend and had been home ever since. He told the officer it was the last time he saw his car. He said his friend was in the living room if he wanted to verify the story. The detective agreed and questioned Robert who confirmed Stenson's version of events; they ran an errand, picked up ice cream, and had been home for several hours. Luna also vouched for the timeline.

When the detective asked Robert what errand they ran, he looked at Luna and said, "I really shouldn't say."

"Why is that?" the detective asked.

"Because it may incriminate my friend," Robert told the detective.

The officer sat up and reminded Robert to impede a criminal investigation was a serious offense that could land him in jail. Robert looked at Stenson and said, "I'm sorry, Stenson."

He told the detective, "We picked up a birthday present for his wife. It is in the car's trunk. Now you have ruined his wife's surprise."

The answer was not what the detective expected. He looked at Luna, then back at Stenson. He closed his notebook and stood up. "I believe I have all the information I need. We'll be in touch if there are any further questions."

Stenson rose to walk the detective to the door. The detective turned to Luna and said, "Happy birthday, ma'am. I am sorry if I ruined your surprise."

The officer apologized to Stenson for his totaled

car and told him to be prepared for what he would see when he picks up the vehicle at the police impound lot.

After the detective left, Stenson plopped into a chair. "That was close," he exhaled.

"You think he bought it?" Robert wondered.

"I think so," Stenson replied. "But I almost choked when you told him we went out to pick up a birthday gift for Luna and hid it in the trunk."

"How did you know I had a gift for her in the trunk?" Stenson asked Robert.

"I didn't," the marine admitted.

"You better be glad I did, in case they check," Stenson told him with a sigh of relief.

"Now you've ruined Luna's surprise," he told Brick.

"I will be surprised if my birthday present isn't filled with bullet holes," Luna joked.

"My poor car," Stenson lamented.

"My poor present," Luna playfully pouted.

"At least I didn't lie to the guy," Stenson admitted.

"Brick and I ran an errand," he said. "And the last time I saw my car in one piece was when it was parked in the driveway. He didn't ask me when was the last time I saw my car in pieces? And when he asked if I knew anything about the arson at Silkroad, I said I had nothing to share."

"You are a smooth operator, Stenson. You should have been a criminal or a politician," Brick suggested.

"Aren't they one and the same?" Stenson replied.

* * *

David Pham phoned a contact at the New Orleans Police Department who Kenny Wu kept on their payroll. He wanted to see if they had any information about the fire at Silkroad or shooting under the St. Claude Avenue Bridge. Specifically, he wanted to know about the black guy and the fat man who was shot.

Even though Detective Crépin Thibodeaux was one of their inside informants, David would have to inquire about the shooting indirectly to not raise suspicion they were involved. Thibodeaux was a source, but he was not a dirty cop. And David Pham wasn't about to test his loyalty to Kenny Wu for robbery, kidnapping, and attempted murder.

"Detective Thibodeaux," the man answered.

"Thib, it's David Pham," he introduced.

"You guys come up with any leads about the fire at Silkroad? Kenny is pretty upset about it," David said.

"Fire Marshall says it's arson unless Kenny keeps barrels of diesel fuel inside," the detective told him with a flat cop sense of humor.

"Any idea who is responsible?" Pham asked.

"We found a shot up car across the street. Checked out the owner and it appears to be unrelated. Looks like somebody stole the guy's vehicle and some kind of gunfight shredded his whip. Too bad. It was a nice car," Thibodeaux said.

He added, "I went over to the guy's house myself and he didn't even know the car was gone. His wife and a friend corroborated his story."

"Mind if I ask the guy's name?" Pham inquired.

"Stenson Beckett. He owns O'Malley's pub in the Quarter. Why?" the detective asked.

"Just curious. With a car like that, I thought I might know him. But his name doesn't ring a bell."

"Hey, I heard about the shooting down by the river. Any luck on that?" David asked.

"No. Probably some drug deal gone bad. It's not high on our list," Thibodeaux told him.

"Who was shot?" David inquired.

"A big guy who was one the owners of that

defunct nightclub Empire. One victim, a black guy who was also an owner at Empire, said something about a kidnapping and ransom, but it seemed too farfetched. Anyway, we are looking into it," the detective told him.

"Okay, thanks. Say hello to the missus and let us know if there is anything you need."

After they hung up, David pondered the information. The most important name Thibodeaux revealed was Stenson Beckett. He needed to check him out to see if there was a connection between him and the Club Empire guys. The good news was the bridge incident was not a serious concern for the police. Just another shooting in the Big Easy, which meant Kenny Wu was in the clear... At least for now.

Chapter 11

David Pham scoured the web for information about Club Empire and its owners. He recalled Kenny had attended a few social events there before it closed after that monstrous disaster. Little did he realize the ironic connections they would have to the place and the owners now. He found a photograph from an event featuring Justin Carter and Zabrina Chao, the woman they smuggled from North Korea.

Justin Carter, the black guy Kenny attacked who went by the name JC, was listed as a partner with a man named Anthony Gallo. He assumed Gallo must be camera shy because he could not find a photo of him anywhere. But in an interview with Mr. Carter, he referred to the man as "Big Tony". David assumed he was the fat guy who had been shot when Kenny robbed them of half a million dollars and kept the girl, which he still didn't understand why?

As far as Zabrina Chao was concerned, she was not listed as an owner of the organization, which David guessed was due to the fact she was an illegal immigrant. However, he sensed she was as heavily involved in their operation because she seemed to be everywhere promoting their activities.

From what he read, the three were building a new establishment. Of course, that was before Kenny went on one of his wild tangents and snatched the girl. He felt a headache coming on. Why didn't Kenny leave this alone? David knew the answer was greed, something Kenny was famous for. He'd worked with Wu long enough to know he will use people, including himself, to get whatever he wanted. It did not take a PhD in psychology to know his boss was a textbook sociopath: egocentric, callous, manipulative, impulsive, compassionless, disrespectful, aggressive, without remorse.

Kenny became worse over the years as he gained wealth and notoriety under the guise of being a successful businessman and philanthropist. If people only knew the gutters Kenny wallowed in, they would run and hide. Everything he did was a scatological ruse.

David searched for Stenson Beckett, the name Crépin Thibodeaux revealed. He was easy to find. Several news articles and videos featured him donating to homeless people, building a church in rural Alabama, and recently becoming the new owner of O'Malley's pub in the French Quarter. From all accounts, Stenson Beckett was an upstanding guy, unlike his boss who was as fake as a three dollar bill.

Fortunately for Stenson Beckett, David could not connect him to the Club Empire people. Maybe he was barking up the wrong tree and the guy's car really was stolen and ended up across the street from Silkroad. But it seemed too much of a coincidence to dismiss. However, he would not give Kenny Wu the guy's name unless he was certain he was involved. As impulsive and irrational as Kenny was, he knew he would do something foolish. He needed more proof before they went down that road.

* * *

Kenny Wu may have fled, but the guy wasn't hiding. He was plastered all over the news after the fire. Luna watched Kenny's response to a reporter's question.

Kenneth Wu
CEO, Silkroad International Shipping

"I am thankful nobody was hurt. Investigators
are looking into the cause of the fire.
However, it will not disrupt our operations
or my generous contributions to the city I
love. Like New Orleans, we are resilient."

"We'll see how resilient you are, Kenny," Luna
said to the television screen as she rewound the
recorder and paused it on a frame of the man's face.
She studied the image for clues where the interview
took place. The building behind Kenny appeared to
be in some nondescript industrial park. She didn't
expect he was keeping Zabrina there. If he was, the
guy was dumber than a sack of bricks.

She searched commercial real estate websites
looking for buildings in New Orleans that were
designed like the one Kenny was standing in front
of. She soon realized it would not be easy because
all the commercial office parks looked exactly the
same as if they were all stamped from cookie cutters.

She knew from previous interviews Kenny
Wu lived in the Garden District neighborhood
popular with celebrities and other notable people.
But exactly where proved to be difficult. Property
records revealed many homes in the area were
owned by limited liability companies to shield the
identities of the owners and Kenny Wu was among
the hidden.

Stenson walked into the kitchen to pour a cup of
coffee.

"Morning, babe," he told his wife when he
returned with a mug that read, "World's Greatest
Dad".

"Why are you up so early?" she asked her
husband.

"Robert is stopping by to take me to the place where they towed my car. It looks like it's going back to the shop," he replied after a sip of his warm brew.

"It's been shot to pieces, Stenson. Why don't you sell it for scrap and get another car?" she suggested.

"I love that car, Luna. It's a classic, and she's got nine lives. Nothing a little Bondo and some fresh paint won't fix," he hoped.

"And a new engine and new interior..." she said. "You could build a new car for what you will spend repairing it."

"Now Luna, if you were shot to pieces would you want me to repair you or get a new model?" her husband comically asked her.

"Well, if you upgrade me, can you give me the skinny version back? I still haven't gotten used to my big rear end after my pregnancy."

"Sure. Might even put some lifters on those chest upgrades you received after our son was born," he teased.

"Watch it, buster. I am a woman, not a car. You with all your funny repair analogies," she playfully reprimanded.

"Yes dear," was his tickled reply.

There was a knock at the door. Stenson let Robert in.

"Make yourself a cup of coffee," he told the big marine. "I'll get your nephew so you can change his diaper."

Brick shook his head and looked at Luna.

"What part of 'I don't do dirty diapers' does your husband not understand?" Robert asked her.

"I bring the toys. He does the diapers," Robert explained to Luna about his made-up baby rules.

She laughed.

"I think he enjoys seeing you dry-heave every time you see baby poop," Luna told him.

"Your husband is a very sick man, Luna," Brick said as he took a sip of coffee from the cup Stenson bought him that read, 'Wild Man'.

Stenson returned with his son and handed him to Robert. "Say good morning to your nephew with his clean diaper, you big baby."

"Ah, the smell of a clean baby," Brick admired.

"You should have smelled him five minutes ago," Stenson replied.

Brick made a silly face at Stenson Jr. In a child-like voice, he said, "See, little Stenson. Your daddy is learning. I am Uncle Presents and he is Daddy Doo-Doo. Can you say Daddy Doo-Doo?"

"Don't teach my son to say that," Stenson warned. "If the first words out of his mouth is calling me Daddy Doo-Doo, you are fired as his uncle!"

The guys noticed the frozen image of Kenny Wu on the TV screen. "Where did you find that?" Stenson asked Luna.

"Morning news," she replied. "He's apparently on his victim tour right now with the media."

"Do you recognize the place behind him?" Stenson wondered, proving he and his wife think alike.

"I was working on it before Daddy Doo-Doo and Uncle Pyro-Presents distracted me," she teased.

"Why don't you two get out of here and buy a bunch of duct tape for Stenson's four-wheel girlfriend so I can get some work done?" she suggested.

"Yes, boss," Stenson replied.

"We'll stop by and visit Big Tony at the hospital after we deal with my girlfriend... I mean my car. Then we'll head to O'Malley's to meet with JC."

Brick laid the child into the crib and told his nephew, "Be good for mommy."

"You two be good!" Luna told the overgrown

kids.

The guys headed to the impound lot where Stenson's car looked worse in broad daylight than the last time they saw it the night before. He had it towed back to the shop, where his mechanic would be pained to restore it again. Afterwards, they stopped by a fast food restaurant for an early lunch. Robert ordered two bags to go. When they arrived at the hospital, Brick attempted to be discreet smuggling the contraband. But all anyone had to do was follow the French fry smell to Big Tony Gallo's room.

Anthony lit up when the guys walked in. The smell of fast food made the big man smile.

"Finally, some real food!" he exclaimed.

"I wasn't worried about surviving after being shot," Big Tony said. "I was more afraid of dying of starvation if I had to keep eating this hospital food. Anybody want my salad?"

Robert laid out two double cheeseburgers, two large fries, a large soda, and an apple pie. If the way to a man's heart was through his stomach, then Big Tony knew who loved him. As he ate, Stenson filled him in on the details of the flammable events at Silkroad and assured him they were doing all they could to find Zabrina.

On the way back to O'Malley's, Stenson phoned JC and asked him to meet them. An hour later, Justin arrived and grabbed a stool next to Stenson. Robert, who was behind the bar, asked JC if he wanted his regular drink? He quietly requested a glass of water instead. Robert and Stenson sensed the burden he carried and promised they were in this together like NATO. If you mess with one, you mess with all.

Unbeknownst to them, they were being watched from across the street where David Pham sat at an outdoor café. He witnessed JC walk into O'Malley's and talk to Stenson and the tattooed guy behind the bar. Now he had confirmation the men knew each other. Even though he couldn't be certain these were the guys who took down Silkroad, David assumed they probably were.

Stenson leaving his car behind in the alley across from Silkroad was the clue he needed. Now he could tell Kenny what he wanted to know. In a small way, he felt sorry for these guys because they did not know the storm heading their way. He drove to Kenny's house in the Garden to relay the news.

The phone rang as David walked into Kenny's home office. He motioned David to take a seat while he took the call.

"Father, what do I owe the pleasure?" Kenny said cheerfully, trying to disguise his fear.

"What is this trouble, Dingxiang?" Wu Kong interrogated his impotent, illegitimate son.

"What do you mean, father?" Kenny sheepishly replied.

"Who burned down your business?" the Rising Tiger asked.

"It was an electrical fire, according to investigators," Kenny lied.

"How many electrical fires start with a tattooed man rolling a barrel of fuel inside a building and lighting it with a cigar?" Kong demanded.

Kenny paused. What else did his father know, and how did he know more about the fire than he knew?

"How do you... I mean," Kenny muttered.

"Do you think I do not know everything you do?" Kong warned. "I have the surveillance footage. I assume you saw it too?"

"The equipment was lost in the fire. I have not seen it," Kenny admitted.

"Who is the girl?" Kong inquired like an FBI investigator.

"The girl?" Kenny fumbled, realizing this snowball was about to burn in hell.

"The girl you climbed out of the window with and fled," revealing Kong knew more.

"Oh, that girl? She's my girlfriend," Kenny lied again.

"Do you bind all of your girlfriends and gag their mouths?" Wu Kong taunted.

"Father, I can explain everything," Kenny trembled.

"I warned you that you are on a very short leash. If you do not resolve this matter quietly and quickly, your time on this planet will be brief," the Rising Tiger growled.

"I will..." Kenny was cut off before he completed the sentence and the line went dead.

He placed the handset down and stared at David. It was a blank stare, as if Kenny was staring at the inside of his own soul. After he gathered his composure, he asked David, "What have you got?"

"Advice," David replied. "End this now. Give them the girl and return their money because if you don't, they will be the last of your worries when you face the wrath of your father."

"I did not ask you for advice." Kenny clarified, "I asked you for information."

"The car they found across the street from Silkroad belongs to a man named Stenson Beckett." David shared. "He owns a pub in the French Quarter named O'Malley's."

"I scoped out the place earlier today and the black guy, Justin Carter, who you ripped off, knows him. There is also an employee who works there, a big dude with tattoos, that matches the description your guys gave us, which I might add, your father knew the person who torched the place had tattoos. But it could be a coincidence."

"Doubtful," Kenny replied. "This Beckett guy owns a bar?"

"Yes. O'Malley's in the Quarter," David confirmed.

"Burn it," Kenny instructed.

"What?" David asked, as if he heard him wrong.

"I said torch the place," Kenny repeated.

"Have you lost your mind Kenny? First, Beckett is well liked around the city. He's a military veteran with a purple heart and this doesn't seem like something he would do. It's just guess if he's even involved. The only thing I can confirm is he knows Justin Carter."

"Burn it, I said," Kenny told him again.

"Absolutely not!" David firmly refused.

"If you want the place burned, then do it yourself or arrange for someone else to do it. But I will not have any part of this. You may harm an innocent person and you are certainly raising the stakes of this dumb game while rattling the cage of your father! I will not be involved in your madness."

"You disappoint me, David," Kenny replied.

"I disappoint you?" David exasperated. "I have been by your side and loyal throughout all of your craziness. But I am telling you, I do not feel right about this. I have a wife and kid to think about. They are where my loyalty lies."

"Leave the information and go," Kenny bemoaned. "I will deal with this matter myself."

"I am warning you Kenny, you are playing a very dangerous game," David cautioned. "You've got half a million dollars of their money and the insurance money from your building. You don't need the girl. Get out of this before it is too late."

"David, this is why I am number one and you will always be number two. You do not see things as I do. You play it safe, whereas I play for keeps. You must break a few eggs to make an omelet and get ahead in this world."

"If you don't watch out, those broken eggs will end up on your face," David concluded as he stormed out the door.

* * *

Stenson's phone rang at 4:15 AM. He answered with a groggy, "Hello?"

"Get over here!" Robert Brickhouse shouted over a chaotic commotion in the background.

"Where?" Stenson asked, looking at the clock. "Do you know what time it is?"

"The bar, now!" Brick demanded before he slammed the phone.

Stenson shook the cobwebs from his head and climbed out of bed. Luna stirred and asked him, "Who was that?"

"It was Robert. Something is going on at the bar."

"Come back soon. I was having sweet dreams with you snuggled against me," she cooed in her sleepy voice.

It did not take long for Stenson to realize the urgency of the call when he saw an orange glow scarring the black horizon. Emergency vehicles formed a block-wide perimeter in the French Quarter. Stenson parked and walked toward the scene where he found Brickhouse standing across the street from O'Malley's engulfed in flames.

"Anyone inside?" Stenson asked.

"No. We closed around 1:30 AM. Slow night. Staff was out by two. Alarm service called me half an hour ago," Brick replied.

"Do I ask if this started in the kitchen or some other reasonable explanation?" Stenson wondered, already knowing the dreadful answer.

"If Molotov cocktails through the front windows qualify as reasonable," Brick remarked as they watched the flames.

Stenson shook his head. "Meet me at the house when this is over. I will put some coffee on."

Luna found Robert and Stenson sitting at the kitchen table at 7:00 am. She smelled the smoke on their clothes and asked, "Did you guys burn something?"

Stenson pointed the remote at the TV and turned up the volume. The fire at O'Malley's was headline news.

"Oh, my god!" Luna exclaimed.

She watched the story. It made Brick and Stenson more nauseous having witnessed it in person.

"Before you ask, it was not a kitchen fire," Stenson told his wife.

She poured a cup of coffee and joined the guys at the table, not really knowing a consoling thing to say. She saw the wheels spinning in their heads. Luna knew they were beyond angry; Stenson and Brick were flamingly furious.

They were out half a million dollars, of which fifty thousand was Stenson's money. Their friend Zabrina Chao was still very much kidnapped, and they did not know where to begin looking for her. Tony Gallo was shot and now Stenson's bar was a pile of rubble. Why? One name came to mind, who, until a week ago Stenson had never heard before. Kenny Wu had turned their lives upside down.

"What can I do?" Luna asked.

Stenson looked at her with steely determination, "Dig up as much information as you can on Wu."

Chapter 12

Kenny Wu watched the morning news with a twisted sense of delight at the sight of O'Malley's Pub burning to the ground.

He told David Pham, "They should get the message not to mess with me."

"I hope so, for your sake," Pham replied.

Secretly, David knew how easily this could spin out of control.

"Are you sure nothing can connect you to this? Two fires of two businesses within days of each other seems suspicious, even for the casual observer," David warned.

"Investigations take forever. Besides, even if they determine both fires were arson, there is nothing to connect my transportation company to a bar in the Quarter. It looks like a serial arsonist is on the loose, burning random businesses," Kenny reasoned.

"What if they trace the people you hired to torch the bar back to you?" Pham inquired.

"They won't. I didn't use our regular people. I brought in guys from out of town and they are long gone by now," Kenny assured.

"Where is the girl?"

"At the safe house," Kenny replied.

"What do you plan to do with her?" David asked.

"I'm not sure yet. I may keep her or kill her just to piss the guys off who thought they could game me," Kenny told David Pham.

"You are nuts, Kenny! As long as she is missing, even if the cops don't make it a top priority, which Thibodeaux said it isn't, you are going to have these other people after you."

"Haven't you realized, David, that I am untouchable? I am so beloved in this town I welcome it. They will lose, not me," Kenny told him confidently.

"What about me, Kenny?" David asked. "I've lived in the same place forever and have a wife and child to think about."

"You'll figure it out," Kenny said uncaring. "Besides, you are a ninja. You can protect yourself."

"I am a mixed martial artist, but that is beside the point. I don't have a good feeling about these guys, Kenny. Let's give them back the girl and money and quit while we are ahead."

"No way," Wu replied. "I am a winner. I will never concede, especially to these amateurs."

David's stomach churned. His gut instincts told him this was a very different situation than anything Kenny had done before. He was playing too close to the fire and his building wasn't the only thing to be burned if he does not quit while he was ahead.

"Don't worry about it, David," Kenny reassured. "We've got the shipment coming soon. It's the biggest deal we have done. Concern yourself with that while I have fun yanking these guy's chain."

"Fine," David said as he got up to leave. "I hope you know what you are doing."

"I always do," Wu bragged.

After David left, Kenny looked at his notes and dialed Stenson Beckett's personal phone number.

"Hello?" the voice at the other end greeted.

"We are even," Kenny said.

Stenson did not have to ask who this was. The Asian accent from a number he didn't recognize told him it was Kenny Wu.

"Oh, we are far from even," Stenson assured him. "You owe me half a million dollars and a girl. Then we'll discuss my bar."

"Do you like games, Mr. Beckett?" Wu taunted.

"Depends," Stenson replied.

"I assure you that you do not want to play with me," Kenny warned him.

"Look Wu, I don't know what you are getting at. You started this. We can end it now if you turn over the girl and return the money," Stenson tried to reason.

"Why are you so concerned with the girl and the black man's money? Is your health and your family's health worth you getting involved?" Wu asked.

"You leave my family out of this! And those people you mentioned are my friends. I simply want them made whole and you will never hear from us again," Stenson angrily proposed.

The offer wasn't true because there were other scores to settle with Kenny Wu, such as a certain fat man being shot. But for now, Stenson was attempting to keep this maniac focused.

"The only way this ends, Mr. Beckett, is if you fold your hand and walk away. Cut your losses before something happens that no amount of money can repay," Kenny taunted.

"Are you threatening me, Wu?" Stenson asked with a voice growing louder as his blood began to boil.

"It's not a threat, Mr. Beckett. It is a promise." Wu assured him, "I know where you live. I know your wife, Luna. I know your child. I know your friends. I will burn them like I burned your bar if you get in my way," Wu warned.

The line went dead. "Wu?" Stenson yelled.

Stenson smashed his phone against the wall. Luna

rushed into the room to see what the commotion was about.

"Who was that?" she asked her husband.

"Don't worry about it," Stenson said as he picked up his keys.

"I am going to see Robert. I will be back in a while," he told her.

Before she could respond, Stenson stormed out the door. In all the years she had known her husband, she had never seen him so angry, nor had he ever spoken to her that way. Whatever upset him was serious. Very serious.

On his way to pick up Robert, Stenson phoned JC.

"Justin, get over to Big Tony and don't let him out of your sight. I think something bad is brewing. I will tell you more when we arrive."

He screeched to a halt in front of Robert's house and blew the horn. The big marine jumped in.

"What's up?" Brick asked Stenson.

"I received a call from Kenny Wu," he angrily relayed.

"How did he..." Brick began.

Before Robert finished the question of how Wu found Stenson, he answered. "The car."

"So they found the car. How does that connect you and me to JC and his crew?" Robert wondered an impossible question.

"I don't know," Stenson replied, "But it has, and now Kenny Wu has threatened me and my family."

"Where are we headed?" Brick asked as Stenson punched the pedal down the highway.

"Paying a visit to Sarge," Stenson told the big marine.

Sergeant John Dean served in the U.S. Army Rangers. Now retired, he runs Gulf Coast Logistics, a front company for his arms sales business. If you need military hardware of any kind, Sarge was a good friend to know. Once, when JC angered Stenson and Brick with one of his tricks before they were friends, Stenson borrowed a tank and blew up his warehouse. After the warning Stenson received from Kenny Wu, he planned to be armed to the teeth and ready for anything that lunatic had up his sleeve.

Stenson honked the horn when they pulled up in front of Gulf Coast Logistics. A semi-truck-sized corrugated door raised, inviting them to drive inside. Sergeant Dean, a burly man in his mid-70s with a thick shock of gray hair, greeted the guys when they exited the car.

"Stenson, what brings you and that grubby marine to this dark side of town?" John Dean inquired.

"We stopped by to see if you were dead," Brickhouse told him with a twisted marine sense of humor.

Robert and John Dean enjoyed sparring with each other about who was better, the Army Rangers or U.S. Marines. It didn't matter because both were capable killers. However, this visit was no joking matter and Stenson wasted no time getting down to business.

"I need some protection, Sarge," Stenson told John Dean. "Seems a certain Chinese guy wants to get friendly with me, and he is threatening my family."

"Yeah, that was after he burned down Stenson's bar last night," Robert added.

"Burned your bar? Why?" Sarge astonishingly asked.

Stenson shared the events of the past few days; the kidnapping of Zabrina, money stolen, and Big Tony being shot. He elaborated the botched surveillance episode where the bad guy got away with the girl. When he mentioned Robert burned the place down, Sarge laughed, not that it was funny, but because it sounded like something that crazy marine would do.

Dean realized the seriousness and told the guys, "Come this way."

They stepped to the rear of the warehouse where he pressed a hidden button. The back wall lifted like a scene from a spy movie revealing a cavernous room filled with deadly goods.

"Let's see what we've got," Sarge told the men as they walked inside.

It always amazed them how an arms dealer could be so inconspicuous sitting under everybody's nose. Dean had every kind of weapon you could imagine. How he got his hands on things, they never asked.

"What do you need, Stenson? I've got a MiG-21. It has a few miles on it, but will do the trick," Sarge said, pointing to a shrouded shape hulking in the back.

"Not sure my homeowner's association will allow me to park a Russian fighter jet in the driveway," Stenson jokingly said.

"Got anything smaller?" Stenson wondered.

Sarge opened a metal crate. "These are MP5K. It's a close protection weapon used by special ops. They aren't much bigger than a handgun and easy to conceal, which is why they like them so much. Fires 9mm at 900 rounds per minute. Basically, it is a saw."

Stenson picked up the weapon and sighted it toward the back wall. "This will work, but I am afraid to ask how much it costs? I'm a little light on funds right now."

"As long as it protects you and your family, call it a gift." John Dean told him with a soldier-to-soldier smile.

"Will six be enough?" John asked, which was more than Stenson would suggest.

"That will allow you to stash a few in different locations for quick access. I will throw in enough of these 15 and 30 round clips so you don't worry about running out of ammunition if things go sideways or if Robert Brickhouse misses the target."

Brick took offense at the suggestion he didn't know how to shoot. "Stenson, hand me one of those so I can show this Ranger the United States Marine Corps can out-shoot anybody in the Army," the tattooed marine boasted.

They continued to browse through Sarge's inventory until they filled two large duffle bags with dangerous wares. When Stenson suggested it might be overkill, Sarge reminded him it was better to have more weapons than not enough.

"Thank you, Sarge," Stenson told the Ranger as he shut the door to the hidden room.

"Now let me get my testosterone filled Marine out of here before he thinks he can fly a MiG-21," Stenson said.

"How hard can it be?" Robert guessed.

They placed the duffle bags in the back of Luna's SUV.

Sarge told Stenson, "I hope your wife doesn't find your toys."

"I will hide them better than her birthday present, so Brickhouse won't spoil our surprise," Stenson suggested.

"Marines. You can't live with 'em and can't shoot 'em," Sarge slyly replied.

"Because we will shoot you before you see us, Ranger," Brick smarted back to Segeant Dean.

After they left Sarge's place, Stenson and Brick drove to the hospital where they found JC in Tony

Gallo's room.

"How are you feeling, Big T?" Robert asked as they walked through the door.

"I won't be dancing with JC for a while, but I'm feeling a little better," Big Tony replied.

"JC doesn't know how to dance," Robert said. "That boy can't even walk straight."

After the laughter settled, Stenson urged the guys, "It's time to get you out of here, big fella. I don't know how, but this Kenny Wu clown car knows we are involved. Now he has threatened my family. Something tells me he is not done with you and JC, either."

"Go into hiding?" Anthony Gallo asked.

"Until we know where this nut job is or more about the gangsters he associates with. You know firsthand how tricky he and his friends are," Stenson reminded.

"Yeah. I never saw that coming," Tony Gallo agreed with a lead belly full of regret.

Stenson said, "Luna is doing everything she can to locate the people involved. But we need to lie low until we know what we are up against."

Robert handed JC and Tony new mobile phones. "These are burners. They won't be track our communications. Turn your other phones off or better yet, toss them in the dump. We cannot risk giving these people any opportunity to know where we are located."

"JC, see what you can do about getting the big guy out of here," Stenson suggested.

"Even if he needs to remain in the hospital, it cannot be this one," Stenson told them.

"I don't need another hospital. But I might need a cane," Big Tony assured.

After they left, Stenson dropped off Brick at his place before returning home. Luna noticed the duffle bags when he walked in. She asked, "What's in the bags, dead bodies?"

"Not yet," Stenson told her with a smile that said he was in a better mood than when he walked out the door earlier.

He said, "It's your birthday present, so keep your nosey nose out of this closet."

Luna knew those bags did not contain her birthday present, but she also knew Stenson really didn't want her snooping around. Instead, she teased him, "You really don't know how to wrap a girl's present, do you?"

"I didn't know how to change a baby's diaper until I met you. I'll figure it out," her husband wryly replied.

He placed the bags inside a hall closet until he could find a more permanent place to store these presents he hoped he would never use. He joined his wife on the sofa where she sat with her laptop resting on her crossed legs.

"Find anything?" Stenson asked.

"Dead ends," Luna told him with a sense of frustration.

As a security analyst, Luna had extraordinary talent. In the tech world, she was known as a "white hat"; an individual who uses hacking skills to identify security vulnerabilities in hardware, software, and networks. "ViciousDelicious" was one of the many identities she adorned while scouring the dark web for criminals. When she couldn't find something, it meant it must be buried deeply.

"I admit whoever is behind this guy is good enough to make him appear legit," Luna realized.

"It's going to take a while to untangle his web. As for the Chinese gang? I have found several members who have been arrested in New Orleans, but it isn't like there is a mailing list with their names. I am trying to track down people associated with Kenny Wu. Here is what I've found."

Luna handed her laptop to Stenson. "See that name at the top of the list, David Pham? He pops up a lot. More than Wu when I cross-referenced things."

"He seems important," Stenson guessed. "What's his connection to Wu?"

"As far as I can tell, he looks like Kenny's number two guy in their operations. The rest of the names seem like underlings who answer to Pham," she suggested.

Stenson replied, "Let's assume these so-called operations aren't exactly on the up-and-up. He gets Pham and his goons to do the dirty work like burning down my bar to keep his hands clean. Since we can't find Wu, let's start with David Pham. Got anything on him?"

"He is interesting. David is from South Korea and went to the same university as Wu. He has a Master's Degree in business and seems to run Wu's company legitimately. Business records, tax returns, public statements all seem on the straight and narrow. It doesn't mean he isn't involved with Wu's shady side, but the guy doesn't hide."

"Were you able to locate him?" Stenson asked.

"I have his address," she told her husband. "He lives a normal life in the suburbs; Has a wife and four-year-old daughter named Miko. The kindergarten she goes to is listed there as well. He seems too open and normal to be a gangster, if you ask me."

"I agree," Stenson replied. "But if it is all we've got, let's begin there."

Chapter 13

Stenson handed a list of Kenny Wu's known associates to Robert Brickhouse. "We need to tail these guys," he suggested.

"The most important person on the list is David Pham. He is Wu's number two. Since we don't have a clue of Kenny's whereabouts or where he has stashed Zabrina, Pham is our primary target. We need to keep tabs on these other gangbangers as well. We don't need more surprises."

"Going to take a lot of bikers to tail 20 people day and night," Brick guessed, as he studied the names on the sheet.

"It's probably not even a complete list," Stenson warned. "Those are the ones Luna could find now."

"I will make some calls," Brick assured him with an emphatic determination in his voice.

Robert folded the piece of paper and tucked it into the top pocket of his black leather biker jacket.

"What will you do?" the big marine asked Stenson.

"I am heading to the house to look after my wife and kid and come up with a plan for Mr. Pham," he said. "But warn the others if we have eyes on them, they probably have eyes on us, so be careful."

"Roger that," Brick confirmed.

Stenson returned home and joined Luna on the sofa. She was sitting with her laptop banging away at the keys. He was struck by her genius as he watched her magical fingers type commands resembling some alien language. He was amused since he could barely type his own email address using two fingers.

"You know what all that means?" he asked the smart woman.

"I do," she said with a genius grin on her face. "That's why I make the big bucks and you own a..." She paused before completing the sentence.

"Say it. I own a pile of rubble, which was formerly my beloved bar. Should I rebuild it or go into the demolition business?" Stenson retorted.

Luna laughed at the sarcastic remark. She knew how much it hurt her husband's feelings to lose O'Malley's. She handed the demolition man her laptop.

"What am I looking at?" he asked her.

She pointed to a spreadsheet filled with colorful charts and graphs.

"I did some cross-checking on Wu's shipping company. I looked at cargo ships over the last two years to see if I could spot any trends or anomalies that stood out. Most of it was standard transport stuff from well-known shippers. However, a few caught my eye," she explained.

"Nestled among the standard shipments, I noticed what I will call 'special' cargo. They were always loaded last, which means they were unloaded first, where their final destinations were is unknown."

Stenson seemed puzzled. "Did they vanish?"

"Well, kind of," Luna explained. "Those shipments hop-skip around through various shell companies and end up in some not-so-friendly places. It's a little sketchy and I don't know the contents of the cargo. My guess is Kenny is smuggling all sorts of illegal things, including humans. Could be drugs, weapons, or currency. It's a lot of shady stuff the way this appears to me."

"We know Zabrina was brought here on a cargo

ship according to JC," Stenson reminded. "Not sure if it was Wu's boat, but you already said Chinese smugglers were caught using one of his ships."

"Right," his wife agreed.

"Where does this lead us?" Stenson asked the genius.

"Down a rabbit hole. But I bet you a kiss. These shell companies are owned by him and may have some connection to his father, Wu Kong."

"That Sun Fang, Rising Tiger guy?" Stenson wondered.

"Yep," the smart girl replied.

She pointed to names on the spreadsheet. "This barely scratches the surface of how many offshore bank accounts may be involved," Luna theorized.

"Sounds complicated," Stenson admitted.

"It is and even harder to track. That is why criminals and other undesirables like them so much," she told her quizzical husband.

"But like a bloodhound, I've picked up his scent. Believe me, I will sort this out," the determined hunter told the man.

"I know you will, genius." Stenson pecked a kiss on her cheek and said, "That's a down payment for the bet I expect you will win."

Kenny Wu stopped by the safe house where Zabrina was held. He noticed two of his guards were covered in bruises and scratch marks.

"What happened to you two?" he asked the battered men.

"Kenny, that woman is crazy and knows how to fight!" one of the banged up guards complained through a bloody nose.

"That little woman did all that to you? Why am I paying you guys? I should hire her," Wu chastised the scrambled men.

"Good luck with that," a guard mumbled under

his breath.

"What did you say?" Kenny questioned.

"Never mind, where is she?" Wu asked because he did not have time for all this madness.

The guards led Kenny down a hallway to a back bedroom. One unlocked the double-bolted door and swung it open to reveal a room padded from floor to ceiling. It resembled an insane asylum. The only thing missing was a straightjacket and if they had one they would have put it on this terror cat.

Zabrina sat in the middle of the room, zip-tied to a chair by her ankles and wrists. Duct tape covered her mouth under a hood resembling something a beekeeper would wear.

"Is all of this necessary?" Kenny asked the banged guards.

"I am telling you, boss, this woman is evil. She screamed so loud even with tape over her never shut upping mouth we had to pad the room to dull her rumble. And the mask over her head is because the woman spits like a viper! I think Won Lee is blind in one eye. And please don't ask us to unbound her feet or hands. She will spring on you like a jackal on a menstrual cycle!" the guard warned Kenny Wu.

Wu shook his head at the wimpy guards. He removed Zabrina's beekeeper hood and the tape covering her mouth. She immediately spit at Kenny who was prepared to duck. Apparently, Won Lee was not, and the projectile hit him in the other eye.

"Aren't you a feisty one?" Wu taunted the crazed woman. "I bet you are good in bed? Oh wait, you are. That is how you made me so much money."

"Let me out of these restraints, and I will show you how good I am!" Zabrina seethed.

"If you ever get out of here alive it will be because of me, not because of your black friend's heroics or his fat buddy. By the way, did I tell you we shot the fat boy? He is dead," Kenny crowed, even though he wasn't certain of the big man's status.

Zabrina quieted momentarily at the thought of Big Tony and worry for JC.

"Well, my little prize, I must go. I am not finished with your other friends."

Other friends? Zabrina knew Kenny must be talking about Stenson and Brick. Somehow, they had become involved.

"Leave them alone!" she hissed. "This is between you and me. I will do whatever you want!"

Wu slapped her hard across the face causing her head to spin. His thin lips pierced into a wicked grin. Kenny said, "I know you will, princess."

He turned to the guards. "Keep a close eye on her. We need this evil woman alive."

After Wu left, muffled yells ensued. It sounded like his guards were losing the battle with Zabrina. He laughed with a sadistic sound of the devil imagining what Zabrina was doing to them as they tried to restrain her again. He did not care or bother. It wasn't his problem. That is what they were paid for. But he had to admit they weren't lying when they said the woman was feisty.

Inside his car, the phone rang. It was his father.

"Yes, father?" Kenny greeted in a fake cheer.

"Have you dealt with the situation?" Wu Kong asked in a prosecutorial tone.

Knowing the only answer his father would accept was not the actual answer, Kenny lied. "Yes father, everything is back to normal. In fact, it is better than normal."

"It better be!" the Rising Tiger warned, before abruptly hanging up.

"It better be?", Kenny thought. He would rather face that crazy woman before the fury of Sun Fang. At least with her, he had a chance. But with Kong, he would swim with the fishes if this went more out of control.

* * *

Brick stopped by Fort Beckett, the nickname he had given Stenson's fortified home.

"Everyone on the list is covered," the tattooed marine informed Stenson and Luna.

"We have also located David Pham," he confirmed.

"Wow, that was fast," his best friend replied.

"Pham wasn't hard to find using the tips your wife provided. She should have been a detective," the gutsy marine said.

Stenson laughed. "She's our detective."

Brick continued. "We found his wife and child easily. She keeps a normal schedule, taking the kid to and from school every day, shopping, and such. David took a few days to spot. He appears to be lying low like you, holed up at home. Probably senses something is heading his way."

"If he's like me, the guy is probably armed and dangerous, waiting for us to strike," Stenson pondered.

"That was my guess too," Brickhouse wondered aloud. "It may take some wit to get to him unless we go in blasting."

"Why don't you go upstairs and say hello to your nephew while I prepare enough food to feed a bullet-proof Marine."

"I may be bulletproof, but I am not inflammable. With my luck, David Pham has a flamethrower." Brick joked.

After Robert was almost burned alive by an improvised explosive device, even birthday candles scared the big marine. He was like the Scarecrow in The Wizard of Oz except with tattoos and cannot dance as well. When Brick returned, he joined

Stenson at the kitchen table.

Stenson said, "Here is what I don't understand, Robert. Why would a guy like David Pham get mixed up with Kenny Wu? He seems like a normal family man to me, not a gangster."

"We are mixed up with gangsters. And you are a normal family man," Robert pointed out.

"Yeah, but we don't set out to get mixed up with gangsters. They always seem to find us. They bring the mixing bowl and we bake their cake."

"Nice analogy, chef," Brick joked. "Hope you made dessert because this conversation is making me hungry."

Stenson laughed, then got serious again.

"What if David Pham went into business with Wu and he dragged him down a road he did not want to go over time?"

"Assuming you are right and he's a normal guy who didn't find out his boss is a sociopath until it was too late," Brick suggested.

"I don't know. It's just a guess. Based on what Luna has come up with about him and what you guys found, does he seem like the type?"

"No. He's not like any of the bad guys we have run across," Robert admitted.

"We won't know until we talk to him," Stenson suggested.

"Kidnap Pham?" Brick reasoned.

"Maybe. Or maybe not," Stenson considered the response of his door-kicking-burn-the-place-down friend.

"If we can find an easier way to talk to him without kidnapping the guy, he might be more forthcoming," Stenson reasoned.

"Remember how our friendly approach interrogating assholes produced better results than doing things the hard way?" Stenson quizzed the bulky marine.

"That's true," Robert responded. "We sure went down some holes when we tried to beat the nonsense out of some of those insurgents," Brick recalled.

"So, what do you suggest?" The marine wondered. "Just knock on the door and say we are friends with the fat dude you shot, and another you stole money from, and the girl you kidnapped, can you help us?" Robert fictitiously proposed.

Stenson laughed at the suggestion. "As long as we don't knock on the door like we did before. You saw where that got us?"

"We're not taking my ride if we do," Brick humorously responded.

"My poor car," Stenson chagrined as he shook his head and looked toward the floor.

"We must get closer to Pham and grab him if he's uncooperative," Stenson suggested. "I have a feeling the guy is in over his head with Wu. He may give us the information we need to save his hide."

There was a knock at the door. Stenson and Brick instinctively pulled their pistols and aimed them at the opening while Luna peered the peephole.

"Relax cowboys," she told the armed men "It is JC and Big Tony,"

She opened the door and welcomed them in.

"Come in before these wild boys shoot you,." she told them.

When JC saw the guns drawn, he told the guys, "I hope they aren't mad at me again."

"I am sure I will find a reason to shoot you JC, but not right now. I am eating and I do not want to ruin my meal with your brains sprayed all over this table," Brick taunted Justin Carter with a mouth full of food.

Stenson and Brick put their weapons away and invited the guys to join them at the table. Anthony

Gallo placed a flashy cane JC gifted him in the corner. The big fella told the guys he felt better, but would not be jogging soon. When JC reminded Big Tony he could not jog before he was shot, Gallo reminded JC he still can't play basketball. What was his excuse?

Luna offered the fellas sandwiches to fill their faces instead of bad jokes. She left the room to check on the baby while those overgrown kids planned their next dangerous adventure. They tossed around ideas for capturing David Pham. JC suggested they go in guns blazing and pull him out like he had seen in a movie.

Brick replied, "Seriously, JC? You couldn't round up a house cat... a dead house cat."

The marine took a bite of his sandwich. Staring at his meal gave him an idea. Why not impersonate a pizza delivery driver and knock on the door? When David Pham answered, show him there is a special on machine guns with extra pepperoni.

Everyone liked the idea, except JC. He complained, "Brick's idea has guns. Why didn't you like mine?" Justin wondered.

Before anyone explained Robert's idea was more subtle and came with an element of surprise, they guessed if it might actually work?

Once when JCs group was getting Stenson back for one of his tricks before they were friends, they broke into to his apartment and contaminated his food with an experimental estrogen, causing him to grow DD sized breasts. It was a simple and a funny way to get their revenge. Of course, Stenson did not find the humor in it when he received a "mansectomy" to correct the problem.

Everybody was chuckling remembering the story when Luna returned to the room. "What are you clowns laughing at?" she asked the guys.

"Stenson's mansectomy," JC told her, causing

everyone to burst into laughter after hearing the word again.

"You are not considering doing that to David Pham, are you?" she asked. Luna hoped they had better ideas than spiking her husband with some estrogen.

They explained the idea to Luna. Big Tony would dress up as a pizza delivery driver who would knock on David Pham's door. Luna agreed it was absurd, but it might work. She liked it better than the estrogen idea because this one did not involve her husband borrowing her bras.

Chapter 14

Somehow, JC found a pizza delivery driver almost as large as Big Tony. He borrowed the guy's shirt and sign from the roof of his car. The term "borrowed" was subjective. The driver called it "armed robbery" after JC used a nine-millimeter pistol to persuade him to give him the stuff.

Justin explained he would bring it back after they were done, and even offered the man a tip. When the driver held out his hand, waiting for JC to place some money, JC explained his tip was to get a different job because this one did not pay enough to be robbed at gunpoint for a pizza shirt and a sign.

Robert Brickhouse was going over the plan with everyone when JC returned. Justin took a seat and watched Brick's presentation. After Robert finished, he asked if there were questions? JC raised his hand and asked, "Do we kill Pham before or after we show him the pizza? And how much pepperoni are we talking about? This sounds like an expensive operation."

The group thought it was a hilarious question. They also wondered if JC was serious or simply yanking Robert's chain. If so, it worked because Brickhouse almost burst a blood vessel in his head while resisting the temptation to leap across the room and choke JC to death. Instead, Robert raised two fingers to his eyes and pointed at JC with a look that said, "Just wait JC. When this is over, it's you and me!"

While Big Tony dressed into the pizza delivery outfit, Robert asked, "Where is the pizza box, JC?"

"You didn't tell me to get a pizza box," Justin replied.

"I didn't tell you to get that sign or the hat or a stack of coupons either. What pizza guy shows up without a pizza box?" Brick thought JC had to be the worst pizza robber in the world.

Before World War III broke out in the living room between Brick and Just Crazy, Luna offered to order pizza for everyone. After all, this was a pizza plan and like actors preparing for a role, maybe a few slices would refocus the guys. Call it "method eating" instead of "method acting".

Brick told her, "At least use some of those coupons he stole."

"Make sure they don't put anchovies on it, Luna," JC requested. "Those are nasty. I mean who puts little fish on pizza?"

Brick glared at Stenson. "I swear I am going to shove an entire fish tank filled with anchovies so far up JCs back side his eyeballs will float if he doesn't shut up!"

When the pizza arrived, Big Tony answered the door wearing the same outfit as the delivery guy, who asked him, "Why didn't you pick these up?"

Big Tony smiled and said, "It's a long story."

They polished off the pies and prepared the pizza box they paid for. The group would take two vehicles; Tony Gallo placed the pizza sign on top of his car and would drive alone while Stenson and Brick followed in Robert's van.

JC pouted when he was told he would stay behind with Luna and the baby until Stenson told him protecting his wife and child was the more important job. It made JC feel important and avoided telling him if he went there was no guarantee Robert would not toss him from a moving vehicle.

Stenson and Robert followed Big Tony to David Pham's house in a suburban middle-class neighborhood on the other side of town. Seeing where the man lived furthered their belief that Pham was not a gangster. If so, he was most boring gangster they ever encountered.

Big Tony pulled into the driveway while Stenson and Brick stayed two houses back, parked far enough away not be noticed, but close enough to rush in if things went sideways.

Tony grabbed the pizza box and walked up the sidewalk to the front door. He knocked and a moment later, a face peeked through the blinds. David Pham seemed puzzled to see a large pizza man wearing a shirt two sizes too small with a hat that barely fit his enormous head. He opened the door.

"Pizza," Tony cheerfully offered.

"I didn't order a pizza. You must have the wrong address," Pham told him.

"I believe this is the correct address, sir," Big Tony confirmed when he lifted the pizza box cover.

David looked inside, expecting to see a pizza he did not order. Instead, he noticed a Mac-11 machine gun with a fat finger on the trigger through a hole in the box's bottom. This was certainly not the pizza he ordered, nor a meal full of lead he wanted to eat. He liked extra cheese on his pizza but did not want his chest looking like Swiss if this pizza guy pulled the trigger.

David looked up at Big Tony with a question mark on his face and the thought of what was now running through his confused mind.

Tony stood quietly smiling, waiting for a response. It wasn't an evil smile. It looked like the pizza guy was enjoying being a gun-toting pizza delivery driver. Unfortunately for David, his environmental outlook was not as sunny. He realized he had no choice but to comply with whatever this meal-on-wheels happy pizza killer desired.

"Turn around," Tony politely instructed.

Pham didn't hesitate. He was still confused by this polite pizza guy's pleasant demeanor. He turned to face the inside of his house knowing this might be the last time he ever saw it again. Tony zip tied his hands behind his back, then spun him around.

"Don't worry, I am not a cop. But I will advise you of your right to cooperate. If you do not, this may become a very unpleasant experience. You don't want a bad day, do you?"

"No," Pham sheepishly replied.

Big Tony escorted David Pham to Robert's van. The door slid open, and Big Tony encouraged the man onto the seat next to Stenson. He squeezed in next to him and shut the door. Brick looked over his shoulder and smiled while gripping the pistol resting on his lap.

Given his predicament, David was eager to cooperate and forthcoming with information about Kenny Wu. He told the guys he did not want any part of Kenny's insanity tried to talk him into returning the money and letting the girl go. While he had no part in the attack on JC and Anthony Gallo, nor was he responsible for the kidnapping of Zabrina, David felt compelled to apologize to Big Tony for being shot. He revealed the location of the safe house where Zabrina was being held and warned the guys about a Chinese gang Kenny worked with who were not nearly as polite as they were.

The frankness of the conversation convinced Stenson that Pham was telling the truth. Either that or he could win an award for lying. But Stenson trusted his instincts and let him go with a warning.

"Don't say a word of this to Kenny Wu. Our beef is with him, not you. Take care of your family and lie low until this blows over or blows up, whichever Kenny chooses. Right now might be a good time for you to take a vacation," Stenson suggested.

Tony opened the van door. After David exited, Big Tony said, "No hard feelings?"

David replied, "None. I just wish Kenny was as reasonable as you guys."

Big Tony removed the constricting pizza shirt as he returned to his car. He shoved the pizza sign into the back seat and drove away. After he passed the van, Robert joked. "Big Tony needs a bra. That guy has bigger boobs than my girlfriend."

On the way back to Stenson's house, Robert suggested, "Let's storm Wu now in case our new friend David Pham tips him off."

Stenson knew David could be playing them for fools and dialing Kenny Wu as they speak. But he had pretty good instincts and believed David Pham didn't want any part of this mess. Also, rushing in like they did last time at Silkroad was not a good idea. They needed a better plan before visiting Kenny Wu again.

"Wu is slippery," Stenson told Brick. "We missed him the first time, and we do not want to miss him again. We can't go in guns blazing. Zabrina will be a human shield or caught in the crossfire. We cannot risk that. There is no telling how many people he has watching the place and this Chinese gang revelation is concerning. We need more information."

It had been several days since Kenny heard from David Pham. He called to invite him to dinner, which wasn't unheard of, but it had been ages since they shared a meal together and the timing seemed suspect.

History said if Kenny Wu ever asked someone to join him for a meal, it was to discuss business. And often, things did not end well for his dinner guests. David had seen it a few times as his right-hand man. So, it was not a good sign when this lunatic invited him to break bread.

David arrived at Kenny's favorite Chinese restaurant at 7:00 p.m. He found Kenny dressed in a black suit with a white open collar dress shirt seated at his preferred table in the back.

A waiter poured a glass of Huangjiu, a Chinese yellow wine after David sat down. Kenny waved the waiter away with a look of do not disturb. Behind a rice-paper partition out of sight and sound of the few customers in the restaurant, Kenny got to the point.

"Word is you met the guys who are causing me trouble," he said as he took a sip of wine.

"If you mean, did a fat pizza guy show up at my house with a machine gun? Yes, I met them," Pham told him curtly.

"What did they want?" Wu asked like an interrogator.

"Isn't it obvious? They want the girl, their money, and interest before they walk away," Pham warned.

Unconcerned, Kenny replied, "And?"

"I told them you are crazy and you would never agree. They advised me to take care of my family. They don't want me. They want you, Kenny."

"I knew you were never loyal, David," Wu said, wiping his pencil thin lips with a black cloth napkin.

He raised from his chair and tossed the napkin onto the table.

"Dinner is on me," the crazed man said as he walked away.

David exhaled a sigh of relief, saying to himself, "That was close."

The next thing that ran through his mind came from a silenced Ruger Mark IV pistol behind his right ear. The well-placed shot from the experienced assassin caused David's eyes to roll back. For a few seconds, he stared at the spinning ceiling before falling face down into a bowl of egg drop soup.

* * *

"Wu is not a gangster," Robert explained to Stenson. "He's a punk who gets others to do his dirty work. We've dealt with killers worse than him. This dude is an amateur, Stenson."

"I know, but there is something sneaky about the guy that tells me he has tricks up his sleeve we haven't yet seen. You saw how easily he snatched Zabrina and jumped JC and Big Tony," Stenson reminded the former U.S. Marine.

"Remember the time we grabbed the guy dressed like a businessman and assumed he would be an easy target to interrogate? Later we discovered a suicide bomb strapped to his chest beneath his suit?"

"Yeah. Glad his trigger malfunctioned," Brick remarked, recalling that lucky day.

"Let's not give Wu the benefit of the doubt. I don't want anymore surprises," Stenson cautiously warned.

Luna walked into the room. Stenson changed topics and asked his wife, "You want to go on a field trip with this crazy marine and me?"

She said, "You are both crazy and I like field trips. So a field trip with crazy guys sounds fun to me. Where are we going?"

"To a firing range," Stenson told her. "Robert and I will teach you how to shoot."

"I already know how to shoot. You taught me last year," Luna reminded her husband.

"I taught you how to use a pistol. The crazy biker

and I thought you would enjoy learning how to fire a machine gun with a lot more bullets and tickly vibrations," he teased.

That got her attention. Luna exclaimed, "Woohoo! Hot guys and automatic weapons? Count me in!"

They smiled at her enthusiasm. Stenson told Brick, "Women... They will ignore you until you mention some wild idea, then they really like you."

"Works for me and the women I tend to date," Robert replied.

* * *

Wu paced his office contemplating his next move in this game of chicken or chess. He realized in hindsight killing his number two was not one of his better ideas. Kenny called the shots and left the minutiae to David Pham. There was no use in crying over spilled milk or spilled blood now that he was dead.

Kenny had 50 gangsters on the payroll watching his back. But there were none he trusted more than David Pham. He felt he had no choice. Cutting off the head of the chicken had to be done because David knew where the skeletons were hidden. Kenny could not risk leaks like that seeing the light of day, or even worse, discovered by Sun Fang.

"I want this guy Stenson Beckett dead!" Wu yelled.

Three goons playing cards in another room overheard the shout and ignored it.

One said, "Never heard boss yell like that to David."

Another replied, "I am glad I am not him. And who is Stenson Beckett?"

When no one responded, Kenny stormed into to the room. He looked at the card players and barked,

"Didn't you hear me?"

One of the braver (or less intelligent) souls said, "David gives us orders. We assumed you were yelling... I mean discussing the matter with him."

Kenny realized his enforcers were idiots. He pointed to the one who spoke up and said, "You are in charge now. David Pham is no longer with the organization. Now do what I said!"

Kenny stormed out of the room and slammed his office door. The men looked at each other confused. None were more so than the newly promoted number two. His better judgement told him to wait for Kenny to calm down before asking what the guy's name was again and if Kenny had his address. Also, it might not be a good time to ask if the promotion came with a raise.

* * *

Robert and Stenson took Luna to meet their favorite arms dealer, Sergeant John Dean, at his private firing range deep in the Louisiana swamps.

The automatic weapons they were about to put through their paces weren't exactly legal for the average person to own. That was precisely why Sarge kept this place so well hidden where only mosquitos, alligators, and snapping turtles knew its location. In this murky, muggy muck, Sarge's clients could test his unique merchandise without annoying federal crimes. At least that was the idea, and it worked so far.

Stenson unzipped one of the black duffle bags and handed Robert an MP5K machine gun and a clip. He grabbed another and showed Luna how to load the magazine. Stenson explained to his wife the switch settings on the side of the weapon. This model had four: 0-1-2-D which stood for Safe, Single Shot, Double Shot, and Continuous Fire.

Why the letter D for continuous fire? Nobody knew or cared. Stenson and Brick assumed it meant "You are dead if we set it to D".

Luna watched like a geek in a science class taking notes. There were three targets set up 40 yards down range. Stenson told her the gun is a close quarters weapon. It is still accurate at a distance, but the people who use this weapon are usually up close and personal. That is why he chose this model if anyone should break into their home. That would be very personal.

"Put these on," Stenson told Luna as he handed her pair of black ear-protecting headphones.

"I look like Mickey Mouse," she said after placing them on her head.

"Mickey's ears were on top. Yours are on the side. Now pay attention." Stenson teased his amusing wife.

Stenson, Sarge, and Robert donned their ear protection as well. Robert raised his weapon and fired a single round, hitting dead center of the target. Next, he switched to the two-burst setting and fired again. "Tap, Tap" in quick succession. Again, Brick was on target with two holes only slightly off center from the other.

Stenson nudged his wife. "Watch this."

Robert switched the weapon to fully automatic. Brick pressed the trigger and ripped bullets until the clip was empty, leaving the target in shreds. It happened so fast before the remaining 27 rounds were expelled that Luna could not believe what she had witnessed.

They removed the ear protectors. Stenson explained to his wife, "You have 30 rounds in a clip. Only go full auto if absolutely necessary."

They replaced their ear protection. Stenson held up the weapon and fired the same sequence as Brick with similar results.

Looking eager for her turn, Stenson handed the weapon with a new clip to Luna.

"Got this?" Stenson asked her.

"What?" she said.

Stenson pulled one of the ear cups away and said again, "You sure you've got this?"

Luna grinned like a little kid and said, "Got it!"

Brick and Sarge were amused by the scene of this tiny Minnie Mouse girl holding a machine gun. Luna inspected the weapon, turned it upside down, and studied the hole where the magazine went. She checked the switches on the side, then inserted the magazine until it make a reassuring click.

She looked up and smiled at the guys with an expression that said, "See, that wasn't so hard."

Stenson smiled and gave her a thumbs up. She adjusted her mouse ears and positioned herself in front of the target. She raised the weapon and pressed the trigger. Nothing happened.

She removed her hearing protection and handed the gun back to Stenson. "I think you broke it."

The guys laughed at the funny girl. Stenson flipped the weapon on its side and said, "Honey, you forgot to turn the safety off."

Luna blushed. "Oops, I forgot that part."

She looked closely again at the switch, then set it to a single fire. She raised the weapon to her shoulder and took a deep breath, then she pressed the trigger. "Pop" came the sound from a single round that surprised Brick and Stenson when it hit only slightly off center. She smiled at the boys, proud of her accomplishment.

Stenson told the men, "I told you the girl can shoot."

Luna set the weapon to the two-shot setting, raised it, and fired again. "Tap-Tap". While the results weren't as close as those of Stenson and Brick, Luna hit the center mass, which would have been a bad day for a bad guy or girl. Next, she set switched it to fully automatic. She grinned like a kid who was about to raid a candy shop. Luna paused for a moment then pressed the trigger and let it rip. Bullets flew everywhere, but most of them hit their mark. Whoever was on the receiving end of this would have surely been dead or regret they ever messed with this Mouseketeer. The guys cheered for her and removed their ear protection.

"That was fun!" Luna squealed.

Stenson explained to his wife, "The only reason you weren't completely on target is you weigh 110 pounds when wet, and this weapon has quite a kick when fully automatic."

Brick told her. "You did great, Luna. You should train JC how to shoot."

"I want to do it again!" she excitedly proclaimed.

The guys smiled as Stenson handed the funny mouse another clip.

Chapter 15

Kenny turned on the TV in his office. A commercial teased an upcoming news exposé titled, "Death & Destruction on Silkroad".

> "Silkroad, the international
> shipping company owned by CEO Kenneth
> Wu was destroyed in a suspicious fire.
> Now his Chief Operating Officer is the
> victim of a suspected assassination.
> We investigate."

Kenny flipped off the television, both physically and metaphorically.

"Great," he lamented as he considered the warming situation.

"The news media is hounding me, investigators are snooping around, and a couple of lunatics want to play games with me ever since I kidnapped a crazy woman."

Things were spinning out of his control. He had to put a lid on this fast. He knew how to manipulate the media; he'd done it for years. Investigations take time and he was well insulated. Nobody had incriminated him of anything yet and the only person who could have exposed him was now dead.

One thing got under his skin more than any other. It was the hornet's nest he stirred up after he kidnapped the girl and extorted her friends. Maybe

David Pham was right about giving the girl and the money back. But it was too late for that now. Kenny had never backed down from a fight and he was not about to back down from this one either.

What bothered him was Stenson Beckett, a man who seemed to come out of nowhere. Who is this guy and why was he involved? The kidnapping was between Pok Kyung-Wook (Zabrina Chao) and her business associates. It had nothing to do with that mild-mannered cowboy. Or was Stenson Beckett as mild-mannered as he believed?

Burning down the man's bar should have been enough warning to anyone sticking their nose into places it did not belong. Others would have run, but not this guy. There was something about Stenson Beckett that was different. Whoever he is, if this wannabe hero wants to play a game with him, then he will be happy to oblige the man. It was time to shut Mr. Beckett down like he did to David Pham.

Kenny's phone rang. "Hello father, how are you?"

"Concerned," Kong said sternly.

"Everything is fine. A new shipment will arrive next week. We are on track as if nothing happened. I will send you money soon."

"You better," the Rising Tiger growled.

"Listen, father, speaking of money, may I get a small loan until my cash flow improves? That incident with the fire caught us off guard and left me in a tight position. With such a large shipment arriving, there is a lot to cover."

"You want money from me after all I have done for you? You have placed me in an unfavorable position. Where did all the money go you've made?" his father demanded.

Kenny attempted to defend himself. "Uh, expenses? It is very expensive to live here."

"By expenses, you mean flashy cars, clothes,

expensive homes, and whores?" Kong roared at his illegitimate son.

"It is only temporary, father. I promise to repay you?"

"How much?" Kong asked.

"Two million?" Kenny timidly replied.

"You better be talking, Won, and not dollars," Kong warned.

"I am afraid it is dollars, father. Like I said, it is very expensive here. Two million is nothing to you."

"Nothing to me, but it's a fortune to you," the growling tiger replied.

"I will have my people wire it to one of the off-shore accounts, and I better get that money back with interest. I don't care if you are my dumbass son. My money isn't free," Kong scorned.

Kenny knew his father meant it. The man did not become successful losing money.

"Yes, father, I will repay you with interest," he assured.

[Click]

The phone went dead.

Kenny leaned back into his chair, staring at the ceiling. It was time to set a trap.

* * *

"Hello?" Stenson answered.

"Stenson Beckett, my friend. How are you?" the taunting voice greeted.

Stenson placed his finger to his mouth, signaling to Brick and Luna to be quiet. He placed the phone on speaker.

"Is this my buddy, Kenny Wu? We were just talking about you. You've been hard to find," Stenson mocked.

"I've been quite busy with your little plaything, Zabrina. It seems you have been busy with my friend too, Mr. Pham," Kenny relayed.

"Oh, we had a friendly conversation. What do you want, Wu?" Stenson sharply asked him.

"We are reasonable men, Mr. Beckett. You burned my business, so I burned yours," Wu acknowledged.

Stenson rolled his eyes as Kenny continued. "I understand you want the girl back and the money. Apparently, the black guy isn't man enough to get it, so he involved you. It was an unfortunate mishap that caused the untimely demise of his fat friend. Mistakes happen. But I want this to end. It's too much trouble for both of us."

"I agree," Stenson said. "What do you propose?"

"Let's have a meeting. I would like to meet you in person, as I am sure you would like to meet me."

Wu continued. "I enjoy meeting other intelligent people like myself. You will get the girl and money. We say goodbye and put this behind us."

"Okay. You are right, I would love to meet the guy who pulled this off. Rarely do we run into gangsters," Stenson faked.

"Great! I will text you the details of the time and place, say, an hour beforehand?" Wu suggested. "It's not that I don't trust you. But for security reasons to protect a man in my position, I must take precautions. You understand?"

"I understand," Stenson said. "I look forward to meeting you soon."

"You as well, my friend," Wu told him before hanging up.

"Have you lost your mind, Stenson?" Brick exclaimed. "You know good and well this is a setup."

"I know it's a trap," Stenson agreed. "So, how do you do to capture a rat like him? You build a better trap."

* * *

Lei Min, the hitman Kenny blackmailed into doing his dirty deeds over the years, including dispatching David Pham, walked into his office.

"You sent for me?" Lei Min asked.

"Yes, Lei Min. Have a seat," Wu said.

"I have a problem," Kenny began, pointing to a computer screen with a photo of Stenson Beckett from an old news story about the guy giving away turkeys at a Thanksgiving event.

"This is Stenson Beckett, my latest problem. Remember the woman we kidnapped from the parking lot?"

"Of course," Lei Min acknowledged.

"Well, she is partners with a pair of gentlemen from whom we secured certain financial assets in which one member of their team suffered an unfortunate injury during the transaction," Kenny whitewashed.

"You mean when you stole a half million dollars in ransom money from two guys, kept the girl and had me shoot the fat one?" Lei clarified.

"I don't like your tone, Lei Min," Kenny complained.

"I don't like you not admitting what really happened," Lei Min scolded Wu.

"Anyway, this Beckett guy is apparently friends with them and he has become a real problem for me." Kenny admitted.

"What do you want me to do about?" Lei Min asked even though he already knew the answer.

"Get rid of him, and I mean permanently," Wu said it so matter-of-factly, as if he was asking Lei Min to pick up dry cleaning on his way home. He clicked another showing the burned remains of O'Malley's Pub.

"I burned this guy's bar before Pham left our organization," Kenny said.

Lei Min ignored, "left our organization." It was more whitewash. He thought, "No, you blackmailed me into killing the only person who could tolerate being in the same room with you."

Kenny clicked another slide with a photo of Stenson's home he found on a real estate website. The modest two story house looked like any other suburban home in New Orleans.

Kenny said, "This is his house. I will text you the address."

Lei Min rolled his eyes, thinking he's a hitman and can find any address he needs. But he let the idiot continue.

"I am setting up a meeting with him in two days. Unfortunately, he will never make it."

"Why? Did you forget to text him the address?" Lei Min chastised.

"No, I have his phone number. I will text him the address," Kenny said, completely missing the sarcastic dig at his lack of intelligence.

"You are making me lose my train of thought," Kenny told the hitman.

"That train left long time ago," Lei Min mumbled under his breath.

"Anyway, he won't make the meeting because the day before, when he thinks I am out of town, you and whatever army of my guys you need will hit him at home and erase his very existence from this earth," Kenny revealed.

Kenny's elaborate plans and long-winded descriptions were getting on Lei Min's nerves. He thought, "Kenny, just say you want me to go to the guy's house and kill him before your meeting."

Instead, Lei Men asked, "Why so many guys? He looks harmless to me. I can pop him and be done with it," Lei simplified.

"I know you could with a normal guy, but don't let his average looks fool you. There is something about Mr. Smiley Face I do not trust. Take my advice and bring more than you need. Cover every exit and means of escape,"

Lei Min looked at Kenny as if he had read, "How to Be a Hitman for Dummies."

"It's going to cost more," Lei told him.

"I don't care what it costs. Just get him out of my life," Wu urged the killer.

Kenny stared at the layout of Stenson's home and wondered where to position six shooters. It crossed Lei Min's mind that it would be easier to kill Kenny Wu instead.

"Seriously, Kenny? Six shooters? He is one guy in a suburban home. How hard can it be?" Lei Min wondered as he saw the layout.

"I don't care if Godzilla is in that house. I don't want this guy getting away. Something tells me if I don't take him out now, he is going to be a bigger problem for me later."

Little did he know this prediction would be the biggest underestimation of his life.

After picking up Stenson Jr. at the babysitter, Stenson, Luna, and Brick headed to Fort Beckett. Luna took the baby upstairs while the guys dragged in the duffle bags filled with weapons.

They laid out the six MP5K machine guns on the table and reloaded the spent clips. When Luna saw the number of weapons, she asked, "You planning for a war?"

"If this is war they want, it is war they will get," Stenson assured his wife.

He picked up the first MP5K with a 30 round clip and two spares, then walked to the sofa where he pushed them underneath. He grabbed another and stashed it in the coat closet in the living room. A third, he placed in a kitchen cabinet under the sink. Stenson grabbed another from the kitchen table with two clips and told Brick to grab the others and follow him upstairs. He hid one under his side of the bed in the master bedroom and instructed Robert to place one under the cabinet in the hallway bathroom while he placed the final one in the baby's room.

"Did I miss anything?" Stenson wondered, looking around.

"Personally, I would have hidden a few more," Brick joked with his best friend.

Panic struck. "Really? Should I get more?" Stenson seriously considered.

Brick laughed. "No, I think you've covered it pretty well. But I am surprised you didn't set up some landmines or booby traps as paranoid as you are."

Stenson chuckled at Brick's remark. "I can always go back to Sarge's place. He has some."

Chapter 16

"Bingo!" Stenson announced after reading the text message he received from Kenny Wu.

"Playing games with the old ladies at the retirement home again, Stenson?" Brick teased his friend.

"No, Wu just messaged me. Looks like he is out of town and wants to meet tomorrow. He did not mention a time or place."

"As Elton John once said, Saturday night's alright for fighting. That gives us time to prepare," Brickhouse suggested.

"Let's visit Sarge again to pick up a few more party gifts. We wouldn't show up without presents, would we?" Stenson asked the crazy marine.

"Of course not," Brick stated. "I am fond of those candles you cannot blow out. I wonder if Sarge has sticks of dynamite with the same fuse?"

"He has everything else, so it wouldn't surprise me," Stenson guessed.

"What are you two up to?" Luna asked when she walked into the room and found the guys laughing.

"We were discussing party favors for our meeting with Wu. Will you be okay if we stop by Sarge's place?" Stenson asked his wife.

"Will I be okay?" she asked rhetorically. "You hid enough weapons around the house for an insurrection. Just tell me where you hid the first aid kit in case I trip over one and shoot my foot."

"The safety switches are on, Luna," Stenson reminded her.

"I know they are. I found the gun you hid in our son's bedroom," she divulged.

"Did you put it back?" he asked his wife.

"Of course, my overly protective husband," she assured.

Luna believed, like Robert, it was overkill. But admired how seriously her husband was at protecting her and their son.

The guys drove to Gulf Coast Logistics in Robert's van. He blew the horn, and the gray corrugated metal door rattled open. Sarge greeted them when they drove inside. "Back so soon?" John Dean asked.

"Yes. Brick wanted more toys. You know he cries when you don't give the big baby what he wants," Stenson chided.

Robert shook his head, tired of marine jokes whenever he was with these Army guys.

"It looks like Kenny Wu wants to meet us tomorrow. He said he's going to return the girl and money then walk away like nothing happened," Stenson explained.

"You believe him?" Sarge asked.

"Of course not, which brings us here," Stenson said.

Stenson explained to Sarge they know Kenny will try to ambush them like he pulled off on JC and Big Tony. He admitted they don't know how many bad guys they will encounter or where and when the party will go down. All he knew was they will be contacted at the last minute with a time and place.

"That is a lot of unknowns, Stenson. Going to be hard to plan for that," Sergeant Dean observed.

"That is why he is doing it, so we won't have time to plan. He thinks he is going to get the jump on us. But I want to make sure we are ready for anything,"

Stenson warned the seasoned military man.

"Well, it seems like you are going to need a variety of party favors for this show. How many people are going with you?" Sarge asked.

"Right now, only four. Brick and me, Justin Carter and his friend Big Tony Gallo, who is still recovering from a gunshot wound he received from the last time we tangled with these people."

"Do the others have training?" Dean asked the men.

Brick laughed. "Well, if you are talking about JC? The only training he has is how to get on my nerves. He is an expert at that. The other guy, Big Tony, is good with a gun. But if you mean professional training, no."

"Sounds like this can get tricky." Sergeant Dean believed.

"We could ask some of Brick's biker friends to give us a hand. They are all ex-military, but I don't want to risk anyone getting hurt who has nothing to do with this," Stenson told him.

"I don't mind giving you a hand. After all, you are using my weapons," Sarge reminded.

As a former Army Ranger, Sergeant Dean had seen his share of hairy situations throughout his long military career.

"We would appreciate having your veteran eyes on things when this goes down. Are you sure?" Stenson asked the Ranger.

"This sales stuff is boring. I miss the dirty work. I'll be happy to watch your six," the sergeant offered.

Sarge looked at Robert Brickhouse. "What do you say, Marine? Want to invite a Ranger to your soiree?"

"Oorah!" Brick exclaimed with a marine battle cry. "It will be an honor to have you riding along."

"Now let's choose some amusing gifts for your

friends," Sarge suggested as he led the guys to the hidden part of his warehouse.

They loaded Brick's van with a large cache of weapons and accessories including night vision goggles, bullet-proof vests, grenades, an RPG launcher, two sniper rifles, and six head-worn radios with encrypted communication so the bad guys could not listen.

"That should cover a few bases," Sergeant Dean surmised as they looked over the haul in the back of the van.

"If this isn't enough, we are in trouble," Stenson told him, amused by the variety of weapons they were holding.

Sarge bid farewell as their rolling armory drove away. Since they did not know what time the meeting would take place tomorrow, Stenson suggested they meet with JC and Big Tony now to prepare. He phoned Luna, who had fallen asleep on the sofa while watching a movie, to let her he would be late.

* * *

The black SUV cruised down Hawthorne Lane past Stenson Beckett's home and circled the block at 11:15 p.m. The suburban neighborhood stood quiet, lit only by an occasional porch lamp, including the one illuminating the entrance to Stenson Beckett's home.

The tinted vehicle parked three doors past its target hidden in the shadows of an unlit home and a Serviceberry tree. Despite Kenny's suggestion to bring six killers, Lei Min brought four. Dressed in black from head to toe, they looked like real-life ninjas armed with silenced weapons instead of swords.

The assassins stealthily exited the vehicle and crept towards the two-story house. Each killer took a predetermined position in the front, back, and the side opposite the garage. The last ninja gymnastically vaulted a wooden privacy fence and swung up to the first of the two-story roof.

Lei Min joined one shooter at the front. He twisted the porch light with his black leather gloved hand. They hid in total darkness as Lei Min peered through the window right of the door. Between slits of the window blinds, he saw a pale blue glow. A television in the living room provided enough illumination to see the room was still.

Lei Min whispered "Qīngchú", which translated to "Clear" in Mandarin over the radio followed by four more confirmations. All the killers had vantage points of the home that were trouble-free. This is how it should be, Lei Min told himself. Kill the man in his sleep and leave as quietly as they arrived.

He twisted the lock that proved the door was secure. Lei Min removed a small kit about the size of a deck of cards from his jacket pocket and kneeled in front of the door to pick the lock.

[Tick] [Tick] [Tick]

Though sound asleep on the sofa, Luna had the awareness of most new mothers hear the slightest sounds babies make or any unusual noise even through the dull monotony of a tv left on. She opened her eyes and listened, unsure if it was a dream or the settling sounds houses make. Her grandmother's antique clock on the fireplace mantle read 11:29 p.m.

[Tick] [Tick] [Tick]

Luna listened.

[Click]

Now acutely aware of sounds that did not fit, Luna's eyes adjusted to the darkness searching for the source of her angst. Unstirring her repose, Luna remained still on the sofa. Was it a movement or a brush of air that tickled her senses? The hair on her neck bristled to attention.

Lei Min gently opened the door and waved the assassin to enter ahead of him. With softly padded feet like a cat stalking prey, the killer slipped inside the home. Greenish gradients of night vision goggles illuminated every detail as bright as day. The laser attached to the HK45 compact tactical weapon swept the room.

A crimson dot dashed across the floor, climbed the far wall, then back down again. Transfixed and terrified, reality set in. This was not a dream. This was Stenson's worst nightmare coming true.

Luna calculated the intruder's distance to be within ten feet of her and instinctively rolled from the sofa onto the carpeted floor with barely a sound. She felt underneath the sofa for the weapon her husband hid only hours before. She grasped the cold steel grip and found the safety switch. Three clicks she rotated to the right. 1.. 2.. D.

When the pinpoint dot met the coffee table inches from her face, Luna raised up and fired.

[ZIPPPPPPP]

[THUMP]

It was that quick when the man's body crumpled to the floor. Lei Min realized not only was someone awake inside, but they had automatic weapons and knew how to use them. He called over the radio, "Qù! Qù! Qù!" which meant "Go! Go! Go!" instructing everyone to enter the home at once.

[SMASH]

Crashed the kitchen door.

[CRASH]

Came another from the other side of the house. Lei Min rushed inside and sprayed a dozen shots throughout the room. He stepped over the body of the ninja laying in the entry and ducked behind a wall next to the stairs. It was silent.

Luna's heart felt like it may explode as she tried not to hyperventilate with tiny sips of breath. The crunching sound of footsteps on broken glass came from the direction of the kitchen warning her now there were two intruders on opposite sides of the room. She listened intently for more clues and heard a bump in the hallway that told her there were now three.

She did a mental check of her ammunition. She'd spent one third of her magazine on the first group of shots. That left her two more bursts before she would have to reload again. She pulled the two magazines hidden under the sofa close to her side and replayed how to load the weapon from her training at the firing range.

An action movie played through her mind trying to present different scenarios where she could dispatch these killers at the same time. She had no time to think if she would to survive. Instinct and adrenaline guided her now.

The assassin who entered from the side of the house joined Lei Min behind the wall. They heard footsteps of their comrade approaching from the direction of the dining room. Lei Min planned to let the other killer draw the shooter out, who he assumed was Stenson Beckett, and catch him from behind.

Luna had another plan. She reached for a large glass candy dish from the coffee table and waited. She watched the dot from the kitchen scan the room until she was convinced the assailant was at the entry to the living room. She took a deep breath, then launched the candy dish over the sofa where it crashed and shattered to the floor.

[Pop] [Pop] [Pop]

Luna stood up and fired a quick burst into the man.

[ZZZZIPPPP]

The MP5K ripped him down. Lei Min signaled the next killer to attack.

[Pop] [Pop] [Pop] [Pop] [Pop]

Flashes of light shocked and shattered the darkened room as the shooter prayed to God his adversary would reveal their hiding place. Luna never gave the killer a second chance as she raised her weapon and unloaded fear and fury into him with the ultimate act of defiance.

[ZZZZIPPPP] [Click] [Click]

[THUMP]

The third killer was down and Luna's weapon was empty. Lei Min could not believe in less than five minutes he'd lost three men. Without time to consider how right Kenny Wu was for telling him to bring more shooters, Lei Min popped from behind the wall and riddled the sofa, missing Luna's head by millimeters.

With no time to reload, Luna dashed for the dining room and slid across the floor. She found another hidden weapon and flipped the safety to fully automatic. She popped out from her hiding place and sprayed the room with all 30 rounds, not caring who or what she hit.

Quick footsteps ran upstairs. She screamed inside herself, "Oh my God, my baby!"

She swapped out the empty magazine for a fresh one and stuffed two more magazines into her pockets. She peered around the corner. Seeing only bodies lying on the floor. She rushed out and headed for the stairs.

Despite the darkness with a pale TV glow, Luna knew every inch of her home. She glanced up the stairway and saw nothing. It was eerily quiet, but somewhere up those stairs was a killer threatening her child. Her son cried. Luna hugged the wall and crept up the steps with her weapon pointed upward. Her heart raced as her trigger finger trembled ready to fire at the first sign of movement. When she reached the first landing of the L-shaped staircase, she stopped again and listened. Footsteps sounded like they came from the master bedroom at the farthest end of the hallway. Between her and the master bedroom was her baby's room in the middle of the hallway.

She crouched and crept up the next flight until she could peer through the bottom railing at ankle height of the second floor. There was a dark shape in motion. A laser dot searched the floor in her direction. She quickly ducked. With her child's life is at stake, Luna raised the weapon over her head and let five shots rip into the hallway. Not waiting for return fire, she bound the last three steps and concealed herself behind the wall in the corner. She held her breath and listened only to realize her child had stopped crying.

Luna was terrified and prayed the child went back

to sleep because anything else was beyond anything she would consider. Three meters stood between her and the baby's room. It remained silent as she tip-toed forward. She peered around the corner to see into the hallway. It was quiet. Too quiet. In a last dash, she rushed toward the baby's room. She froze when she reached the doorway to see a silhouette of a figure holding her son.

"Put him down!" she screamed with her weapon pointed at the head of the killer.

"Such a sweet child," the shadowy figure said quietly as he caressed the child's head with a silenced pistol.

"I said put him down! Please, I beg you. Do what you want to me, but leave my baby alone!" Luna pleaded.

"I don't want you or your child. I want your husband," Lei Min said ominously. "Where is he?"

"He's not here!" Luna screamed. "Now give me my son!"

Luna laid her weapon on the floor and raised her hands into the air in complete submission. "Please, just give me my child and leave. My husband and I have done nothing to you. He is a good man. Don't hurt him or my baby," she begged.

From the bathroom behind her, a figure emerged.

[Pop] [Pop] [Pop] [Pop]

Four close-range shots rang out. Luna dropped to her knees, blankly staring at the shadowy figure who stood before her. With outstretched arms, she cried, "Please do not hurt my son."

Luna fell face-forward into the blood-soaked carpet as her mind faded to black.

"You fool! What have you done?" Lei Min shouted at the shooter.

"You said take them out, so I did," the killer replied. He turned on the bedroom light and saw Luna lying face down with three crimson-colored holes soaking her white Snoopy t-shirt. He looked up to see Lei Min holding the dead child in his arms. One shot had missed its mark and struck the little boy in the head.

Without a word, Lei Min raised his pistol and fired into the killer's forehead. The man fell backwards into the hallway with a thud.

Lei Min was petrified by this turn of events. This was not the way this was supposed to happen. He stepped forward and gently laid the baby into Luna's outstretched arms. Lei Min did not come here to kill a woman and a child. Even killers abide by certain rules.

Chapter 17

Brick and Stenson wrapped their meeting with JC and Big Tony at 12:30 a.m. Everyone agreed they believed the rendezvous with Kenny Wu was a setup. There was no way the crook would say, "Sorry about kidnapping the girl, stealing half a million dollars from you, and shooting the fat guy. My bad. Please accept my apology. Here is your stuff back. Have a nice day."

No way. This was a trick, and the guys spent two hours discussing any scenario, no matter how off-the-wall or outrageous the psychopath may decide to go to get the jump on them again. JC even wondered, "Let's say he drives an ice cream truck to the meeting. You know the one that plays music and tries to sell us poisoned ice cream. He would kill us and steal more money at the same time."

Brick asked JC, "What kind of ice cream do you want?"

"I would get a fudge bar. What would you get?" Justin answered, as cool as an ice cream bar.

The room burst into laughter at his response. There was something so gullible and naive about Justin Carter. Half of the time, the guys did not know if he was really that simple-minded. Or was he smarter than them and they were the brunt of his jokes? In some ways, that was the genius of JC. He could be the smartest guy in the room and nobody would notice how clever he really was.

Stenson mentioned to Robert as the marine drove him home how ironic it was that two years ago, JC and his friends were their sworn enemies. Now they were helping the group get out of this terrible mess. Two police cars with flashing lights and blaring sirens flew past them. As they approached Stenson's neighborhood, they spotted a helicopter flying above, using a spotlight to search the ground.

"Looks like a manhunt is going on in your neighborhood, Stenson," Brickhouse joked to his friend.

Little did they know how true that statement would be. Their jovial moods instantly switched to terror after they saw police cars blocking Stenson's street. Stenson jumped from Robert's van before it stopped moving and sprinted toward the line of police cars. Six houses down Hawthorne Lane Stenson could see a mass of emergency vehicles congregated in front of his home.

Robert caught up as an officer attempted to prevent Stenson from going further. Stenson yelled at the officer barring him, "That is my house!"

He pushed the cop's arm away and sprinted toward his home. Robert also brushed past the officer, hot on his best friend's pursuit. Stenson was stopped again when he reached the conglomeration of emergency personnel. His house was marked off with yellow police tape and lit like the sun from lights on two firetrucks parked in the street. Stenson was stunned to see throngs of police and emergency crews entering and exiting his home.

He begged an officer, "What's going on? Where are my wife and son?"

The officer informed him this was an active scene, and he did not have the authority to release information. Seeing the fear in Stenson's eyes, the officer radioed for someone more senior than him to assist. A moment later, a detective arrived. After he confirmed Stenson's identity, the detective said, "Sir, there has been an incident at your home. I regret to inform you there have been casualties."

"Casualties?" Stenson repeated in shock.

"Your wife has been transported to Tulane Medical Center with gunshot wounds," the detective informed the fearful man.

"My son?" Stenson asked.

The detective briefly looked away. This was never easy to say no matter how many times he had done it before. He turned back to Stenson and said, "I am sorry, Mr. Beckett. Your son did not survive."

Stenson dropped to his knees and cried to the sky, "Oh my God, why?"

The detective placed a consoling hand on Stenson's shoulder. "I am truly sorry for your loss, Mr. Beckett. May I drive you to the hospital to be with your wife?"

Brick stepped forward and informed the officer he was his best friend and he would take him to the hospital instead. Robert helped Stenson to his feet. Together, they watched paramedics carry a stretcher down the front steps of Stenson and Luna's home. The small form under the sheet confirmed it was Stenson's infant son. After they placed the stretcher inside the ambulance and closed the doors, Stenson leaned into Robert's shoulder and cried like he had never cried before. As Brick embraced his friend, the big marine wept, too.

Stenson was silent, staring out of the car window as they drove from the scene. He was lost in a fog as dense as the one pouring over Lake Pontchartrain. There were no words to comfort his broken heart. Robert was not much of a praying man, but tonight he prayed Luna would survive.

The only information Stenson received for

several hours was that his wife suffered multiple gunshot wounds and was in surgery. The waiting. The worry. The unknown tortured Stenson Beckett's ripped soul. Robert was angry. He phoned JC and told him to get his ass to the hospital now. When Justin walked through the doors, followed by Big Tony, Brick leaped from his chair and slammed JC with his full force into the wall.

He screamed, "You did this! I should kill you right here and now!"

Brick continued to yell. "Ever since we first laid eyes on you, JC, you've been nothing but trouble! If it wasn't for Stenson, you would have been dead a long time ago! Look what you have done to Stenson and his family! You are a worthless human being!"

Big Tony pushed himself between the pair and used his enormous size to pull Brickhouse off. "Let him go, Robert! It is both of our fault. So if you kill him, you'll have to kill me, too!"

JC was in tears. He knew this was his fault. He never wanted Stenson or Robert involved. But he had no place to turn. It was his problem, not theirs. And the words that cut him most were Robert reminding him he was a worthless human being; something he had told himself his entire life.

Stenson was oblivious to the commotion. Robert regained his composure and pointed to JC and Big Tony. "You two stay out of my way. Especially you JC!"

Robert stormed outside to calm down while Big Tony and JC walked over to speak to Stenson. They sat on either side of him. Stenson held his head in his hands. JC placed his arm around Stenson's shoulder. All he could say was, "I am so sorry, Stenson."

Stenson did not reply. The apology did not register. JC's arm around him did not register. This hospital did not register. None of it registered.

Stenson was lost in a dark tunnel where nothing in the world made sense. If there was a Hell, he was walking those burning halls right now.

"Mr. Beckett?" came a voice from a doctor wearing green scrubs and cap.

As if some unseen ghost lifted him from the chair, Stenson rose to meet the doctor in the corridor. The physician escorted Stenson to a small consultation room nearby.

"Sir, I am Doctor Michael Conrad, chief surgeon on duty. I attended to your wife's injuries when she arrived. Your wife has sustained three gunshot wounds to her back. She's in critical but stable condition. We have placed her in a medically induced coma and will monitor her closely. The next 48 hours will be crucial to her survival."

"What about my son?" Stenson asked.

"Unfortunately, your son did not survive. He sustained a fatal gunshot wound to the head. There was nothing we could do. I am sorry."

"I want to see my son!" Stenson demanded.

"I will arrange for a nurse to take you to him," Dr. Conrad promised the grieving husband. He placed his arm on Stenson's shoulder and said, "Again sir, I am very sorry for your loss."

A few minutes later, a medical administrator entered the waiting room to take Stenson to see his child. Stenson asked Robert Brickhouse to accompany him to the morgue. Inside the sterile, stainless steel room laid a tiny bulge covered with a white sheet. Before going any further, Stenson paused.

"Stenson, you don't have to do this," Robert Brickhouse insisted.

Stenson ignored Robert's suggestion and stepped toward the edge of the table. He nodded to the pathologist to pull back the sheet. His son,

Stenson Beckett, Jr., was wearing the same baby blue pajamas with little yellow trains Stenson had dressed him the day before. The child appeared to be sleeping except for the hole in his tiny forehead. Tears streamed down Stenson's cheeks, and his lips quivered. He placed his hand on the baby's tummy and said, "I am sorry I did not protect you, my son."

Stenson leaned down and kissed the infant's cheek and nodded to return the cover. He turned and quietly left the room while Brick thanked the doctor and followed his friend down the hall. JC and Big Tony watched Stenson walk by, completely numb. Brickhouse glared at them, believing they should have been the ones to see Stenson's dead child. It was all Robert could do to keep from ripping this hospital apart. He knew there would be time to vent his anger later. But right now, he had to keep it together for Stenson and Luna's sake.

Robert sat next to Stenson in the waiting room. Neither said a word. Stenson was lost in his thoughts while Brick knew the only comfort he could provide was being there for his friend. Nothing would bring his child back or undo the damage done.

An hour later, a medical assistant entered the waiting area to inform Stenson he could visit his wife in the intensive care unit. As if on auto-pilot, Stenson arose to his feet and followed her down another sterile hallway. After Stenson entered the room, the assistant closed the door, leaving Stenson alone with Luna. Seeing her laying there attached to so many tubes and machines made him feel as helpless as her. The rhythmic pumping of oxygen and chirps of a heart monitor were the only signs his wife was alive. He held her hand. Luna looked so frail. And though she was unconscious, he prayed she could hear his words.

"Luna, when we were in kindergarten and I met

you the very first time, I knew we would be friends forever. If it wasn't for you, we would have never dated because my friends knew I was too shy to ask you out."

"I never told you how nervous I was when I asked you to marry me. I was afraid you would say no. I didn't feel worthy of your love."

"You know my damaged parts and the life I came from. Yet you've always loved me and understood me like nobody ever could."

"The day you told me you were pregnant, and I dumped you onto the floor. You giggled at how silly I was when I heard the wonderful news. We've always had fun like that Luna. You are my best friend. We laugh and cry together. There is nothing we can't do."

"I have never felt so blessed when our son was born and you insisted on naming him after me. All I have ever wanted was to be is the best husband, father and friend I can be."

"Yet, here I sit Luna, holding your hand, and I am terrified. I have failed you and our son with my promise to protect you. I hope one day you will forgive me."

"Please be strong for both of us, Luna. Because right now I am weak. Without you, my love... my life is incomplete."

Chapter 18

"What do you mean his wife and child are dead?" Kenny Wu shouted at Lei Min, not believing the fatal news.

"I sent you to kill one guy. You said I was overreacting when I told you to bring more men. So you brought four instead of six? And you are telling me that all four of your guys are dead, killed by one little woman who had automatic weapons?"

"I wasn't expecting it," Lei Min defended.

"That is an understatement," Wu agreed.

He flipped on the television in his home office. Of course, the news was splashed across the screen with the charming slug, "Terrorism in the Suburbs."

The news story drew a connection between Stenson Beckett's O'Malley's bar fire and the slaying at his home. Camera crews caught him leaving the hospital and one brave reporter attempted to ask him a question by sticking a microphone in his face. His large tattooed friend was having none of it and quickly dispatched the reporter with a shove and a stern warning, "Leave the man alone!"

Kenny Wu turned off the television and yelled at Lei Min. "See the shit storm you created?"

"I created? You are the one who ordered the hit with no intelligence and did not know the man wasn't home or his wife had automatic weapons and knew how to use them!"

The hitman continued, "It would have been

helpful if you had told me there was a child in the house. I would never have agreed to this because I am not in the business of killing kids. David Pham would have never let this happen," Lei Min pointed out.

"David Pham is dead! And you better watch who you are talking to or you may find yourself with a similar fate," Kenny Wu warned the Lei Min.

"You are the one who should watch what you say, Wu! Because not only will you have to look over your shoulder every day of your life wondering when that Stenson Beckett man is going to kill you, and believe me he will. But you'll have to watch out for me too if you dare threaten me again!"

Realizing he just told a hitman he would be killed was not a good idea.

"I am sorry Lei Min. This has spun out of control like I did not plan. I need your protection. Whatever it costs I will pay," Kenny Wu begged.

"It is going to cost you dearly, Wu. You have knocked over a hornet's nest with this," Lei Min warned.

He advised Kenny, "You better get out-of-town. And I mean now. Lie low and I will too. I doubt they can find me, but these guys definitely know you are behind this. You better come up with some good alibis if the cops also find out."

Kenny reached into his desk and handed Lei Min an envelope filled with cash.

"Looks like you get a bonus, since your other guys are dead. I will be in touch," Wu said to the hitman.

* * *

Brick drove Stenson home to retrieve clothing and other essentials. Stenson planned to stay with his wife for as long as it took for her to recover, or God forbid, die.

Robert sensed Stenson still did not want to talk, so he kept his conversations brief only inquiring if he needed this or that. Inside, Brick burned with fury at the perpetrators who committed this crime. To witness firsthand the harm it caused his friend and family was more than Brick could bear.

After they returned to the hospital, Brick headed to Gulf Coast Logistics to visit Sarge. He needed help and an arms-dealing ex-Army Ranger was a good place to start.

Sitting in John Dean's office, Robert told the Ranger he blamed himself for not anticipating this double-cross move when they had planned for every other possibility. One thing he knew for sure was Kenny Wu was behind this and as God was his witness Robert Brickhouse promised to get his revenge.

The problem now was lack of intelligence. Luna had been their source of information as a security analyst who could hack and track anyone or anything. Without her, he did not know how he would find Kenny Wu. His biker friends had kept tabs on every known associate and their patterns had not changed. He had confirmed they were all accounted for last the night. So he did not know who the trigger men were other than the four dead were members of a local Chinese gang. Police suspected one had gotten away.

John Dean leaned back into his chair. He told Brick he knew people who worked in intelligence for the U.S. military and said he would call to see what they could find.

When he asked how Stenson was doing? Robert said, "Not good, John. I have never seen him like this before and he's been through some scary situations. He is deeply hurt."

"I understand, Robert. I know how close you

two are. I will do whatever I can to help. Please give Stenson my best."

* * *

Kenny Wu reached the safe house where Zabrina Chao was being held. He was not in the mood for her antics today. He stormed the padded room and kicked over the chair she was handcuffed to onto its side. Kenny stood over Zabrina and hissed, "You've caused me a lot of trouble and you will pay for it dearly!"

He slammed the door, leaving Zabrina crumpled on the floor, feeling terrified. Kenny plopped onto the sofa and turned on the TV. Now the story had become national news of a gangland gun battle in a New Orleans home that killed an infant and left another person critically wounded with four assailants dead.

At least the woman has survived for now, Kenny thought. But Lei Min was right. He had to get out-of-town and cover his tracks. New Orleans was too hot for him to stay.

"Get the girl!" Kenny yelled to the guards.

One of his cargo ships was preparing to depart New Orleans in two hours. He would make sure Zabrina Chao was on that boat and out of his hair. The only reason he didn't kill her now was she was his bargaining chip, and he had a sick feeling he would need it later.

The only thing for certain in this spinning madness was Kenny and Zabrina were heading in opposite directions. She would take a long, slow ride back to Asia while he relaxed on a beach. He had arranged his alibis to vouch that he had been in Florida on business when the attack on Beckett's home occurred. Plenty of people would cover for him because they had too much to lose in business and their life if they betrayed him. Kenny knew where his alibis hid their skeletons as well.

* * *

Stenson did not leave Luna's side for three days as she laid in a coma. He talked to her like they would often do, telling funny stories or dreaming about vacations they would soon take. He could not allow himself to believe she would not recover or always be by his side in the journey of life. It was too devastating to think that way. All Stenson could do was hope and pray, which he did like he had never done before.

His friends called every day to check on him and ask about Luna. The calls were brief, and the answers were the same. Brick stopped by on the third day and persuaded Stenson to join him in the hospital cafeteria for a bite to eat. They grabbed a couple of sandwiches and sat at a quiet spot in the cafeteria's rear. After several minutes, Stenson finally spoke.

"There is so much to do and all I want is to be here with Luna and not think about the rest." He told his best friend.

"They want me to plan my son's funeral," he said. "I can never step foot in my house again, so I must move. I don't have a job and my wife is in a coma. I don't know how to feel or what to do. I am numb, Robert and my world is upside down. Part of me died when I lost my son and the other half is hanging on by a thread."

Robert took a bite of his sandwich and thought about what he said.

"Stenson, I wish I could rewind the tape on many things in my life, as I am sure you do too. But we cannot change what has happened. Everybody who knows you and even those who don't share your heartache," the big marine told him.

Stenson replied, "I wish I had a magic wand, Robert. There are a few things I would change."

"Would you change being friends with JC?" Robert asked him.

"No way. This was not Justin's fault. It was caused by an evil man. And if we didn't help JC we might have lost him too. I know you don't like the guy, but I am telling you, Robert, he's a good person."

Robert listened as Stenson continued to explain.

"Think about us, Robert. We wouldn't have become best friends if it wasn't for that IED attack on you. Being blown up almost cost you your life, but would you trade our friendship for that?" he asked.

"If I had a magic wand, I would make people like Kenny Wu disappear. He has hurt not just us, but many others. Think about the harm he caused to Zabrina. Those are scars she will carry for the rest of her life. Within our little group alone, he has irreparably hurt each of us. Can you imagine how many others he has done that to?" Stenson wondered aloud.

"Then let's make Wu disappear," Robert suggested.

"Robert, all my energy is focused on my wife. I can't even think of that right now," Stenson admitted.

They ate in silence until Brick spoke again. "As far as the funeral arrangements for your son or dealing with the house, we will all help you any way we can. I will look for houses you can rent and get into quickly when Luna is discharged. We will get movers to pack up your house so you never have to step foot in it again."

"Thank you, Robert. But I am not burying my son until Luna is with me," Stenson quietly replied, almost in tears at the thought.

"Doctors have told me she will have another

surgery tomorrow to remove the bullet lodged near her spine," Stenson informed.

He paused. "Luna may be paralyzed, Robert."

When he bowed his head, a teardrop fell upon his plate.

The only thing Robert could say was, "Damn."

Chapter 19

Specialists performed the delicate four-hour surgery on Luna to remove the bullet lodged near her spine. Afterwards, chief neurologist Dr. John Graham briefed her husband.

The surgeon extended his hand. "Mr. Beckett, I am Dr. John Graham, chief of neurology."

"Sir, your wife has sustained an injury to her spinal cord. Specifically, the bullet has fractured a vertebral body in the mid-thoracic region of her spine, which has caused a spinal cord contusion."

Spinal cord, vertebral, thoracic raced through Stenson's confused mind.

"What does that mean?" he asked the surgeon.

"It means, while the bullet has not penetrated the spinal cord itself, the trauma from the broken bone has severely bruised the nerve tissue. As a result, your wife has lost the ability to control or sense her lower limbs," the surgeon clarified.

"Does that mean she is paralyzed?" Stenson fearfully asked.

"From the waist down, yes," the surgeon acknowledged.

A chill froze Stenson like a statue as he stared at the doctor for several moments.

"Will she ever walk again?" the terrified husband hesitantly asked.

"I regret to say, it is unlikely," Dr. Graham replied.

The gravity of the words struck Stenson to his

core. He looked down at the tiled floor feeling like he might pass out. The doctor, who was married understood Stenson's despair. He offered an ever-so-slight glimmer of hope.

"However, with intensive physical rehabilitation, we have seen remarkable improvements in some patients."

Stenson thanked the surgeon for sharing the devastating information. After he left, Stenson thought of what he said. He did not focus on the negative, rather he hung onto the words, "remarkable improvements in some patients."

Stenson knew his wife is remarkable and strong. And while her recovery will not be easy, there is hope. But Stenson also had to come to terms with the reality Luna may never walk again. If that was the case, then they will accept their fate. For better or worse, through sickness and health, Stenson vowed to always be by her side.

There was a knock on the ICU room door. Pastor Samuel Jackson, the pastor who married Stenson and Luna with the funny wedding vows, walked in.

"Pastor Jackson," Stenson said with the first smile he had managed since this horrific tragedy.

"I hope you don't mind I stopped by?" the pastor said.

"There is no one I would rather see more than you right now," Stenson told him as he looked at Luna lying unconscious in bed.

The pastor walked over and took Luna's hand into his own. Then he reached for Stenson's hand and said a quiet prayer for healing of hearts, mind, body, and soul. Stenson wished the prayer would go on forever; he would take all the prayers he could get right now.

"How is she?" the pastor asked.

"She is in a medically induced coma. Luna came

close to losing her life. Doctors tell me she may be paralyzed," Stenson informed the pastor.

"I am terribly sorry, Stenson. How are you?" he asked.

Stenson's heart weighed heavily, like a dam ready to burst. "May we talk?"

"Of course, Stenson. Shall we go to the chapel to speak more privately?" Pastor Jackson suggested.

"Yes, please," Stenson humbly replied.

The hospital chapel was an intimate room with a single stained glass window and four rows of pews. It was empty and quiet, similar to how Stenson felt inside. They took a seat in the front row but did not speak. Stenson stared ahead looking at the colorful window. While the pastor allowed him to collect his thoughts, he reflected on the respect he held for Stenson Beckett from the moment he met him a few years ago.

"What's on your mind?" Pastor Jackson asked.

Stenson's gaze remained focused on the window as he began, "I am lost, like I have never been before, pastor. I am hurt. I am terrified. And I am angry."

He said, "I have never wanted to harm another soul. My father destroyed everything around him and almost destroyed me."

"When you tried to fight him back as a boy?" the pastor recalled the story of Stenson's young life before he met him.

"That was physical," Stenson said. "I am talking about how he almost destroyed my soul. It was a dark time in my life when he killed my mother and my grandparents. He stole my innocence and everything good I believed in."

Stenson paused, then said. "My life could have gone another way, pastor."

"But it didn't," Pastor Jackson replied.

"I have always wanted to be a better person than

him. I have done things I am not proud of and I have killed before. But that was war and I defended myself and my country then. Still, I have prayed for forgiveness. But now there is such darkness in my heart. I cannot find the light. I want revenge."

Pastor Jackson felt the honesty in Stenson's words.

"Stenson, we often turn the other cheek," The pastor explained.

"They murdered my son and almost killed my wife, Sam!" Stenson exclaimed, raising his voice.

"What happened to an eye for an eye? I believe I read that somewhere in the bible," Stenson quoted.

Pastor Jackson searched for the right words to say.

"Stenson, before I was a pastor, prayer got me through many troubled times. I have had my own transgressions, for which I have asked for forgiveness. It was only through my faith that I stand here today. I wish I could offer you a magical solution, but it doesn't work that way."

"Well, I hope God forgives me for what I may do."

Stenson stood up and walked out of the chapel, leaving Pastor Jackson to pray for the young man's broken heart and his wife's broken body.

* * *

Kenny Wu's henchmen struggled to get Zabrina Chao out of the white panel van. They wish they had restrained her ankles after she kicked Hou Tao in the nuts. And even with duct tape over her mouth, they understood the unpleasant things she was saying to them.

The men shoved the wildcat into an open shipping container sitting on the dock at the Port of New Orleans next to a large freighter named,

"Precious Cargo". They rolled two barrels of water inside along with several bags of non-perishable food, a thin blanket, waste bucket, and a flashlight. Kenny expected Zabrina Chao would suffer, and that was his intention, especially after the fiasco she caused him now. But he needed her to survive the perilous month-long trip to Asia, since this bargaining chip would be more valuable alive than dead.

Kenny watched a giant gantry crane clamp the top of the container with metal claws and lift it high into the air. The crane transited the container over the port side of the ship and set it on a stack of thousands of other containers destined for Asia. It seemed ironic to Kenny that he was a human trafficker who smuggled people into the United States. This time, he was smuggling someone out. Zabrina Chao never suspected she had a round-trip ticket.

Satisfied she was out of the way, it was time to smuggle himself out of New Orleans. He ordered the driver to take him to the executive airport where a private jet awaited his departure from the Big Easy that had become a big problem.

* * *

It was quiet in the hospital room except for the tiny chirps of a heart monitor and the rhythmic mechanical whoosh from the machine helping Luna breathe. Doctors reduced the medication keeping her in a medically induced coma earlier that morning. All Stenson could do now was wait.

For the first time in more than a week, he saw his wife stir. It was a brief gasp of air that startled him. Luna raised head slightly in an involuntary movement. He clinched her hand while she was still unconscious.

A few minutes later, she stirred again, trying to cough. It appeared to Stenson his wife was in distress. He rushed to find someone to help. When a nurse returned with Stenson, she assured him this was a normal response for patients with a breathing tube to experience these symptoms during recovery. A respiratory therapist entered and skillfully removed Luna's breathing tube from her trachea.

Undeterred and overly protective, Stenson kept a keen watch over his wife as he sat by her bedside. An hour later, Luna's eyes flitted under her eyelids as if she was having a vivid dream. He watched her eyes flutter back and forth, then she opened them and blinked several times. He squeezed her hand. Finally, Luna turned her head to look at Stenson as if he was a stranger. He offered her a gentle smile that reminded her of a long-lost friend. Gradually, her mind cleared the fog.

In a weakened, gravelly voice, as if her throat were filled with sand, she squeezed his hand and whispered, "Stenson."

"Hi, sleeping beauty," Stenson said as he fought back tears.

"Where am I?" Luna asked.

"You are in a hospital, dear," Stenson told her.

A nurse walked in after being alerted to a change in Luna's vitals. She came over a pressed several buttons on the machines and introduced herself to the patient.

"Hi Luna, I am Angelina, I am your nurse. How are you feeling?"

"I hurt all over," Luna replied.

"Here, let me help you," the nurse said as she adjusted the morphine drip into Luna's arm. "Would you like something to drink?"

"Yes, please?" Luna whimpered.

It never occurred to Stenson that Luna had

nothing to drink in seven days. Nourishment had come from an intravenous drip. The nurse returned a few moments later with ice water in a Styrofoam cup. She held the straw to Luna's mouth so she could take her first sips.

The nurse sat the cup on a tray attached to the bed and said, "Get some rest. I will be back to check on you soon."

The nurse handed Stenson a control lying on the side of the bed and instructed him to call her if they needed anything before then. After the nurse left, Stenson held the cup up again for Luna, who almost emptied it in one gulp.

"I will get you more," Stenson offered.

"No, stay with me," She told him.

Luna squeezed Stenson's hand.

"I want to look at you," she sweetly told her husband.

Her mind had cleared enough to know why she was here. Luna remembered the attack and death of their child. Tears welled in her eyes.

"I am sorry, Stenson. I tried to protect our son," she said.

Hearing those words coming from the bravest woman he had ever known crushed him. He knew how hard his wife had fought, taking out four killers, and she almost won.

"I know you did, honey. There were too many," he said.

Luna was not to blame. Stenson blamed himself.

"I am the one who is sorry, Luna. I should have been there to protect you and our child. If I had not taken that meeting, I would have been there. Will you ever forgive me?" he asked his wife with love in his broken heart.

"Honey, it's not your fault," she consoled.

"I am as heartbroken as you. But I love you with

all my heart and we will get through this together," she told her husband.

Stenson leaned down and kissed her cheek.

"Let me get you more water," he said.

After this brief talk of forgiveness, she released his hand. Stenson dialed Robert after he left the room to share the news that Luna had awakened. He returned a few moments later with a fresh cup of water. All he wanted to do now was to spend every moment with this brave woman who he was blessed to call his wife.

* * *

The next morning, Luna's surgeon arrived to check on his patient. Stenson watched Dr. Graham perform a series of tests on his wife. She had no feeling from the waist down when the doctor pricked her thigh, calf, foot, and big toe, revealing no sensation.

His heart sank, but Luna remained optimistic when the doctor told her it could be temporary considering the seriousness of the surgery she had undergone. He explained it takes time for nerves to heal, but there were no promises; only time would tell.

Stenson was quiet after the doctor left the room. Luna sensed his anxiety and asked what was bothering him even though she already knew. He looked up, trying to feign bravery. But Luna knew her husband too well and what he was thinking since they'd been friends forever. Long before they were boyfriend and girlfriend or husband and wife, Luna knew the heart of this thoughtful man.

"Don't give me that pouty look, Mr. Beckett," Luna said wryly. "You are not the one laying in a hospital bed unable to feel your toes or pee involuntarily into a plastic bag."

Normally, a remark like that would have made Stenson laugh. But right now, humor could not break through the concern for his wife's health and her recovery.

"I would do anything to trade places with you, Luna," Stenson said. "It hurts me to see you this way."

"I know, Stenson," Luna replied. "And I think of all the challenges you've faced in your life and how you have always come out on top. Like you, I will work my butt off (when I can feel it) to overcome this challenge, too."

"When you can feel it?" he said, catching her funny joke.

"Look, if I cannot walk, it is what it is. We cannot change what has happened. I am happy knowing I have you. And if this is the price I pay for the gift of your love, I will never trade it. We cannot change the past, only move forward without fear," she bravely concluded.

His wife's optimism encouraged Stenson; it was one of the many qualities he admired about Luna. When times were tough, she showed enormous strength. No challenge seemed insurmountable to her, not even this one. Now it was his turn to be strong for her. Hard days lay ahead for both of them.

There was a knock at the door. It was Larry McMaster, the owner of Fairhaven Memorial Park & Mortuary. Stenson had asked him to stop by to help them plan the funeral for their son. Larry shared a leather binder containing photographs of caskets for children and infants. Luna carefully studied every picture and read the descriptions. Stenson knew how important this decision was to his wife. It was not lost on him she was burying part of herself.

How many parents buried a child, not because of some unfortunate malady or misfortune, but murder? Their little boy would never grow up to...

"I like this one, Stenson. What do you think?" she asked.

Luna pointed to a photograph of a small casket with the heading, "Sweet Prince". The container, half the size of an adult casket, was powder blue with nickel plated handles and accents. Above the white crepe lining and matching pillow was a scene of an angel inside the lid, surrounded by clouds and a crescent moon. Below it read, "Good night Sweet Prince: May flights of Angels sing thee to thy rest."

The casket was beautiful, he agreed. But quietly inside, it took all his strength to resist screaming, "I can't do this!"

They finished planning a small memorial service for family and friends to take place the following Saturday, a week from today. After the funeral director left, Luna told Stenson she wished she could attend.

"Oh, you will attend young lady, even if Brickhouse and I have to push this bed all the way to the chapel," He assured her.

"Besides, Brick needs exercise. He's getting fat," Stenson said, making the first joke since this tragedy occurred.

Luna chuckled. In reality, it was the reason the service was postponed for a week. Stenson hoped Luna could attend. Unfortunately, that decision would be left to the medical professionals caring for her.

"Will you do me a favor, Stenson?" Luna asked.

"Of course," Stenson replied.

"Go home for a while and don't worry about me. I am in expert hands and I know you haven't left my side since I arrived. Have a beer with Brick and the guys. It will do you some good," she encouraged her husband.

"I don't want to leave you. And I haven't spoken

to JC or Big Tony since this happened," Stenson admitted.

"Stenson, do not blame them," Luna said. "You did what you always do and help your friends. What happened was not their fault. I am sure they feel terrible about this."

Luna said, "Remember how you reached out to JC after we destroyed Club Empire? And you gave him back their money so they could rebuild?"

"Yes," Stenson said.

"Then I am asking you to reach out to them and tell them I am okay and you forgive them," she pleaded with her beautiful blue eyes that Stenson could not refuse.

"I will, Luna," he promised and sealed it with a kiss.

Chapter 20

Stenson left the hospital at Luna's insistence. He followed the GPS to an address of a rental home Robert had leased for the couple. It was owned by a family with a disabled son who had recently passed away. Equipped with wheelchair access and other accessibility features, it would be suitable for Luna's long road to recovery.

Everything seemed foreign to Stenson when entered the home. Except for a few scattered boxes, nothing belonged to them. It was a strange sensation of feeling out of place. The furniture was not theirs. Even the smell was the scent of another person; a dead, crippled person, which Stenson put out of his mind. This would have to do no matter how awkward it felt, because their previous home was a house of horrors. Neither Stenson nor Luna had any intention of stepping foot (or wheelchair) into that place again.

He wandered around the home inspecting each room. The master bedroom was filled with boxes of clothes. One had a post-it note stuck to it with a message from Soni James offering to help organize the place. The next room held Luna's office equipment with boxes of computer books Stenson would never understand. The third room caused him to stop at the doorway. He did not bother walking in. This would have been his infant son's bedroom. Gone were the cheerfully painted walls he and Luna had spent so much time lovingly creating. There was no crib or musical mobile decorations. The endless toys from family and friends were not there. The room stood as empty as Stenson's broken heart. He closed the door, for it was too painful to see.

Stenson returned to the living room and noticed a box labeled "Photos". He used his car key to slice the tape and open the cardboard container. He pulled the carton closer to the sofa where he sat down. One-by-one he removed picture frames and stared at each. The first was a picture of him standing with his mother when he was eight years old wearing his Cub Scout uniform. He remembered that day and wished his mom was here to comfort him like she did whenever he scraped his knee. But this pain was much greater than anything he had ever felt before.

There were photos of Luna in college and his official Army portrait taken when he first joined the service. Oh, how young he looked and how much he had grown since then. Pictures of him and Luna before they were married enjoying dinners, sporting events, and the time he proved to her he could not ice skate when he fell flat on his butt. Someone had captured the moment and caught Luna when she was in full giggle. Oh, how he loved her laugh.

Photos captured special times with their friends like the wedding photographs that proved this motley bunch could dress nice once in a while. He stared at a picture of Luna beaming when she was pregnant and showing off her enlarged tummy. He smiled remembering how happy she was then.

The last frame he removed was a photograph of Luna holding their son in the delivery room shortly after the baby was born. Stenson was leaning into the photo by her side. Their smiles as new parents radiated from ear to ear.

Stenson wiped away a tear that dripped onto the glass with the cuff of his shirt. He sat the picture frame on the coffee table and thought how it seemed like a million years ago. As he stared at the photos, he wondered what they would do now?

Nassau, Bahamas

Kenny Wu sipped a tropical drink by the pool at his private villa on Paradise Island in Nassau, Bahamas. The six bedroom, eight bathroom estate had been used to entertain guests and business associates during better times. Now it was his refuge from the madness in New Orleans.

His accountant purchased the property several years ago through one of his off-shore shell companies using cryptocurrency. He was an early adopter of the financial technology and made a significant amount of money providing illicit services on the dark web. Crypto was his untraceable slush fund spread across many digital wallets and platforms. Even his father did not know where some of his money came from. When he mentioned crypto to the old man years ago, his father did not understand. He was a dinosaur who preferred cold hard cash.

Kenny traveled to the Bahamas under an assumed name using one of the many fake identities he had stashed away for situations like this. Good luck finding him, Kenny thought. So what if Stenson Beckett's kid is dead? It wasn't his problem now. He warned the man if he wanted to play a game with him, then Stenson Beckett would lose. And now here he sat in the lap of luxury while Beckett cried over spilled milk... or an infant's blood.

New Orleans, Louisiana

The memorial service for Stenson and Luna Beckett's son took place on a cold, gray Saturday morning at Fairhaven Funeral Home. Doctors allowed Luna to attend with the aid of a wheelchair and a medical assistant.

Everyone who knew the couple paid their respects including many they did not know. The tragedy befallen the couple resonated with the residents of New Orleans. Media outlets covered the event respectfully by keeping their distance. Brick's biker friends reinforced the lines they could not to cross.

Stenson felt as dull as the gray, rainy day. He only spoke briefly to those who offered their condolences. Luna was more engaged when visitors encouraged her to get well soon and conveyed their sorrow for her loss.

Pastor Jackson had driven from Alabama to New Orleans the night before to officiate the funeral. Even for a man of faith who shared the highs and lows of people's lives, this was an especially tough task for him today. He considered Stenson like a son and knew the deep pain he felt.

After the funeral, Luna and Stenson stayed under the tent covering the gravesite and stared at the tiny casket. They realized the finality of the moment. Luna was sad at losing her child, unable to protect him as every mother should. But she was more saddened for her husband. This wonderful man she was so honored to bear a son with and named after him was hurting. And here she sat in a wheelchair with the harsh reality that she may never bear another child again truly broke her heart.

Stenson did not deserve this. Never in her life had she met such a gracious human being. She felt tears well up inside. But she would not allow herself to cry. She vowed to remain strong. Stenson was fearlessly protective of her. Now it was her turn to do the same for him.

Stenson was quiet as he held the umbrella over Luna's head as the medical assistant wheeled his wife to the van. He leaned down and kissed Luna, telling her he had things to do and would visit her later.

Brick walked over and stood by Stenson in the drizzling rain after the van drove away. JC and Anthony Gallo watched the scene from a distance. Robert had not spoken to the men after the blowup at the hospital. Stenson knew it was time to honor Luna's wishes and bury this misunderstanding like he buried his son.

"Let's talk to JC and Tony," Stenson suggested.

When Stenson and Robert walked over, JC and Big Tony did not know what to expect. With the emotion of the day, maybe Stenson and Brick were going to kill them now to save themselves a trip to the cemetery later.

Instead, Stenson said, "I want you to know Luna and I do not blame you for what happened to our son. It has forever changed our lives, but it was not your fault. We know who is to blame. We remain your friends including this hotheaded marine. Right Robert?"

Robert was not nearly as forgiving as Stenson, but since this is what Stenson wanted, he said, "Right."

JC burst into tears. He had carried this burden blaming himself since the tragedy occurred. Stenson reached over and embraced Justin Carter in a brotherly hug.

JC said, "I am sorry, Stenson,"

"We all are, JC," Stenson replied.

Big Tony and Robert Brickhouse shook hands.

In that rainy cemetery. These tough men who had been through so much together reaffirmed their friendship with a bond that was stronger than ever.

Stenson visited the hospital from sun up to sundown every day the following week as Luna's condition improved. He took part in her rehabilitation and learned how to get her in and out of bed, change her clothes, and bathe her. Luna teased him once when he was giving her a bath. "I can reach that part, pervert. Now wash my toes. I can't reach them."

Stenson took Soni James up on her offer to unpack and decorate their rental home. JC and Big Tony offered to help as well. He wasn't worried about Anthony Gallo, but JC's taste in anything was always over the top.

The hospital released Luna on Easter Sunday. It was not lost on Stenson this was the resurrection of his wife. He drove the van he'd purchased to accommodate her wheelchair to their new home. When they arrived, a sign in the yard read, "Welcome Home Luna!" in big pink letters with colorful balloons attached. JC, Big Tony, Soni, Sarge, and Brick were waiting in the yard and cheered when Stenson opened the van door and lowered the ramp.

Luna guided her powered wheelchair out of the van and onto the driveway as she had practiced the last couple of days. Stenson smiled at all the attention his wife received. No accomplishment was too small. When she approached the house, Big Tony told her he built the ramp leading to the front door and hoped it wasn't too steep. Luna joked that the wheelchair Stenson bought was powerful enough to carry him if he wanted to sit on her lap. When he told her he was too heavy, she reminded him she could not feel her legs. Stenson did not know how his wife kept her sense of humor, but it certainly cheered him up.

Now the rental house felt more like their home. Soni had impeccable taste. Gone were the boxes, and the furniture was moved to allow Luna's wheelchair easy access around the house. An aroma of Italian food filled the air from a giant pot of spaghetti Big Tony had prepared.

Stenson asked JC, "I have seen all the work they've done. What did you do?"

He replied, "I supervised and was in charge of the most important room in the house," JC said proudly.

"Did you decorate a dog house? By the way, I hope someone told you we don't have a dog," Stenson joked.

JC waved his arm toward the hallway, inviting Luna to go first. Stenson followed, with JC and the rest of the crew crowding behind. Luna stopped her chair in front of the closed master bedroom door.

"Cover your eyes," JC encouraged Luna.

Stenson shook his head, expecting the worst.

JC opened the door and yelled, "Surprise!"

"Oh, JC! I love it!" Luna exclaimed.

Stenson was less impressed. "My bedroom looks like a brothel."

The bed was adorned with a purple bedspread and matching silk sheets with leopard spotted pillows. Candles of different shapes and sizes were lit around the room. A large wedding portrait of the couple adorned the soft gray walls, and a photograph of their infant son sat atop the dresser.

"Most of the credit goes to Soni," JC admitted.

She replied, "Girl, I wanted to liven up this room up for you. Your last bedroom must have been decorated by Stenson. It was as boring as vanilla ice cream with no sprinkles."

"Hey, I have sprinkles," Stenson defended his

decorating style.

"I love it Soni, thank you," Luna gushed. "And thank all of you who've helped us get through this difficult time."

"By the way, JC. What did you do since Soni did all the bedroom design?" Stenson asked Justin Carter.

"I decorated you, bro," JC proudly crowed. "I bought you new clothes. Check out your closet."

Stenson reluctantly opened the door and peered inside.

"Oh, hell no!" Stenson exclaimed.

He walked out wearing a leopard spotted evening jacket. "You expect me to wear something like this? I look like Hugh Hefner went on safari."

"You have no style, Stenson," JC said.

"I think you look hot, Stenson," Luna teased her husband.

"Take it all back, JC. I like my boring style," Stenson told the wannabe fashion designer.

"JC can return your clothes, Stenson, but I am keeping the bedroom just the way it is." Luna declared.

Soni winked at Luna who admitted the bedroom had more style. They returned to the dining room where Big Tony served everyone food. While they chatted across the table, Big Tony noticed Justin did not touch his plate.

"JC, you aren't eating. You don't like my cooking?" Tony Gallo asked.

"Oh, it's good. I am just not hungry right now," JC replied.

Justin always had an appetite. He was a human vacuum cleaner when it came to food. Yet JC's mind was elsewhere. The mood changed when everyone realized why JC was sad. There was one person missing from this feast. Their friend Zabrina wasn't there.

Luna broke the silence. "Does anyone want to talk about the elephant in the room?"

Everyone looked at each other knowing what Luna meant. Stenson wiped his mouth and placed his napkin on the table.

"I have tried to wrap my head around this," Stenson began.

"We were going about our lives until one day a psychopath showed up. All JC and Tony wanted to do was get their friend back even if it cost all the money they had. We see how that went," Stenson plainly said.

"JC didn't want me involved and certainly not Brick. But he had no place to turn but us. And we did what friends do; we helped. There is no way any of us saw what was coming for Luna and me."

He continued. "Let's look at the score. Zabrina is gone. The money, which is the least of our problems, is gone. Tony was shot. My wife almost lost her life and is paralyzed. And my son is dead."

"We are dealing with a lunatic. And what has puzzled me from the beginning is I don't know why Kenny Wu did this or what he has to gain? The more we go down this rabbit hole, the more people have gotten hurt. We have lost so much already. I don't want to lose anymore. Do we let the cops handle this and cut our losses?" Stenson asked.

Everyone looked at each other not knowing what to say.

"You mean after all this, we just walk away?" Brick wondered.

"I mean yes, I guess?" Stenson replied.

"What about Zabrina?" JC asked the group.

The question made everyone sick. Because they all knew the likelihood of the police recovering Zabrina alive was not in their favor.

Robert said, "Let me ask you something, Stenson. When have we ever walked away from anything? In combat, we didn't. We ran into the flames. When I almost lost my life, you risked yours to save mine. When JC and his crew screwed us before we were friends, we did not give up. We outwitted them and finally won."

"I know, Robert. But nobody died," Stenson replied. "This is deadly different. It's not like playing some joke on JC where the damage was not permanent. "

"It doesn't matter, Stenson. The same rules apply," Robert explained. "We have always won because we were smarter than our opponent. The only reason this happened was because we underestimated Kenny Wu."

"Nothing is going to stop him from being a psycho," Stenson pointed out.

"Exactly!" Brick exclaimed. "So, let's use that fact to our advantage. This guy is bound to have many skeletons buried some place. We just need to find his weaknesses and turn the tables on him."

"Wu has more resources than us," Stenson reminded.

"He's a millionaire and in case you didn't notice we are broke. How do we compete with that?" Stenson questioned.

"With our wits, like we always have. Money can't buy you street smarts," Robert replied.

The big marine said, "We've got more resources than you think, Stenson. One is sitting next to you. Your wife may be in that wheelchair, but I bet if you ask her, she's willing to help us dig up a quarry full of dirt on Kenny Wu. And we've got Sarge. You wanted a tank, and he gave you one, remember? Anything we need Sarge can get. And don't forget the Mystery Man. Maybe there is something we ask that phantom to do for us. And more importantly, Stenson, you have me, JC, Big Tony, Soni and an entire gang of bikers at our disposal who love you and are loyal to you and Luna."

Stenson looked around the room. Everyone nodded and seemed to agree, including his wife.

"This will be dangerous," Stenson warned.

"No, son," Brick said with a steely look in his eye.

"For love and friendship, this will be Vengeance!"

Chapter 21

Stenson placed a large whiteboard upon an easel in the living room. Their rental home would serve as command central for the lost and found; where they were lost with much to be found before they killed, captured, or brought to justice those responsible for this mayhem.

Stenson began with the obvious. He taped a photograph of Kenny Wu in the middle of the board. From this Black Widow, everything radiated outward from this tangled web. Before he psychoanalyzed the Latrodectus Hesperus, he tacked another photo of the most time-sensitive problem they faced. They must find Zabrina Chao. The clock was ticking and time was not on her side.

Luna sat in her wheelchair behind Stenson pecking keys on her laptop. She was determined to track Wu and Zabrina. Her former enemy was now the friend Zabrina needed most. Despite Stenson's plea, Luna would not rest until she found them both.

Next, Stenson placed a photo of Wu's number two on the board. His operations guy, David Pham, was a contact who may help. Other pieces he drew on the board: the stolen money, attack on Big Tony and JC, fires at Silkroad and O'Malley's. And a question mark represented the most painful of all, the unknown assassins who killed his son and left his wife paralyzed.

He took a deep breath and focused before a fuse

blew in his head. There were other pieces he wasn't sure where they fit. Wu Kong, the man they call Sun Fang, is Kenny's father. Stenson suspected he may have a financial interest in his son's activities. For all he knew, the elder Wu may pull his son's puppet strings and bet the master behind this madness. Finally, there was the Chinese gang who were involved in Wu's human smuggling operations, and maybe more.

Luna watched Stenson attempt to make sense of it all as he drew lines between the pieces to visualize the connections.

"What is that?" she asked, pointing to a drawing on the board.

"It's a beehive, representing the Chinese gang," he said.

"Looks like a pile of dog poo," Luna scrutinized.

Stenson looked at the drawing, then back at Luna as if she was some sort of paraplegic art critic who did not approve of his drawing skills. He erased the illustration and told her she would be terrible at Pictionary. Then he redrew the illustration with little bees and the word "Buzz" so Luna would not mistake it for canine excrement.

"Why did you draw flies around the poo?" she teased her husband.

"Really, Luna?" Stenson said, laughing at her silly joke.

"What's that other thing?" she wondered, pointing at another Stenson masterpiece drawing.

He said, "It's a bag of money representing the cash that they stole."

"It looks like a bag Santa would carry," his wife observed.

"You should add a sleigh and reindeer. Maybe a couple of elves," the comical art critic suggested.

"I am glad you said that instead of telling me I

should draw 500,000 one dollar bills so it would be clear to you how much money we lost. And before you ask, that would require a bigger whiteboard and green markers. Although I wouldn't mind if Santa Claus brought me a bag of cash for Christmas."

"Have you been naughty or nice this year, Mr. Beckett?" Luna playfully teased.

The wheelchair-bound comedian returned to her work after Stenson did not answer the question. He guessed she was probably coming up with more corny jokes to distract him later.

Kenny Wu, the braggadocious man about town, was conspicuously absent since the attack on Stenson's home. Stenson knew this was by design as much as the St. Valentine's Day Massacre on February 14, 1929. While it was widely believed Al Capone was behind the attack, Scarface was conveniently in Florida and never convicted of the crime.

Nobody had seen or heard from Kenny Wu since the attack. It seemed the man had simply vanished. Stenson knew things were getting too hot in New Orleans for Wu with the media snooping around and authorities connecting their dots, too. He was convinced Kenny left New Orleans, but where he had gone was anybody's guess.

David Pham was their best lead because he did not want any part of this madness. However, they had not spoken to him since the "pizza delivery" meeting a few weeks ago. JC and Big Tony went out to locate him so they could talk to him again.

"He's dead." Luna interrupted.

"Who's dead? Kenny Wu?" Stenson hoped.

"As if we could be so lucky?" Luna replied. "David Pham is dead. It seems he had an unfortunate dinner date that left him with extra ventilation in his head."

She turned the laptop around to show Stenson

the news story. Somehow, it did not surprise him. But he felt bad for David Pham, who seemed like a reasonable guy. He suspected Pham knew too much and Kenny erased him to cover his tracks.

"What happened?" Stenson asked his wife.

"The article says it was an unknown assailant," Luna read. "Says David was eating alone at a Chinese restaurant when someone assassinated him. There were no witnesses or suspects according to police."

"Of course not," Stenson said sarcastically. "Like it's a regular day in New Orleans when somebody walks into a restaurant and shoots a person in the head and nobody sees or hears a thing."

"What about his family?" Stenson inquired.

"No mention of them other than he leaves behind a wife and daughter," Luna shared. "Big Tony and JC drove by their house a while ago and found it empty. Neighbors said they left the day before David was killed."

"At least David's family got out of town. I wish he had done the same," Stenson regretted.

"Any mention of Kenny Wu?" he asked Luna.

"The only thing it says is David Pham was the Chief Operations Officer at Silkroad International Shipping. It mentioned the recent fire at the business, which the article said is still under investigation, but nothing about Kenny Wu."

"Now what?" he wondered aloud.

"It looks like we are heading further down the rabbit hole," Luna believed.

Everything about this chaos with Kenny Wu felt like a giant rabbit hole.

Luna suggested. "Why don't we contact the reporter who has been covering this and see what she knows?"

Luna emailed the reporter who immediately phoned her. She was very interested in speaking with them. They had not spoken to the media after the O'Malley's fire, leaving Robert Brickhouse to release a brief statement. And nothing had been said regarding the attack on their home.

Out of an abundance of caution, Stenson agreed to meet the reporter at a restaurant in the French Quarter. Only a handful of their closest friends knew where they lived now, and Stenson intended to keep it that way as long as Kenny Wu was on the loose.

Erin Collins, a tall, slender woman in her late 20s with caramel-colored hair, approached the table at the Green Curry restaurant where Stenson and Robert were seated.

In an off-the-record interview, Stenson explained the timeline of events that led to the ambush at his home causing the death of his son and injuries to his wife. He revealed the fires at Kenny Wu's Silkroad International Shipping and O'Malley's Pub were related. He told her of the kidnapping of Zabrina Chao, and the attempted murder of Anthony Gallo. He explained the extortion and stolen money, and how Justin Carter identified Kenny Wu as the perpetrator. He also revealed they had spoken to David Pham, Kenny's Chief Operations Officer, days before he was assassinated. He told the reporter they suspected Pham knew enough to expose Kenny Wu, which is why he was no longer among the living.

The revelations left the reporter speechless. She thought she was simply interviewing the victim of a tragic crime. She was not prepared for the flood of information she just heard.

"This is a major story!" Erin Collins exclaimed.

"If you can prove it." Stenson said cautiously.

"The problem is Kenny Wu is so well insulated and connected to insiders that nobody wants to go near this. I feel certain if you dig enough there is more to this story. We do not know where to find Wu. But maybe an investigative story by an aspiring reporter will rattle his cage and flush him out."

"Wow!" she said. "I will do everything I can to help you if you promise me an exclusive. This could make my career."

"Of course," Stenson replied. "Let us know of anything you find, and we will do the same."

The reporter rushed out of the restaurant, eager to get started on this major scoop. Stenson and Brick discussed their next move. They needed more information. Since David Pham was out of the picture, Stenson suggested grabbing one of the foot soldiers from the Chinese gang that Brick's biker friends were tailing to see what they may know. It wasn't much to go on, but it was worth a try.

"I'm on it," Robert affirmed. "You want him delivered on a silver platter or in tiny pieces?"

"You should probably keep him in one piece. It's easier to talk with a jawbone attached," Stenson humorously replied.

Panama Canal, Panama

"Help!" Zabrina rasped in a scratchy voice reminiscent of the first phone call by Alexander Graham Bell in 1876. It was a plea of desperation more than any hope someone would hear her scream. How many days had she been trapped inside this floating prison? She had lost count.

The ship was motionless; silent except for random creaks and groans when a wave nudged the monstrous ship. The sun scorched at high noon 650 miles from earth's equator as "Precious Cargo" awaited passage through the Panama Canal.

Zabrina roasted inside the torturous sweatbox of corrugated metal. Dangerous conditions left her so dehydrated she no longer sweat. Heat stroke was a life-threatening concern, but Zabrina knew she must conserve water. She only allowed herself a few sips a day from the two five-gallon containers that were now close to one.

She stripped her clothes and sat nude in the center of the tomb on a thin blanket folded four times into a small square. She dared not move because walking across the metal was like walking across a grill sizzling her feet. To further her misery, the heat amplified the rancid odor of the hellish environment since the small bucket provided for her waste tipped over during a storm and sloshed about the floor before the liquid evaporated, leaving only a foul stench behind.

Her only gauge of night and day in the pitch black box was the changing temperature. Nights were as frozen as the days were blazed. If not for curling into a fetal position covered completely by the soil-soaked blanket and using her breath for extra heat, she would have frozen to death.

Her food comprised 30 pouches of tuna, two bags of dehydrated bananas, and a three boxes of saltine crackers. The flashlight died days ago leaving her in this darkened filth with nothing but bad dreams to keep her company. She ate a single banana chip, holding it on her tongue until it melted in her mouth.

She imagined in her nightmarish dreams Kenny Wu laughing at her fate, sitting on a beach with a cocktail in his hand. Seeing his taunting face dance through her mind did not make her cry, even if she could produce tears. Wu's face made her angry and gave her the will to survive.

The Happy Monkey
Jefferson Parish, New Orleans

Robert parked his matte-black van in an alley next to a laundromat across the street from The Happy Monkey, a bar and restaurant in Jefferson Parish where members of the Chinese gang who were believed to be associated with Kenny Wu hung out.

Brick chewed his cigar and studied the place. A dozen Kawasaki and Honda motorcycles were parked in front of the two-story brick building that looked like it was a former grocery store with apartments above. A few Asian men mingled outside.

He did not like the place already. Who names a social club, "The Happy Monkey"? He wondered if the gang was named "The Chimps"? As far as motorcycles were concerned, Brick preferred his black and chrome, slow-rolling Harley Davidson over those flashy crotch rockets. Not only did his bike have style, it held sentimental value since it was a gift from Stenson after they took down Club Empire.

He would have enjoyed riding it on a night like this, but he brought the van because of passenger requirements. Besides, nobody rode on the back of his bike unless it was an attractive woman. Once, he gave Stenson a ride home before he cut his long hair. People wondered who his new girlfriend was. After that, Brick never gave a guy a ride on the back, even if it was his best friend.

Brick puffed the cigar and scanned the crowd in front of the Monkey bar. He searched for a guy who appeared to be the loudest and most cocky. They were the fun ones to play with, and by play he meant to beat the crap out of until he got the information he needed. One man stood out, and it was no surprise when he climbed onto the flashiest bike.

"Figures," Brick said as he tossed the cigar out the

window and watched the man drive away. He turned on his headlights and eased out of the parking lot. With a wicked grin, the marine smiled and said to himself, "Let the fun begin."

Chapter 22

Robert Brickhouse phoned Stenson. "Meet me at the warehouse," he said with a hint of mischief in his voice.

Stenson arrived half an hour later. He found Robert in the cavernous warehouse that JC and his team used to store equipment and supplies. The big marine was standing next to a man who was bound to a chair.

"Why are you wet?" Stenson asked.

"Went for a swim," Brick replied with a Cheshire cat all-knowing grin that told Stenson there was more to this tale.

"With your clothes on?" Stenson clarified.

"I forgot to bring my bathing suit and nobody wants to see me naked," the burly marine replied.

"Who is he? And dare I ask why is he wet, too?"

"He is one of the Chinese gangsters Kenny Wu is so fond of employing. Seems he wanted to take a swim in Lake Pontchartrain with his motorcycle after he took a flying leap like a stuntman into the lake. It took me a while to fish him out. Unfortunately, that piece of junk crotch rocket he was riding did not survive," Brick explained with the satisfaction of knowing he'd never see that ugly bike again.

Stenson pulled up a metal chair and sat down across from the man. He said, "Hi, I guess you met my friend Robert. My name is Stenson. What is yours?"

"Cào ni mā!" ("F**k your mother") the man said in Mandarin.

"Sorry, I don't speak Chinese. Is that your full name? May I call you Cào (F**k) for short?"

"Ni tā mā de qù si ba!" ("You f-ing go to hell")

"Wow, that's even more difficult. I will stick with the first one if that's ok with you?" Stenson said.

"Ni shìgè báichī!" ("You are an idiot!") the defiant Asian replied.

Stenson looked at Robert Brickhouse. "Too bad he doesn't speak English. I wanted to tell him we meant him no harm. We simply wanted to ask him a few questions."

Brick laughed. "Yeah, it's too bad. Like when he did an Evel Knievel jump into the lake. All I wanted to do was tell him he had a tail light out."

"You know Brick, I always tell people bad things happen when you don't communicate," Stenson mused.

Stenson looked around the room and said, "It seems a little bleak in here. We should make the place more comfortable for our guest. We should add some plants or something to liven this place up."

Brick knew exactly what Stenson had in mind.

"That is a good idea," Robert agreed before returning a few minutes later with a potted plant in his hands.

"Ah, that is much better," Stenson said approvingly.

The captive gangster must have been thinking, "I am tied to a chair after a manic ran me off the road into a lake and these guys are decorating a warehouse with plants?"

Stenson explained to the gangster, "My wife gave me this plant for my birthday. I asked her for a Venus flytrap, but she said this was more exotic. They say the fragrance is amazing, but I have a sinus problem that impedes my sense of smell. Care to smell it and tell me what you think?"

The man turned his head away from the kidnapping florist.

"Come on," Stenson encouraged. "You may never smell something this rare again."

Finally, if either out of curiosity or he simply wanted Stenson to shut up about a stupid plant, the gangster agreed to sniff it. Brick held it close to the gangster's face while Stenson encouraged him to take a deep breath because the scent was said to be faint.

The man took a whiff, then let out a blood-curdling scream. "Aaagh! My face is on fire!"

"Oh look, Brick. Cào ni mā speaks English. I thought he only spoke Chinese."

"Since he didn't tell you he speaks English, maybe he will forgive you for not telling him this is the most venomous plant in the world." Robert deviantly suggested.

"Oh yeah. Cào ni mā, I forgot to mention this is the gympie-gympie plant. It's poisonous," Stenson informed the agonizing gangbanger.

"My name is not Cào ni mā, you idiot! Make it stop! My nose is swelling and my face feels like I am being burned with hot acid and electrocuted at the same time!"

Stenson offered his sympathy when he explained, "I am afraid it will get worse over the next 20 to 30 minutes. But they say the pain will go away in a few weeks or months if you don't die before then. People have committed suicide over the agony and their inability to sleep."

Robert chuckled. "Sleep is overrated. Did I ever tell you, Stenson, about the time we were training and our instructors kept us awake for four days straight? That sucked."

"I can imagine. Do you sleep well now?" Stenson asked.

"I sleep like a baby, especially tonight when we finish with this guy. Did I tell you I bought a new mattress?" Brick asked his friend.

"Would you two shut up about sleep and mattresses and take me to a hospital or shoot me?" the man begged, unable to wipe the tears from his eyes or snot running down his chin.

Stenson told the agonizing gangster, "I am personally against violence. However, my friend might shoot you since he is not sympathetic towards people who kill his friend's child and paralyze his wife."

Brick gave the man sinister smile that said he would be happy to kill him.

"Please! I will tell you whatever you want! Just take me to the hospital!" the man pleaded.

"Where is Kenny Wu?" Stenson demanded with a much more serious tone.

"If I wasn't about to die a miserable death right now, I would tell you I don't know him. But since I feel like I am being cooked alive, I will tell you I work for him indirectly. But I promise I have never met the man. I am too far down the food chain."

"Who do you work for?" Stenson forcefully inquired.

"Danny Oh! Ask him about Wu, but that is all I know! Now take me to the hospital!"

"One more question? Where do we find Danny Oh?" Stenson asked.

"He hangs out at The Happy Monkey. He's easy to spot, but good luck getting in there," the snotty-nose gangster warned him.

"Oh, we will get in there. Don't you worry about that," Brick said. "But you won't be there to see it with your eyes swollen shut."

"Now, will you please get me an ambulance? I am truly suffering. This pain is insane!" the gangster cried.

"I will call you an ambulance after we drop you off," Brick informed the crybaby.

"Drop me off?" the gangster astonishingly asked.

"Yes. And you better hope the ambulance arrives before your lungs swell up and explode inside your chest," Robert told him. "We better hurry. Take off your clothes."

"Take off my clothes?" the confused gangster repeated.

"Yeah, I don't want any of those gympie-gympie stingers in my van," Robert told him.

With no time to argue, Brick untied the man who quickly stripped off his flashy, waterlogged clothes. Robert guided him to the van and shoved him inside. They drove to Bourbon Street where Robert let the man out behind the dumpster of a voodoo shop. Robert dialed 911 and held his phone up to the suffering man's ear and instructed him to explain his situation to the operator.

"Hello... please help me. I am dying! Where am I located? I am naked on Bourbon Street with a nose swollen the size of a circus clown and eyes the size of golf balls about to pop out of my head. Come quick!" the gangster blurted.

After a pause, he said, "No, I am not drunk or high on drugs! I inhaled a gympie-gympie plant. No, it is not a hallucinogenic the Mayan people used in ceremonies. Why am I naked? I don't have time for 50 questions! Please send an ambulance immediately!"

The call abruptly ended. The gangster squinted at Brick through his golf ball eyes and repeated what they already knew.

"She hung up on me. I don't think she believed

a word I said," the naked gangster conveyed in an astonishingly painful voice.

Robert said, "Yeah, it is New Orleans and I bet she gets a lot of crazy calls. I am sure yours was one of the more unusual ones she's received today. But you will be fine. Cops are all over the place. I am sure somebody will help you eventually."

The man was dumbfounded and speechless.

Robert bid him farewell. "We have to leave now. Thanks for your cooperation. Good luck with your messed up face and breathing normally again."

* * *

It was no exaggeration when Luna suggested they were headed down a rabbit hole in their search for Kenny Wu. Now it seemed they were after a guy named Donny Oh. If the guy with the messed up face and breathing problems told the truth, Mr. Oh was not a person you could walk up to and ask if he knew where they could find Kenny. They needed a creative way to flush that gangster out with as little gunfire and casualties as possible.

The Chinese gang, of which Mr. Oh was believed to be in charge, had their sticky fingers in many unsavory pies. Smuggling, prostitution, bookmaking, drugs, and extortion were their stock in trade. How much money Kenny Wu made from the gang was unknown but it was not Stenson's concern. Their priority was to find and rescue Zabrina Chao and to do that they had to find Wu. The rabbit hole kept getting deeper.

Luna continued her quest to track Wu's digital footprints; his movements, financial dealings, and family ties. Meanwhile, the guys needed a plan to get to Donny Oh. The Happy Monkey, the social club where the gang hung out, seemed like the place to start. Stenson, Robert, Big Tony, and JC drove over to get a better look.

"It is a hornet's nest," Robert observed.

"There are at least 20 guys in there and I guarantee you they are all packing heat. Look at the roof. There are a few up there too. And there is no approach to the building where we wouldn't be exposed," Brick evaluated.

"Come on, Robert. You are such a friendly guy. Why wouldn't they let you in?" Stenson sarcastically asked.

"I don't know. Maybe somebody told them I like to set buildings on fire. Gangsters can be so picky," Robert mused.

Stenson studied the surroundings on a map. Robert was correct, there were too many watchful eyes and blind spots where they could be picked off before anyone got closer than twenty meters without drawing suspicion.

"What if we were invited?" JC asked, reminding Robert he was sitting in the back seat.

"Where do you plan on getting an invitation, genius?" Brickhouse replied to what he considered was another of JCs preposterous pontifications.

"Did you see the poster in the window?" Justin asked.

"What poster? The one I made for you with my reward for you dead or alive?" Robert taunted.

"No, the one promoting a band performing Friday night," Justin said.

"JC, we need to infiltrate a club filled with gun-slinging gangsters. Why are you are talking about some band they have playing Friday night? This is a military operation, not some dance party," Brick warned him, not believing he was explaining this to the Disco Duck sitting in his back seat interrupting his concentration.

JC was undeterred and tried to explain.

"Remember how you fogged us out with that funky smell at Club Empire and caused all the black tie guests to flee?"

"Yeah, that was funny," Brick recalled the disaster.

"Why don't we do the same to them?" Justin proposed.

While Robert searched for some pain medication in the glove compartment of his van for the headache Justin was causing him, Stenson considered the idea.

Stenson said. "JC may be on to something, Robert. Instead of funking the people out with a vile smell like we did at Club Empire, why don't we knock them unconscious with gas and slip out with Donny Oh?"

Brick popped a couple of aspirin in his mouth then thought about the idea, not because JC came up with it, but because Stenson believed it might work.

"Well, that would eliminate a gun battle. But how would we get inside? We cannot get close enough to rig the place with Nitrous oxide," Robert noted.

"We impersonate the band," JC suggested.

"We what?" Brick looked over his shoulder at JC like he had lost his mind and wondered if he should have swallowed a few more pain relievers before he replied.

"In case you didn't realize, bozo, none of us plays an instrument or can sing or dance," Brick pointed out while wondering why he's even having this conversation.

"I can sing," JC boasted. "You should hear me in the shower."

"No thanks," Brick replied. "I've seen you in a leopard print robe and that was more than enough for me to see."

Big Tony and Stenson laughed at the back-and-forth conversation between Robert and JC.

Stenson said, "It's unconventional, but I think JC is onto something. We could impersonate the band as a ruse to get inside and set off some kind of gas to knock them out."

Robert looked at Stenson as if he drank the same crazy Kool-Aid as Justin Carter. Then he remembered it was some of their dumbest ideas that actually worked.

Robert said, "JC, the only reason I will consider this wild idea is because Stenson believes it might work. But if this does not go well, then I promise you I will kill you sooner rather than later. Do you understand?" Brick warned him.

"Not if I kill you first," JC taunted the marine.

Stenson and Big Tony roared with laughter. Before things got out of control and they had to clean up pieces of JC, Stenson said, "Calm down killers. Save it for the gangsters. We have work to do."

The Happy Monkey

"Absolutely not!" Robert emphatically told JC. "I am not wearing that!"

"I didn't know it was an 80s cover act, Brick. But we've already paid the band to take the night off, and these are the costumes they wear when they perform," JC explained.

"These costumes look like something drunk Aussies wore at a disco in the '80s after mating with some equally drunk kangaroos!" Robert complained.

"Probabally a Koala Bear too," Stenson said.

"Aren't those the cute little Australian bears?" JC asked. "I want one of those for a pet. I thought about a panda, but those are harder to clean and feed that a little bear.

"Would you two shut up?!" Robert barked while staring at the clothing he could not believe he was about to wear.

"Hey, my outfit doesn't fit," Big Tony said while looking in a mirror. His shirt was too tight, exposing the lower part of his stomach, and the vest looked like an adult put on an infant's clothing. Even the hat was too small.

"I am sorry, Big T. They didn't have anybody in the band as big as you, so you'll have to go with it. We will stick you in the back," JC told the biggest member of their fake cover band.

"What is a Gap Band, anyway?" Brick asked Justin. "Sounds like a band you would be in with that enormous gap between your ears where your brain should be."

"Look them up," JC suggested. "They were a popular band back in the 80s."

Robert searched the internet on his phone for the Gap Band. After he found a video, he said, "JC, the Gap Band are black guys. Did it occur to you we are all white except for you?"

"That's why I am the singer. We'll just tell them I am the only surviving member and you are the replacements," he suggested, having clearly thought of this beforehand.

Robert shook his head and looked at Stenson, who was already dressed in his costume.

"This might work. Now put on your outfit and stop whining," Stenson told the unhappy marine.

Robert begrudgingly put on the costume and said, "If photos of me wearing this outfit get out, I am killing somebody."

Brick noticed four pumpkins sitting on the floor.

"What's with the pumpkins?" he wondered.

"Remember smoke bombs when you were a kid?" Stenson asked.

"You mean those little balls with the fuse that set off colored smoke?" Brick recalled.

"Yeah, those. These are bigger versions with a twist. At the end of the last song, we will each set a pumpkin at the foot of the stage and light the fuse, which are just sparklers we placed in the stems for dramatic effect."

"That was my idea," JC offered. "Big Tony and I carved the pumpkins, too. Do you like them?"

Now Robert was completely confused. He was standing there looking like a crocodile hunter who mated with a disco ball, trying to follow Stenson's explanation about how this was going to work before JC interrupted.

"JC, where did you get pumpkins when Halloween is months away and had time to carve them? And where did the tank of Nitrous oxide come from?" Robert questioned.

"Jesús knew where to get them. He's got some friends in Mexico who sent them to us. We carved them when you were taking a nap for your headache. And we borrowed the tanks of Nitrous from a dentist office," JC explained.

"You borrowed laughing gas from a dentist office, like they just let you walk in and say you needed a couple of tanks of Nitrous oxide?" Brick asked, not waiting to hear the answer.

"Come on Brick. I got a teeth cleaning last week and let Big Tony in the back door when they were out of the room looking at my x-rays. I left the dentist a note saying we would bring them back later," he told the marine with a grin of bright, shiny teeth.

"Forget it. I am sorry I asked," Brick told him, exhausted from hearing Justin's crazy adventures while he was taking a nap from the last headache JC caused. He felt a stronger one coming on now.

"Stenson, please continue before I strangle the dental thief over here," Robert begged his friend.

"So, on the last song, we light the pumpkin fuses

like it's part of the act and set them at the foot of the stage. Then we dance off and exit the building through the back door while Nitrous fills the room," Stenson explained.

"That's clever but the most absurd idea I have ever heard," Brick admitted.

"That's why I am the brains and you are a backup singer," Stenson joked.

"We should watch a few videos," JC suggested. "The Gap Band were talented dancers. We will lip sync the songs, but you can't lip sync dance moves. By the way, Brick. The first song is Burn Rubber. Can drive your motorcycle on stage and do a burnout in the beginning? That should get their attention."

"I should burn rubber all over your face, JC. But yeah, if that's the way we want to start the show, I can do it. At least I'll look cool for a minute before you make me look like a dancing Koala bear."

"Alright, follow me. I will teach you some moves, especially for the last song," JC offered the group.

"I don't like this plan one bit," Robert complained.

Stenson laughed. "Pay attention crybaby. Or your bad dance moves might get us killed if we aren't convincing."

When the show was about to begin, JC peered at the audience from behind the curtain. The place was packed with gangsters and their dates. He noticed one man surrounded by gorgeous women and an equal number of gun toting bad guys. That must be Danny Oh.

"Everybody take your place," JC instructed.

Brick rolled his bike quietly onto the stage. When everything looked ready, JC cued the DJ, who announced the band.

"Ladies and Gentlemen, put your hands together for GBR — The Gap Band Revival!"

JC pointed to Brick who started the throaty

engine of his motorcycle and roared it a few times. The curtain raised, and the crowd cheered when he drove the bike onto the stage. Then he held the brake and cranked the throttle, causing the back tire to screech and create a large plume of smoke that filled the stage.

The audience reacted wildly as the music to the song "Burn Rubber" played. Big Tony and Stenson entered the stage with their arms rocking back and forth like discotheque robots, followed by Brick who fell in line behind them.

JC, appearing as the star of the show, entered the stage, waving to the crowd and blowing kisses to the women in the audience. He stood behind the microphone, gyrating his hips to the music, then began to lip sync to the song.

The crowd loved it. Nobody seemed to notice how poorly the backup singers were dancing. All eyes were glued on JC as he worked the crowd. Even Robert Brickhouse loosened up when he realized this stunt was actually working.

By the end of the show, the crowd was in a drunken frenzy. Women were dancing. Gangsters were slinging drinks. Everyone enjoyed themselves, including the band of misfits on the stage.

The curtain came down to rousing cheers. The audience clearly wanted more. The guys picked up their pumpkins and cued the DJ to begin the final song. Each lit a fuse, causing the pumpkin stems to sparkle.

When the curtain rose, the guys strutted on the stage to the opening notes of "You Dropped a Bomb on Me". The crowd roared at the sight of the sparkling pumpkins, not noticing the hoses attached to the bottom or the evil carved faces as they sat them down at the foot of the stage.

The guys resumed their positions dancing while

JC took the mic to lip sync again. Nobody noticed Stenson dance off stage mid-song to open the valves of the Nitrous oxide canisters. They had it timed so they would exit within two minutes before gas filled the room.

Stenson returned to take a bow with Brick and Big Tony. They danced off stage and ran out the back door as planned. Once outside, they celebrated their success. This was one of the easiest and funniest tricks they had ever played. A few minutes later, they realized JC had not left the building.

JC reveled in the adulation from the audience. He kept saying, "We love you New Orleans. You are the best. We will see you soon. You are amazing. I wish I could take you home with us. You are great. This is pretty funny. You are pretty funny. The world is funny, don't you think?"

By this time, JC was overcome with the intoxicating gas as much as the audience who were euphoric. Gangsters were laughing with JC and offering to buy him drinks. Five minutes later, everyone was unconscious.

Brick looked at his watch. "Let's round them up."

They donned gas masks and returned to the building where they had no trouble locating Donny Oh. He was slumped in a chair with JC passed out in his lap. It looked as if they fell unconscious before the drinks arrived.

"I am taking a photo of this," Brick told them as he pulled out his cell phone and snapped a shot.

"JC, with his face in this guy's lap is priceless!" he exclaimed.

Stenson and Big Tony lifted both men and hauled them out of the back door of the club and into Robert's van. Meanwhile, Brick went around the room confiscating gangster toys while his biker friends carted off the other gang members into a semi-tractor trailer parked outside.

They laughed as they drove away. Robert said, "I owe JC an apology. That was the funniest way we've ever kidnapped people."

Chapter 23

Donny Oh and Justin Carter were in a hazy state of mind after they regained consciousness in the back of Robert's van. Unaware of their surroundings or what had transpired, they looked at each other with the feeling you get when you are certain you've met someone before but do not remember where.

"Hey, you are singer," Donny Oh said in broken English with a heavy Chinese accent when he recognized JC.

"You dance good. Other guys bad. You should replace them in band. Fat guy dance ok, but other two terrible. Especially tattoo guy with ugly motorcycle. Tell him Kawasaki is better," the inebriated gangster critiqued.

Brick looked over his shoulder ready to jump into the back of the van and whip Donny Oh if he said one more word about his motorcycle or his dance moves that were acceptable enough to kidnap his high-as-a-kite ass.

"I like your suit," Donny told JC. "Where can I get one?"

"I'll ask the guys we borrowed them from," Justin replied, still as delirious as Donny Oh from the laughing gas.

"Want to try on my hat?" JC offered the gangster.

"Would you two shut up?" Brick shouted from the front seat. "I'm tired of listening to your craziness!"

"Hey, it's ugly guy from band," Donny Oh

exclaimed when he recognized Robert Brickhouse, "You should take dance lessons from him. He is great dancer. You suck."

Brick slammed on the brakes and jumped from the van. He stormed to the rear, flung open the doors, and climbed inside. He tore a piece of duct tape from a roll he found on the floor and placed it over Donny's mouth. Then he ripped another strip and covered JCs yapping trap as well.

When Robert returned to the driver's seat, the annoyed marine told Stenson, "I should have done that sooner."

They arrived at South Shore Harbor half an hour later. The laughing gas had worn off and Donny Oh's joyous mood had become more concerning after he realized the predicament he was in.

Brick parked near the pier where JC's shrimp boat, the "Wicked Witch" named after Zabrina, was docked. He and Stenson muscled the gangster out of the van and up the ramp while JC and Big Tony hauled their gear to the boat.

Brick secured Danny Oh's hands above his head attached to the port-side fishing net boom. He started the winch lifting Donny Oh until his tiptoes barely touched the deck. Robert patted the gangster on his cheek and told him to enjoy the ride.

He yelled to JC who was on the bridge, "Yo! Dancing Machine, take this rust bucket out to sea!"

JC fired up the diesel engines and slowly backed the aging vessel away from the dock. They headed into the pitch black darkness of the Gulf of Mexico.

"I need a beer," Robert told the guys as he headed below.

"Get one for me," JC hollered to the big marine.

Robert replied, "You've had enough intoxicants for one night, JC. So shut up and drive the boat and try not to run into anything."

"We are in the middle of the Gulf of Mexico. What could I possibly hit?" JC asked.

"How about that oil rig straight ahead if you don't turn this shipwreck starboard," Brick replied.

"Which way is starboard? There are a million stars out here." Justin replied.

Robert shook his head. "Turn right, moron!"

The guys returned an hour later ready to interrogate Donny Oh. The stress position Robert left him in was a technique he learned from his time interrogating prisoners in the corps. While persuasive, this was not all Brick had in mind for the gangster. He lowered the rigging to allow the Donny's feet to touch the deck and arms fall to his side. He ripped the tape from Oh's mouth and impolitely asked, "Are you ready to talk?"

"Who are you?" Donny Oh wondered now that the fog had cleared his terrified mind.

"I'm the lunatic that will make your life hell if you don't tell me what I want to know. So let's skip the introductions and get to the point. Where is Kenny Wu?"

"I don't know who you are talking about," Oh replied.

"Wrong answer," Brick said as he pressed a button, lifting the man's arms over his head higher than before.

"Let's try this again. Where is Kenny Wu?" Brick demanded.

Donny realized from the look on Robert's face this would not go well if he did not tell the madman what he wanted to know.

"Wu skipped town after he put some girl on a cargo ship," Donny Oh revealed.

JC asked with a sense of concern, "What girl?"

"I don't know. Some Asian chick. Kenny left after they loaded her and we haven't heard from him since."

"How did he leave town?" Robert interrogated.

"How do I know? Do I look like a travel agent?" Donny defiantly replied.

"Wrong answer again," Brick said as he winched Donny higher into the air.

"Okay, okay! Let me down!" Oh pleaded.

"Kenny took a car to the airport. That's all I know. I swear!"

Brick lowered the man down then asked, "Who were the hitmen who killed my friend's child?"

"It wasn't us. We answer to David Pham. He must have ordered the hit," Donny presumed.

"Pham is dead and we know it wasn't Kenny. So who else could it be?" Robert pressed.

"I don't know, and if I did, I wouldn't tell you because I would be a dead man. Kenny Wu doesn't mess around," the gangster replied.

"I don't mess around either," Robert said as he pressed the button and held it down as the Donny Oh raised ten feet off the deck.

"You must like pain," Robert told the man.

"You are going to end up dead if you don't tell us what we need to know. We are your only hope for survival," the marine admitted.

"Okay, I will tell you if you let me down," Donny pleaded. Brick waited a few moments before he lowered him back down to the deck.

"There is a hit man Wu has used before. His name is Lei Min, a real killer. But don't ask me where to find him. I have never met the guy, just heard the name."

"Do you want to live?" Brick asked.

"Yes," Donny Oh sheepishly replied.

"Can you swim?" Brick questioned.

"No," Donny said as he worried what was next.

"Stenson, give the man a life jacket," Robert

instructed.

Stenson placed a life jacket over the Oh's head and pulled the Velcro straps tightly around his chest. Robert hit the switch winching Danny Oh to the top of the boom high into the air. While Donny screamed, Robert pulled a lever, swinging the arm 90 degrees over the side of the boat. Danny Oh panicked as he dangled over the black water.

"Wait! What are you doing?" the gangster screamed.

"I am taking out the trash and letting you live unless the sharks are hungry for a snack tonight."

Robert warned him, "If we ever see you in New Orleans again, we may not be as generous next time."

"My guys will get you! You are all dead!" Donny Oh vowed.

"I don't think so," Brick said with a sinister grin before pressing the switch dropping Donny Oh into the ocean with a mighty splash.

"Don't worry, Donny," Brick yelled over the side of the boat. "The current is in your favor. You should be in Mexico in a few days."

Robert turned around and yelled up to JC. "Take us home, Dancing Machine. Our work here is done!"

Danny Oh bobbed up and down like a cork helplessly watching the boat lights fade over the horizon. His terror had only begun when something under the water bumped his leg.

Back at Stenson's House, Luna found the guys drinking coffee at the kitchen table when she wheeled in at 6 am. She was amused to see them wearing costumes from the night before.

"Did you boys have fun at your little dance party last night?" Luna slyly asked.

Stenson replied, "JC has a new career in a cover band, but the rest of us need different jobs."

"Yeah, the gangsters were not impressed with

Robert's dance moves," JC remarked.

"My dance moves may not be good, but my taste in motorcycles and interrogation skills are priceless," Robert bragged to the chuckles from the other guys who were there.

Stenson shared how they captured Donny Oh and left him in the ocean. When she asked about the rest of Donny's crew, Robert explained.

"I doubt we will hear from them again," he said while taking a sip of his coffee. "The Mexican cartel was extremely interested in meeting those guys after my biker friends dropped off a truck load filled with them."

It never ceased to amaze Luna at the creative ways these guys got things done. Loading the people who attended the show at The Happy Monkey into a tractor trailer and driving them to the Mexico border was Robert's twisted idea. He had contacted a Mexican gang who they dealt with years ago after he found out they had been muscled out of New Orleans by the Chinese gang. Rounding them up and dropping them off to their Mexican enemies was a fitting way to ensure the gang stayed out of their way while they searched for Zabrina.

"We have a new name for someone to find," Stenson told his wife.

"Who?" she asked.

"Well, if Donny Oh was telling the truth, his name is Lei Min. He's a hitman Kenny Wu has used before and could be involved in the death of our son. But finding him may be more difficult than finding Wu."

"Sounds like it might be a job for the Mystery Man," Luna suggested.

Stenson and Robert glanced at each other when they heard that name.

Stenson said, "You may be right. We'll have to put the word on the street. It's not like we can pick up the phone and call him."

"That dude freaks me out," Robert admitted.

The Mystery Man spooked Stenson and Robert every time they had encountered him in the past. The hooded character was a phantom who could sneak in and out of places without ever knowing he was there. If anybody could find a hitman, it was the Mystery Man.

The guys went home to get some rest while Stenson and Luna discussed the eventful evening. Capturing the bulk of the gang was a last-minute idea. And while Stenson knew they did not round up everyone, it was 20 fewer flies in the soup. He placed a bag on the kitchen table containing identifications of everyone they found at the social club. Maybe it would help Luna connect some dots leading to Kenny Wu.

Luna dove into her research after Stenson went to bed. While the identifications provided a treasure trove of leads, she would save them for later. Finding Wu would not bring their child back or help her walk again. But now that she knew Zabrina had been placed on a cargo ship, her priority now was saving her life.

She searched for cargo ships affiliated with Wu's Silkroad logistics company departing New Orleans within the past two weeks. One vessel named "Precious Cargo" was destined for Asia. If Zabrina was on that ship, it would not be easy to find her. Unless she was stowed in crew quarters, it would be like searching for a needle in the proverbial haystack; the ship held 24,000 containers.

Luna turned her attention to private flights leaving New Orleans around the same time as the ship. It was not clear who chartered the flights. Celebrities, executives, and wealthy people didn't advertise their movements. All she had to go on were the flight logs she uncovered and aircraft destinations. Like Stenson, she assumed Wu fled the country. The publicity from recent events would have made Kenny easy to find; especially with resources like the FBI or Luna LeRoux-Beckett.

Fourteen private flights departed New Orleans in a two-day window destined for other countries. None went directly to Asia, except for that of a high-profile tech tycoon. The others transited to typical vacation spots in the Caribbean, Central or South America, London, Paris, and Hawaii.

Like throwing darts with a blindfold on, she tried to get into Kenny Wu's head. Hawaii seemed out of the question because it was still part of the United States and within reach of federal authorities. The others destinations, she could not be sure of. Would he go to Europe and transition to somewhere else? Anything was possible, she told herself. She doubted he would travel to Central or South America, since he did not appear to have any dealings there that she could find. After learning of Kenny's unwelcome relationship with the Mexicans, she doubted the coward had a death wish to hide there. The Caribbean stood out. It was close enough to the U.S. yet out of reach of federal agencies. She also knew from several shell companies she located that Kenny Wu had businesses there.

There were five flights to the Caribbean. One contained a passenger list with names which appeared to be a family. Unless the bachelor hid himself disguised as a husband with a wife and kids whose last name was Sepinaccio, she doubted it was his flight. Luna did not believe Kenny Wu was that creative.

The only information she gleaned from the four other flights were the counts of the passengers and crew. She jotted down tail numbers of the aircraft and the charter companies who owned them. If they wanted to find out more, it would require feet on the ground.

She looked at the stacks of identification collected from the social club. With so many to track, Luna enlisted reporter Erin Collins' help. Maybe she would turn up something for the story she was working on about Kenny Wu.

Fallon O'Malley, the former owner of O'Malley's Pub, visited that afternoon. It was a welcome distraction from the chaos to see an old friend. He'd brought Stenson a check he received from the insurance company for the fire that destroyed the bar.

"One-point-two-million?" Stenson repeated after reading the number.

"I forgot the insurance for the building was still in my name. You planning to rebuild?" Fallon asked Stenson.

"To be honest, Fallon. I don't know what I am going to do. My wife is a paraplegic, my child is dead, and I'm up to my ears in gangsters. We do not know where the guy, Kenny Wu, who we suspect is behind the bar fire and the attack on my family is hiding. We found out last night our friend Zabrina Chao is apparently on a cargo ship headed for Asia. Now we've discovered the name of a hitman Wu may have hired to take out me and my family."

"Wow, Stenson. Why don't you use the money to help you get by until then? The bar is the last thing you should worry about right now," Fallon suggested.

"It's your money, Fallon. I am sorry about your pub," he replied.

"Nonsense, Stenson. That was your pub they burned to the ground." Fallon insisted. "I have money set aside. The missus and I will be fine. You need that money more than me right now."

Seeing the humility in Stenson's eyes when he took the check touched the Irishman's heart. Luna gave him a warm smile of gratitude that said more than words.

"Is there anything else I can do to help you two?" Fallon asked the couple.

"Pray for us," Stenson humbly replied.

With a reassuring pat on Stenson's shoulder, Fallon said. "Always, my boy. Always."

Chapter 24

St. Louis Cemetery No. 1 was eerie during the day and spookier at 2:00 am. With above ground burials and monuments dating back to 1789, you felt the spirits walk among you. One tomb was believed to be the final resting place of Marie Laveau, a powerful voodoo princess who lived in New Orleans in the 19th century. It was here that Stenson and Robert waited for a different ghoul.

No matter how many times they had encountered the apparition in the past, the visits always made them feel uneasy. The phantom accomplished feats that seemed impossible or unexplained. No one knew who he, she, or it was, hence the epithet Mystery Man. One thing was certain: Stenson and Brick were glad the ghost was on their side.

The arrivals were always mysterious. Would the boogie man walk through a wall, float from a tomb, or vaporize from the moonless sky in the wee hours of this spooky night? They never knew. It was always a surprise.

Brick felt a tap on his shoulder causing the big fellow to jump and blurt, "Whoa!"

Stenson and Brick peered over their shoulders. Dressed in black from head to toe and wearing a hoodie with shadows hiding his face, stood the infamous Mystery Man.

The phantom did not say a word. He simply placed a folded piece of paper in Stenson's hand.

When they looked up, the ghost had vanished. Stenson opened the note and read it aloud.

```
Follow the money.
Follow betrayal.
Follow true love.
I will follow death.
```

The guys weren't sure what to make of the ominous message. They shared it with Luna when they returned to Stenson's place.

"The Mystery Man isn't much for words, but when he speaks, it says volumes," Luna remarked.

"What do you make of it?" Stenson asked.

"I think it means if we follow the money it will lead us to Kenny Wu. Follow betrayal probably means we should look into the connection between Kenny and his father," his genius wife guessed.

"What about following true love?" Robert asked her.

Luna smiled. "I believe it means we need to help JC find Zabrina."

"And the last part of the message... I will follow death?"

"I think it means the Mystery Man will find our son's killer," Luna said with a look of chagrin.

"I was afraid of that," Stenson replied. "The Mystery Man intends to go after Lei Min alone."

Robert said, "If anyone can find a hitman, it would be the Mystery Man. We don't know where to begin."

Stenson seemed concerned.

"I don't have a good feeling about this, Robert."

"Oh, and you have a good feeling about us finding this Wu character, his infamous father who is worse than him, and boarding a cargo ship already at sea to rescue Zabrina while we don't get killed in the process?" Brick asked him sarcastically.

"Basically, yes," Stenson replied at the absurd observation.

Luna interjected. "Speaking of ships, I located a cargo vessel Zabrina may be on. A ship named Precious Cargo left New Orleans two weeks ago. The final destination is Hong Kong where it is scheduled to arrive in 34 days. According to a tracking website, it traveled through the Panama Canal and is making its way across the Pacific Ocean now. The next stop is Seoul, South Korea, in two weeks."

Brick looked at Stenson hoping he wasn't thinking of landing a helicopter on a cargo ship or some other crazy idea. Actually, Stenson had thought of that and already put it out of his mind; not because he couldn't get a helicopter, but because he was certain there must be a simpler way to board a cargo ship.

Luna informed them. "Coincidentally, Hong Kong is the home of Sun Fang International and Wu Kong, Kenny's father."

"Have you had any luck locating Kenny?" Stenson asked.

"It is coming together in drips and drabs," Luna replied. "I've narrowed down four private flights to the Caribbean. There are others that flew to Europe and elsewhere, but the Bahamas made more sense to me. I uncovered some of his shell companies that are based there."

"You mean to tell me he is enjoying life on a beach while we are hanging out with ghosts in a cemetery?" Brick humorously wondered.

Luna laughed. "I can't be sure. It's only a guess based on all the flights out of New Orleans that night. It will take feet on the ground to verify if he is there. Do you guys need a vacation?"

Robert replied enthusiastically. "I will start

packing now!"

Stenson was more uncertain. Considering his wife's recovery and rehabilitation, he didn't want to leave her alone after what happened before. However, Luna insisted she was in excellent hands with the private nurse and physical therapist Stenson had hired. It would give her more time to find the missing pieces to this puzzle with them out of her hair. Besides, Stenson had waited on her hand and foot since the tragedy. It would be good for him to get away for a while.

Stenson hesitantly agreed to go. They left Luna to work her magic while they met with JC and Big Tony to let them in on their plan.

Even though this was considered a surveillance mission, the guys would not miss a chance to grab Kenny Wu if they had the chance. They still had a stash of Sarge's weapons prior to the phony meeting with Kenny Wu and might have a chance to use them this time.

While they were away, Luna received a call from the reporter, Erin Collins. She had located two women who were smuggled to the United States by a Chinese gang on a cargo ship from Asia. Like Zabrina Chao, the women were forced into prostitution after they arrived. Erin learned the shipping company handling the cargo was Silkroad owned by Kenny Wu. The women were prepared to go public with the accusations and agreed to appear in her investigative report provided their identities remained anonymous.

While it was no smoking gun, Erin's editor would allow the investigation to air. The recent arson of Wu's offices in New Orleans, a smuggling operation with foreign gang links, prostitution, and a missing owner were enough to raise suspicious questions that only Kenny Wu could answer.

That should rattle his cage, Luna thought. Now it was time to flush Kenny out of his hiding hole. Luna played a hunch and arranged a chartered flight to the Bahamas. Meanwhile, she turned her attention to Kenny Wu's finances, which was no simple task. Luna was not an accountant, but she was an expert at digital forensics in her role as an I.T. security analyst. She knew the dark corners of the web to search where the bad guys like to hide.

It was common practice for companies to use offshore bank accounts to avoid paying taxes. In Kenny's case, it was the preferred method of concealing income from his nefarious activities. To complicate matters further, Kenny converted most of his ill-gotten gains into cryptocurrency.

Essentially, the funds were moved into anonymous black holes making them even more difficult to track. Luna knew a little about Crypto and while the technology behind it had real-world applications; she believed its viability as a currency was fraught risk and bad actors. There was nothing supporting digital currency except the last person who dumped money in. Without oversight or protections for investors, Luna considered it a Ponzi scheme. At some point, the house of cards would come tumbling down.

As Luna pieced together Kenny's financial pie, it made sense to her how he became so wealthy. It wasn't because of his transportation company, Silkroad, or even his criminal enterprises. Those simply funded his other endeavors into crypto. She realized Kenny was an early adopter of the technology from interviews he had done in the past, promoting it as a revolutionary shift in the financial system. It was a public relations spin to get others to invest. In Luna's mind, it was a traditional pump-and-dump scheme that's been around forever. She wondered why others did not see things as plainly as she did?

One thing soon became clear; Kenny Wu was a prolific gambler. He bet early and often on new cryptocurrency and realized amazing profits. Like pump-and-dump or a Ponzi scheme, it's always the early investors who make money. Maybe she could use that crack in his psyche to her advantage. The reason casinos were so profitable is the gullibility of their customers. Everyone believes they will be a winner and even when they occasionally win, the euphoria makes them believe they can run the table. Most times, they play until they lose it all. In the end, it is the house that always wins.

Cryptocurrency presented additional challenges. One of its selling points was the owner of the currency remained anonymous and it was why criminals liked it so much. To the public, that much was true. Individuals were known simply by a mathematically generated identifier. But exchanges where real money became cryptocurrency knew where the trail began. That was where Luna needed to be if she was to uncover Kenny Wu's digital wallets.

She recalled a friend from college created his own crypto currency exchange as a proof-of-concept for his post-doctorate degree. She wondered if it would be possible to use his technology to create a "honey pot"? The "Honey Pot" concept was quite simple. Spy agencies used it all the time. They set up fake websites on the "dark web" to advertise things like drugs, weapons, credit cards, or pornography. Unsuspecting customers would purchase from law enforcement posing as the criminal. The idea was the same as an individual purchasing something illegal from an undercover cop on the street.

She reached out to Tommy Tucker to see if he still had his crypto platform running. When she explained she was trying to catch the guy who murdered her child and left her paralyzed, Tommy Tucker was all in.

Her idea was to create an exchange with a new coin that promised high returns. She would create a buzz and marketing hype on channels she expected Kenny to watch in the crypto world. Maybe it would lure him into purchasing tokens on the new platform with the proposition of getting rich quick.

Tommy loved the idea for the name of the new coin. They would call it "LSAdavantage".

Luna said, "It stands for Luna-Stenson Advantage. You don't think it was too obvious for Kenny Wu to figure out?" she asked.

"Not if he is as dumb as you think, Luna. Maybe you should have gone into psychology," Tommy Tucker joked.

It was a simple yet ingenious plan. They had a head start using Tommy's PhD project with previously minted coins. In a few hours, Luna created a website and enough hype to offer LSAdvantage coins. Customers were feeding like sharks trying to get in early on the new coin. If this wasn't a trap to capture Kenny Wu, Tommy and Luna would be millionaires overnight.

Tommy altered the exchange to capture meta-data such as IP addresses and location information, and link it back to new registrations that provided more personally identifiable information, including bank accounts and other crypto wallets a person used. This was the holy grail for Luna to help her identify Wu if he should fall into their trap.

If Kenny Wu caught wind of this exchange and began investing, Tommy would use Kenny's coins to purchase more. This, along with other investor contributions, would cause the value to rise quickly. And like a gambler, Luna bet Kenny would not walk away and continue to invest.

Since the terms dictated funds could not be accessed for 90 days, there would be no way for Kenny to retrieve his investment. By the time they shut down the exchange, they should have uncovered many of the hiding places where Kenny stashed his money.

To protect other investors who got caught up in this ruse, Tommy and Luna would return their funds leaving Kenny the only one holding an empty bag. The brilliance of the plan is Kenny's greed exposed his secrets he thought no one could find while bankrupting himself. It was perfect.

Chapter 25
Nassau, Bahamas

Kenny Wu took a long, satisfying sip of pina colada from his cozy spot beneath a breezy palm tree at his home on Paradise Island. He surfed his laptop rather than a surfboard as the turquoise waves licked the beach. Surfing like this was much more profitable and less likely to cause him bodily harm. The only drowning he intended to do was in a sea of cash.

Watching his crypto empire grow gave Kenny a bigger rush than any giant wave. What a life he enjoyed now; nice weather, Zabrina Chao, and her meddlesome friends were out of the way. Authorities could not find him. Even if they did, he was out of their jurisdictive reach. The media and his father were radio silent. He had enough money to never work another day. Life was good.

Crypto was the easiest way to make money. He knew it was a perfectly legal Ponzi scheme. As an early adopter, Kenny Wu admired his own genius. Like other young tycoons, he would be a billionaire before he was 30 years old if he played his cards right; half the age of his father when he reached that symbolic height.

His assets were scattered around the globe and difficult to track. It was a shell game to stay ahead of authorities, since much of his wealth was earned through illegal means. But it would not be long until he turned his cryptocurrency into cold, hard cash. Just a few more plays adding more coins to the coffers and he would be untouchable even by the infamous Sun Fang.

His dad. That old-world traditionalist did not know how to operate in the new world he would soon conquer. The ancient man knew nothing of technology and did things the hard way. Sure, he had been a gangster when he was younger, growing up poor in communist China, with few opportunities to rise.

He gave the old man credit. He toiled and built an empire of legitimate companies, one brick at a time. But few people knew where it all began with Sun Fang. Those founding bricks were started with rackets no different from his own.

His father talked about providing him with a better life than he had growing up. It's why he'd sent him to expensive private schools and an Ivy league university. But Sun Fang didn't care about him or his mother. He was simply an asset his father could use in the United States. That's why he had abandoned them there so many years ago. Kenny didn't even know the man until a few years ago. And despite his father setting him up in business with Silkroad, he did not want, need, or appreciate Sun Fang meddling in his charmed life now.

Kenny Wu was his own man. Soon he would be more wealthy and powerful than his father. He used people and then discarded them when they fulfilled their purpose or became an obstacle. And if anyone thought he lost sleep over killing David Pham or that infant child of Stenson Beckett, they were seriously mistaken. Emotions like empathy or sympathy were for the weak. The only love he had was for himself, and he had no problem admitting that simple fact.

Kenny continued surfing the usual boards, looking for new crypto opportunities. His philosophy was to buy low and sell high. That was how he had gained so much wealth in such a short amount of time. A new currency caught his eye. It claimed to be a patented blockchain pegged to the U.S. Dollar with guaranteed returns. LSAdvantage looked like a prime target to invest. Why not throw a few darts at the proverbial dart board and see where they might land? He could handle a financial hit if things don't turn out well. But if this gamble paid off, he could make a fortune like he had done many times before.

Kenny sipped his drink and signed up for a new LSAdvantage account. He used one coin from another digital currency valued at $32,000 to purchase 10,000 LSAdvantage coins at $3.20 each. If his strategy was successful, the investment could be worth millions after the 90-day lock-out window when he could withdraw the funds.

* * *

The foursome of Stenson, Brick, JC, and Big Tony flew from New Orleans to the home of powdery beaches, bikinis and rum. The plane landed at the same Nassau, Bahamas airport they believed Kenny Wu had arrived 10 days ago.

It was a wild goose chase since Kenny could have traveled to any place in the world. But Luna had great instincts. They were grateful the search began in the Bahamas instead of somewhere less hospitable and cold like Antarctica.

Upon their arrival, the team spread out across the airport. Each carried a photo of Kenny Wu and began asking baggage handlers, maintenance workers, and employees at the private terminal if they had seen the man. It became apparent either nobody knew anything or were unwilling to talk even for cash.

When they regrouped two hours later, Brick looked around and asked where was JC? Big Tony told him he wandered off when he was speaking with a member of the ground crew who fueled the planes.

Brick was annoyed. "We've been here two hours and already lost JC. He's like a little kid. We should have put a leash on him."

Robert's annoyance was only made worse by the heat of the tropical sun beating down on the black tarmac. "Let's find him before I bake to death or get a suntan as dark as JC."

They spotted him sitting outside a café 20 minutes later. He was having a lively conversation with a Bahamian man and did not notice when the group walked up. Robert cleared his throat to get Justin's attention.

JC looked up and said, "Hey everyone, this is my friend John Hilton."

"I didn't know you had friends in the Bahamas, JC," Brick said in a perturbed tone.

"Oh, we just met," JC cheerfully admitted.

Justin introduced everyone. "John, this is Robert. That's Stenson, and the big guy is Big Tony Gallo,"

"Which is the guy who is dumb as a brick?" John Hilton asked JC.

Justin choked on his drink. "No, his nickname is Brick."

"That's not what you said a minute ago," John clarified.

Big Tony and Stenson tried their best to contain their laughter while Robert grew hotter by the second, and it wasn't because of tarmac heat. Stenson attempted to diffuse the microwavable situation.

"JC, we should go. We are hitting dead ends here."

"Grab a seat," JC suggested.

"Robert looks like he could use a drink."

The men sat down with Brick nearest to JC in case he didn't like his drink or felt the need to toss the social butterfly into traffic if he had one more dumb thing to say.

JC told the guys, "John recalled a plane landed here 10 days ago. He recognized the photo and believes a passenger may have been Kenny Wu."

"Any idea where he went?" Stenson questioned.

"No, but the driver might," John replied. He removed a business card from his wallet and handed it to Stenson.

"Here's her card. She drives for many of the wealthy visitors to the island. By the way, JC told me about your son. I am sorry for your loss."

"Thank you, John. You've been a big help. Can I offer you something?" Stenson asked, reaching into his pocket for cash.

"No. JC bought me a few drinks. That's good enough." John reassured.

Robert mumbled as they walked away, "Unbelievable. We sweat for two hours and JC gets information for the price of a couple of drinks?"

Stenson chuckled. "See why I told you not to kill him?"

Robert handed JC his phone. "Since you are on a roll, call the driver."

A black SUV arrived at the airport 15 minutes later. The men were stunned when Sylvia Sumner, a statuesque woman of African descent, stepped out of the vehicle wearing a white blouse, black skirt, and smart-looking chauffer cap with matching black high heels.

"Mr. Carter?" she asked the group.

Justin enthusiastically extended his hand.

"You can call me JC."

"You can call him idiot," Brick said under his breath.

"May I get your bags?" Ms. Sumner asked the group.

"No, I will let my boy Mr. Brickhouse get them," JC replied.

Robert elbowed Stenson. "Did he just call me his boy?"

Stenson laughed, then told Sylvia, "We will get them Ms. Sumner. It is a heavy load."

Actually, they did not want Sylvia handling duffle bags filled with illegal weapons. Brick was still fuming when they went to retrieve the bags.

He told Stenson, "I hope these are loaded. I am going to shoot JC in five minutes if he doesn't shut up."

When they returned, Justin was seated in the front seat of the SUV, chatting with Silvia like they were old friends. The sight of JC with an attractive woman while he was relegated to the role of sweaty bellhop did not improve Robert's mood.

Inside the SUV, JC told the guys Sylvia also recognized Kenny Wu from the photograph. She said she had driven him to an isolated estate at the end of the island. What she found unusual was how heavily guarded it was. Sylvia assumed the visitor was an important figure and asked no questions.

Sylvia said the only way to access the estate was from a two-lane road, boat, or helicopter. Stenson joked they left their helicopter at home. The reality was they could not drive to the estate in an SUV loaded with weapons acting like they were lost and asking for directions. Although the thought crossed their minds. They needed a better plan and since this was technically a "vacation", Stenson asked Silvia to drop them off at the resort hotel instead.

JC palmed a wad of cash into Silvia's hand when they arrived and thanked her for the ride and information. She asked him to call her later if he wanted to get together for drinks.

Overhearing Sylvia's offer, Robert interrupted.

"I am sorry. Our friend will be dead later."

"Excuse me?" she asked.

"I mean Justin will be dead tired later. He's had a long day and needs his beauty sleep... a lot of beauty sleep," Robert clarified.

"Speak for yourself old man," JC quipped. He gestured with his hand to his mouth like he was holding a phone, telling Sylvia he would call her later.

After the guys checked into the resort and checked into their rooms, they returned to the pool area to plan surveillance of the estate where Kenny Wu was suspected to be hiding. Brick did a double-take when JC joined them.

"Did you forget your pants?" Robert flabbergasted.

JC lifted his Bob Marley t-shirt to show him his attire.

"I am wearing a bathing suit," JC said.

Robert was horrified when he saw the neon blue bikini bathing attire.

"That's not a bathing suit. It's a banana hammock!" Brick exclaimed.

"You are out of touch with the latest fashion old man. Look at your tired shorts. This is the new hotness," Justin confidently educated the big marine.

"No, that is an idiot wearing a thong. Put on some real pants or you are not sitting with us," Brick demanded.

Two women walked by and said hello to JC. Robert shook his head in disbelief. "How did you meet them?"

"We rode down the elevator together. They said I have nice legs," JC bragged.

"Whatever," Robert barked. "Sit away from me and keep your legs closed. I don't need to see your junk."

After Robert and JC worked out their seating

arrangements, the team looked at a map of the island Stenson had displayed on his tablet. They realized the most covert way to reach the home would be by water. It was a brief ride from one end of the island to the other. But a trip like this would have to wait until after dark. With several hours before nightfall, Robert and Big Tony set out to secure a boat while Stenson went upstairs to chat with his wife. JC planned to invite Sylvia over for drinks and a trip to the casino.

* * *

Kenny was three sheets into the wind by late afternoon. Alcohol wasn't his only intoxicant. He was high from watching his wealth rise at a record pace after purchasing LSAdvantage crypto-currency. The new coin was red hot, and it was moving fast. Other investors must have caught on and were buying in a frenzy. Kenny worried if he didn't go all in now he would lose his advantage as an early adopter, a technique that rewarded him handsomely in the past.

Throughout the day, he continued to move coins from other digital wallets to increase his stake in LSAdvantage to the tune of $2.5 million. On paper, it seemed like a lot of money, but it was air as far as he was concerned. He likened it to picking up his chips from one casino table and moving to hotter one. Without risk, there could be no reward. It was the reason he was so rich and even richer in 90 days when he could cash out. He had always been a winner and had every intention of running the table with this new coin.

Call it over-stimulation or exhaustion that left Kenny bored of sitting around the house. It was time to hit up the casino and win some actual cash. What was the point of being rich if you could not enjoy the spoils? He grabbed a set of keys to a white Lamborghini and told his henchman stay behind. He was tired of the babysitters and wanted to go alone.

* * *

JC sported a crème colored jacket and matching slacks with a white open collar shirt and tan loafers when he met Sylvia Sumner at the hotel bar. She was stunning in a coral blue dress which fell just above the knee with matching heels that highlighted her long, taut legs.

"You look nice," Sylvia complimented Justin.

"You too, Miss Sylvia," JC cooly replied with a Southern gentleman's twist.

They sat a table in the rear of the bar with overstuffed chairs where they ordered drinks. The conversation was light-hearted and friendly, as if they'd known each other for years. Sylvia liked Justin. He was down-to-earth and funny; a big kid with a sweet heart. He wasn't like other men who ogled her or tried to impress her with their wealth. JC was simply a nice guy with a genuine smile and mischevious twinkle in his eyes that told her he knew how to have fun.

She shared stories of moving from Haiti to the Bahamas when she was a child; how she felt nerdy because she loved books and the arts; of how people could never get past her looks and appreciate her for who she was as person, something she valued more.

JC told her of his tough upbringing and stories of his life; how he had started an amazing business with friends and lost it all because they betrayed Stenson Beckett and Robert Brickhouse. They had become friends since then. At least Stenson was a good friend. The verdict was still out if the crazy tattooed marine would ever forgive him. He told

Sylvia about the kidnapping of his business partner, Zabrina Chao, and the tragedy that led them to the Bahamas now.

Something caught Sylvia's attention when JC spoke of Zabrina. "I wish someone cared about me like you care for her."

"I am sure many people care for you, Sylvia," JC reassured her.

"Not really, JC. Most people want something from me. But few care for me on the level you care for Zabrina. Anything romantic between you two?" she wondered.

"No way!" JC exasperated. "I can't stand the woman. I just want to find her because she owes me money."

"Come on, JC. I am a smart woman. I think you like her more than you are leading me to believe," she challenged him.

"Let's change the subject and hit the casino," JC suggested, eager to move on from the awkward conversation.

It was JC's first time in a casino, but he didn't tell that to Sylvia. Instead, he acted as if he was a savvy gambler. But when they went to the slot machines, Sylvia noticed JC watching others to see how it was done. Not wanting to embarrass him, she offered to go first so JC could watch her and maintain his coolness, which she found cute.

There was a commotion coming from a nearby craps table. It sounded like somebody was winning big. The pair walked over to check it out. A high roller immediately noticed Sylvia in her low-cut dress and shapely legs. The man called her over and asked her to blow on his dice for good luck.

Sylvia smiled at JC, then obliged with a puff on the dice. Justin was in shock. Not at Sylvia blowing on the dice, but whose dice she blew. Standing 10 feet across the table from him was Kenny Wu. There was no mistaking the face of that Asian gangster burned into his mind. He remembered clearly those evil eyes and wicked thin smile from the night they shot Big Tony, beat him up, and stole their money.

JC knew he must react fast. With Brick and Big Tony away and no time to locate Stenson, Justin knew this was his chance to grab the man who caused such irreparable harm. When Sylvia returned to his side, JC whisked her away.

He exclaimed in a hushed voice, "That's him! That is the guy we've been looking for!"

Sylvia glanced over her shoulder and confirmed it was indeed the man she had driven from the airport to the compound at the end of the island.

"What are you going to do?" Sylvia asked JC, seeing the wild look in his eyes.

"I need your help. Sylvia. I don't care what it costs." JC said. "Use your charm to woo the guy back to my room. Tell him it's your room and you want to invite him for a drink. When you arrive, I will be waiting. Nothing will happen to you. I promise."

"If it will help you get your girl back," Sylvia said.

"You mean get my money back?" JC lied.

Sylvia winked coyly. "Whatever you say, JC."

She sauntered back to the craps table holding a glass of wine. It did not take long for Wu to notice her again. JC would have liked to watch Sylvia work her magic. Instead, he made a hasty retreat upstairs to prepare for a surprise Kenny Wu would never forget.

The room was dark when JC heard the click of the hotel card release the lock. He gripped the handle of his Glock 9mm and waited in a chair hidden in the shadows. Before he knew what happened, Kenny Wu turned on the light and pointed his pistol at him while holding Sylvia around the waist.

"Hello, JC. Did you think I didn't recognize your black ass when you recognized me?" Wu taunted.

"I am sorry, JC," Sylvia exclaimed. "I didn't know what was going on until we got to the door. He said he was going to kill me if I didn't do as he said. He promised me he won't hurt you."

"No, I won't hurt you now, JC," Kenny assured.

"But I don't need her now that I've got you," Wu said.

Kenny lowered the pistol into Sylvia's back and fired. Sylvia Sumner crumpled to the floor.

JC screamed, "No! You are a madman!"

"You do not know how mad I am, Justin Carter. But you and your friends will soon find out how fiendishly sideways I can be. Drop the gun and let's go!" Kenny demanded as he waved his gun toward the door.

JC let his gun fall to the floor and walked past Kenny Wu. The gangster marched him to the end of the hallway and into a back stairwell where they took five flights down to an underground garage.

Stenson returned to the hotel after sightseeing around the island and picking up gifts for his wife. From the corner of his eye, he saw two men hustle through the parking lot. He did a double-take because one man looked like JC. It took a moment to register until he realized the man behind him was Kenny Wu! He watched in disbelief as Justin was forced into a white Lamborghini at gunpoint.

It happened so fast. With little time to react, he spotted member of the hotel staff drive up with a guest's car. Stenson ran over and grabbed the keys and said, "I'll take that!"

He jumped into the metallic blue Bugatti Veyron and threw it into gear, leaving the valet without a tip and very confused. Stenson tore out of the hotel driveway in pursuit of the Lamborghini. He speed dialed Robert Brickhouse.

"What's up?" Brick asked nonchalantly.

"I am in a stolen car chasing JC!" Stenson yelled over the phone.

"JC stole a car?" Brick repeated.

"No! I stole a car. I am following a white Lamborghini with JC in it and Kenny Wu is driving! He's heading for the bridge. I think he's trying to get to the airport!"

The call left Brick as confused as the valet. He asked, "Why is JC going to the airport with Wu?"

"Dude, Kenny kidnapped JC at gunpoint and I am chasing the car! Get to the bridge and cut him off! We cannot let him get to the airport with JC!"

"We're on it!" Brick said.

Stenson clicked the phone and yanked the car to the right. He barely missed another vehicle and a light pole as he weaved his way through traffic on the congested two-lane road, trying to catch up to the sports car.

Kenny Wu noticed a vehicle in the rearview mirror gaining on him. Then he recognized the face of the driver was Stenson Beckett. He punched the gas.

"What the hell? Where do you people come from?" Wu asked rhetorically.

JC looked over his shoulder and saw it was Stenson coming up fast in the Veyron. He smiled, then defiantly answered Wu's question.

"From your mama's house!"

"That makes no sense. My mother is dead," Kenny Wu said while trying to concentrate on the road.

"I bet your dead mama drives better than you do!" JC taunted the man after Wu crashed through a flower stand, causing people to scatter.

Stenson stayed tight on his tail. The Lamborghini hung a quick left as Stenson flew by. He yanked the emergency brake and spun the sports car 180 degrees in a J-turn. Stenson buried his foot into the accelerator and roared the car in an adrenaline pumping, heart thumping, gear thrashing, tire burning frantic pursuit.

The Lamborghini flew over a hill causing sparks to fly like the Fourth of July when it landed and crunched the pavement. Tourists dove for cover as the two sports cars sped by. They made another tire-squealing left and right turn as Kenny tried to lose Stenson Beckett. Up ahead was the Paradise Island bridge. Both men encouraged their cars to give it all they had. It was an all-out sprint for the next 1,500 hundred yards until they reached the end of the bridge.

Stenson laid into the Bugatti, like jockey in a championship race begging his horse for more. He pulled alongside the Lambo. The men glared at each other eye-to-eye as they sprinted toward the finish line. Kenny raised his pistol and fired through the passenger window, shattering glass across JC's face.

Stenson slammed the brakes enough to attempt a pit maneuver police use. He tapped the bumper of the Lamborghini causing it to go into a 360 degree spin. JC's terrified face whizzed by in slow motion as the Lamborghini launched airborne, tipping over end-to-end nose, tail, then nose again before sliding 150 yards and coming to a screeching halt remarkably on what was left of its mangled wheels.

Stenson screeched to a stop and jumped out of the Bugatti. He ran over to check on JC who was banged, bruised and bloodied but conscious. Kenny Wu was in worse shape. A white jeep roared up moments later with Brick and Big Tony.

"Get Wu!" Stenson yelled.

Robert and Anthony Gallo ran over and untangled Kenny Wu from the mangled wreck. They dragged him to the jeep and tossed him inside while Stenson assisted JC. In less than 90 seconds, the pit stop was over with the only casualties being two exotic sports cars... at least for now.

Chapter 26

Racing from the crash scene at break-neck speed through downtown Nassau, Robert Brickhouse cursed oncoming traffic who were flipping him off as he passed them by. Stenson calmly pointed out that he was driving on the wrong side of the road. The revelation cleared things up for the big marine, who thought he had rented a mail truck because the steering wheel was on the wrong side.

After jumping a median into the correct lane of traffic, the big marine screamed, "Have you lost your mind, JC?"

Justin was dazed from the movie-stunt-worthy somersault crash.

He replied quietly, "I was trying to capture Kenny Wu."

"I thought if I grabbed him, you would stop making fun of me and thinking I'm an idiot," JC justified.

Stenson glanced at Robert.

"JC, that was way too dangerous and you could have been killed!" Brick yelled, not out of anger but more out of brotherly concern.

"You wouldn't care if I was dead, Robert," Justin told him in a defeated tone as he stared at the floor.

Nobody had to tell Robert his teasing had gone too far.

"Look, JC, we love you. You get on my nerves most of the time. But never try a stunt like that again.

We are a team and we will always have your back."

This the first time Robert Brickhouse admitted he even liked JC, much less love him. Now he had let his true feelings show.

"Wu killed Sylvia." JC said quietly.

He reached into his pocket and handed Stenson his cellphone he had covertly picked up without Kenny noticing before they left the hotel room.

Robert swung into a parking lot where the guys viewed the video in disbelief. JC had placed his phone on the dresser and started recording before Sylvia and Kenny entered the room. He filmed the entire encounter. His initial motivation was to prove to the guys he was as capable and cunning as them. JC certainly did not plan to witness a murder. Yet here it was for all to see. Kenny Wu killed Sylvia Sumner in cold blood.

There was a long pause before Stenson finally said, "This has become much more complicated. We have a murderer and the suspected murderer in the car. The dead woman was in JC's hotel room and law enforcement will comb this island to find him."

"What should we do?" Brickhouse asked his friend.

"Get the hell out of this country and sort this out later on our turf. No telling how many cops and judges Wu has on the payroll if his track record is anything like New Orleans. They will try to pin this on JC."

Getting to the Bahamas was simpler than getting out. The weapons they brought were stashed in Anthony Gallo's hotel room. By this time, the resort would be crawling with police. Then there was the automobile crash site with Stenson's fingerprints all over a stolen car. Also, they had two injured people in the vehicle. JC was dazed and bruised, but Kenny required medical attention.

Stenson would not entertain the idea that things could not get any worse because in his experience they can and probably would. The first thing they needed to do was to get off the road. Stenson told Robert to find a motel where they could lie low until they figured a way out of this mess. Next, he phoned Luna to update her on their situation and arrange another charter flight back to New Orleans. He told Luna to be prepared for a video he was about to send.

He turned his attention to Kenny Wu. The immediate issue was Kenny's whining in the back of the jeep about a broken collar bone sticking out of his shoulder. The man almost killed JC a few minutes ago and Robert Brickhouse wasn't having any of this whiney gangster's complaints. He'd seen bones stick out in combat and was more than happy to let Wu suffer for a while.

After they checked into the motel, Robert attended to the crybaby's injury. He was angry and told Kenny Wu to suck it up when he shoved the collar bone back under his skin. Brick took pleasure in hearing the man yelp like a puppy whose tail was caught in a door. Actually, the pain was worse than that, but Robert did not care.

Kenny Wu's cell phone chirped. Brick grabbed it and saw "Find My Phone" displayed on the screen. Somebody was trying to locate Kenny Wu and Robert was certain it wasn't anybody they wanted to see.

"He has a tracker on his phone!" Brick realized.

"Who is tracking this?" Robert demanded of Kenny Wu.

Kenny looked at Robert defiantly and said something in Mandarin. Brick did not have time for this and if Kenny thought he was playing games, Robert cleared it up by twisting the man's broken arm causing the bone to pop out again. Unfortunately, the agonizing pain caused Kenny to pass out, which was counter-intuitive and did not answer Robert's question.

"Now what?" Big Tony asked.

"All our weapons are at the hotel," Stenson reminded everyone.

"We can trash his phone and split before his friends get here," Big Tony suggested.

"I am tired of all this hunting, chasing, and moving around," Brick aggravatingly complained.

Brick had an idea. He told the guys, "I'll be right back."

Robert dashed out the door leaving everyone to wonder what he had in mind. He returned five minutes later and picked up Kenny's phone. He told Wu, who had regained painful consciousness, to call his guys and tell them not to come or he was dead.

Kenny dialed a number with his remaining unmangled hand. Robert turned on the speaker as it rang. When the other side answered, Kenny said something that sounded like "macka-lacka-wacka" excitedly in Chinese. Brick hung up the phone.

"Perfect!" Brick exclaimed.

"You speak Mandarin now?" Stenson asked.

"No, but I understood two-ten. He gave his guys our room number," Brick explained.

Kenny was as puzzled as the rest.

Robert said, "I guess you forgot to say the room number in Chinese. That's the problem with being bi-lingual. Sometimes you mix up the languages."

Brick told the guys, "I've changed our room. Let's go."

Robert laid Kenny's cell phone on the bed while they moved next door to room 208.

Now Stenson was confused. "You got us the room next door?"

"Trust me," Brick said slyly.

"Tony, grab a couple of those fire extinguishers hanging on the wall outside. JC, if you are well enough, go to the jeep and get the gas can and buy a pack of condoms. You can find them at the front desk of this fine establishment that charges by the hour," Brick instructed Justin Carter.

"What should I do?" Stenson asked the marine.

"Babysit our friend. I'll be back," Robert replied as he dashed outside.

Big Tony brought two large chemical fire extinguishers into the room and sat them on the floor. JC and Brick returned a few minutes later. Since they did not have any weapons, Brick improvised. It wasn't much, but it would have to do on such short notice.

Robert gagged Kenny Wu to keep him quiet while they waited. Brick handed one of the fire extinguishers to Stenson who was still trying to figure out what Brick was planning.

A few minutes later, they heard a commotion coming up the stairs. Brick peered out from behind the curtains and showed four fingers to let them know there were four bad guys. As they approached room 210, Brick held up his fist, telling them to stand by. It sounded like a bomb exploded when the door next to them bashed in. It was followed by unintelligible screaming that probably meant something like, "Get down" or "Hands up" in Mandarin.

Robert flung open their door and rushed out, followed by Stenson and Big Tony. When they arrived at the entrance of the smashed door, Stenson and Brick vomited the white chemical foam from the fire extinguishers into the faces of the four unsuspecting gangsters.

Covered in white foam in what looked like a shaving cream plant exploded, the four men fired blindly at the door, igniting condoms filled with gasoline. That miscalculation set the room ablaze and blocked their exit. Panicked, the men continued to fire hitting each other instead of their adversaries. Three clumps hit the floor. The last gangster took a chance and rushed through the flames and out the door directly into Big Tony who lifted him like a rag doll and tossed him over the balcony where he landed on the roof of a car below.

"Let's get out of here!" Brick commanded as he and Stenson tossed the fire extinguishers into the burning room. They grabbed Kenny Wu, and piled into the jeep, then tore out of the parking lot, leaving the inferno behind.

"That was your plan?" Stenson exclaimed.

"It worked didn't it?" Brick said with a chuckle.

"Yeah, but how are we going to explain that we didn't kill those guys or set the room on fire? Who would believe us?" Stenson asked the crazy biker-marine.

Brick replied, "Maybe the guy Big Tony tossed over the balcony will tell them."

The team checked into another seedy motel hoping there would be no more dangerous encounters with Kenny's friends. The list of things to do was long and getting longer with every second. It began with getting out of the Bahamas with a murderer in their custody. Their weapons were at the resort in Big Tony's room, and Kenny required medical attention. Brick suggested letting him die and dumping his body into the ocean, but Stenson knew they had to keep him alive at least until they rescued Zabrina.

Recovering Zabrina presented an entirely different set of challenges Stenson didn't have the brain capacity to consider those right now. The weapons were a gigantic problem. They were already facing enough charges in the Bahamas. How would they get the weapons out of the hotel? They checked in together and paid for theirs rooms in cash. However, each were required to provide identification.

It was obvious Stenson could not go back to the hotel after he stole a car from the valet. JC was suspected of murder, so he could not go. Brick stuck out like a sore thumb with his tattoos and poor attitude. That left Big Tony. While he was easy to spot because of his enormous size, maybe his friendly nature would allow him to get inside.

Then there was the matter of Kenny Wu and his injuries. Even though Robert believed Kenny only suffered broken bones in the crash, it was the open wound complicated by Robert shoving the man's bones in and out of his body that presented the problem. The gangster could die from infection. At the very least, they had to pump the man with antibiotics if he was going to survive the return trip to New Orleans.

They could not take him to a clinic. After running his mouth about the room number, they wouldn't risk him talking to anyone again. Brick offered to get the antibiotics. He didn't say how he would do it, but after his trick at the motel, nobody doubted his resourcefulness.

Transportation presented another problem. They could not use the jeep in case witnesses from the last motel got the license plate number after an unfortunate fire and a mass murder they did not commit. Stenson made a note to get everyone false identifications next time, if they make it out of this mess alive, because Robert had used his real id to rent the jeep too.

"Take a vacation," Stenson recalled Luna saying. Since when did anyone take a vacation like this, he wondered?

JC offered to ditch the vehicle and pick up food on the way back. How he could think of food at a time like this was anybody's guess. Maybe the car wreck scrambled his stomach as much as his brain, Brickhouse suggested. But they were hungry and food was one thing less on the list.

Big Tony and Brick set off in hired cars while JC left with the jeep. With Kenny Wu bound and gagged in the bathroom, it was finally quiet enough for Stenson to call his wife.

"Oh my God, Stenson!" Luna said when she answered the phone. "I saw the video!"

She asked why they did not go to the police. Stenson admitted there were too many unknowns. If they got caught up in multiple investigations defending JC, or the hotel fire and dead gangsters, or the stolen car, they would never find Zabrina in time.

Luna did not like it but she knew her husband was right. They had done nothing wrong, but to the outside world, or at least the Bahamian authorities, they were guilty until proven innocent.

Until she saw the murder video, she had been in an upbeat mood. Erin Collins investigative exposé on Kenny Wu was a powerful story that aired the night before. She also wanted to tell him about the progress she made uncovering Kenny's money. But all that mattered now was getting the team out of the Bahamas... and fast.

Stenson sensed her mood.

"Are you okay?" he asked his wife.

"I am fine, just worried about you," Luna replied.

"I wanted to give you some good news, but it can wait," she said.

"I could use some good news," Stenson said.

"It's no big deal. I just wanted to tell you I can

wiggle my toes," Luna relayed.

"You can what?" Stenson exclaimed.

"Wiggle my toes," she said in a sweet voice.

Stenson cheered.

"That is the best news I have heard all day!"

Chapter 27

Robert returned to the seedy motel with a doctor who made house calls, paying extra for him to forget the visit and their faces when he left. The physician stitched, bandaged, and injected Kenny Wu with antibiotics and a powerful sedative. Despite the doctor's suggestion to take Kenny to the hospital to check for internal injuries, Robert assured him Wu would be fine as long as he did not bleed all over the airplane or turn green until they returned home.

After they freed Zabrina, Robert did not care if Wu turned into a zombie. Then again, he realized becoming a zombie was not a good idea because that would require him to kill Wu again after he was already dead. He made a mental note to research how to kill zombies, just to be safe.

Big Tony lugged in three heavy duffel bags and clunked them onto the floor. The metallic rattles caused the group to jump because the bags were filled with weapons. Robert reminded the big fella to be more gentle since one bag contained grenades and he did not want to be blown up in a low-rent motel.

Gallo explained how he retrieved the weapons. When he arrived at the resort, police were on the scene investigating the crime. Instead of risking walking into the lobby, he waited in the garage until he saw a maintenance worker leave and paid him to borrow his uniform and laundry cart. Luckily, nobody spotted him because the shirt did not fit and his stomach hung out. He lamented there were never clothes in his size. Big Tony suggested next time they should send a smaller guy or steal bigger clothes.

JC walked in with bags of food. He told the team he dropped off the jeep. Then he explained by "dropping off" he meant the vehicle "accidentally" rolled over a cliff and fell into the ocean. He rationalized by the time authorities found it, they would be out of the country. But he warned Robert he may not get his rental deposit back.

JC passed around boxes of food. He handed Robert a container that he said contained a dish named after him. Brick was not impressed when JC told him it was Jerk Chicken. He ignored the dumb joke because he was too hungry to beat the comedy out of "Just Crazy" right now.

Stenson opened a video Luna sent him on his tablet. It was the Erin Collins investigation into Kenny Wu that aired the previous evening. Everyone watched as they ate. When it was over, they looked at Kenny Wu, whose face was pale, not only from his injuries, but from the shock of what he had just seen.

"This looks bad for you, Kenny. But not nearly as bad as when people see the video of you killing Sylvia," Brick warned.

Kenny gulped. "I will pay you anything! Just let me go. I promise you will never hear from me again. You can have the girl. I will help you get her. Please!"

Brick replied, "That ship sailed a long time ago. And make no mistake, we will get the girl. And when this is over, I promise we will never hear from you again. No one will because you are going to be locked up tight, or dead."

Luna arranged for a charter flight out of the

Bahamas to New Orleans leaving in two hours. The sedative the doctor gave Kenny had finally kicked in putting him to sleep, which gave JC and Big Tony time to grab a few winks. Stenson and Brick stepped outside to talk.

Robert lit a cigar. "What are we going to do with Wu?"

"I'm not sure yet," Stenson said as he stared into the tropical sky.

"I say we dump his carcass in front of a police station and email that murder video anonymously," Brick suggested.

"I thought of that," Stenson agreed. "But we should hold on to him until we find Zabrina. I don't know why, but with our bad luck we need all the insurance we can get."

Precious Cargo, the ship they suspected Zabrina was on, was not due to arrive in South Korea for another week. After unloading there, it would set sail to its final destination in Hong Kong. As of this moment, nobody had an idea how to catch up to a cargo ship at sea, board it, find Zabrina, and get out of there in one piece. But like always, they would somehow pull several more rabbits out of the proverbial magic hat.

Hong Kong

"There is no sign of him," a voice over the phone said. "Nobody has seen him in two weeks. No activity on his credit cards, either," the man informed Wu Kong.

"Keep looking," the Rising Tiger instructed.

The elder Wu looked over Victoria Harbour from his 80th floor executive suite at Sun Fang International headquarters on Hong Kong Island. His son, Su Dingxiang or Kenny Wu, as he was known in the U.S., dropping out of sight warned him of the strong possibility that larger problems loomed ahead.

He watched the news investigation from New Orleans. The mention of his company formerly owning Silkroad International Shipping was troublesome. The human trafficking incident the story uncovered occurred long after he turned the company over to his son. And while Kenny and his company were never charged with the crime, it remained a stain on his reputation to even be associated with Silkroad.

Kong read the dossier compiled by his security team about his son's recent activities. The normal rackets he was into were nothing new. But what concerned him was the murder of a child. Rule number one; never leave loose ends. And killing a man's child and leaving the father alive was a certifiable mistake.

Kong was not sure how Kenny ran afoul of the man named Stenson Beckett or the people surrounding him. But the more he read about Mr. Beckett was cause for concern. Intelligence told him Stenson Beckett was considered by many to be an honorable man, a quality his son did not possess. Even among thieves there was honor. Wu Kong suspected this would be a battle his son could never win. If Kenny did not put an end to this, maybe his father can.

Stenson's phone rang from a number he did not recognize.

"Hello," Stenson answered.

"Mr. Beckett, my name is Wu Kong. I am Kenny Wu's father."

"Oh, really?" Stenson said, somewhat astonished. He placed the phone on speaker so Robert Brickhouse could hear the conversation.

"Well, let me tell you that you are a horrible

father. Your son killed my child and paralyzed my wife. What do you want?" Stenson demanded.

"I want my son, Mr. Beckett. He has caused great dishonor to me and my family's name."

"Your family name? Dishonor?" Stenson said raising his voice. "Do you think any of that compares to the harm he has caused me, my family, and my friends?"

"I understand Mr. Beckett," Wu Kong said in a genuine tone. "You seek justice. I promise if you deliver my son to me you will receive the justice you and your family deserve."

"Believe me, Kong, you could never repay the loss of my child!"

[Click]

Stenson hung up the phone clearly upset by the call. He shouted, "Give me my son? I will give you your son in a box!"

San Francisco, California

Lei Min immigrated to the United States with his wife and child from Beijing, China in 1989. With little money and unable to speak the language, the couple found support among the large Asian community in San Francisco.

For the first ten years in the U.S., they worked menial jobs in Asian restaurants and small markets until they saved enough to open a market of their own. Lei Min imported goods from Asia, which is how his path crossed with Kenny Wu.

Kenny lured him in with his Chinese heritage and offer to provide low-cost transportation services through his company Silkroad International Shipping. Their relationship became more intertwined when Lei Min accepted a loan from Kenny to purchase inventory to expand his business.

It appeared to be a wise investment at the time. But as the saying goes, if it's too good to be true, it probably is. And that was the case with Kenny Wu. Soon Lei Min owed more money than he made.

This was a common practice for Kenny Wu. He built great wealth indenturing the Asian immigrant community by stealing their businesses no matter the damage it caused. He used intimidation, violence, or even death to get what he was owed. It was loan-sharking 101.

Before Lei Min met Kenny Wu, he had a reputation as a hard-working and honest businessman. People admired him and often asked for help to resolve business matters or disputes. He did this with such finesse that it caught Kenny's attention.

Unlike other debtors who owed him, Kenny used Lei Min's unique abilities to his advantage. If Lei Min could resolve issues without resorting to violence, then it was better for Kenny. Most times Lei Min collected debts diplomatically. But when a troublesome borrower would not submit to his normal means of persuasion, Kenny made Lei Min an offer that he could not refuse.

He instructed Lei Min to kill the man and dispose of his body. In doing so, Kenny promised to clear Lei Min's debts. If he did not, Kenny threatened Lei Min's family would pay the price with their life.

With little choice, Lei Min agreed. Even though he'd never killed before; to save his family, he did the deadly deed. Lei Min cleared his conscience by convincing himself it was justified. The guy he dispatched was a drug dealer corrupting his community. The way Lei Min looked at it, he was cleaning up the streets for the people he loved.

Unfortunately, it did not end there. Kenny used the murder to blackmail Lei Min. Whenever Kenny called a shot, it was Lei Min who executed it, literally.

It was not something Lei Min was proud of or would ever admit. He conducted this business with the utmost discretion. His wife was unaware that her husband led a double-life as a contract killer. And as far as Lei Min was concerned, it would remain that way.

It had been two years since Lei Min's son and his wife tragically died in an automobile accident, leaving behind their six year old daughter. Since then, Min and his wife raised their granddaughter as their own. When Kenny Wu called for the hit on Stenson Beckett, it was business as usual. But killing a child was never part of the deal. It did not bother Kenny Wu in the least that the child was dead, outside of the initial shock at the news. He was a psychopath without remorse. However, the vision of holding Stenson Beckett's dead child and laying the baby in the mother's outstretched arms made him think of his grandchild. It was a vision that would be forever burned into his memory.

It was 7:45 a.m., and the store opened at eight. His wife was late. She was normally here by now after taking their granddaughter to school. He opened the register to add currency to the days till. Suddenly, his heart skipped a beat when he found an instant photograph of his wife and granddaughter sitting atop the black plastic box separating the bills and coins. He looked at the photo and realized they were wearing the same clothes they were wearing when he left for work this morning. He turned the photograph over and read.

        You for them.

Below the ominous message was an address and time. Midnight tomorrow at an abandoned amusement park in New Orleans.

Chapter 28

If this was their idea of relaxation, they needed a different travel agent. At least they captured Kenny Wu and got out of the country relatively unscathed. Relative was the key word since JC was slightly banged up and Kenny Wu's clavicle bone popped out a few times. They also avoided becoming guests of the Bahamian police in a one-star jail.

On the return flight to New Orleans, JC and Big Tony played cards in the back of the Cessna Citation. Strapped in a seat across from them was a sedated and drooling Kenny Wu. Robert browsed a biker magazine in the front row while Stenson stared out the window, contemplating life.

Brick broke the silence. "Can I ask you something?"

Stenson glanced over. "Sure," he answered.

"We both know Wu was behind the attack at your home. Why haven't you beat him until he revealed who the shooter was?"

"What good would it do? It won't bring my son back," Stenson replied.

"Revenge?" Robert suggested.

Stenson considered the idea more than Brickhouse knew. He struggled with those dark emotions in a battle between right and wrong. It was as if he had a devil on one shoulder screaming "kill" while the other held an angel steering him in an opposite direction.

Stenson told him, "Robert, I have seen too much death in my short time on this earth. I will always miss my mother and son. Nothing will bring them back. But I will not allow myself to be like those who stole their lives. I am angry and hurt to the core of my soul. I would not be human if I did not consider vengeance."

He continued. "All I want is to find Zabrina and end this madness. I don't want anyone else to get hurt, especially those I love. It was a close call when Big Tony was shot and by some miracle my wife is alive. This has been dangerous from the moment we heard the name Kenny Wu. We were lucky to capture him and there is enough evidence to put him away for life. I don't care about the money. If I could have paid Kenny's extortion to prevent any of this, I would have."

"JC and Big Tony tried that. You see where it got them?" Brick reminded his best friend.

"Yeah," Stenson agreed. Paying extortion, whether it was him or JC, he was certain would have led to the same outcome.

"What about how you dealt with your father?" Brick asked Stenson an off-limit question he had never broached before.

Stenson glared at Robert incredulously. It was a touchy subject that few who knew the truth were sworn to secrecy and were never to mention again. Robert, JC, and Big Tony were accomplices to the crime the night Stenson dispatched his evil father with a shotgun blast to the head. They helped bury Tug Beckett on Haggerty's land.

"That was not revenge, Robert. It was preventing my father from harming another boy, as he had done to me," Stenson clarified.

"I understand that. But what if Wu gets away with this? He has enough money. Could you live with yourself if he was on the streets ripping the world apart because you would not deal with him when you had the chance?" Brick pressed.

"Of course not, Robert. I don't even know what I am going to do with him once we arrive in New Orleans. We've been thinking on our feet all this time and my feet haven't gotten that far," Stenson admitted.

He was right. They were like this aircraft flying on auto-pilot. It was one step at a time, and the next step was where to stash Kenny Wu once they reached New Orleans.

"I have an idea what to do with him," Brick slyly said.

Stenson sipped his drink and saw the mischievous look in Robert's eyes. Recalling his last plan burned up a motel room and tricked guys into shooting themselves, or when he torched Kenny Wu's business, Stenson was afraid to ask what other wild ideas floated around the wild man's head.

Sergeant John Dean and Soni James met the guys at the airport when they touched down in New Orleans. JC and Big Tony loaded the duffle bags filled with weapons into Sarge's black SUV. Stenson and Robert muscled Kenny Wu into the back and climbed in beside him.

John offered to watch the prisoner while the guys caught up on much needed rest. Soni drove JC and Big Tony to their homes while Brick suggested another idea that did not require John Dean babysitting a murderous gangster. He directed Sarge to an abandoned amusement park off Interstate 10.

When they arrived, Robert manhandled Kenny out of the SUV and grabbed a pouch of zip ties. He told John and Stenson, as they ambled through the desolate park, how he often visited the place when he was a child. He pointed at his favorite rides among the ghostly remains. They finally stopped when they reached the "Big Easy" Ferris wheel.

Brick continued talking as he pulled Kenny close to the rusted hoop. He said the ride scared him as a kid because it rose so high in the air and he was afraid of heights. Robert forced Kenny inside the lowest basket. He zip-tied Kenny's arms above his head and spread his legs wide and tied each to the side in a pose reminiscent of Leonardo da Vinci's drawing of man.

He strolled over to a control panel as if he were the conductor of this terrifying rig. Using all his force, he freed the rusted latch that kept the giant wheel locked in place. He asked John and Stenson to help him push the wheel. They spun it around until Kenny reached to the top. Over Kenny's screams and pleas, Robert mentioned he was only stuck on the wheel for 10 or 15 minutes when he was a child; it was a much shorter stay than Kenny Wu would get to hang out now.

Sergeant Dean was impressed with Robert's humorous imprisonment, while Stenson believed Brick should see a therapist about his fear of Ferris wheels.

As they walked back to the SUV, Stenson asked, "That was your plan? Strap him to a Ferris Wheel?"

Robert laughed. "You got a better idea?"

"No. But if I did, I am sure it would be more boring than yours."

Sarge dropped Brick and Stenson off before heading back to Gulf Coast Logistics. Even though they had only been away for two days, it felt like an eternity. Both men were glad to be home with their body parts still intact.

Luna greeted Stenson from her place on the sofa when he walked in. With her funny sense of humor, she said, "Welcome home, honey. I would get up to kiss you, but I am stuck on the couch."

Only Luna could tell a joke about being paralyzed and make Stenson smile.

He replied, "I guess that means dinner is not ready?"

"You are the chef in the family. I provide the good looks and comedy, and you provide the food," she teased.

Stenson plopped onto the sofa and gave the comedian a long kiss.

"You look worn out," she noticed.

"I'm okay. Just a little tired from harboring a murderer, a high-speed car chase, burning down a motel full of gangsters, and fleeing international prosecution. Normal day for me," he supposed.

"Where is Kenny Wu?" Luna wanted to know.

"He's hanging out," Stenson said.

Luna appeared confused until Stenson explained the Ferris Wheel.

She laughed at the revelation. "What are we going to do with Robert?"

"I don't know, but I am glad he's on our side. That boy is devious," he replied.

Stenson filled her in on the missing parts of their recent activities. Now that they had Kenny Wu, Luna shared the progress she had made while they were away. She had located several of Kenny's offshore bank accounts and crypto networks he used. The crème de la crème was Kenny Wu transferred millions of his other cryptocurrency to purchase LSAdvantage coins.

Stenson knew nothing of cryptocurrency or the high-tech world Luna purveyed. He considered himself lucky to operate their overly complicated television remote. After she explained how she pulled it off, Stenson was amused, especially when she told him the meaning of LSAdvantage was

"Luna and Stenson Advantage".

"You are a genius," he told her.

"And don't you forget it, buster. Now where's my dinner? I haven't eaten in two days," Luna joked.

"Right away, boss," Stenson said as he headed to the kitchen to whip something up for the hungry techno-wizard comedian.

In a house full of mirrors,
twisted, and strange,
Your reflection starts to change.
The world around you takes new guise.
Can you tell your truth from lies?
Amidst the laughter and the screams,
A voice inside you whispers bad dreams.
It speaks of justice and revenge,
Of settling scores for righteous amends.
Eye for an eye. Tooth for a tooth.
The voice intones,harshly uncouth.
Feel the weight of impending fate,
Closing in with unwavering hate.
For in this hall of distorted glass,
Your past misdeeds will come to pass.
All the harm you've caused before,
Will return with fury to pay you more.
So, as you stumble through this maze,
See your sins return their gaze.
Remember this and heed it well,
The road to Vengeance ends in hell.

Lei Min closed his phone. Whoever authored this sick riddle was toying with him like a cat with a ball of yarn. The thread of his nerves were quickly unraveling as he raced to save his wife and grandchild. On the red-eye flight from San Francisco to New Orleans, Lei Min wondered who this could be?

This perpetrator had to be a professional with even more dark art skills than him. How he found him and his family was unknown. In fact, it was terrifying. In all the years he had worked for Kenny Wu, nobody suspected he was a hired assassin. To kidnap his wife and granddaughter and whisk them away to New Orleans was something he could not wrap his head around. Why New Orleans? If he wanted revenge, the stalker could have easily taken him out in San Francisco.

Lei Min arrived at the abandoned amusement park at 11:00 p.m. His hand gripped the Ruger Mark IV pistol hidden inside his jacket pocket as he walked through the graffiti covered park. It was an ominous backdrop for what was certain to be an epic showdown. Among the trash strewn lanes, he envisioned the ghosts of revelers past laughing and taunting him like the giant Mardi Gras jesters standing guard above the entrance. His senses were highly acute; aware of every crackling step and the long shadows being cast by the foggy moon.

Once the predator and now the prey, Lei Min's stomach was tied in knots. Soon, he would face a foe as worthy as him. Only one would leave this devil's lair alive. Silently, he slipped through Main Street Square. The buildings resembled Bourbon Street after a bomb exploded. Past the Zinger, Scrambler and Lafitte's Pirate Ship; the Joker's Jukebox, the Invertatron, and Zydeco Scream, he cautiously walked.

"Help!" a voice yelled in the distance.

Lei Min froze.

"Help Me!" came the call again.

Lei Min scanned the darkness searching for the source of the plea. It was not the voice of his wife or grandchild. It was the voice of a fearful man.

"Please, somebody help me!" the voice begged.

Lei Min inched toward the sound with his pistol drawn.

"Help!" echoed through the empty park.

The hitman looked around, then up. He spotted the source of the distress hanging in from the top a Ferris wheel. To his surprise, it was Kenny Wu.

Lei Min fired a shot, missing Kenny's head by inches.

"I will kill you!" Lei Min shouted.

"Who is there?" Kenny searched the darkness below.

"Where are my wife and grandchild?" Lei Min yelled at the splayed man.

"Lei Min, is that you? I don't know what you are talking about! Get me down from here!" Kenny begged the hitman.

Lei Min fired another round that sparked the metal and ricocheted away.

"I swear Kenny, if anything happens to my wife and grandchild, you are dead!" he shouted.

"I don't have them, Lei Min. It's the people whose kid you killed. They have them and they will be back. Get me down from here and I will help you find them!" Kenny yelled below.

"I did not kill the kid. One of your incompetent men did!" Lei Min roared clarification.

"They don't know that, Lei Min. And they don't care! They want you and me dead. Get me down. There are at least four of them after us, and I have a broken arm. I can still fire a weapon. You won't be able to get them all yourself." Kenny appealed.

Lei Min believed Kenny for no other reason than Kenny could not have attached himself to a Ferris wheel and spun himself to the top. It must be the father of the dead child and his accomplices. He dialed his phone and called for reinforcements from the Chinese gang. He quickly realized he never should have come alone.

"I will be back!" Lei Min shouted to Kenny Wu.

"Wait! Where are you going?" Kenny cried.

Lei Min did not reply as he returned to the park entrance to await more men. Fifteen minutes later, eight Asian gangsters arrived in two SUVs armed with automatic weapons. Lei Min laid out the situation and told four to come with him and left the rest to cover the park entrances. It was time to turn the tables on Stenson Beckett and his friends.

The hitman made it back to the Ferris wheel and released the switch holding the ride in place. He and the other men spun Kenny to the ground.

"Thank you. Now give me a gun," Kenny demanded.

Reluctantly, Lei Min nodded to a gangster behind him who handed Kenny a .45 pistol. Gun or not, Lei Min vowed to kill Kenny Wu after the rest were dead and he got his family back.

"Spread out!" Lei Min told the men. "If you find my wife and grandchild, do not engage. Call me over the radio. I will rescue them myself."

Chapter 29
New Orleans, Louisiana

Bashed and bedraggled. The misfits caught up on their sleep. Odds were it would be their last chance before setting out on the next wobbly leg of a journey that would take them halfway around the world. How they would board a cargo ship to find Zabrina Chao trapped inside a metal box stacked among thousands of others were details they had not worked out. Despite the danger and impending danger heading their way, this barrel of monkeys were committed to rescuing the girl no matter the consequences they would face.

Wheelchair-bound and paralyzed from the waist-down did not stop Luna. She worked out the logistics that would catch them up to the container ship Precious Cargo, which was due to arrive in South Korea in less than a week.

After Robert's persistent nagging, Stenson agreed to interrogate Kenny Wu. He needed to confirm they were looking for the right boat. Nobody was in the mood for another goose chase, dead-ends or surprises. However, Mr. Brickhouse was more motivated to learn about the assassination attempt at his best friend's house. Even if Wu revealed the shooter (and Stenson was certain he would considering Robert's persuasive charm), he did not to want to think of what it would take to capture a hitman.

Stenson felt a headache coming on. With so

much to consider, he was afraid one more thought might cause his brain to erupt. Their current headache was strapped to a Ferris wheel 50 feet in the air. Robert, Stenson, JC and Big Tony returned to the abandoned amusement park a few minutes before midnight. They were in no rush to free Kenny Wu, as Robert reasoned, the longer he suffered, the easier his interrogation would be.

No Trespassing and Beware of Alligator signs warned the rule-breakers of dangers ahead when they entered the park through a rusted fence. As they strolled along the trash-strewn paths, past graffiti covered buildings and broken rides, they joked how Kenny's suffering had only just begun. While JC pondered if the park really had alligators or they put those signs up to scare people away, shots rang out. The guys scattered like cockroaches surprised by the kitchen light.

"Ambush!" Brick yelled as he dove for cover next to a ticket booth.

He whipped out his pistol from the back of his jeans and returned fire into the darkness. The rest of the guys appeared dumbfounded wondering what to do.

Brick hollered, "Why aren't you shooting?"

"You are the only with a gun!" Stenson yelled back.

It never occurred to anyone except Robert to bring a weapon. With four of them there to untie one guy from a Ferris wheel, how hard could it be? They would discuss their incorrect assumption later if they survived.

"Get to the van and see what we've got!" Robert told Stenson over the pinging and plinking sounds of whizzing bullets.

Stenson stooped down and duck-waddled his way back to the van while Robert played bullet-tag with bad guys. Stenson opened the rear doors and found a duffle bag. He unzipped it and assessed the unpromising contents. He phoned his wife as bullets tinkled Robert's van.

"How's it going?" Luna cheerfully greeted.

"We are at an abandoned amusement park filled with the most unfunny clowns trying to shoot us, and we have no weapons!" Stenson humorously summarized.

"I thought you were there to get Kenny Wu down from a Ferris wheel to interrogate him. Who is shooting at you?"

"I don't know, Luna. I forgot to ask them before I ran head first into a trash can while trying to find cover and not get shot."

"Are you okay?" she asked.

"Well, I wasn't shot. But I have a large knot on the top of my skull. Other than that I am fine."

"How did Kenny get down from the Ferris wheel?"

"I don't know Luna. I will ask him after we find him for the tenth time."

"This will be the third time, Stenson. Once at Silkroad, when you lost him and Brick set his place on fire. Then when you found him in the Bahamas, after you wrecked an expensive car you stole from a hotel. So, if you find him again, this will be the third time. Just saying."

"Okay, third. But it really feels like the tenth time we have tried to catch this guy. Just saying."

"Why didn't you bring your guns?" she asked.

"Because Sarge has them at his place and we didn't think we would need them. But as much as I love you, I do not have time to explain all of this right now. Please call Sarge and politely ask him to get his ass to the amusement park and bring us an arsenal... and quick!"

"Why didn't you call him instead of me?" she

quizzically asked.

"I am wondering the same thing, Luna. It certainly would have been a shorter call with fewer explanations."

Stenson hung up the phone and waddled back to Robert's position with the bag slung over his shoulder. Meanwhile, "Chatty Kathy" (otherwise known as Luna LeRoux-Beckett) called John Dean. Unfortunately, he was on the other side of town and informed her it would take at least an hour before he would arrive. It was not the answer Luna had hoped for when she texted Stenson the bad news. Soni James, who had stopped by to visit Luna overheard the conversation and jumped from the sofa.

"I am going! Nothing is gonna happen to my boys!" she exclaimed.

Soni ran outside and grabbed a bag from her SUV then rushed into to the bedroom to change clothes. Like Superman, emerging from a phone booth, she sprinted out the door and flew from the driveway.

Stenson shook his head when he read Luna's message. He told the guys they were on their own as he unzipped the bag and inventoried what they had.

"We've got five night vision goggles, five headset radios, a couple of smoke grenades, two paintball guns and a tranquilizer dart."

"Paintball guns?" Robert repeated not believing what he heard.

"There are four or five guys shooting at us and this is all we've got? Where is the gun for the tranquilizer dart?"

"I don't know, Robert. I didn't pack your bag," Stenson sarcastically replied.

A car roared up behind them and screeched to a halt. A tall figure jumped out and sprinted in their direction. Brick spun around and took aim, ready to fire.

"Don't shoot!" a voice shouted with hands in the air.

It was Soni James wearing a t-shirt, jeans and running shoes. It was the first time they had ever seen her without a wig, dress, or high heels.

Brick was bewildered. "Soni?"

"I thought you boys might need some help," Soni replied in a baritone voice they had never heard her speak in before.

"But..." Robert stuttered.

Seeing the surprise on the tough guy's face was priceless. Never one to miss an opportunity to joke with the big marine, Soni said, "I might dress like a woman, but I assure you I am all man. What do you need me to do?"

The answer caused Robert to pause and reevaluate his opinion of Soni James. She threw off his train of thought. Finally, he said, "We are short on weapons. Did you bring anything?"

"I have a can of pepper spray in the car. You never know when some frisky marine might hit on me," Soni wittily replied.

Brick laughed. "These guys are hitting us with real bullets. They are friskier than you, so get your mace!"

Soni ran back to the car while Robert handed out the sad stash of weapons. Stenson and JC received paintball guns, while Big Tony got the tranquilizer dart. Since Robert was out of bullets from his unfriendly exchange with people who did not like him. He was left fending for himself with bare hands or whatever weapon he could find. Maybe he could use the trash can Stenson ran into since it already had a dent.

They all donned radios and checked their comms, then placed the night vision goggles over their heads. Robert drew an imaginary map of the park on the palm of his hand. He and Stenson would use the smoke grenades to conceal their entrance through the front of this jacked up park. JC and Big Tony were instructed to enter from the East and West sides while Soni James would cover the rear. The goal, as Robert explained, was to keep the gangsters bunched together where they could surround them in a pincer move.

"What's a pencil move?" JC inquired.

"I said pincer move. Nevermind JC. Just take out anybody you see on the west side."

"Which side is west?" JC asked the marine.

Brick waved his exasperated empty gun and pointed it to the left. "Over there, moron. By the roller coaster."

"Why didn't you say, by the roller coaster?" JC naively asked.

Brick looked at him clearly unamused.

The park had grown quiet. Experience told Brick and Stenson this meant their opponent was regrouping for another attack. Everyone illuminated their goggles and pulled them over their eyes. There was no time to waste. JC, Big Tony, and Soni headed off in opposite directions. Stenson and Robert waited until everybody was in place.

"You sure you don't want to wait for Sarge?" Stenson asked Robert.

"Do you want to wait an hour and risk losing Kenny Wu again?"

"No, but considering they are using live ammunition and all I have is a paintball gun, it would be nice if we had a few of Sarge's toys to play with."

"The bad guys don't know it's a paintball gun. If you've ever been hit with one, it hurts. That should stun them enough for you to perform one of your wrestling moves and take their weapon."

"Why is everything more complicated and dangerous than the last thing we did?" Stenson wondered.

"That is a rhetorical question, Stenson. At least we aren't dressing up in costumes and dancing this time," Robert said.

"Ready," Big Tony radioed.

"I'm in place," Soni confirmed.

"Hey Robert, do you know how to turn this roller coaster on? I might want to take a ride when this is over," JC said.

"JC, if we survive this, I will figure out how to turn it on so I can strap you to the tracks and amuse myself when I run over you and slice you in half," Brickhouse joked.

Another volley of gunshots rang out through the darkness Lei Min was on the other side of the park and paid no attention to the commotion. He was laser-focused on finding his wife and grandchild. He, along with Kenny Wu and four more gangsters combed the park, while the others kept Beckett's group occupied at the front of the park. Building by building and ride by ride, they continued to search.

Stenson informed the guys over the radio, "We will pop the smoke on three."

He counted down. "Three... Two... One... Go!"

Robert and Stenson pulled safety pins and tossed two smoke bombs over the ticket booths landing on the other side of the entrance. Gun shots pierced the wall of smoke revealing shooter locations from the muzzle flashes. Stenson and Brick sprinted through the cloud and found cover on opposite sides. A few more shots, then it grew quiet again.

Despite not having weapons they wanted, they had one advantage; they could see in the dark and the bad guys could not. In shades of green and black, Stenson and Brick scanned the night lit as brightly as day.

Robert saw a shooter searching for them standing ten yards away. He snuck over and tapped the gunman on the shoulder. When the startled man turned around, Brick said, "Hello."

Robert cracked his face with an elbow harder than a concrete block. The blow knocked the man to the ground with an "oomph" and a thump. Robert leaned over and picked up his weapon.

He told the unconscious man, "I'll take that."

Robert zip-tied this hands and legs. This guy wouldn't bother them again unless he knew how to hop.

"One down," Brick radioed.

Another gangster popped up and looked around for the source of the commotion. Stenson waited for the moment to "paint" his forehead.

[Splat!]

The man let out a puppy dog yelp. He immediately dropped his weapon and reached for his eye.

"Uh oh," Stenson uttered as he ran toward the gangster and picked up his gun.

"Uh oh, what?" Brick asked.

"This guy is going to need a patch. I was about to pop him in the forehead but he turned at the last second and the paintball struck him in the eye."

"I bet that hurt," Brick jokingly replied.

"Yeah, he's crying and saying something about eye of the tiger or where is my eyeball? My Mandarin is a little rusty."

"I have another problem," Stenson said. "His gun is out of bullets. Is it a foul to shoot a guy in the eye with a paintball when he couldn't shoot back?"

Brick chuckled "I don't know? We'll have to check the rule book on that. You might have to sit in time-out like they do in hockey."

Three more gangsters took off running when

they realized things weren't going their way. Stenson called over the radio to the others, "Keep your eyes open. They've scattered and heading your way."

"Got one! I am chasing him now. He's headed for the roller coaster," JC replied.

"I see another coming toward me," Big Tony informed the crew.

"Another is coming this way," Soni relayed.

"This joker is fast!" JC said over the radio. "The idiot is running up the roller coaster tracks!"

Big Tony squawked. "My guy just ran into a pirate ship."

"Did you say pirate ship?" Brick repeated.

"Yeah, there is a ride over here built like a boat. Skull and crossbones flag.... It's a pirate ship," Gallo described.

Stenson laughed. "The guy I shot could be the captain of the boat with his new eye patch."

How this team had so much fun in dangerous situations was a testament to who they were as friends. They trusted each other and nobody panicked. Humor was a way to deal with the stress and a key to their success. If one needed help, they were always there for one another. And most times, it was accompanied with a joke.

"Anybody spot Wu?" Stenson asked.

"Negative," they all replied.

"Keep looking. He has to be hiding somewhere around here," Stenson replied.

JC called over the radio, "Wow! This guy just took a swan dive off the top of the roller coaster. He missed the turn and didn't realize he cannot fly. By the way, it's a nice view up here. Pretty moon tonight."

"Get off that damned roller coaster JC and help us, you sightseeing moron!" Brick roared.

"You are no fun," JC taunted. "I'll be right there."

Big Tony stood outside the pirate ship, tucked within the shadows, and calmly waited. There was only one way in and out, and he was tired of running after the guy. He could hear him scurrying inside the ship. Ten minutes later, the gangster thought the coast was clear. He casually rounded the corner and walked past Big Tony, who he did not see. The big man stepped out of the shadows and wrapped his massive right forearm around the gangster's neck. He stabbed the tranquilizer dart into his shoulder and said, "Goodnight sweetheart."

Tony called out, "My guy is taking a nap. He won't bother us again for several hours."

Soni dodged bullets while chasing another shooter throughout the unamusing obstacle course. When the gangster realized after he ran out of ammunition that he could not outrun the six foot seven Soni James, he dove off a bridge into Gator Bait Lagoon and tried to swim away. Suddenly, he let out a terrifying scream and rolled over in the water several times. Through gurgles and gasps, he flailed his arms in desperation until there were only chunky pieces of the gangster left.

"That is something you don't see every day," Soni said over the radio.

"What's going on Soni?" Brick asked.

"The guy I was chasing jumped into the lagoon. Tell JC there really are alligators here and they are hungry," Soni warned.

The gunfire died down and screams subsided, leaving the place eerily quiet again. Lei Min had separated from Kenny Wu to cover more of the condemned park. Alone in the company of ghosts from his past and mounting fear, bad voodoo filled the air.

A shiver zipped up his spine when he saw two Mardi Gras masked characters staring from above the entrance to the House of Mirrors. "Sock and Buskin", the comedy and tragedy masks, welcomed him with a sinister grin and a sad frown. It was if to say, "Wait and see the fun we have in store for you tonight."

Lei Min adjusted his grip on the Ruger Mark IV pistol, taking a moment to compose himself before stepping into the glass maze. Silver slivers of moonlight intruded holes in the storm-ravaged roof, trading shadows for brief respites of light. Adding to the dizzying effect, the floors, walls, and ceilings were covered in mirrors, causing Lei Min's head to spin with a stomach-churning sense of vertigo.

The hitman became more unnerved after he saw six copies of himself looking back at him. Something seemed out of place. He creased his eyes, straining to find the difference. His stomach knotted when he realized a hooded figure stood before him, holding a pistol in a gloved hand down by his side. Silently unmoving, the figure stared. Lei Min swayed left to prove his mind was not playing tricks on him. Five reflections imitated. The sixth did not budge. Unflinching, the phantom dared Lei Min to move again.

Before he processed the challenge, the phantom disappeared.

"Grandfather!" a child called out from deep inside the labyrinth, proving to Lei Min this was not a dream.

He yelled, "Ài!"

"Please help!" the child pleaded again.

Lei Min rushed forward and crashed into a mirrored wall. He felt around the walls until he found an opening to only be blocked again a few steps later. From the corner of his eye, he saw the hooded figure flash by in a daring move to tempt him to play this deadly game of hide and seek.

Lie Min fired two rounds shattering glass to no avail. He turned to see the phantom rush by, toying with him again.

He screamed, "Let my family go!" then he rapidly fired three more shots. Mirrors came crashing down, yet the mysterious villain appeared on the other side of the room, unfazed.

He crept deeper into the house of terror shooting every mirror in the wicked place. He was on the hunt to kill this mysterious predator if it was the last thing in life he would ever do.

Stenson and Robert followed the gunfire sounds to its source. The rest of the team were on the other side of the park heading the same way. Stenson reached the building first and drew his empty gun. He was going in and prayed surprise was on his side.

"Robert, cover me. Do not let anyone sneak up behind me," Stenson instructed his friend.

"Roger that," Brickhouse said as he reached the building moments later and posted himself outside.

Broken glass and shuffling steps guided him through the shattered maze. Each time a shot rang out Stenson moved closer toward the sound. He heard the cries of a child and pleas of a man. Neither voice he recognized.

Lei Min continued to the center of the maze, lit only by streams of moonlight casting through the broken ceiling. There they were, eight mirror images of his wife and grandchild kneeling on the ground. Behind them stood the hooded figure holding a pistol to his wife's head.

With a silent stare, the phantom raised his other hand and waved, "come closer". Lei Min fired point blank at the shadowed man. The reflection shattered, yet there he stood. Another round, another shot, and another the hitman fired. The only thing more shattered than glass were his nerves.

Lei Min screamed, "Let them go! I beg you!"

The Mystery Man stood unflinching with a cold, dark stare. He fired again. Another mirror shattered, then a shot rang out. Lei Min felt a piercing sting in his back. He turned and fired erratically. This time, his shot rang true and the hooded man fell.

Lei Min dropped to his knees from the gunshot to his back. It was then he realized in his fit of fear; he had struck his wife and grandchild too. As he started at the terrifying sight, the shadowy figure raised his weapon one last time. Lei Min knew his fate when the shot fired into his heart.

He fell forward landing face down. There he stared until his last breath with eyes wide open. For all eternity, hell would know the price he paid for the harm he had caused to an innocent child.

JC followed the sound of gunshots and crouched down across from a building where he saw a man holding a gun. He took aim and fired.

The man doubled over and JC exclaimed, "Got one!"

"I've been hit!" Brick yelled over the radio.

"Where are you?" Justin Carter asked.

"The south corner of the Mardi Gras town. Outside the House of Mirrors." Brick confirmed.

"I am across from you. That's where I just shot the bad guy," JC told the marine.

"You didn't shoot the bad guy, you dumbass! You shot me!" Brick exclaimed.

Robert didn't have time to worry about being shot with a paintball. He had to get inside now that JC arrived. "Cover the outside, JC. I've gotta get to Stenson."

Stenson made it to the open area to find Lei Min's body. A few feet away, he saw three more casualties. It did not register to him at first who the people were until he noticed the hooded figure.

"Stenson Beckett," a voice behind him said.

Stenson slowly turned around. It was Kenny Wu with his one good arm raised with a pistol pointing straight at his head.

"Wu," Stenson calmly said.

"Drop your weapon," Kenny instructed him.

Stenson let the gun fall to the floor. "It was empty anyway, Wu."

"You thought you could win this game? Such a shame," he taunted. "In life, there can only be one winner. You should have walked away when you had the chance. Maybe your son and wife would be alive today."

"My wife is alive, jackass," Stenson corrected.

"Ah well, then I must take care of her after I rid this world of you. I'll make sure you hear her scream from the depths of the hell I am about to send you to."

[Chock] [Chock]

Kenny Wu turned to stare into both barrels of a shotgun pointed inches from his face.

"It will be you going to hell," an old man with a long gray beard said.

"Haggerty?" Stenson said in disbelief. "I thought you were..."

"Dead?" the old man replied.

"No, son. I am not dead. But he soon will be," Haggerty told Stenson as he stared down Wu.

"Don't do it Haggerty! I don't want his blood on your hands," Stenson begged. "We need him a little while longer before he faces his doomed fate."

Haggerty stood there, a hair-pull trigger from blowing Kenny Wu to eternity. Brick arrived a moment later, followed by JC, Big Tony, and Soni

James. Kenny looked around the shattered room and realized he was the one who had lost this game. His head lowered, and he dropped his weapon in an act of shame. JC and Big Tony grabbed Kenny and hustled him outside. Soni and Robert watched the encounter between Stenson and his mentor and savior.

Stenson looked at the old man who he believed to have been dead for many years. He pushed the barrel of the shotgun down to the floor. Both men knew the relevance of this weapon and how it had changed Stenson's life in countless ways.

"Thank you, Haggerty," Stenson told the old man.

Lucious T. Haggerty smiled and placed his weathered hand on Stenson's shoulder. "You are a good boy, Stenson." That was all he said. Soni followed him outside, leaving Stenson and Robert alone in the maze.

They surveyed the casualties lying on the floor. Lei Min, the hitman, was dead. Across from him, in a tragic embrace, were an older woman and a child who were as important to him as Stenson's son and wife. Karma had its day. Then they noticed the hooded character and their hearts sank.

"Is that who I think it is?" Robert asked a question he hoped was not in the affirmative, but they both knew the answer was true.

"I believe so," Stenson sadly replied.

They walked over and solemnly stared. Robert leaned down and carefully rolled the hooded man onto his back. In all the years the Mystery Man helped them accomplish impossible things, they had never known his identity. While they often speculated who it might be, they preferred the anonymity of the benevolent ghost.

Stenson kneeled down and gently pulled back

the hood. He paused before lifting the mask to reveal the face. Their hearts dropped when they discovered the Mystery Man was Fallon O'Malley.

Chapter 30

Staring with heart-broken disbelief at their fallen friend lying dead upon the ground left Robert and Stenson without words to describe the immense loss they felt. Fallon O'Malley, the former owner of O'Malley's pub in the French Quarter, gifted his business to Stenson when he retired to spend more time with his family and friends. Some retirement, they thought, seeing Fallon lying there wearing the hooded masquerade.

How could it be? He was the Mystery Man, and just like Superman, he was never supposed to die. Over the years, Stenson and Robert had tried to guess the identity of the phantom, but never suspected it was Fallon. As the hooded character, he had helped them many times in mysterious ways. The disguise proved he never wanted credit for any of the good deeds he had done for them.

Looking back, the Mystery Man's identity made more sense. Fallon had been a member of the British SAS where covert missions were their modus operandi. And like the Mystery Man, they operated in dangerous shadows. Often going unnoticed and uncredited; where success was expected and death an ever-present danger.

How tragic it was that Fallon gave his life, seeking justice for the murder of Stenson's child and injured wife. For Stenson Beckett and Robert Brickhouse, it was a sad day to know the Mystery Man lost his battle, helping them.

"What should we do?" Robert asked.

Stenson considered their options, which were few.

"As much as I hate to admit it, there is nothing we can do for him now." Stenson sadly replied. "It's not like we can drop him off at the hospital and say, 'Hey, we found a dead guy at an abandoned amusement park and thought we'd save you a trip.' How would we explain all the carnage around this park and risk losing Wu again?"

"We've never left a soldier on the battlefield," Brick reminded his friend.

"I know, Robert. Do you have a better idea?" Stenson asked.

Robert searched his mind hoping to find another option. Regretfully, he replied, "Unfortunately, I do not."

Stenson placed his hand over Fallon's heart and closed his eyes. He reverently said, "Thank you Fallon for all you have done."

He rose and told Brick, "Let's go."

Stenson noticed as they walked out, Robert had a pronounced limp and a florescent yellow splotch on the crotch of his jeans.

"Why are you limping?" Stenson asked him.

"Your buddy shot me with a paintball in the catcher's mitt. I think JC broke my bat and balls." Brick explained. "He thought I was a bad guy and caught me in friendly fire. Just when I started to like him, I'm ready to kill that lunatic again."

Stenson said, "Any other time, that would be funny. But pardon me if I'm not in the mood to laugh right now."

Sarge raced over when they reached the parking lot. "Did I miss all the fun?"

When nobody smiled, Sarge knew something

had gone terribly wrong. He noticed Kenny Wu bound in the back of Robert's van. An unhappy JC and Big Tony sat across from him not saying a word.

Stenson asked, "Sarge, would you mind watching Wu for a few days? It's been an extraordinarily long night and there is much more we must do."

"Sure, Stenson," John replied without asking why.

Stenson and Robert piled into the van and pulled out. They were followed by Sarge and Soni James. After they arrived at Gulf Coast Logistics, Big Tony and JC muscled Kenny Wu out of the van to the back of the warehouse where they strapped him to a chair. Stenson told Sarge he'd call him in a few days. With little ado, they bid farewell.

On the way to Stenson's house, Robert asked his friend, "Why didn't you let Haggerty blow Kenny away? By the way, where did the old man come from? I thought he was dead."

"So did I," Stenson replied. "And where did he go after he left? He didn't stick around."

"I guess the old man figured his work was done. I would have liked to meet him. That is the second time in your life he saved your ass," Brick recalled.

"Yeah." Stenson remembered. "The first time was when I was 10 years old."

Stenson said, "For the longest time, I thought Haggerty might have been the Mystery Man. And then I saw him in that crazy dream where I had a conversation with him and his words lifted me out of that dark place I was in after my son was killed."

"That dream you had of him was wild. I remember you telling me about it. When even I couldn't get through to you, Haggerty did. Are you sure it was a dream?" Brick wondered.

"Right now, I don't know what is a dream or reality. But to answer your question why I didn't let Haggerty blow him away? We need Wu to find

Zabrina. And if by some miracle we rescue her, something tells me there is a person much worse than us who wants Kenny."

"Sun Fang?" Brick answered.

"Yeah, Kenny's father. The Rising Tiger," he confirmed.

"It seems like a lot of trouble turning him over to his father, but it's your call. I would have dusted him off this planet a long time ago." Brick assured.

"Just because he has blood on his hands doesn't mean I want his blood on mine," Stenson explained.

"Well, you are more forgiving than me," Brick replied.

"I did not say I forgive him. I am simply doing what I feel is right. I'll let God and his father judge that killer. My conscience is clear," Stenson clarified.

"You are a good man, Stenson," Brick said, repeating the same sentiment Haggerty told him a while ago.

"You are alright yourself, Robert. I couldn't ask for a better friend. Although you might have to explain your injured crotch to your lady friends." Stenson joked.

Robert pulled a cigar from his breast pocket and lit it. After a long puff, he said, "I am so going to kill JC when the time is right."

Stenson laughed. "Maybe he was getting you back for the time we hired the Mystery Man to put those bullet ants in his underwear drawer."

Robert chuckled fondly remembering how the Mystery Man helped them pull off that stunt. "Yeah, that was a good one."

Robert dropped Stenson off at his home, declining an invitation to come inside. He was as exhausted as Stenson, and more than a little sore. He said he was going to soak in a hot tub and think of creative ways to get JC back when he could walk properly again.

Luna was waiting up when Stenson arrived. She learned of the devastating news about the Mystery Man from Soni James when she called a short time ago. Stenson dropped his keys on the hallway table and gave her a kiss. His melancholy mood told her he did not feel like talking. With a heavy heart, he told his wife goodnight and went to bed.

Her husband slept restlessly throughout the night. Luna heard him talking in his sleep. It broke her heart to hear his dreams; those private things he kept inside. He asked his deceased mother what he should do? He apologized to Fallon O'Malley for leaving him behind. He wept when he talked to their infant son and prayed for forgiveness.

Luna loved her husband for his tender heart. In many ways, he was the same little boy she fell in love with so long ago. And even though this madness happened because he helped his friends. Luna knew if Stenson was asked, he would do it all over again. That is who he is a person to his core. And every day, she adored her husband even more.

Luna and Stenson were practical people. It was not they were unemotional, but realistic about things they could not change. There was no point in looking back when what was done could not be undone. Their personalities were such that no matter what, they always looked ahead. And like her husband, Luna held onto hope, especially now. While she may be stuck in a wheelchair, she was more determined to walk again. Luna vowed to be there for Stenson no matter the challenges they faced. Although they were lovers, husband and wife, more than anything, they were best friends. There is no mountain high enough or valley low they could not conquer together.

Stenson looked like he hadn't slept a wink when

he walked into the kitchen later that morning. He poured a cup of coffee and joined his wife at the kitchen table. He leaned over and kissed her cheek.

She closed her laptop where she had been reading about the mass shooting at the amusement park. She did not want to start his day by telling Stenson the story was national news.

"I need to call Fallon's wife," Stenson said, staring down at his coffee cup.

"She phoned while you were asleep and is obviously devastated. She asked me if you were okay," Luna shared.

Stenson looked toward the ceiling and shook his head. "How did this go so wrong?"

"I don't know, Stenson. None of us saw this coming. It's not your fault," She assured her husband.

"What happened to me, our son, Fallon..." Luna's voice trailed off, then she paused before saying, "However this ends, Stenson, I am with you all the way. Let's focus on getting Zabrina back."

"How long before the ship docks in South Korea?" Stenson asked his wife.

"Five days," Luna replied.

"Can you arrange a flight to Seoul in a couple of days? We've got a funeral to attend before we can leave," he sadly realized.

"Of course," she replied, reaching for his hand with a comforting smile.

Stenson picked up his phone and walked into another room to make the difficult call to Fallon O'Malley's widow. He offered his sincere condolences and offered any help he or Brick could provide.

Fallon's body was released to the family after the autopsy was complete. Fallon had wished to be interred in his native Ireland according to his will. A memorial service was planned for family and friends to pay their respects in New Orleans before Fallon O'Malley's final journey home.

It was gray and dreary the morning of the service. It fit the somber mood Stenson and Robert felt. The men wore their military dress uniforms in honor of the fallen soldier.

"I bought a new dress coat," Brickhouse told Stenson. "Seems I've put on weight since leaving the corps."

"It's all that beer you drink," Stenson sarcastically replied.

Stenson and Robert learned from Fallon's wife about his terminal cancer diagnosis. Fallon did not even reveal the diagnosis to his children, so they would not worry. Only his wife knew the severity of his illness. It was one reason he wanted to get rid of the bar. He knew his time on this earth was short and he wanted to make the most of the time he had.

She assured the guys that Fallon would rather go out as a soldier than to succumb to a deadly disease he could not fight. She did not blame them for his untimely demise.

"My husband loved you blokes, especially you, Stenson," she said. "He was proud the day he told me he was leaving the bar to you. He knew you would take care of it as he did. He considered you like a son."

"Some son I am. The bar burned to the ground," Stenson replied.

"That wasn't your fault, Stenson. Fallon knew it, and it was another reason he wanted to help you. When he heard what happened to your family, he was deeply hurt."

"There will never be another one like him, Mrs. O'Malley," Stenson said as Robert nodded in agreement.

"I know," she replied. "I will miss him for the rest

of my life. But I will cherish the wonderful years we spent together. He's in a much better place now and no longer in pain."

Stenson hugged her. A gesture she returned with a kiss to his cheek. At the conclusion of the memorial, Robert and Stenson saluted Fallon's casket wrapped in the British flag. It was a fitting tribute to a life well lived.

* * *

Everyone gathered at Stenson's home after the service. Stenson, Brick, JC, Big Tony, Sarge, and Soni were all there. They were scheduled to depart for the long flight to South Korea that evening, and there were still things left to do.

An old friend of Stenson's stopped by. It had been several years since Charlie Whitehorse and Stenson had seen each other. The professional car thief and Stenson had a humorous past. They were arrested together when Charlie hot-wired a car in the middle of winter so he and Stenson would not freeze. It was a time when Stenson was a runaway and they were both homeless teens. Charlie served time for the crime while Stenson chose a different path when he got his GED and joined the United States Army.

Charlie's business now was shipping high-end cars to Asia and the Middle East to sell. Coincidentally, he had several containers of vehicles aboard the ship, "Precious Cargo". Charlie offered them to the team if they needed transportation when they arrived in Asia.

Everyone staked claims on the vehicles they wanted when they saw the list of what was on board. JC wanted the candy-red Ferrari. Big Tony a 4x4 truck. Sarge got the Humvee. Stenson went for a 1970 Camaro. Brick chose a Harley Davidson motorcycle, and Soni the pink Cadillac Escalade. They weren't sure how they would use them. But if needed, they would roll in style.

The same went for the weapons. Sergeant Dean brought enough for a small army. After everything they had been through so far, this army of misfits weren't taking any chances and would be armed to the teeth.

"What about food?" JC asked.

"How do you stay so skinny as much as you eat?" Brick asked JC.

"I am athletic and burn a lot of calories. Why do you think I run so fast?" He asked Robert.

"Because you are afraid of me," Brick replied.

"I bet I can outrun you," the mocha man joked with the marine.

"I bet you cannot outrun my gun," Robert said. "By the way, Sarge. Do not give him a gun. Do you have anything safe enough for Just Crazy?"

"Party sparklers?" Sergeant Dean offered.

"No, he'll figure out a way to set me on fire and I've been burned enough for one lifetime," Brick replied.

Everyone laughed, recalling the time Brick was blown up in a Humvee in Iraq and almost burned alive until Stenson saved him.

"I'll get the food," Big Tony offered.

"At least we will eat well before we are killed," Robert remarked.

"Luna, anything else to add?" Stenson asked his thoughtful wife.

"I will be here running logistics. Wish I could come with you guys and girl," she told the team.

"You'll be our eyes and ears. That is important considering JC doesn't know directions." Stenson remarked.

"Or what time it is," Brick added. "I told him to

meet us at 1800 hours and he said there were only 12 on a clock."

After a chuckle at JC's expense, they went their separate ways to prepare for the dangerous trip ahead. On the way to pick up food, Big Tony noticed JC was unusually quiet.

"You okay, JC?" Tony Gallo asked.

"I'm fine," his best friend replied.

"Thinking about Zabrina?" Big Tony wondered.

"I'm thinking of us not getting killed trying to rescue her," he said unconvincingly.

Big Tony knew there was more on JC's mind. But he didn't press the subject.

"Hey, pull over. I need some cash," JC instructed.

They stopped at an ATM outside a local bank. After receiving his money, the ATM would not release JC's bank card. Frustrated, Justin began rocking the machine back and forth and cursing aloud. The sight of JC screaming at an inanimate object amused Tony until JC returned to the truck to and retrieved a hammer. He marched back to the uncooperative money dispenser and began whacking it into submission, using more colorful words than before.

Finally, the card reader fell to the ground. JC picked it up and strolled triumphantly back to Tony's truck. He tossed the hammer into the back and removed his card from the defeated card muncher.

Big Tony looked at JC as if he had lost his mind. He asked him, "Do you feel better?"

"Yeah. Now drive before the cops arrive," JC urged the large driver.

"You know you were on camera, right? I bet the video goes viral on the internet and you will have to pay for that ATM," Big Tony warned his psycho friend.

"I don't care. At least I got my card back," Justin

reasoned.

"You are nuts, JC!" the big fella said as they sped away.

Chapter 31
Seoul, South Korea

The Bombardier business jet flew from New Orleans in route to Seoul, South Korea. The team comprising Robert Brickhouse, Stenson Beckett, Justin Carter, Anthony Gallo, Soni James, and John Dean. Their banged up prisoner, Kenny Wu, was their special guest on the flight. The team was scheduled to arrive at 8:15 p.m. local time, a few hours before the container ship "Precious Cargo" docked at the port of Incheon.

During the flight, Robert and Stenson reviewed their plans with Sergeant Dean. Nobody wanted a repeat of the disasters they had encountered thus far. While the rest of the team played cards, watched movies, or caught up on their sleep, JC was unusually reserved in the back of the aircraft.

Robert noticed. "Just Crazy sure has been quiet."

Stenson looked over his shoulder to see JC staring out the window.

"He is worried about Zabrina," Stenson guessed.

"That boy is in love," Robert suggested.

"Maybe, but he has reason to be concerned. Z has been trapped in that container for weeks. I hope, for all our sake, she is alive."

The reality was nobody wanted to think of the hell Zabrina had endured in that torturous floating prison. It was only after Brick beat the information out of Kenny Wu that they learned South Korea and Hong Kong were not the only destinations for the cargo. Several containers, including the one holding Zabrina Chao, were destined for North Korea. In an act of spite, Kenny had shipped Zabrina back to the place she had escaped. If they did not intercept the ship in Incheon, they would be in serious trouble.

Turning his attention to Kenny Wu, Stenson asked Sergeant Dean, "How is our prisoner?"

"Sleeping like a baby," he replied. "I checked on him an hour ago. If I got the dosage right, he should be awake by the time we land. If not, we may have to carry his carcass off this aircraft."

It was nice having Sarge along for this dangerous trip. Besides providing weapons and combat experience, he had contacts in South Korea. Meanwhile, Luna had been tracking the ship since they left New Orleans. It was anchored several miles off the coast of Incheon awaiting clearance to dock.

After they landed and unloaded the plane, Sarge's contacts drove them from Seoul to Daebudo Park. The location gave them a clear view of the Port of Incheon where would stage their launch. The hair-brain plan was for Stenson, Brick, JC and Big Tony to take a Zodiac boat under the cover of night out to Precious Cargo where they would pull along the starboard side of the ship. Out of sight from the loading docks, they would use a "can" cannon to fire a grappling hook with a carbon fiber line to grasp the main deck. If that was successful, they would monkey their way, hoisted 190 feet above the waterline and board the ship unnoticed.

It was a terrible plan, but it was the best terrible plan they could come up with. They had discussed other bad ideas before settling on this one. Bribery would have been an obvious approach, but after giving money to Chinese gangsters back in New Orleans only to be ripped off and almost killed, they weren't willing to try that again. Fast roping down from a helicopter was talked about. That idea was quickly dashed because they were not insane and didn't have a helicopter on hand. Then there was landing on top of the ship from a midnight sky dive. But since nobody knew how to sky dive and they did not have parachutes, that left them with bad option number one.

The dimensions of a cargo ship on paper did not do justice compared to seeing how massive cargo ships are in real life. Precious Cargo was a Panamax class ship, the largest able to traverse the original locks of the Panama Canal. The vessel was 294 meters (965.0 ft) in length, 32 meters (106 ft) wide, with 12 meters (39.5 ft) of draft and a height of 58 meters (190.0 ft). It was longer than three NFL football fields and nearly as wide. As far as container ships go, Precious Cargo was small compared to some of the other 163 ships docked at Incheon. Many of those vessels carried upwards of 20,000 containers. Fortunately for these guys, they only had to search 12,000 of them to find their friend.

They could see from their vantage point through binoculars that the port was lit like daylight and bustling with activity. It operated around the clock with thousands of people scurrying around like worker ants. It was another reason they could not simply board the ship in the normal way. Even if they would have bribed someone, none of them would pass for Asian. These misfits stuck out in a crowd.

Luna phoned to tell Stenson Precious Cargo had been cleared to enter the port. That was their cue to prepare. Soni helped Sarge load weapons onto the Zodiac boat while the boarding party dressed all in black; boots, pants, shirts, jackets, knit caps and gloves. Stenson, Brick, and Big Tony rubbed black paint on their faces. Robert noticed JC doing the same.

"What are you doing?" Robert asked JC.

"Painting my face like you," he replied.

"You know you are black, right?" he asked Justin, as if he was teaching a one-year-old about color.

"We are doing this because we are white and will glow in the dark," the exasperated marine explained.

"Oh, I thought we were doing it to look cool," JC replied.

Brick did not know if JC was serious or messing with him. Nobody could be that dumb. Either way, he shook his head and asked Stenson rhetorically, "What am I going to do with him?"

Everyone chuckled.

"Let him have his fun," Stenson said. "You must admit he is entertaining."

Sarge spotted Precious Cargo through his binoculars in the distance.

"There's your boat," he informed the motley crew.

Stenson looked at his watch. "According to Luna, we've got 19 hours to board, find Zabrina, and get out of here alive."

"No problem," Brick replied. "Why don't we throw in a big party and have some fireworks too?"

"Watch what you ask for," Stenson told the humorous marine.

He acknowledged in a backhanded way there would be a hell of a party and plenty of fireworks if this did not go well.

"You sure you don't want me go?" Soni asked the guys.

"No. Stay here with Sarge in case something goes wrong," Stenson told her. "Which with us lately seems to be every time."

The mood became more serious as they prepared to depart. They had their game faces on as they double-checked their gear. The ship had reached its berth. It would not be long before cranes began removing containers. Stenson, Brick, JC, and Big Tony climbed into the Zodiac and tested their radios a final time.

"See you on the other side," Stenson told Soni and Sarge as Big Tony started the outboard motor and guided the rubber dingy into the chilly blackness of the Yellow Sea.

Gallo killed the engine when they were 100 yards away. As they coasted closer to the ship, the more incredible the size of the hulking vessel became.

"That is a big boat," Brick remarked with a tinge of awe in his voice.

"What have we gotten ourselves into?" Stenson asked rhetorically as he stared up at the stark reality of how high 190 feet was.

"Drop the anchor here," Brick instructed Tony Gallo.

They were 20 yards from the aft of the ship, hidden in the shadows. The Zodiac was a speck against the giant backdrop of the busy port. There wasn't much chance of being discovered unless someone was specifically looking for them or they had terrible luck. As dangerous as this stunt would be, they needed all the luck they could get.

Brick calculated the angle he would need to fire the cannon to reach the main deck. They only had three charges to catch the grappling hook. This would be the easy part if they actually grabbed hold of the ship. After that, they had to shimmy 190 feet above the water to board the vessel. Since they didn't have a clue where Zabrina's container was, they planned to start at the rear of the ship and work their way toward the bow. The task was even more challenging since the containers were stacked eight-high and ten-wide. And if that wasn't complicated enough, they had to do it without being spotted by the crew or crane operators.

Sarge had devised a system of mirrors they would hide behind to avoid being spotted. If someone on the bridge looked out, or a crane operator looked down, they would see a reflection of containers like a magic trick. At least that was their clever, untested plan.

Robert loaded a charge along with a coil of carbon fiber line with the grappling hook. He took aim and said, "Here goes nothing," and fired the cannon with a muffled "pop".

They watched the grappling hook soar through the air, unraveling line as it flew. It had the distance, but the angle was wrong and the hook clanked the metal side of the ship and fell into the water. Like a fisherman reeling in a line, Brick wound 200 feet of cable back into the cannon. He loaded the second charge, then took another aim at a higher angle than before and fired again. This time, the hook made it onto the deck but did not clasp the rail. It fell helplessly over the side into the water again.

The guys were tense. There was no point telling them this was their last attempt. Failure now and they would have to scrub this insane mission and call it a night. JC secretly crossed his fingers when Robert fired the last shot. This time, it hit the deck and scored when the grappling hook held firm. Brick leaned back with all his weight and confirmed they were good to go when the line stayed taut.

"Okay, Big Man, get over here," he told Tony Gallo.

Anthony Gallo stood next to Robert who ran the line through one eyelet on the Zodiac, around Tony's back, and tied it off through another.

"Keep the engine running as we cross. That anchor may not hold. If the line slacks, back away and keep us tight. We don't want JC swimming with the sharks."

"They'd probably spit him out," Big Tony joked.

Brick stepped into a harness and secured two C-clamps to the line with a pulley system mountain climbers use to scale rock faces. He stood on the edge of the Zodiac and tugged the pulley, slowly lifting off the boat with a muffled zipping sound. He made it to the top of the ship in two minutes. He waved to the boat then slid the harness down to the Zodiac.

"You are next," Stenson told JC,

"You got this?" he asked.

"I would be lying if I didn't tell you I'm a little scared. But yeah, I got this," Justin replied.

"Good luck," Stenson encouraged.

JC hesitated for a moment, then he tugged himself off the boat into the air as he had seen Brick do. He was slower to shimmy up the line than Robert, but he made it to the top without becoming a tasty snack at a shark buffet. It was quite an accomplishment for a guy who had never rappelled before. Finally, Stenson glided his way up to the ship. He waved to Big Tony who lifted anchor and moved the boat further into the shadows. Now it was time for their search to begin.

Looking up at the stack of containers made them realize it was higher than they thought. Each container was 8 feet 6 inches tall, adding another 68 feet they had to climb. They hid in the darkness listening to crew talking on deck. Brick held a knife ready to slice someone open if they got too close; an outcome they hoped not to resort.

After the ship workers walked away far enough to feel the coast was clear, Robert tossed a grappling hook up to the top container. It made a loud "clank" before catching hold. It briefly caught the workers' attention, but luckily not an odd enough sound for someone to investigate. They guessed the crew was used to hearing things bump, bang, and rattle on a ship like this.

Brick was first to scale the stack. He was close enough to the bridge that if someone looked out, they could not see him. He unpacked and unfolded four mirrors, which were three feet tall and two feet wide. They formed an upside down L shape with two wings on each side. They were held in place with Velcro straps around his waist, chest, and forearms. He folded the top mirror over his head and said to himself, "I hope this works."

JC and Stenson scaled the containers and assembled their optical disguises the same as Brick had done. Standing together they looked out over the dock to see the activity below. There was no time to waste as they spread out across the first row of containers.

As rudimentary as it was, each man stomped their foot on top of each container causing a dull thud. It was loud enough to be heard in the box, but quiet enough not to reach the crew down below. The hope was they would get a response if Zabrina was inside. Despite having the container identification number, it was placed on the doors and impossible to be read because of how the containers were stacked.

Stomp. Wait. Listen. Move on to the next row. Stomp. Wait. Listen. They continued this down the entire 20 container length. Nothing on the first pass.

The gantry crane was now in place hovering over the ship. Luckily, the crane started near the bridge removing the first cargo box. They watched a container lift 40 feet in the air, slide out over the dock and lower down onto a truck. When the truck drove away, another moved into place. After watching the process several times, they scaled down the stack and returned to the starting point to do it over again on the tier below.

After four hours of this, everyone was feeling nervous. At least now, they could see container numbers each time another box was removed. They prayed, for JC's sake, they would find Zabrina soon. They were lucky so far that their optical trick had worked. But all it would take was a misdirected angle of light for them to be discovered.

There were six more stacks on the deck and another five stacks below in the ship's hold. They began again on the third level. When they reached the 10th row, right in the middle of the ship, JC stomped. He thought he heard a reply. He stomped again. He heard two more knocks and a raspy voice. He stomped again. Then came more frantic knocking. JC held his hand up and pointed to the container. Stenson and Brick rushed over. Justin jumped down to the stack below and verified the number on the container. It was her!

He removed a pair of bolt cutters from his backpack and crushed two locks. JC swung the door open and by some miracle, there she was. Tattered, emaciated, bedraggled, and smelling of her own human waste, JC did not care. He rushed inside and embraced Zabrina.

There was no time for celebration. A commotion and loud voices in a foreign language came from below. Men were climbing the stacks to investigate something the crane operator saw. Could it be one of the container doors had come open on its on?

They didn't plan to stick around to find out, except for JC.

"Shut the doors!" Justin demanded.

"JC, what are you talking about? Get out of there!" Stenson told him in a hushed yell.

"I am not leaving without Zabrina! She is too

weak to get her out of here before the crew arrives. Shut the doors and go!" he insisted again.

They had no time to debate the matter. Stenson and Brick closed the doors and latched them shut. They hustled away from the noise of the crew approaching. Stenson and Brick slid off the side and crashed onto the deck.

"Now, what do we do?" Robert wondered. They had not thought that far ahead.

"I don't know, but we've got to watch that container or we've just lost JC and Zabrina!" Stenson realized.

"Tony!" Brick whispered over the radio. "Get into position where you can see the dock. When I tell you, the container being raised by the crane has both JC and Zabrina in it."

"Did you say it has JC and Zabrina in it?" Gallo repeated.

"You heard me. I will explain it later," Robert replied.

"Radio Sarge tell him to get some wheels over here right now because we do not know where that truck is going and if we lose the truck, we've lost our friends."

Brick looked at Stenson and said, "Now what?"

"We've still got this mirror setup, and it's worked so far. I know you won't like this, but I am going to get on that container and ride it down with JC and Zabrina."

"That's insane! And you are right. I don't like it at all!"

"What choice do we have? You rappel down to Big Tony and hook up with Sarge and the rest. I will stay in contact with you over the radio."

"Dammit Stenson, don't make me worry about you too!"

"When have we ever failed?" Stenson asked

Robert.

"Never. But we have also never hijacked a shipping container in mid-air in a foreign country. You better be careful, for Luna's sake!"

"I will. Now go!" Stenson insisted.

Robert attached the grappling hook to the deck rail and repelled down the side of the ship. Stenson scaled up the stack again and sprinted toward container holding JC and Zabrina.

When Brick reached the Zodiac, he said, "Tony, get me to that dock! I've got to find a way up there to watch that truck!"

Risking being discovered, Big Tony zoomed the Zodiac closer to the docks. Luckily, there was so much activity above, nobody paid attention to a small rubber boat.

"There!" Brick exclaimed when he spotted a ladder leading up to the dock a few hundred yards from where they were unloading containers. He removed the mirror contraption as they moved closer.

"JC, can you hear me?" Robert Brickhouse radioed to Justin.

"I... you..." a broken response came between static. The metal container was interfering with their communication.

"Stenson!" Robert called out.

"I hear you, Brick," Stenson said in a hushed reply.

"Hang in there, buddy. The calvary is on the way!"

"Sarge! Where are you guys?" Brick radioed to Sergeant Dean.

"We are on the way. But it's going to be at least 20 minutes before we reach the port."

"I don't know if we have twenty minutes," Brick warned.

Big Tony pulled the Zodiac closer to the ladder. Robert climbed up and ran down the dock, dipping and dodging his way around containers. He stopped when he was 40 yards away. There was nothing between his hiding place and the truck holding the container with two of their friends inside and a mirrored one on top.

He heard the truck engine start. He could not let this truck get away. Slowly, the vehicle pulled away, moving toward him. As it passed, Robert told himself, "This is a terrible idea," and took off running alongside the vehicle. Before the truck built up speed, he leaped for the bottom edge of the container. Holding on for dear life with his fingertips, Brick's feet dragged the pavement.

There was no way he could hold on to this position for long before his fingers lost their grip or 1,000 people saw a crazy man being dragged along the pier. He looked under the container and grabbed hold of a rail, then swung beneath the truck. With a vice grip hold, he lifted his legs and clamped another rail with both feet.

"Brick, where are you?" Stenson radioed.

"I'm under your truck," he said, out of breath.

"You are what?"

"Where you go, brother, I go," Brickhouse replied.

"Remind me when this is over to discuss your choice of travel options," Stenson joked.

"Tell me about! But then again, why would I take travel advice from you? We are in South Korea and you are riding on the roof of a shipping container wearing mirrors. Your options aren't so bright, either."

The truck slowed down. Robert and Stenson saw it approaching another smaller ship at a different dock.

"Now what?" Stenson wondered over the radio.

"I don't know, but I am glad we are stopping because I wasn't sure how much longer I could hold on." Brick admitted.

Robert lowered himself to the pavement and rolled to one side. He could see two dockworkers' legs walking nearby. The driver stepped out of the truck to speak with the men, then they walked away.

"Stenson, can you get down here?" Brick inquired.

"Not right now. Still many people around," Stenson relayed.

"Sarge, where are you guys?" Robert asked over the radio.

"We just arrived at Incheon. Where are you?" he questioned the marine.

"I don't know. We drove North for 10 minutes. It appears we are at another dock. They look like they are planning to transfer this container to another ship."

"North Korea?" Dean asked.

"I hope not, but I have a feeling that is exactly where it's headed," Brickhouse surmised.

"We'll head that way, but all these trucks and containers look the same. How will we know which one is yours?"

"We'll figure something out," Brick ensured. After all, they boarded a cargo ship, found the girl, and made it this far. Flagging down Sarge and Soni should be easy compared to the rest.

Chapter 32

Port of Incheon—South Korea

Robert found himself pinned beneath the truck holding the container with JC and Zabrina trapped inside. The transport was not literally sitting on top of him preventing his movement, rather he was surrounded by hundreds of dockworkers in a foreign port who might find it suspicious if a tattooed white guy rolled out from under one of their trucks. The cavalry of Sarge and Soni, along with a couple of friendly South Korean drivers, were charging toward his location. He had to figure out a way to signal them without alerting every shuffle-nut puttering around this busy dock.

He removed his black nylon backpack, unzipped it, and looked inside. There wasn't much to work with, he quickly surveyed. He briefly considered using the flare gun, but for reasons other than his fear of catching himself on fire, he decided it was an option of last resort. Duct tape, zip ties, and not much else occupied the bag. The only viable solution he determined was to use the mirrored illusion contraption.

Maybe he could use the magical device to create an opposite effect; instead of hiding him, it would reveal his location. He folded the mirrors into a tent shape and placed it in front of the rear axle between the wheels.

Robert called John Dean over the radio to inform him of his masterful improvisation. "Sarge, look for a truck reflecting your headlights as you drive down the pier."

"Clever, Robert. Let's hope I am the first to see it. Otherwise, you just signaled everybody in Incheon."

"It's the best I could come up with on short notice," the marine replied. "I considered shooting JC with a flare gun and letting him run around screaming he's on fire. But unfortunately, he is currently detained."

Sarge and Soni laughed at the suggestion. They were glad they were not on Brick's bad side like Justin Carter. It would be awhile before Robert Brickhouse forgave the man for shooting him where the sun doesn't shine.

Sarge replied, "Funny. But it's a bit obvious, don't you think? By the way, where is Stenson?"

"He's grabbing a moon-tan on the top of this box. How's the weather up there, Stenson?"

"Can somebody remind me why I am on the roof of a shipping container in South Korea?" Stenson replied.

"Maybe it's because you are friends with Justin Carter and enjoy traveling unconventionally?" Brick suggested.

To the outside observer, they may believe all these guys do is joke around. But there was method to the madness for this comedy team. Levity calmed their nerves and allowed them time to think. They all knew one false move, misstep, or bone-headed miscalculation and somebody could end up dead and that was no joke.

When the coast was clear, Stenson slid down the dark side of the cargo container and rolled beneath the truck next to Robert Brickhouse.

"What's up?" he said nonchalantly.

"Nice to see you again. How was your trip?" Brick said.

"Better than yours it seems," Stenson told him

as he noticed Robert's shoes. They were hanging by threads with a big toe sticking out of one sock.

"I just bought these boots," Robert stated in a perturbed tone.

Stenson chuckled. He envisioned Brick shredding his boots with smoke pouring off his feet as he ran alongside the truck like Fred Flintstone peddled a caveman car. As they pondered new dangerous ways to get JC and Zabrina out of the box perched above their heads, a gigantic clank rattled the truck and shook the ground.

"No way!" Brick exclaimed.

He notified the rest of the team over the radio. "Guys, a crane has grabbed this container and we won't be here long if you don't get here quick!"

They watched the metal box lift from the trailer high into the midnight air. Instantly blinded by the intense shipyard lights and completely exposed, Robert yelled, "Run!"

They log-rolled from beneath the truck and took off in a blind sprint, fearing they would be the next victims gobbled by the transformer-like claw machine. Unable to see, they did not notice when in thirty yards they ran out of pier. Doing their best Wile E. Coyote impersonation in a Roadrunner cartoon, their feet were spinning in mid-air when they splashed into the harbor.

Their shocked, dazed and confused heads cork-popped from the oil-slicked freezing drink. It would have been a viral moment to capture them spitting water out of their mouths like porpoises in an aquatic show. Treading, trying not to drown with all the extra gear they wore, Robert called over the radio to warn their rescue team of their new location.

"Hey guys, forget looking for us under the truck. We are in the ocean now," Robert said.

He waited for a moment and when no response came; he informed Stenson of the obvious. "Apparently, our radios aren't waterproof. What should we do now?"

Stenson approached ice cube status and was clearly not in the mood for Robert's question.

"Why do you always ask me what to do?" Stenson asked him with more than a hint of annoyance in his voice.

"You are the one who yelled run and failed to mention we'd be taking a midnight swim. You figure it out, genius!"

Brick reached into his pocket searching for a cigar; something he did whenever he contemplated a terrible situation, and this one certainly required a moment of self-reflection. He pulled out a mushy wad of tobacco and brown paper, then he washed his disgusting hands in the ocean and said, "JC owes me a box of cigars and a new pair of shoes when this fiasco is over."

Robert and Stenson swam to the pier and waddled up a ladder. They sounded like a pair of squishy ducks as they sloshed behind a stack of shipping containers to spy on the scene they fled. It was no surprise when they discovered the container had disappeared.

"Don't... say... a..." [shivering] "word... Stenson... I... know... the... container... is on.... another boat..." Brick chattered.

Sure enough, there was another ship docked across the pier being fed containers by the orange monstrous crane 100 yards away. Before either said the words, "Here we go again", two white SUVs rolled up and parked behind the empty truck. The Asian drivers stepped out of the vehicles and struck up what sounded like a friendly conversation with the dock workers standing nearby. Behind them, Sergeant Dean appeared and walked over to inspect the mirror contraption between the wheels of the empty container truck. He looked around, wondering where the guys were. Robert shot out from behind the stack and waved his arms franticly over his head like the next contestant on a TV game show.

"Psss... Sarge, over here!"

John noticed the excited tattooed contestant and casually strolled over like it was a normal day, which wasn't day or normal by any stretch of the imagination.

"I thought you were waiting by the truck? And why are you two wet?" Sarge asked.

Stenson and Brick looked at each other not having the time or patience to explain their icy adventure.

"It's a long story," the pair said.

"Where are JC and Zabrina?" John Dean asked.

They pointed to the cargo ship on the other side of the dock receiving regurgitation from the box munching crane.

"They are on another ship? I thought the plan was to get Zabrina off the cargo ship and bring her back in the Zodiac?" Sarge verified.

"Well, that was the plan," Stenson said. "Now it looks like we need another plan."

"And why is JC in the box with Zabrina, and where is Big Tony?"

It was too many questions, with little time to discuss the finer details of how this cockamamie plan went wrong. As far as Big Tony was concerned, he was probably floating around the harbor somewhere. They did not know because their waterlogged radios did not work. And while everybody else was having a good time, Stenson and Brick were trying to not be run over or fall off the roof of a container truck, or getting caught by dock workers in a foreign port, or dying of hypothermia. It was far too much to explain, so the status of their enormous boat driver was the least of their concerns especially after hearing more bad news.

"No freaking way," Stenson said after hearing the information John's contacts shared.

"Yeah, according to the dockworkers my guys spoke to that boat our friends are now on is heading to North Korea," John revealed.

"But it's in a South Korean port. What about sanctions and those two countries are technically still at war?" Stenson asked.

"The flag on the boat may not be North Korean, but my contacts assured me that is where this one is going. Don't ask me how or why."

Brick looked at Stenson shaking his head. While Robert kept his mouth shut, Stenson imagined the string of curse words stitching together inside the marine's skull. Dealing with South Koreans was one thing. But as soon as that boat crossed an imaginary line not far away, the rules will change.

Everyone was quite aware North Korea did not have the best relationship with the United States. In fact, the North Koreans (or at least their despot leader) hated the country they were from. And here they were, a bunch of ragtag Americans showing up to rescue a black guy and a North Korean woman who fled their country only to return? Yeah, this was not good.

Now they were about to be in more perilous position than their previous dangerous feats; firing squads or worse if they were caught. They had to get JC and Zabrina off that boat before it hit North Korea. Stenson borrowed Sarge's satellite phone to call Luna in New Orleans to see if she could give him some information.

Sarge, Soni and Brick stood by and listened to one side of Stenson's conversation with his wife:

"Hey babe, where are Charlie's cars?"
"Yeah, I'm fine. Brick is fine. Everybody is fine."
"Did we get Zabrina? Well, sort of..."
"It's complicated Luna. JC is in the box with Zabrina, and now we are heading to North Korea."
"I know North Korea doesn't like Americans."
"How did JC get in the box? I know he was supposed to get her out of the box..."
"Look babe, I don't have time to explain all of this right now. I simply need to know where Charlie's cars are?"
"Okay, thanks. I love you too. Yes, I will tell Brick to look after me, but who will look after him?"

[Click]

"I like Luna," Robert told Stenson after he hung up the phone.

"I like her too, Robert. And I would like to see her again if we can impossibly rescue JC and Zabrina, dispose of Kenny Wu, and get back to New Orleans in one piece."

Stenson returned his attention to the business at hand.

"According to Luna, the manifest says Charlie's cars were loaded after Zabrina. They were some of the last containers to go on before the ship departed New Orleans, which means they've been unloaded from Precious Cargo and are somewhere around this port."

Brick asked, "Why do we need the cars?"

Stenson glared at him.

"I don't know, Robert. But the way this is going I want to know where those vehicles are. I'm pretty sure they don't have car rental places in North Korea should we need a ride."

"But Zabrina and JC are on the boat. Where do the cars come into play? You lost me," Brick persisted.

"Look Robert, I don't know where the cars are or what we are going to do with them if we find them. And I don't have time to answer your twenty questions. This is a fluid situation if you haven't noticed."

Their next insanity was figuring out how to intercept another cargo ship. North Korea was not far away. They had the Zodiac, which could hold eight people. Stenson counted: Sarge, himself, Brick, Big Tony, Soni, and Kenny Wu... that's six. It left enough room for a small cache of weapons.

Stenson explained the best of their worst options was to follow the cargo ship to North Korea and figure out how to board the vessel along the way. Maybe they could grapple hook this one like they did with Precious Cargo. Then it occurred to Stenson they had no more explosive charges for the "can" cannon used to fire the grapple hook. So Brick, or whoever wanted to try their luck lassoing a cargo ship in the open sea was their only shot.

It was a terrible plan. In fact, it was no plan at all. It was a suicide mission. But like always, they would do whatever it took, no matter how dangerous or crazy the idea was to save their friends.

While Stenson was telling himself, "I wish our friends would stop getting caught," Sarge made a suggestion.

"Why don't we bribe the captain to let us search the boat for Zabrina and JC's container and get them to unload it?"

That would never work. Or could it? There was one way to find out. Sarge walked over and spoke to the South Korean drivers, who in-turn spoke with the boat crew who notified the captain. The captain, a portly, balding man with an unsteady gait, shuffled down the boat ramp and spoke with the South Koreans. Money exchanged hands and Sarge came back and told the team they were good to go.

"No way!" Brick exclaimed. "Stenson, you and your elaborate schemes of following the ship in a rubber dingy, grapple hooks, and whatever else you planned to get us on board. This is much easier than your bright ideas."

"Well, I... uh... nevermind," Stenson fumbled. Finally, he said, "Grab your stuff and get on board before somebody changes their mind."

Since none of the crew spoke English, Sarge asked a South Korean driver to assist them as a translator. More money exchanged hands with the stipulation the translator would not leave this port. The only people North Koreans hated more than Americans were their rich cousins from the south.

With that out of the way, Brick and Stenson searched for JC and Zabrina's container while the others combed the docks looking for Charlie Whitehorse's stolen cars. Thankfully, Stenson and Brick found Zabrina and JC in short time before the container was loaded. This might be easier than they thought, since the box wasn't on the North Korean ship yet.

When the large metal doors flung open, Robert and Stenson were gob smacked by the overpowering stench of urine, feces, and musty sweat; a smell so close to death. However, seeing JC hold Zabrina in a comforting embrace made the foul odor fade away. Well, not really. Love or no love, JC and Zabrina stunk. But after several torturous weeks at sea under inhumane conditions, everyone was thankful to see Zabrina Chao alive.

Stenson and Brick entered the container and offered to help JC carry her out. He waved them away as if to say, "No, I've got this."

They watched him gently lift her up like a precious porcelain doll. Zabrina was fragile and very weak, barely able to speak. She had lost considerable weight from her already petite frame as she wrapped her pencil-thin arms around Justin's neck. Like a groom carries a bride across the wedding threshold, JC stepped out of the metal prison giving Zabrina a taste of freedom's fresh air.

This was the moment that cracked Brick's steely heart in his opinion of Justin Carter. JC was a hero now and worthy of the soldier's respect. In Robert's mind, and Stenson's too, heroes were the ones who risked their lives to rescue you no matter what it took. However, the joy was short-lived when they discovered four men pointing AK-47 weapons at them. Across the way, they saw another group threatening the rest of their team.

"We've been double-crossed!" Brick exclaimed.

"Well, this wouldn't be the first time it's happened to us," Stenson said as he raised his arms over his head.

"Hey Big Tony, where did you come from?" Brick wondered when he saw their big boat driver standing next to Sarge, Soni and Kenny Wu.

One of the Asian guys holding an AK-47 on Robert told him to shut up, or Robert guessed that is what they said since he did not speak their language. He pushed the guy's muzzle down to the surprise of the man holding the gun. This was apparently not how they do things in Asia, but it's exactly how Robert did things and he wanted an answer before he was shot.

Big Tony said, "I waited by the ship for you with the engine running. But you guys took hours up there and the Zodiac ran out of gas. Apparently, nobody thought to fill it up. Then I heard some little girls screaming in the water saying it was cold and cursing each other. I paddled the boat back to the dock and lost 50 pounds doing it. Not the best way to lose weight, but whatever. Then I climbed my fat ass up a ladder and ran into Sarge."

The gunmen pointing weapons looked at each other with an expression of, "Who are these crazy people and what are they talking about?"

Brick asked, "Who was in charge of gas for the Zodiac?"

"I thought it was full, Robert. I mean, who rents a boat with a half tank of gas?" Sarge admitted it was on him.

In his defense, Robert felt compelled to set something straight before this conversation went any further.

"Those girls you heard screaming, Big T? That was Stenson when he was in the water. He sounds like a pubescent girl when he is cold. I am manly, so it wasn't me."

Soni James chimed in, "Robert, remember that time I saw you in the shower? You screamed like a little girl."

Brick choked recalling the embarrassing moment. "I thought door was locked, Soni. That was a foul."

They could have gone on with this conversation, but their gun toting captors were not amused. It seemed hostages were worth more in ransom than they were paid to get these bad joke people on board their ship. The only consolation was they would die together if this did not go well.

As the group was being marched up the plank to board the North Korea-bound cargo ship, Sarge said, "By the way, we found Charlie's cars. They are sitting over there waiting to be loaded onto this boat."

Robert looked at Stenson, trying to process what was about to occur. They found JC and Zabrina and rescued them before they were loaded onto this boat. They should have all been happily on their way home by now sipping champaign. But no, that is not their kind of luck. Nothing with them was easy or predictable. Now they were held hostage and forced to go to North Korea despite really not wanting to go to North Korea. Brick was still puzzled why Stenson cared about Charlie's stolen cars. None of this made any sense. However, one thing was certain; Brick and Stenson would have a conversation about this turn of events before they died.

The armed men escorted the group downstairs into the bowels of the ship. They were forced inside a pale green cabin, fluorescently lit, with double bunk beds on each side. Everyone took a defeated seat on the bunks except for Kenny Wu who Brick pushed to the floor for causing all this trouble. The metal door slammed shut, and a lock clanged tight. One armed guard remained posted outside the door.

With no phones, weapons, bathroom or food, they were more than a little concerned about the predicament they found themselves in. It was ironic that this gigantic mess began with one of their friends being trapped in a box, then there were two with JC and Zabrina. Now they were all trapped in a box, albeit a larger one. Except for Luna who was back in New Orleans trapped in a wheelchair, the equivalent of a prison on wheels. And Charlie Whitehorse who was probably stealing more high-end cars or Lucious T. Haggerty wherever he may be. But for Stenson Beckett, Robert Brickhouse, Justin Carter, Zabrina Chao, Anthony Gallo, Soni James, John Dean, and the criminal who started this affair, Kenny Wu, their fate was all the same. They were stuck in a box headed in the wrong direction.

Nobody was angrier than Justin Carter who sat on a bunk next to Zabrina who was in desperate shape. Without immediate medical attention, she might die. And JC did not come this far to lose her in some nasty cargo ship heading to North Korea.

There was something different about JC's attitude from the moment that door closed; something they had never seen in him before. Brick recognized the look of a wild animal in his eyes. He had seen the same look from soldiers in combat when they were pinned down. It was not fear. No. This was furious anger that said they were getting out of here alive.

The normally mild-mannered jokester shot forward without warning, as if something snapped inside of him. He kicked the metal door with heroic strength.

[BOOM!] [BOOM!] [BOOM!]

The guard peered through the small, round window to see what caused the stir.

JC glared at the man through the circular window. Their eyes locked on each other, separated by thick glass only inches apart.

JC yelled, "I need water!"

The guard kept his eyes laser-focused on JC unfazed by his plea. Then he turned away. It was not because he didn't speak English. Rather, the guard simply did not care what the crazy black man wanted. Meanwhile, Brick considered teaching JC more of the colorful language he used to get the guard's attention. While Brick couldn't hold a conversation in Korean, he certainly knew their curse words.

JC smashed the door again and again in the same booming manner. He finished with a Kung Foo kick and a louder demand, "I need water, now!"

The guard looked back at JC with a devilish grin

daring him to do it again. JC returned the glare ready to burn the glass window the guard was peeping through with his eyes. But if that is what the guard wanted, daring him to hit that door again, then JC was more than happy to oblige. He drum rolled the door like a heavy metal concert that would not stop until the guard's ears were bleeding.

[BAM] [BAM] [BAM] [BAM] [BAM] [BAM]

Robert told himself, "JC is living up to his nickname right now because he has lost his mind. He really is Just Crazy."

Finally, it was enough to annoy the guard. He was fed up with JC and the commotion he was causing. The guard flung open the door with every intention of shutting that black guy up. In a split second, JC sprang forth with such fury and quickness the man never had time to react.

In one swift move, JC wrapped the guard in a headlock and yanked him down, cracking his head on the hard metal floor. Like a prison riot, Stenson, Robert, Sarge, Soni, and Big Tony leaped into the fray. Brickhouse wrestled the weapon free while the rest whaled, kicked, and screamed obscenities at the terrified man. Like a pack of wild animals, the attack was over in seconds.

"Quick! Shut the door!" Robert insisted.

In case the ruckus was heard by other gunslingers on the boat, they quickly reset the room. Big Tony dragged the beaten guard and propped him in a corner where he would not be seen from the porthole window. Robert moved to the opposite corner on the hinge-side of the door with the seized weapon. The rest returned to the bunks and sat down.

Minutes later, a crew member came by and noticed nobody was guarding the door where the prisoners were held. He looked through the porthole and everything seemed normal.

JC yelled again, "We need some water!"

Whether he did not understand what JC said or was incredibly dumb, the crew member opened the door and stepped inside.

[CRACK!]

Robert smashed the butt of the rifle into the man's skull causing him to crumple to the floor. Stenson grabbed the gun while Big Tony dragged the unconscious guard and stacked him atop the other. Remarkably, the ruse continued two more times. Now they had four firearms, four prisoners, and fewer places to hide bodies.

With odds now in their favor, it was time to search the ship and find the betraying captain. The vessel was already underway to North Korea and there would be some convincing to do to get this ship turned around before they crossed the point of no return.

"Zabrina is not doing well," JC said. "She needs food and water."

"Stay with her. I will find it," Big Tony told his best friend.

"Sarge, watch Kenny Wu and these clowns until Big Tony returns. Soni, help JC take care of Zabrina. Stenson and I will scope the ship and deal with any crew we find," Robert informed the team.

Big Tony was first out the door carrying an AK-47 in a search for the galley. Stenson and Robert followed him out and headed down hallways in opposite directions. One-by-one they cleared each room gathering more prisoners along the way. Remarkably, the crew they encountered did not put up a fight. They were as surprised as anyone that the hostages were now the hostage takers.

Anthony Gallo returned with food and water. JC

grabbed a bottle and twisted it open. He gently lifted Zabrina's head to help her take a sip. She finished the bottle and JC handed her another. She could probably have drank the entire case as dehydrated as she was. JC encouraged her to pace herself. He peeled an orange, tearing away a tiny slice, and placed it against her lips as if he was feeding a child.

"Eat this. You need vitamin C," JC encouraged Zabrina.

Soni, Sarge, and Big Tony were mesmerized watching how tenderly JC cared for her. But there were other things to do now.

Sarge told them, "I am going to take these four and locate Stenson and Brick. Keep an eye on Kenny Wu until I return."

Sergeant Dean ordered the four crew members up with some automatic lead encouragement he held in his hands. The crew filed out followed by John Dean. He soon found Stenson and Brick who were shoving a couple of guys into a refrigerated compartment. Dean stuffed his prisoners in to join the others.

They continued searching the ship for more crew members covering three decks, including offices, a gym, cabins, infirmary, recreation room, common rooms, laundry, and galley. They searched the garbage disposal system, freshwater system, sewage treatment plant, refrigeration system, multiple electrical, engine, and cargo compartments. By the time they finished covering all the hiding places on the hulking ship, they had rounded up 19 men. Now it was time to find the hostage-taking Judas who was in charge of this boat.

Chapter 33
Port of Incheon—South Korea

"The guy must be Chinese. There is no way he is North Korean," Stenson bet.

"Do you think for one second the South Koreans would allow North Koreans to use their ports?"

"Chinese, Japanese, Pekinese, or Chimpanzees, I don't care," the annoyed Marine replied.

"You know Pekinese is a dog that originated from China?" Sarge educated the marine after learning the information from one of the animal shows he likes to watch.

"Yeah, and Chimpanzees are primates," Stenson offered after apparently watching the same programs as Sergeant Dean.

"Whatever. I am going to find that fat monkey who drives this boat and betrayed us!" Brick retorted.

The captain was not on the ship's bridge. In fact, nobody was there to mind the myriad of dials, knobs, video screens, and levers scattered around the brains of the boat. They looked out the large windows perched high above stacks of multi-colored shipping containers carpeting the herculean deck like Lego bricks.

The new morning painted the sky with a palette of pinks and blues, with the occasional puff of white clouds floating over the horizon of Incheon, South Korea. The pier was a tranquil oasis compared to the frenzied chaos they encountered a few pitch-black hours ago.

It was a relief to see the ship was still in port and not halfway to North Korea. The question was where is that son-of-a fortune-cookie who thought it was a bright idea to take them hostage for a dictator's ransom? The guys were more than ready to have an impolite conversation with him, especially an angry marine named Robert Brickhouse.

In a stateroom off the bridge, they found the little fat betrayer passed out drunk in bed. In some ways, it was his good fortune because the Benedict Arnold of Asia was so intoxicated that he did not realize his entire crew was missing. It also made it easier for the guys to deal with the tub-thumper without breaking a sweat.

Brick sat on the bunk next to the sleeping man. With the tip of his gun, he swished the captain's sparse hair. He leaned over and whispered into his ear with a soothing growl, "Good morning, Cookie."

Stenson and Sarge snickered as the captain stirred and romantically clutched his pillow as if to enjoy the second act of a sweet dream. Robert noticed a metal trash can in the corner by a small desk scattered with maps and an empty bottle of the Chinese liquor Baijiu. It gave him a sadistic idea. He walked over and picked up the container, dumping its guts onto the floor. Using the steel barrel of his confiscated AK-47, Robert rattled inside the can so loudly that it reminded the guys of the first rude day of boot camp when they were awakened by an unpleasant drill sergeant who possessed the gentleness of a chainsaw.

Brick yelled in his best United States Marine Corps voice, "Wake up you scum-sucking piece of panda dung!"

The captain flew upright into a sitting position with a look of confusion wondering why sleeping beauty left just when they were getting to the good part of his dream. Slowly, the captain's foggy eyes cleared enough to see the beauty queen was now an angry bearded man with tattoos smiling at him with an AK-47 pointed to his head. Then he realized the dream had become a nightmare. It was not the best way to wake up with a hangover. His head banged like Big Ben ringing between his ears.

"You are lucky I am ready to get off this boat and go home that I not wasting my time killing you today," Brick told the hungover man.

The captain gave Brick a look of a puppy when it does not understand by cocking his head. While amusing, Robert was not interested in searching for a translator to explain it again. The marine waved the barrel of his gun at the fat captain's face and pointed it toward the cabin door, suggesting he better get his chunkiness off that bunk and march. Otherwise, there was no telling what Brick would do that did that did not require a mop and bucket.

Chunky monkey wisely rose from the bed and did as he was told. Stenson, Sarge, and Robert continued to persuade the man forward with some automatic AK love until they reached the refrigerated cargo hold below.

"Put him in the fridge along with the others so we can go!" Brickhouse instructed Stenson and Sarge.

They dumped him into the refrigerated compartment to join the rest of his frozen crew. One icicle asked a question in a language they did not understand. However, Robert got the gist of what the beggar wanted and replied.

"No, you cannot have coats. You cannot call your mama. And you cannot show me how well you ice dance. You snow monkeys can freeze to death for all I care after what you did to us!"

Now whether any of them understood what the marine said did not matter, because they clearly got the point when Brick slammed the windowless door shut and locked it with a rusty "Clank!".

Muffled yells and girly screams could be heard as they walked away. Maybe the crew were beating the pinyin out of the drunk captain, who knows? Robert Brickhouse did not care. He and Stenson still had not thawed out from their late-night aquatic adventure. Needless to say, Mr. Brickhouse was unsympathetic to their frozen plight.

The group returned to the drab green room where the rest of the team awaited. With a triumphant smile, Brick announced, "We're outta here!"

"What about Wu?" Big Tony asked, staring at the source of their troubles sitting on the floor, chained to a bed post.

"We're dropping him off and then we're heading home," Stenson informed the group.

Brick did not know what "dropping him off" meant. Drop him off a boat into the ocean? Throw him out of the airplane as they flew home? He made a note to ask Stenson to clarify his intentions later.

While Brick pondered colorful ways to dispatch Kenny Wu, the announcement brought a sigh of relief to the rest of the team. The effort to track down these criminals went beyond anything they could have imagined. Everyone was glad, except Zabrina. Her face was the only one without a smile. She stared at the floor, holding back her tears.

"What's the matter, Z?" Stenson asked Zabrina.

"What about my parents? I haven't spoken to them in years and we are so close," her voice whispered as she shared her desperate feelings.

Stenson looked around the room and saw the shared disappointment everyone's eyes hearing her that lossful confession. Stenson, more than anyone, knew what losing family meant to him.

Zabrina's parents lived in North Korea. Soon

after she departed for the United States, which was a perilous journey not unsimilar to the one she had been rescued from now, authorities discovered her parents paid smugglers to get their daughter out of the country in the hope she would have a better life than them. Since that time, Zabrina had not heard from her parents and feared for their lives.

Stenson kneeled in front of Zabrina and took her hand into his own. He looked into her brown eyes and wiped away a tear. He said, "We've come this far, Zabrina. We will find your parents."

Robert could not believe the promise his best friend made. He motioned Stenson outside to have a word with him.

"Listen, I know how soft-hearted you are Stenson. But how do you think we are going to find her parents and get them out of a country that hates Americans?"

"Sun Fang," he said, as if he had already considered this scenario.

"Wu's father?" Brick asked in disbelief. "He lives in Hong Kong. How can that gangster help us?"

"He is the ultimate gangster and a billionaire. We have what he wants sitting in that room. I bet you a million-to-one that Kong has connections in North Korea. We trade his son for Zabrina's parents," Stenson considered.

"You are insane!" Brick admitted. "I guess it's worth a try. But we keep ramping up the level of gangsters we are dealing with. Those other guys were nothing compared to these."

Stenson retrieved Sarge's satellite phone, which they had found on their search for crew along with the rest of the stuff they stole when they were kidnapped. He and Brick went upstairs to the top deck where Stenson could get a clear signal. Since Kong had called him before, Stenson had his personal number. He dialed Hong Kong and waited for an answer.

"Stenson Beckett, what do I owe the pleasure?" Kong cheerfully greeted as if he and Stenson were best friends planning a golf outing or some family gathering (which in some ways, they were).

"I need your help," Stenson told the billionaire. "I have something you want and you may know how to get something I need."

Stenson explained the situation. For reasons of honor, the Rising Tiger agreed to see what he could do. Kong revealed not only did he have contacts in North Korea; he had the most important one. He knew the Supreme Leader personally.

He did "special" things for the reclusive despot over the years. Mostly, it was importing indulgences such as liquor, food, electronics, cars, and other things not readily available to dictators banned by most countries around the world. But even with his billions, Kong warned he could not ask the Supreme Leader for a favor. Everything he did with him was transactional and done in trade. It was one favor for another, and he wasn't sure what this would cost.

"Did you say he liked cars?" Stenson asked Wu Kong.

"Oh yes. It's one of his favorite indulgences," he replied.

"What if I told you I've got a boat loaded with high-end vehicles ready to deliver right now?" Stenson tempted.

"You are off to a good start," the elder Wu replied. "I will reach out to his people and see if he is interested. What are the woman's parents' names?"

Stenson gave him Zabrina's family names, the village they lived in and their ages. Kong told Stenson to stand by, then hung up. Twenty minutes later he phoned back.

"You are in luck. The Supreme Leader was in a good mood and a little tipsy. He agreed to your proposal. Your friend's family are being kept at a re-education camp in Wŏnsan in Kangwŏn Province on the eastern side of the country."

"We are in South Korea on the western side at the Port of Incheon. That could take days," Stenson replied.

"I know exactly where you are, Mr. Beckett. I have been tracking you and your friends since you left New Orleans," the billionaire revealed.

He continued, "That is one of my ships you are on. You are to take it to the Port of Nampo on the western coast of North Korea. They will off-load your vehicles and you and your friends will be escorted to Ryongsong District in northern Pyongyang to the presidential palace as guests of the Supreme Leader."

Stenson was flabbergasted. "Let me get this straight. You want us to take your boat to North Korea and drive a bunch of stolen cars to the North Korean capital and drop them off at the guy's house and then we get Zabrina's parents and leave?"

"Yes," Kong said, "He likes some Americans, just not most politicians. Also, he wants to meet you since you are bringing him nice cars."

"Pardon me if I don't believe you, because we've been screwed by your son at every turn and we were almost kidnapped by some North Koreans a few hours ago. Why should I believe you?"

"Because, Mr. Beckett, I am an honorable man. It is something my son has never learned."

Somehow, Stenson believed him. Either that or he and his friends were about to the most dead idiots for believing the word of a man whose nickname is the Rising Tiger.

"Do your business and you will leave safely,"

Kong told him. "All I want is my son returned and my honor restored."

"Well, I don't know why I should believe you, but I guess I do," Stenson said. "But I warn you my friends won't be happy if we end up on the wrong end of a firing squad."

"You have my word," Kong promised before ending their call.

Robert Brickhouse was astonished. "You are out of your mind, Stenson! We are taking this boat... his boat, the one we were almost kidnapped on to North Korea. Then we are going to drive stolen vehicles to the most dangerous dude's house who will kill his own people for listening to K-Pop music. Then we say hello and pick up Zabrina's parents, then waltz out like we are going back to Kansas in a hot air balloon at the end of the Wizard of Oz?"

"Basically," Stenson replied. "Except for the balloon and the Kansas part. We are returning to New Orleans on an airplane if we live. But I can get you a balloon. Maybe even some flying monkeys to take back as souvenirs."

"Boy, that cold bath last night scrambled your brain," Brick mocked his best friend.

Robert knew they had no choice.

He said, "Oh well, let's do something even more dangerous and crazy than before because you are such a good guy and want to rescue somebody's parents. And may I remind you Zabrina tried to kill us two years ago?"

Stenson shrugged. It was water under the bridge as far as he was concerned because that bill had been paid in full when they took Club Empire down. They were friends now, and it was the right thing to do. He would do it for Brick. But Robert was right. He must be as crazy as JC.

"Let's see what Big Tony cooked up before we get

underway," Stenson suggested. "I have a feeling this will be a long night,"

"That's an understatement," Brick deadpanned as they returned downstairs. "And where do you think you are going to get flying monkeys?"

* * *

"Wake up!" Brick yelled at the frosty covered snow captain as he kicked him with a new pair of boots he requisitioned at gunpoint from the only crew member who wore the same size shoes as him. It was 5:00 AM.

The other snowflakes barely stirred at the commotion. They were various shades of blue and Brick wondered if this was the dead color blue or iceberg blue. He hoped it was the latter because he needed these popsicle sticks to run the boat or else he'd have to find another crew.

"Tell him to take us to Nampo," Brick instructed their translator who was more cooperative now that he was on the team with guns.

The translator repeated Brick's command, followed by the captain saying something in return.

"What did he say?" Brick asked.

"He said that is where they were going in the first place before you kidnapped him and his crew."

"Hold up. We kidnapped them after they kidnapped us. Now I am in charge and I need him and his little dumplings to thaw out and get us to Tampon. We have places to go and people to see. Chop! Chop!"

"You mean Nampo? Tampon is a feminine product women use during menstruation," the translator clarified.

"What are you, a dictionary? Nampo, Tampon, whatever. We are going somewhere. Tell them to get their little ding-a-longs up and come along. I don't have all morning to discuss women's reproductive health with you!" Brick growled.

Stenson laughed at the interaction.

"Should I tell them about reproductive health or just the come along part?" the translator asked.

Brick looked at Sarge. "Where did you get this guy from? I feel like shooting him and throwing him in with the rest of these slip-n-slides and find another crew,"

Brick looked back at the translator and said nice and slow, so there was no mistake. "No, please tell them the big nice man with the gun in his hand requests them to un-stick their lollipops from the floor and get this boat underway or I will shoot them."

It probably wasn't a direct translation of what Brick said, but whatever the translator told the crew seemed to work. They all stiffly shuffled out the door as if you caught a fish in the ocean and threw it in the cooler, then told the fish later it was time to swim again, you were only joking about freezing it to death. At least until Robert Brickhouse and company got to their destination, then all bets were off as far as Mr. Impatient was concerned.

Sarge, Soni, and Big Tony followed three groups of men to various stations. The AK-47s reminded them if they did not drive this boat correctly, sabotage anything, or cause a mutiny, then Captain Brickhouse would have them walk the plank. Stenson was convinced Brick had been possessed by a dead pirate from the mid-1500s. All he needed now was a patch over one eye, a hook for a hand, and a wooden leg.

JC stayed behind to nurse Zabrina and watch over Kenny Wu. Zabrina's spirits had lifted knowing they were attempting the impossible feat of rescuing her parents. The fact they were trying rapidly improved her health along with Justin's tender loving care.

Meanwhile, Stenson and Robert followed the captain and a first mate upstairs to the bridge. Brick found another bottle of the Chinese booze in the Captain's stateroom and poured himself and Stenson a drink.

"Cheers," he toasted his best friend. "Here is to the most outrageous thing we have ever done."

"Salut!" Stenson said with a reassuring grin, hoping it will all work out for everyone's sake.

The ship raised anchor and departed Incheon at 6:30 AM. Even though they were only traveling 267 miles (or 430 kilometers), the trip took 17 hours at 15 knots. They arrived at 11:30 P.M.

As the ship approached the Port of Nampo, everyone noticed the dock was filled with North Korean soldiers. They really did not know what kind of welcome to expect. But it certainly looked like half the North Korean Army awaited their arrival.

Robert asked Stenson, "Are you sure about this? We can turn around."

Stenson gave Brick a sheepish smile and replied, "We will soon find out."

After they anchored, a senior military officer from the North Korean Army met them on the bridge. With a chest full of medals and a stern look on his face, his appearance took the translator by surprise. He was more intimidating than Brick and Stenson seeing his country's foe standing so close.

"Lái!" the officer commanded.

The translator told Brick and Stenson, "He said to come with him."

As they followed the medal guy, their translator did not budge. Robert asked him, "What about you?"

"He said nothing about me. I am South Korean. I am staying on this boat!" The translator fearfully reiterated his previous position that had not changed from when they negotiated this deal.

Robert and Stenson had no choice. They followed the officer off the bridge and onto the main deck where they met their friends. Whoever this officer was must be important, because every North Korean soldier on that dock was afraid of him when he barked. He turned to the team and announced in perfectly accented English, "You are a guest of the Democratic People's Republic of Korea. The Supreme Leader welcomes you!" Then he saluted.

Surprised, Robert asked. "You speak English?"

"Of course," the officer confirmed. "Your vehicles will be unloaded immediately. We will escort you and your friends to Pyongyang."

Hearing "Pyongyang", the capital of North Korea, left the team slightly uneasy, especially Zabrina. Reality set in to remind them they were about to embark on a trip with the possibly of no return.

After what seemed like an eternity to ponder the situation, everyone knew they could not back out now. The chances of being shot, imprisoned, or whatever else they do to people who change their minds in North Korea was certainly on their minds.

The group walked down the gangway to the pier where they watched a crane remove five containers and place them on the dock. The first one held the black Humvee. Sarge grabbed Kenny Wu by his shirt collar and stuffed him in the back. Next was Stenson's 1970 Camaro followed by Robert's Harley Davidson motorcycle, then Big Tony's 4x4 truck. When Soni saw the hot pink Cadillac Escalade, she exclaimed, "Yeah baby, that's my ride!" Finally, the container holding the candy red Ferrari was unloaded. JC opened the passenger door for Zabrina, then climbed into the driver's seat of the exotic sports car.

Six gun-mounted military vehicles, three in the

front and three in the rear, led them off the pier and into the pitch-black night. As they drove through the countryside, the Americans noticed a stillness and darkness like they had never seen before. The only sounds came from the engines of the vehicles in the convoy. They were the only ones on the road, and there were no lights anywhere to be seen. The country was completely void of any street lights or even a single illuminated house.

The scenery changed as they approached the outskirts of Pyongyang ninety minutes later. It was a completely different place; well-lit with more modern buildings (by hermit nation standards), public transportation hubs, and stores. Yet, it was a ghost town with nobody on the streets except for this caravan. It was spooky and way too quiet for their taste with a gut wrenching feeling something was about to go wrong, like a bad horror film.

They approached Ryongsong Residence or Residence No. 55, known by the locals as Central Luxury Mansion. It was apparent this was an important place after all the military checkpoints they passed through. While nobody but their translator who stayed behind could read Korean, pictures warning of electric fences and land mines were easy to understand. Everybody knew what lightning bolts and explosions meant, and they had no intention of finding out if the proclamations were true.

When they reached the mansion, they remarked it wasn't as big as Buckingham Palace, but it was close. The military vehicles stopped past the main entrance in front of the building, with the Americans halting their cars in single-file line behind them. The highly decorated officer ordered everyone out and instructed them to stand next to their vehicle.

Two enormous doors opened at the top of a flight

of red-carpeted stairs. A group of armed soldiers stepped outside and formed lines on each side of the entrance. The next moment, the Supreme Leader of North Korea stepped out. He was dressed exactly as any image seen of him on television. He wore black pants with a black top and shoes, with that famous haircut; tight on the sides and high on top. He even wore the same smile you saw whenever he waved to crowds. However, this time they were the audience, and it was uncannily surreal.

The Supreme Leader casually strolled down the steps in front of the line of cars. He said in heavily accented English. "Welcome to my country."

The first thing that ran through their minds was, "How many people can say that?" The guy owns an entire country. It was bizarre. In the back of Robert's mind, he could hear JC said, "Hey Brick, One day I'm going to own a country."

The Supreme Leader inspected the Humvee first and looked Sarge up and down. He didn't even acknowledge Kenny Wu as if to say he'd met enough Asians and was more interested in these Americans bringing him nice cars. He nodded at Sarge and moved onto the Stenson's Camaro.

"Classic," the Supreme Leader said and moved on.

He looked at Brick and the Harley then shook his head with disapproval. "Should have been Kawasaki, but it will do."

Robert resisted the temptation to reach out and choke the man for disliking his motorcycle. But he refrained since he didn't want 50 guys to fill him and his bike full of holes.

When the leader reached the pink Escalade and saw Soni James, he said, "You are more beautiful than the car." She smiled, and he moved on.

He looked over the 4 x 4 truck Big Tony drove.

The Supreme Leader approved of the vehicle but was more impressed with Anthony Gallo's enormous size.

"You are a big man. You like food like me," the Supreme Leader told the gentle giant, who returned the leader's smile.

Lastly, he reached the red Ferrari and Justin Carter. The Supreme Leader seemed impressed with this car over all the rest.

JC nodded to the Supreme Leader and smiled like they were old friends and said, "'Sup?"

The Supreme Leader paused and said, "What is your name?"

The team tensed, not believing JC spoke when they had all remained quiet. But this was JC and he would open his mouth when you least expected it. And this was one of those times they hoped his big mouth did not get them killed.

JC replied, "My name is JC."

"'Sup, JC. Nice to meet you. I like your taste in cars."

Now Brick was thoroughly confused. The Supreme Leader returned to the front of the group. "Thank you for the cars except for the motorcycle. I will probably use that for scrap metal."

Before Robert blew a fuse in his head, the Supreme Leader announced. "Join me in my home." Then he proceeded up the steps.

Everybody looked around wondering what to do now? The military officer with the chest full of medals extended his arm suggesting they should follow, which for obvious reasons they did. After all, now they were in the middle of North Korea with no getaway cars, and if this adventure went sideways, they were totally screwed. And if they had to run out of this place on short notice, Big Tony knew he would be shot first. Sprinting was not one of his stronger qualities.

When they entered the palace, they were immediately struck by its opulence. Forget what you see on TV. This leader was rolling in style. Of course, Robert was still fuming about the guy not liking his bike.

He whispered to Stenson, "Who decorated this place? It looks like Elvis Presley's jungle room at Graceland from the 1970s. I didn't know shag carpet was still in fashion."

"Maybe Elvis moved here to get away from the demands of being a celebrity," Stenson suggested.

"Well, Haggerty rose from the dead, so it wouldn't surprise me," Brick noted, since after that, anything seemed possible.

They entered room large enough to hold several hundred guests. There was a bar in the rear, with sofas and plush chairs. Beyond that was a dance floor with a stage at the other end. This must be the Supreme Leader's disco, Brick thought.

Everyone was served their choice of drinks. JC cozied up to the leader at the bar.

"I like your place," Justin said. "I used to own a nightclub called Club Empire in New Orleans. You ever hear of New Orleans?"

"Of course, JC. It is marked on a map to destroy if the United States invade us," the Supreme Leader informed him.

JC choked on his drink, which made the Supreme Leader chuckle.

"I am kidding JC. Maybe you can give me some tips on how to liven this place up. It seems kind of dull to me."

"I will be happy to help you out, my man," JC offered.

"Do you play basketball?" the Supreme Leader asked.

"Why, because I am black?" Justin quipped.

The supreme leader said, "Well, yes."

JC replied, "Okay, I play a little basketball. But it's not because I am black. Those white guys play too."

"Great! Let's play a game before the festivities begin," the leader suggested.

"Really? Let me ask the guys," JC replied

Justin walked over and told the fellas the North Koreans wanted to play them in a game of basketball.

"Oh, this should be fun," Robert said. "I am going to check that short son-of-a-dictator for not liking my bike."

"Calm down, Cowboy. You better let him win. Remember the firing squad?" Stenson reminded the zealous marine.

The men were led to a locker room where they were given shorts, t-shirts, and shoes. Unfortunately, they had nothing remotely close to Big Tony's size, so he played in his boxer shorts and a t-shirt, barefooted because he was wearing boots and did not want to scuff the Supreme Leader's basketball court.

When they walked out of the locker room, they were met by the Supreme Leader's team, who were all wearing military uniforms except for the leader who had changed into black shorts, black tank-top, and black Air Jordan shoes.

The game was rude where the normal rules did not apply. Robert Brickhouse was fouled so many times that he was ready to toss every one of the military guys into the small set of stands. It went without saying; they lost the game 102–4. The Supreme Leader congratulated them for a good game.

Brickhouse mumbled, "You cheating son-of-a-bitch."

The leader asked Robert to repeat what he said.

Robert replied. "My crotch has an itch."

"Would you like some ointment?" the leader asked the frustrated marine.

"No, I'm fine," Brick replied.

For entertainment, a troupe of North Korean women performed traditional songs and dance.

"JC, your friend is beautiful," Kim admired, while staring at Soni James.

Soni overheard the compliment and told the Supreme Leader, "I have a boyfriend," then quickly grabbed Robert's hand.

"Oh, I am sorry. At least he has better taste in women than motorcycles," the leader quipped.

Brick's blood closed in on the boiling point. He calculated ways in his twisted mind how to snap this guy in half. But then he realized it would be difficult to explain how World War III broke out. Soni sensed his hostility and squeezed his hand like a vice grip and smiled at the angry marine. As soon as the leader was out of sight, Robert shook off Soni's grip and told her after that encounter, he needed another drink... or three.

They watched the entertainment for two hours where delicacies were served that no normal North Korean had ever seen. The alcohol flowed freely, and they were all a little tipsy, especially JC and the Supreme Leader. While the rest of the team were huddled together, JC sat next to the leader, chatting and laughing like they had known each other for decades. The sight did not improve Robert's grouchy mood.

"You like music, JC?" the Supreme Leader asked.

"Yeah, but not this crap," he replied with drunken honesty.

"I agree, this sucks, but it's the only music my people know, so I go with it," the leader explained.

"I like hip-hop," the Supreme Leader revealed.

111

"Can you rap and dance?"

"Why, because I am black?" JC asked incredulously.

"Yes," the leader admitted.

"At least you are honest," JC replied with a laugh, then clinked the leader's glass with his own.

"Let's do karaoke together. We will be like Milli Vanilli," the leader suggested.

"Well, your skin tone is lighter than mine, so you get to be Vanilli," JC drunkenly suggested.

"Come with me," the leader instructed JC. He had words with one of his minions in charge of sound and lights. A few minutes later, a military officer walked onto the stage and announced, "All rise and welcome the Supreme Leader and his guest, the most dignified, Justin Carter."

Robert was sufficiently buzzed and could not believe what he just heard. "Did he say most dignified?"

Stenson laughed. "Apparently they don't know JC like we do."

The lights went down and smoke rolled onto the stage from a fog machine. The music started and blue lights illuminated the stage. The Supreme Leader wearing an over-sized puffy silver coat reminiscent of the female rapper, Missy Elliot, stepped out. JC followed wearing a silver metallic jumpsuit with white, untied high-top sneakers. The song they chose was "Mo money, Mo problems," by Puff Daddy and The Notorious BIG.

As the leader and JC danced around the stage and lip-synced together, Brick shook his head and told Stenson, "We really are in the Twilight Zone."

"Hey, they are pretty good. Let's dance," Stenson encouraged the marine.

Brick took a slug of his Jack Daniels and said. "Why not? I know I am going to wake up tomorrow and tell you about this wild dream I had where I was dancing at a dictator's house."

Before long, the entire team were dancing along with the North Korean performers from earlier and several of the military guards. It was outrageous.

When it was over, JC told the leader, "I would like you to meet someone."

JC walked over to Zabrina and took her hand. She was terrified to be in her home country standing in front of the man who persecuted her family.

"This is Zabrina. I mean, Pok Kyung-Wook. It is her parents we've asked you to help us find," JC said.

Zabrina bowed.

"You fled our country?" the leader asked sternly.

Zabrina paused before admitting, "I did."

"Your family means so much to you that you would risk your life to come back here to save them?" the Supreme Leader asked her.

"Yes," Zabrina quietly replied.

"You can take my life instead of theirs," Zabrina humbly offered in trade.

"You are brave, Pok Kyung-Wook. You know the price of escape is death?" the Supreme Leader reminded.

JC became nervous hearing the exchange.

"And why should I grant this exception to you and your family?" the Supreme Leader asked the trembling Zabrina.

JC interjected before Zabrina could answer.

"Because I've asked you to do it as a friend to me," JC blurted.

"You can take me instead of her if you will free her and her family," JC suggested.

"I would die for her," he said.

"JC, do you love this woman?" the leader asked Justin Carter.

"More than you know," he replied glancing at Zabrina.

"Very well. For family, friendship, and love, which you have proven, I will grant your request," the Supreme Leader said with a broad smile to the couple.

JC sighed in relief. "Thank you."

"I like you JC," the leader said. "Pok Kyung-Wook is lucky to have a man as brave as you, willing to risk his life for the one he loves. You are an honorable man and my friend."

The leader reached for Zabrina's hand. "Join us in celebration tonight. You will be reunited with your parents in the morning."

Zabrina bowed her head in respect. Quietly she said, "Thank you."

The festivities continued for several hours. Everyone, including Robert Brickhouse, had good time. When nobody was looking, JC and Zabrina slipped away to a quiet terrace. Underneath a full moon. JC reached for Zabrina's hands and stared into her beautiful brown eyes. Each fought back tears wanting to cry.

The dam broke when Zabrina said, "I love you, JC. I always have."

This was the first time in his life a woman who wasn't his mother had uttered those words to him. JC burst into tears and felt embarrassed for Zabrina to see him weep. His heart broke open revealing a truth he could no longer hide.

JC wiped away his tears, then wiped hers, too.

He asked, "Zabrina, why do you love me? I am a broken toy. I am not very smart. I have a disease I can never rid of. I am the worst person in the world for you to love. I don't even love myself."

Zabrina looked deeply in to JC's kind eyes and said, "JC, from the moment I met you that rainy night when I lost everything and felt hopeless in the world, you were there for me. You protected me.

You shared your friendship with me and your silly sense of humor. In this dark, inhospitable world, you were the brightness who showed me the light."

She continued, "Like you, I am a broken toy. I've been a prostitute, not by my choice. What should have been a beautiful gift shared only with the one I love was callously stolen from me. I am dirty and used. I am ashamed of the person I see in the mirror. But somehow JC, none of that mattered to you."

JC bravely leaned forward and gave Zabrina a gentle kiss on her lips, hoping he did not unjustly cross the line. It was the first time he had ever kissed a girl. He was terrified of rejection like he had experienced in life when his mother abandoned him as a child and nobody wanted to adopt a sick black boy or because he felt like he never fit in.

Zabrina wrapped her arms around his shoulders and returned his kiss more passionately. It was the first time in her life she had kissed someone she loved. Now tears of happiness flowed freely between these two beautiful misfits. By some miracle, these broken toys found the impossible. They found each other. They found true love.

Chapter 34
Pyongyang, North Korea

Robert's head banged like a Chinese gong after he was rudely awakened at 11:00 AM. Anything more than a beautiful woman cuddling next to him, whispering sweet nothings in his ear, was too much to process right now. It was far too early to consider doing anything productive besides stumbling out of this opulent bed. The party did not end until five or six... or 30 minutes ago, for all he knew. The details of the evening were sketchy in his fuzzy brain.

He looked down and noticed he was wearing black silk pajamas. He had no recollection of putting them on or where these silky garments had come from. He was more of a boxers and t-shirt kind of guy when he slept (or naked if there was a special friend in bed with him). But there were no special friends this morning. Just him and his banging head that checked out shortly after seeing JC and the Supreme Leader dancing and rapping to karaoke songs.

"Can you believe that?" he asked himself. "Rapping to karaoke songs with a dictator. Only JC could pull off a stunt like that and not get us killed."

It struck him that he was literally in the Supreme Leader's house, in his bed, in North Korea, and apparently wearing his pajamas. If this was a dream, he needed to see a therapist. If it wasn't, they all needed psychologists because this was absolutely bat-guano crazy.

Where did these pajamas come from? And where did the Supreme Leader get this comfortable mattress? If he had the brain capacity, Robert would figure out a way to steal this comfortable bed. Call it a going away present, easier to attain than Stenson's flying monkeys.

Flying monkeys? Mattresses theft? Silk pajamas? Robert shook his head, hopelessly trying to clear the cobwebs from his mind. He was spooked when he looked over and saw the same humorless North Korean official he first met on the boat was standing in his room, there to inform him they would dine with the Supreme Leader this morning.

Robert looked at the medal-wearing man waiting for him to leave. He did not budge. He just stood there staring even when Robert said, more like a question, "Okay?" waiting to see if the tin man wanted anything else. He knew the guy spoke perfect English, but he did not say a word in any language; English, Korean, Chinese or Swahili.

"Swahili? This isn't Africa, Robert. This is North Korea," he reminded himself.

Still, the medal-man remained stoic, silent, and robotic, with a look that wasn't quite a smile or a frown. Just these thin lips drawn tightly on his un-smiling-un-frowning face. There was something suspicious hidden behind his dark piercing metal eyes that told Robert the robot knew something he wasn't telling him.

It was too early and brain-fogged to worry about this medal-man right now, so Robert ignored him. He tried to imagine he was a statue, like the Chinese buried all those clay soldiers in an emperor's tomb centuries ago.

"Clay soldiers in a tomb? Wonder what they will bury me with if I don't get out North Korea," Robert asked himself.

"They will probably bury me with JC and Soni for all eternity. Wouldn't that be my luck?"

He shuffled into the equally opulent bathroom with gold fixtures, paintings, and more shag rugs. He decided it was a better idea to change clothes in here because he had no intention of doing it front of a clay soldier or real-life creepy man standing in his room. His clothes were laid out nicely washed and pressed. Who washed and pressed his clothes? When did that happen? And if North Korea ever needed money all they had to do was sell this bathroom. Where did they get this much gold for a toilet and faucets?

How did he get into these pajamas? It better not have been the guy in his room with the suspicious look. The way he was staring at him made Robert feel uneasy. He hoped it was nausea. Either way, he questioned which side of the border that guy was on? And where did they get all this gold? Who washed his clothes and did they wash anything else he was unaware of?

Robert had more questions than answers this morning. While sitting on the golden toilet putting on his stolen boots, he recalled the "Medal Man" was the only guy who did not have a good time last night. He remained stoic throughout the evening watching over them like a hawk or a chaperone at a high school dance. But even the chaperones at Robert's high school dances were cool. They just kicked him out of the dance after he spiked the punch.

Robert shook his tangled head. How did he go from who pressed his clothes to high school dances and chaperones? He seriously wondered if someone spiked his punch last night. He had never had a hangover like this before. And if it was that "Medal Dude" he was going to need a lot more aspirin and possibly a Penicillin shot.

Robert guessed the gaudy man was the one who held the nuclear codes, if they had codes, which was probably just some guy sitting in a hole waiting for a smoke signal so he could hot-wire a rocket to life with some jumper cables. There had to be a reason the soldiers feared this man. Maybe he changed their pajamas, too.

It was too much to think about. He decided this guy hated his life because he was a glorified butler with a chest full of medals. But Robert was too hungover to consider what awards they give out for "butlering".

As the group straggled into the dining hall looking worse for wear, each person was directed to an assigned seat at the long table that looked like it could feed 20 people. Brick was too malfunctioned to count the number of chairs and did not care where he sat. They could have put him on the roof with an ice pack and a vomit bag, and he would have been fine. Instead, the biker-marine was shown to the far end of the table with none of the aforementioned accouterments.

Robert surveyed the room with a hand over one eye to stop his brain from spinning like a merry-go-round. He noticed JC and Zabrina sitting at the head of the table, between a gilded chair. He was convinced the chair was stolen from a medieval king's throne or was a movie prop.

"Where do you buy thrones?" he wondered.

He still had not forgotten, despite missing pieces of the oatmeal between his ears, how the Supreme Leader dissed his choice of motorcycles last night.

"Use my motorcycle for scrap? I'll scrap you," he told himself.

Robert was tempted to get up and sit in the fancy man's chair at the other end of the table and dare one of those medal-wearers to move his hungover carcass. But after some consideration, that would require too many steps and a ruckus, none of which he had the energy for, so he dismissed the idea.

A bevy of attractive women who looked like the same members of the dance troupe from a few hours ago offered mimosas in champagne flutes along with assorted tropical fruits. Maybe this was their day job, Brick thought. Then he wondered if they were as hungover as him. They didn't act like it. They were chipper. He considered asking if they knew who changed his pajamas? But it was another idea he quickly put away because he did not speak Korean, nor he did not want to know the answer if it wasn't one of them.

A macaw was perched in the corner at the other end of the room near a window overlooking plush gardens and a swan-filled lake. The red, green, blue, yellow, pink, and white bird with a black beak looked like a mascot from a gay pride parade. It annoyed Robert because the bird kept squawking with a grating voice like fingernails on a chalkboard or an annoyed granny. Not his granny, of course. She was sweet. But he was sure somebody's granny sounded like that bird and the sound was not improving his clanging head.

The parrot entertained everyone except Robert. As a matter of fact, the creature was testing his very last nerve. He was tempted to walk over and choke the flamboyant animal and eat it if they didn't bring him a proper breakfast soon besides this fruit. It wasn't your normal oranges, strawberries or bananas (although they had bananas). This was exotic fruit: Jackfruit, Starfruit, Breadfruit, Dragon Fruit, Snake Fruit, Lotus Fruit, Passion Fruit, Kumquat, Mango, and Guava. The only fruit that really shocked Robert and made him want to throw up was Durian.

He and Stenson had a history with that funky, sweaty sumo wrestler jock strap, stinky sock smelling fruit. It went back to the early days when they first met Justin Carter, Anthony Gallo, and Zabrina Chao. Durian has one of those smells you will never forget. It was like a woman's perfume except as far opposite that end of the spectrum as you can get. If you smelled it once, you will never forget the funky scent. It was interesting how smell can transport you back in time to recall the moment you inhaled it. And recalling the smell of Durian reminded Brick of how he met JC and why he wanted to kill him so badly.

He wanted to hurl. He wanted to kill JC. He wanted to extinguish that loud bird. He wanted to murder anyone who thought Durian fruit was some sort of delicacy.

"Maybe that fruit is a delicacy in hell," Brick thought.

He was ready to snap and to go on a rampage if they didn't bring him something other than this crap to eat; or at least bring him the hair of the dog that bit him last night to calm his nerves. But then again, it required too much energy; certainly more than he had at this all-too-bright-funky-smelling moment. Between the Durian fruit that would remain in his nostrils for a month and that loud screeching bird at the other end of this table, something had to give before he completely lost his mind.

Maybe he could throw a fork? He looked at the table setting and noticed all he had were chopsticks. Those didn't carry enough mass to fly across the room and annihilate the annoying creature or JC. It would probably just upset the bird and cause it squawk more. Then JC would tell him to stop throwing sticks, or whatever nonsense came out of that lovebird's mouth. None of it would improve his headache. So, he scratched those bad ideas, too.

Finally, he had enough of the raucous sound and said in a commanding voice, "Can somebody shut that bird up, or at least turn it down?"

The only people in the room who spoke English were his friends and that "Medal Guy". His friends ignored him, but the soldier smiled, which made him feel even more nauseous. A petite dancer from the night before asked if he wanted another Mimosa? Robert told her to bring the entire bottle of Champaign and skip the mango juice. Of course, she did not speak English. She simply smiled and walked away.

While Robert prayed the woman would not bring him more Durian fruit, the Supreme Leader entered the room wearing a colorful Hawaiian print shirt, khaki cargo shorts, and sandals with straps around his ankles.

"Really? Sandals with straps?" Brick fashion critiqued.

The shirt was as loud and annoying as that parrot and as bright as the sun. After he could not find his sunglasses, he suspected the medal-wearing suspicious guy stole them; so, he added him to his growing list of hate.

Before he would waste his time getting rid of that guy, he had to do something about that blinding garment. He reconsidered the density and flight path of his chopsticks. Maybe if he threw them with the proper trajectory, it would turn the volume down on the Supreme Leader's shirt or at least get him out of eyesight. But then again, it would probably start World War III and the last thing his head needed were a bunch of explosions or somebody scolding him about how he didn't have decorum and you don't throw chopsticks at foreign leaders.

It was nonsense. Everyone stood except

Brickhouse, who was slower to rise while looking for his sunglasses while wondering if they were going to the beach after breakfast based on the way the Supreme Leader was dressed. He grumbled something about formality and why should he have to stand and where was the champaign he ordered 10 minutes ago?

Everyone ignored him.

"Good morning, my friends!" Kim said in a cheerful tone that annoyed Brick even more.

For a guy who partied harder than the rest last night, the Supreme Leader was in a remarkably upbeat mood. Brick made a note to ask him later what hangover relief he used and if he knew who changed his pajamas.

"I would like to make an announcement," the Supreme Leader said. "I have sent a personal message to the President of the United States stating that any further communication with my country shall be directed through our new envoy, the most honorable Justin Carter."

Everyone clapped except for Robert Brickhouse whose mouth fell agape. He asked Stenson, "Did he just make JC a diplomat to North Korea?"

"It seems he did," Stenson said with a laugh.

"Unbelievable," Robert said.

Brick waved for a waitress or servant or whatever the person was called who brings food and drinks in this joint. And wouldn't you know the "Medal Guy" walked over and asked Brick if he could help?

Robert thought, "I am pretty sure you helped me enough last night." But he bit his tongue and said, "Bring me a double Vodka and make it quick!"

After lunch, the group were escorted by military personnel to the front of the palace. The Supreme Leader accompanied JC and Zabrina down the hall. To everyone's surprise, Justin and Zabrina were holding hands. It appeared to everyone they were a couple now.

Guards swung open the massive doors, where the leader stepped outside onto the portico to the sound of applause and cheers from other members of the military and the same dance troupe from the night before. JC and Zabrina were welcomed by his side, and the rest of the misfits followed and lined up behind them.

Stenson held Robert's arm and guided him out the door as if he was leading a blind man with Tourette Syndrome who would blurt anything without checking his brain before it exited his mouth. Brick mumbled something about the noon sun was even brighter than the Supreme Leader's shirt and the annoying colorful bird and he thinks some "medal guy" stole his sunglasses and had his way with him last night. He said something about pajamas, and high school dances, and chopsticks don't make suitable weapons unless you are up close and personal. Stenson didn't know how much Robert had to drink last night, but it clearly affected his twisted mind. He suggested Robert should be quiet and everything would be fine.

After Brickhouse returned from puking in the Supreme Leader's bushes, they watched a black Rolls Royce pull in front of the mansion to great fanfare worthy of a state visit. Robert asked Stenson how the North Koreans could afford a Rolls Royce when they could not feed their people? Then he mentioned something about a gold bathroom and how he was going to steal a mattress later. The mattress was about the only thing Robert said that made any sense. The big marine desperately needed a nap.

A military officer opened the rear door of the car inviting Zabrina's parents to step outside. Upon seeing them, Zabrina broke protocol and rushed down the steps. It was the first time in eight years she had seen her parents. The moment was priceless.

"Mother! Father!" she exclaimed as she embraced them both. Everyone, including Brickhouse, smiled witnessing the beautiful moment. Zabrina took her parents by the hand and led them up the stairs. They were fearful and humbled at the same time to see the leader of their country face-to-face. They bowed in his presence.

The Supreme Leader extended his hand to her father and then leaned over and hugged Zabrina's mother. With a broad politician's smile, cameras clicked away. Surely this was a publicity stunt they would use to show the world what a benevolent leader he was. Really, it did not matter what they did with the photos. For all this group cared about was they accomplished what they came for. Zabrina Chao was now reunited with her family.

Zabrina said, "Mother and Father, I would like you to meet my friends."

One-by-one she walked down the line and introduced them all. Sarge, Soni, Big Tony, Brick, and Stenson. When she reached JC, she said, "Mother and Father, this is Justin Carter. He and his friends saved my life and yours."

Her parents, unable to speak English, bowed their heads in the same reverence they showed the Supreme Leader. However, this time they covered their hearts as if to say they recognized the importance of their deeds.

"My soldiers will escort you to an airbase where a plane awaits your departure to Hong Kong," the Supreme Leader informed them.

He walked down the line and shook each member's hand. When he reached Robert Brickhouse, he said, "Next time bring Kawasaki motorcycle and learn how to dance. You suck."

Brick laughed. "To anybody else, I would kick their nagwi for saying that. But you have more guns than me."

The Supreme Leader chuckled. "And nuclear weapons," he reminded the marine, then patted Brick on his shoulder.

When the leader reached JC and Zabrina, he took Zabrina's hand and said, "May your life be filled with joy."

He turned to Justin Carter. "JC, thank you for your friendship. Take care of this beautiful woman."

"I will," JC promised with a broad smile and a bow.

The group descended the stairs and boarded a military bus. Kenny Wu was already strapped inside, released from his overnight stay in one of their prisons. As they pulled away, the Supreme Leader, soldiers, the dance troupe / waitresses, photographers, and even the medal-covered pajama-changing butler waved goodbye. Twenty minutes later they arrived at a military base where a private jet provided by the Rising Tiger awaited them on the runway.

Three hours later, the plane landed at Hong Kong International Airport. It was decided on the flight only Brick and Stenson would go on the ultimate mission to deliver Kenny Wu. It was time for the source of so much tragedy to meet his maker; Wu Kong, Sun Fang, the Rising Tiger.

Standing next to the SUV, Kenny Wu begged. "I will pay you whatever you want! I have millions!"

"Not anymore," Stenson informed him. "My wife, whom you almost killed, took care of that. You are broke."

This was news to Kenny Wu, but he had no time to ponder his financial situation as Brick unceremoniously shoved him into the backseat of the black SUV. Stenson and Robert climbed in on both sides of the man in case Wu had any intentions of jumping out of the car window. The rest of the team watched as they drove away, knowing this would be the last time they would ever see Mr. Kenny Wu.

The car left the airport at the end of Hong Kong island. It headed toward Victoria Peak, overlooking the financial capital of Asia. Kenny again attempted to plead his case.

"You know this is a trick! My father plans to kill you. Please let me go and you'll never see me again."

"Oh, we'll never see you again, I promise," Stenson reassured.

Brick chimed in. "You have nowhere to go, Kenny. You have no money. You've got no friends. We have video of you murdering a woman in cold blood in the Bahamas. Your businesses and reputation are ruined, including that of your father's reputation, which I might add, he is not happy about. Trust me, Kenny, outer space is not far enough for you to hide."

Kenny knew they were right. He had nowhere to go. All he could do was pray for forgiveness and hope his father will have mercy on his soul. But Kenny forgot one very important fact. The man he should ask for forgiveness was sitting next to him. Kenny had never apologized to Stenson Beckett for the harm he had caused to his family; for being the one responsible for the death of his son and life-changing injuries to his wife. While he may not have been the one to pull the trigger, he was absolutely the true killer. Sooner or later, everyone sits down to a banquet full of consequences. And that day had come for Kenny Wu.

The SUV drove through the iron gates

emblazoned with gold emblems of tigers, past security and up a winding driveway of Wu Kong's mansion at the top of the peak. When the car stopped, they were greeted by unfriendly looking black suit wearing men who opened the car doors. Stenson, Brick, and Kenny exited the car where they were frisked for weapons.

"Hey! Watch where you are grabbing me, partner. That's not a gun down there. But if you touch it again, I will show you how quick I will toss you over that cliff," Brick growled.

The hotshot sunglasses wearer got the message loud and clear and did not test Robert Brickhouse again. Being groped while having the remnants of a supreme hangover was not happening today, or any day. After they cleared that up, the guards led the men through the imposing white front doors of the enormous house. They walked down a long corridor that emptied into a marble reception area with a large fountain and double curved staircases. There, they were told to wait.

To break the tension, Robert told Stenson, "Wu's got a better interior designer than the Supreme Leader."

"Because he's got more money than him," Stenson guessed.

A few moments later, a guard returned and motioned the men to follow him upstairs. Not a word was spoken as they approached two well-armed men posted outside a pair of heavy mahogany doors. In silence, they waited for a cue. Maybe the men wore radios in their ears, because there was nothing Stenson, Brick or Kenny heard before they opened the doors and led them inside a richly appointed library with a large presidential-looking desk positioned in the center of the room at the end. From a side door, a well-dressed Asian man wearing a crème-colored western-style suit entered the room and took a commanding position behind the resolute desk. He waved the guards away, who closed the doors, leaving the men face-to-face with the infamous Rising Tiger.

"Gentlemen, welcome to my home," Wu Kong said without making eye contact with his son. "Please, have a seat."

The three obliged with Brick on the right, Stenson on the left, and Kenny Wu hesitantly sitting in the middle. Kong sat down in a large executive chair. He crossed his hands and stared directly into the eyes of all three men.

"Father..." Kenny Wu interrupted the silent assessment.

Kong raised his hand to his son that said to any casual observer, "Shut up".

Wu Kong paused before returning his hands to their crossed fingered clasp on his desk.

"Mr. Beckett, we finally meet in person," Kong began.

Stenson didn't bat an eye or utter a single word. It wasn't for fear, rather he knew Kong was not done.

"As you know Mr. Beckett, I am a powerful man. I have built an empire. I began from humble beginnings and I admit I am not proud of some of the terrible things I have done."

"Desperate times required desperate measures in the early days. But as I dug myself out and rose to power, I made a vow to live my life in more honorable ways."

"Do not mistake this admission as a sign of weakness. I use my power with an iron fist and a steel heart. I will do whatever it takes to get what I want."

"But I have rules, Mr. Beckett that I follow and I have tried to instill the same in my son."

"Things such as honor mean more to me than the average man. While I am well known to be quite ruthless, I have never harmed a man who did not deserve it. And unfortunately for you, this was a rule my son so carelessly broke when he harmed you and your family."

"But father..." Kenny interrupted.

Kong glared at his son and continued.

"I am a wealthy man. But I am not a greedy man. What caused this harm to you was my son's greed and disregard for your life. I know enough about you to understand you did not deserve what he has done."

"I also know how, despite how dangerous this has been for you and your friends, you are sitting here talking with me as an honorable man."

"You are a rare breed, Mr. Beckett, as are your loyal friends. If circumstance were different, I would want you to work for me. Unfortunately for my son's deeds, that will never be so. Too much damage has been done that cannot be undone. Apologies are only words said in vain."

Kong said, "My words will never restore the life of your child or the harm that has come to your wife. But in the name of honor from one father to another I share your loss as you will soon share mine."

Kong removed a gold-plated pistol from the center drawer and raised it to Kenny's head.

"But father...." Kenny begged.

[Pow]

A single shot. The chair flipped backward rocking Kenny Wu to the floor. Brick and Stenson were shocked, speechless, and stunned. They looked down at Kenny Wu whose eyes were wide open staring at his fate. His life was gone. He was stone-cold dead. The Rising Tiger ensured this would never be undone.

They returned their eyes to the elder Wu who rose from his desk and retrieved a silver suitcase from a cabinet hidden beneath a bookcase. Kong walked back and sat it on the desk.

"Mr. Beckett, you have shown honor throughout your loss. This is a small gift to you and your family in the hope you may rebuild your life and forgive me for my failure as a father."

The men stood up, and Stenson extended his hand to the Rising Tiger. There were only three words left to say.

"I forgive you."

Stenson picked up the briefcase from the desk, turned around, and walked with Robert past Kenny Wu out the door. They never looked back as the guards escorted them to the waiting SUV. As remarkable as what they witnessed, it was surreal they had traveled around the world for Kenny to face his judge, jury, and executioner in less than 20 minutes.

"Where to?" the driver asked.

Stenson pulled out his phone and called JC.

"Where are you?" Stenson asked.

"We are across the harbor, on the mainland. They have a Walk of Fame for Asian actors like Hollywood. You should see it."

"We'll be right there," Stenson said as he hung up the phone while the car continued down the peak.

The driver dropped them off across the harbor to the mainland of Hong Kong. Robert and Stenson found JC, Zabrina with her parents along with Big Tony, Sarge, and Soni James snapping pictures like tourists on the Walk of Fame next to a bronze statue of Bruce Lee.

"How did it go?" Sarge asked.

"We won't be hearing from Kenny Wu again,"

Stenson told the group without going into details of what occurred.

"What's in the case?" JC asked.

"I don't know. It was a gift from Kong," Stenson said.

"Well, open it up!" the lovebird encouraged.

Stenson sat the case on a picnic table, flipped two latches, and raised the lid. Everyone's eyes widened when they saw the contents. The case was filled with bars of gold.

"Wow!" Brick said. "That is almost as much gold as was in the Supreme Leader's bathroom. By the way, do any of you know who dressed me in pajamas?"

Soni James laughed. "We will tell you on the way home, sexy legs."

"Oh lord," Brick said with rolling eyes. "Do I really want to hear this?"

They laughed at Brick's embarrassment while Stenson phoned his wife in New Orleans.

"Hey Luna, care to get a bunch of misfits on a private flight out of Hong Kong? We're coming home."

Chapter 35

New Orleans, Louisiana

The fifteen hour return flight to New Orleans was uneventful, which, after all this crew had been through was a welcome relief. JC and Zabrina sat alone in the back of the plane talking to each other like they had never done before, smiling and holding hands. It was a beautiful sight and a miracle that two people who thought there was nobody in the world who would love found each other.

Robert Brickhouse finally got a much-needed nap after overcoming the shock of finding out it was Soni James who dressed him in those silk pajamas. It wasn't until they were on board the plane that she revealed the reason she did it was because Robert was running down the hallway drunk and naked chasing a North Korean soldier, telling him he wanted one of his medals as a souvenir. To prevent Robert from waking up with a metal pinned to his naked butt, Soni carried him to the bedroom, dressed him a pair of her pajamas, and tucked the drunkard in.

Big Tony and Sarge played cards and discussed the merits of various weapons and how running a successful logistics business selling military hardware like tanks, helicopters, and fighter planes had its pros and cons.

Zabrina's parents did not know what to think. Having left such an impoverished and reclusive nation to flying on a Gulf Stream jet to a new home in the United States would be an adjustment for anyone. Needless to say, they were overjoyed to be reunited with their daughter. Now they believed, especially after meeting JC, she had found the happiness they had dreamed for her.

Stenson was the quietest of all during the flight. He thought of his wife and child as he stared out the window. He was relieved they were all returning home safely, especially as risky as this affair had been. He thanked the crew for risking their lives for him and his family. Knowing he never had to worry about Kenny Wu again was a relief, though he was not sure how he felt about the ending. Part of him had simply wanted the man to go away to some prison and pay the price for the damage he had done. But as he had seen many times before, life doesn't always work out the way you plan. Sometimes there are other plans you can't control, as they found out in difficult and sometimes humorous ways.

He laughed thinking back at how he thought they could lasso a cargo ship. They had done it once, but never twice. He thought of the freezing swim with Robert in the Incheon harbor. How they ended up getting drunk with the leader of North Korea and dancing the night away to karaoke songs was a bizarre surprise. JC became a diplomat to a reclusive nation and fell in love. Who could come up with crazy plans like that?

He thought of Fallon O'Malley and all he had done both as the friend and as the Mystery Man. It was a loss he and Robert would carry for the rest of their lives. Stenson smiled, thinking of old man Haggerty and how he showed up again with a gun to save his life at the perfect time, especially since they thought he was dead for the past two years. How lucky was he to have a car thief friend who he met as a teenage runaway who had the cars they used to save Zabrina's parents lives.

No, you cannot plan that. It was fate guiding this motley crew, and Stenson Beckett could never ask for more colorful and funny friends as them. Most of all, he was thankful for Luna LeRoux, a woman who had seen something in him when he was a little boy and been by his side through the good times and the bad. For her, he would do anything. How lucky he was to have a girl like her as a lover, wife, and best friend.

One thing Stenson knew with all his heart is to never take life, or friendships, or love for granted. They are so hard to find and easier to lose. For love and friendship, these misfits proved they would travel to the end of the earth for vengeance.

As for the stolen mattress and flying monkeys? Robert and Stenson had not forgotten. They told JC they would pick them up next time they traveled with him to North Korea with his new diplomatic credentials because they would be easier to smuggle out of the country then.

The plane became livelier after the pilot announced they had entered U.S. airspace. Soon they would be home.

"What are you going to do with the money?" Robert asked Stenson.

"According to Luna, there is about $25 million she recovered from Kenny Wu through her crypto ruse and his offshore accounts."

"I was wondering if you are going to rebuild your bar?" Robert asked Stenson.

"You mean rebuild your bar," Stenson said. "I am giving it to you. I want to spend time with my wife and pick up the pieces. You will be a great owner and maybe you'll give me a free beer from time to time."

"As for the rest of the money, I plan to split it with the team. JC, Zabrina, and Big Tony can finish their new venture. Sarge can replace all the weapons we lost. Soni can buy some new outfits and maybe a pink Escalade since she loved the one we left in North Korea. And I'll repay Charlie Whitehouse for the money he lost giving us those cars."

"What about you?" Robert asked.

"I don't know, Robert," Stenson said. "Money's never meant that much to me. As long as I have Luna and we can pay our bills, we will be fine. I may donate some to charity. I really don't know."

"What about the gold?" Brick wondered.

"You still feeling like a pirate like you were on that cargo ship?"

"Always," Brick said. "By the way, whatever happened to that captain and his crew?"

"They were part of the deal for Zabrina's parents. I traded them to the Supreme Leader along with the cars." Stenson revealed.

Brick laughed. "Kill two birds with one stone. You are a smart cookie and slightly wrong in the head, Mr. Beckett. That is why I enjoy having you as a best friend. It's never a dull moment. Anyone else would bore me to death."

"The feeling is mutual, Robert. But we really need to work on your temper. I thought you were going to start World War III at the Supreme Leader's house," Stenson joked.

"Believe me, I thought about it!" Brick said. "If that bad-haircut-tropical-shirt-wearing-son-of-a-wonton dissed my motorcycle one more time, it was going to be on!"

A few days later, after everyone had rested, Luna rented a bar to celebrate. The gang was all there, including a few unexpected guests.

"Lucious T. Haggerty, I would like to introduce you to my best friend, Robert Brickhouse. He is as bad and quick-tempered as you with a gun."

Robert said, "Mr. Haggerty, it is nice to meet you. Stenson's told me a lot about you over the years. But I thought you were dead."

"Why does everybody think I am dead? I live in Florida now. Nice weather, pretty girls. I even took up golf," the old man explained.

"Girls?" Stenson questioned. "You've gotta be 90 years old."

"92. But that doesn't mean I've lost my eye for pretty women," Lucious corrected them.

"Haggerty, did I ever tell you about a wild dream I had one night? You visited me in my room when nobody could reach me and you told me to fight, which set all this in motion?" he asked the old Casanova.

"Boy, what have you been drinking? That was no dream," the old man revealed. "I visited you in your bedroom. You were kind of delirious that night."

Shocked at hearing the news confirming he wasn't crazy. Stenson wondered if this was a dream? He made a note to cut down on whatever he was drinking.

"How did you get in my house or know where I live?"

"Fallon O'Malley gave me a key," Haggerty told him.

"How did Fallon have a key to my house?" Stenson wondered.

"Fallon was the Mystery Man in case you didn't notice," Lucious told him. "Did you think we float through walls or come down a chimney like Santa Claus?"

Stenson and Robert looked each other. That was exactly how they thought the Mystery Man got around, not to mention how Haggerty rose from the dead to some retirement home in Florida.

"Well, I... uh..." Stenson mumbled.

Across the room came a boisterous voice. "Just Crazy! Get over here, boy!"

JC's face lit up when he saw it was Pastor Samuel L. Jackson. He walked over with Zabrina and embraced the pastor. They had both imbibed a few cocktails, reminiscent of the first time they met.

"They tell me you are some kind of diplomat now?" the pastor said. "How can your dumbass be a diplomat? You can't even tie your shoes."

"I am a diplomat. Want to see my papers?" JC crowed.

"Boy, the only papers you need are to a dog pound," the pastor told him before taking another slug of his drink.

"After all the money Stenson gave me, I bet I have a bigger house than yours and a hotter car and hotter girlfriend," JC countered.

"Meet my girlfriend, Zabrina," he proudly said.

"Just Crazy, you ain't ever going to be as good as me! But I give you credit. Your girl is fine. The poor thing must be blind."

"I think he's kinda cute, pastor. But so are you," Zabrina flirted.

"Well, she got one part of that right," the pastor replied. "I am much better looking than you, Just Crazy."

"Are you sure you are not the actor, Sam Jackson, playing a preacher because you realize you're going to hell for all the bad things you have done in your lifetime?" JC drunkenly asked, tempting the pastor not to fly off his seat.

"Boy, I have been a preacher my entire life. Praying for simple-minded idiots like you!" Jackson said, taking another swig of his whiskey.

JC replied, "I'm saying you look like him and sound like him, so I assumed."

"Just Crazy, let me tell your mushy mind

something. You are plain dumb. You never asked me if I have a twin brother," the pastor revealed. "He's over there."

JC looked to his right to see the actor Samuel L. Jackson leaning against the bar. He raised his glass to JC and gave him a wide, gap-toothed grin reminiscent of the killer in Pulp Fiction.

"I've had too much to drink because I am seeing double," JC admitted. "They should call you Just Crazy, pastor Jackson, not me."

Soni and Brick were shooting pool. When Robert bent over to take a shot, Soni leaned her seven-foot-tall frame over the big marine wearing a long sequined gown, high heel shoes, and bright pink wig.

"You need a bigger stick, Robert?" she whispered in his ear. "I'll let you use mine."

Brick nervously squirmed away. "My stick is fine, Soni."

He missed the shot so badly the ball bounced off the table. Soni cued up and ran the rest of the table, winning the game. It was fun to see some things never change between those two.

Charlie Whitehorse explained to Sarge and Big Tony the best places to scope out high-end cars for "acquisition" were usually nightclubs and bars. Big Tony said it made sense unless it was his club.

Anthony Gallo was now a celebrity since Fats opened. All the girls wanted to take a picture with him when they walked in the door. He explained the place was named after Fats Domino and his nickname was Big Tony, not Fat Tony. But it did not matter. He was a famous now and all the cute girls wanted to hang out with him.

Luna and Stenson sat at a table taking it all in. They were more in love than ever with a twinkle in their eyes like the one they've shared since they were kids. Tonight, they were happy to be surrounded by all their wild misfit friends.

The music abruptly stopped and JC popped on the stage and announced, "For an encore performance, I present to you, Robert "Sexy Legs" Brickhouse, Big Tony "What's for Dinner" Gallo, and Stenson "I've Gotta Plan" Beckett, along with me, the one and only handsome Justin "Just Crazy" Carter!"

The guys looked at each other with an expression of, "Oh no he didn't!"

The sound of a motorcycle engine revving roared over the loudspeakers.

Stenson glanced at Robert and said, "He did."

The song, "You Dropped a Bomb on Me" by the Gap Band, began to play. Knowing they had no choice and enough to drink for this stupid idea, the guys made their way onto the stage. As they had done when they captured an entire Chinese gang in their club weeks before, Brick, Stenson, and Big Tony lined up behind JC, who was in front of the mic. He handed them the same hats they wore the first time, and the guys began the choreographed dance no better than they had done before.

It was hilarious, corny and totally fun. The crowd enjoyed it with whoops and hollers. Soni James threw dollar bills at Robert Brickhouse. Luna stuck two fingers in her mouth and whistled like a country girl loudly at her husband. Quite a few girls were enjoying Big Tony's moves. And Zabrina had a giant smile on her face watching JC lead them all.

For the rest of the evening, they danced the night away. It was a fitting end for these friends.

Luna was feeling especially adventurous when she and Stenson returned home. She told him she wanted to show him a trick she learned while he was away. He was curious when she asked him to push her wheelchair into the dining room. There was something in the corner covered in a blanket.

"Closer," she directed.

Stenson pushed the wheelchair until something metal bumped against the footrests.

"That's good," she said.

Luna removed the blanket to reveal a walker underneath, the kind you might see old people use to assist them when they walk. Before Stenson could question the device, Luna leaned forward and placed both arms on the walker and lifted herself out of the chair.

Stenson was astonished and immediately afraid she would fall. Instead, Luna said, "Move that," pointing to her wheelchair.

Stenson did as he was told, though somewhat hesitantly. He was amazed to see Luna move her legs, albeit stiffly, not really bending at the knees. But in total surprise, Luna was moving her legs! The walker was only there to keep her from placing her entire weight on them. But there was no mistaking, Luna was walking on her own!

He was overjoyed and instinctively hugged her, almost knocking her down.

Luna giggled. "Watch it there, buddy. Haven't you ever seen a girl walk before?" She loved seeing the happiness on her husband's face.

"That is amazing, Luna!" Stenson exclaimed.

"I thought you knew I was amazing already?" she teased.

"Not that amazing!" he replied enthusiastically.

More determined than ever to put the tragedy behind her, Luna had worked her tail off with a physical therapist while he was away learning to walk again. She was ready to be the wife her husband deserved.

"I'm feeling a little frisky," she said with a coded

come-hither gaze.

"I think you've had too much wine tonight, young lady. It's your bedtime," Stenson suggested with a silly grin.

"I've had the perfect amount of wine, mister," Luna slightly slurred.

"And you are right, it is my bedtime," she said with a wink.

"It's great you have feelings in your legs now, Luna. But you haven't fully recovered. I'm afraid I might hurt you," Stenson tried to reason.

She wasn't taking no for an answer and egged him on. "Listen big boy, if bullets couldn't hurt me, do you think my husband can?"

"You are incorrigible Mrs. Beckett," Stenson submitted.

Eight Months Later...

Chapter 36

New Orleans, Lousiana

Things had returned to normal, relatively speaking. Robert Brickhouse was rebuilding O'Malley's bar in the French Quarter. With the blessing of Fallon O'Malley's widow, the place would be renamed "Brick's Biker Bar".

JC and Zabrina were a hot commodity, inseparable and in love. Zabrina moved in with JC. And through the unlikely request of the Supreme Leader, JC received a special envoy status with the hermit nation. Zabrina and her parents were granted asylum and were now U.S. citizens living in New Orleans.

Big Tony, JC, and Zabrina finally opened "Fats New Orleans" to great success. What happened to Club Empire was long forgotten. JC was practically a celebrity in town, which did wonders for his confidence. He'd come a long way from the scared little runaway boy. He was a man now and a folk hero. That did not stop Robert Brickhouse from teasing him from time-to-time. But JC had earned Robert's respect and admiration. More importantly, JC was proud to call Brick a loyal friend.

Charlie was still exporting stolen cars. However, with the money Stenson gave him, he went straight for a moment and legally purchased everybody the same cars they left behind in North Korea. JC had the red Ferrari, Sarge the Humvee, Big Tony the 4x4 truck. Stenson loved his 1970 Camaro and anytime you see a hot pink Cadillac Escalade rolling through New Orleans, wave to Soni. And yes, Brick got the Harley Davidson motorcycle, flat black and chrome, with a throaty roar that commanded respect. He emailed a photo of himself sitting on the bike holding up two middle fingers to the Supreme Leader with the caption, "Screw Kawasaki!"

Luna continued to make remarkable progress. She ditched the walker for a fashionable cane Stenson found that had a knife hidden in the handle. He was not taking chances in case he was not around. He knew his wife could defend herself.

After they shut down the LSAdvantage crypto coin, they returned the previous investors' deposits with a tidy interest. They cashed in Kenny's coins and hid the money in a Swiss bank account. Authorities considered it simply another failed crypto and since nobody complained and were made whole when it closed, they moved on.

Of course, the only person who could have complained was no longer alive. Kenny's money disappeared like a bad casino bet. The gangster had played the wrong hand and Luna proved the house always wins.

As for Stenson, he wasn't sure what he wanted to do. He was content spending time with his wife. They didn't need money. He had about $10 million left of Kenny's money after giving away $15 million of it to their friends, including a large donation to Pastor Jackson's church, which he used to buy a new car so JC would stop busting him about who had the better ride.

And the gold? Well, Stenson considered it blood money and wanted nothing to do with it. But his best pirate friend, Mr. Brickhouse, wouldn't let him just throw it away, so they buried it one night. You never know when they might need a treasure map the way their luck went.

It was the following day after they buried the treasure when they received a surprise nobody expected. Robert was there when the package arrived. The odd thing was the package, wrapped in brown craft paper, had no return address. Stenson casually unwrapped it. When he opened the box, both men said, "Whoa!"

It was a black hoodie the Mystery Man, Fallon O'Malley, had worn. Mrs. O'Malley found it when she was cleaning her husband's closet and thought it would mean something to Stenson and Brick as a keepsake.

The implications were impossible to know, but Robert and Stenson had a feeling they might see this hoodie again one day and it would not be in a box or on a shelf. Of course, it wouldn't be the first guy coming back from the dead they knew. They were sure Fallon O'Malley was up there somewhere planning another trick as the ghost of the Mystery Man.

That was about as normal as things would be for these misfits, and it was fine with them. Like Robert said before, anything less would bore them to tears. They hoped things will be less dangerous next time.

As he snuggled on the sofa with his Luna, Stenson turned on the news. Since things died down, and they weren't the center of attention anymore. The news was a regular affair. But one story caught their attention. Stenson turned up the volume.

"In an unusual turn of events, a Chinese-American named Donny Oh washed ashore on the border of Peru's Amazon rainforest where he was rescued by hunters of a little-known tribe called the Matsë, also known as the Jaguar people. However, the celebration was short-lived when Mr. Oh was attacked and mauled to death by a jaguar."

Stenson had forgotten about Donny Oh, the Chinese gangster they set out to sea in a life jacket. But he and Luna immediately knew which jaguar killed him. They looked at each other and exclaimed, "Mi Amiga!"

Stenson told her, "That cat protected you then and now. I am glad the animal liked me."

"Only because I told her to like you, remember?" she reminded her silly husband.

"Yeah, that cat was going to eat me alive if you had not stopped her. Thanks, Luna."

"Just don't get out of line, Mister. You may have friends in low places, but mine come from jungles," she teased.

Stenson kissed his wife and smiled at the silly girl.

"I am so happy Luna. I was in such a dark place after our son was killed and terrified I would lose you. But sitting here now after all we've been through? Nothing in this world could make me happier."

"That's too bad," Luna said sadly looking down.

Stenson was puzzled. "Why?"

Luna paused and whispered, "Because I am pregnant."

Stenson jumped from the sofa, dumping his wife onto the floor, causing Luna to laugh out loud.

Well, maybe he could be happier...

About the Author

Author Tony Gray was raised in the city of Blues, Soul, and Rock & Roll, Memphis, Tennessee and calls another Music City, Nashville, Tennessee home.

His career spans television, radio, recording, and software development before he became an author. He is a graphic designer, professional photographer, musician, and former club DJ who knows how to mix vinyl music.

Reach out to Tony on social media and say hello or meet him in person when he has a book-signing event in your town.

Vengeance is the follow-up to his first novel, Double Crossed : Play the Hand You Are Dealt.

To learn more about Tony Gray and his novels, visit:

https://sinceritypress/tonygray

https://double-crossed.com

Acknowlegements

The author wishes to thank the following for their support and inspiration during the writing of Double Crossed : Vengeance

Beth Anthamatten

Belinda Dwyer

Dustin Goforth

Roni Williams

Bruce Baber

Brent Stidham

Alejandro Romo

Ofc. Stephanie Cisco

Ofc. Ryan Frazier

Dr. Dan Collins

The John P. Holt Brentwood Library

Franklin, Tennessee Police Department

Brentwood, Tennessee Police Department

And to the real Double Crossed guys...

Connor Puckett

Frank Jones

Bryan Boyd